GW00703191

Also by Elaine Hankin

Flatmates
Laws are Silent
House of Secrets
Portrait of Rosanna

THE SPANISH TWIN

Elaine Hankin

With best wishes
from
Elaine Hankin

Published in 2013 by FeedARead Publishing

British Library C.I.P.

A CIP catalogue record for this title is available from the British Library.

With grateful thanks to family and friends for their patience and encouragement during the writing of this novel

While the author has tried to be accurate with regard to the events of the Spanish Civil War, will the reader please bear in mind that this is a work of fiction. The same goes for the characters, which bear no relation to any living person.

PROLOGUE

March 1937

He felt himself being launched through space. In a split second he landed face-down in a hollow. Drawing his knees up to his chest, he covered his head with his arms, convinced that his last hour had come.

Despite being deafened by the first explosion, he was conscious of minor blasts shattering the air around him, and knew he was being pelted by flying debris. Random thoughts flashed through his mind: a list of things he hadn't done and would like to do; the face of the person dearest to him. Would she ever discover his last resting place?

Mayhem subsided and he knew he had survived. Lifting his head, he squinted, blinded by rising dust. His eyes watered, his ears rang, his limbs were numb. It seemed the only sense functioning was his sense of smell as he recognised the pungent odour of burnt foliage mixed with charred flesh. He drew his arm across his face to clear the dirt, becoming aware that he had been holding his breath. Exhaling brought on a bout of raucous coughing as he gulped down a lungful of smoke.

His hearing began to return, and from a distance he could make out the roar of retreating vehicles. When silence finally descended, he struggled to his feet and stared around, still unable to focus properly. He stumbled over chunks of rock and clods of turf until he reached the peak of the hillock. His foot knocked against something and he saw that it was a rifle. Stooping to pick it up, he recoiled in horror when his fingers touched something soft and damp. Part of a hand was still clamped around the trigger guard. Turning his head, he vomited into the grass. Recovering, he was unable to stop himself from taking a second look, and recognised the shiny wedding ring on the third finger: Luis Sanchez, married only a month ago. How was he going to break the news to Consuela?

A young girl found him when she went to check on her goats. In panic, she ran to find her mother, returning with several older women. Together they carried him across the rough terrain down the slope into the village. They took him into a house and helped him onto a bed. Hours passed before he woke up.

'Where am I?' His words were a mere whisper.

A woman seated beside the bed leant over him. 'Don't worry, you're safe,' she said. 'My daughter, Jacinta found you.'

He tried to raise his head only to experience a stab of pain through his shoulder and down his arm. He closed his eyes and allowed memory to flood back: the discovery of the fate of his companions; the frantic scrabbling at the bare earth as he tried to bury body parts; the realisation that the task was futile; the long trek across the plain.

'You were injured,' explained the woman. 'Nothing serious, but we had to dig out some shrapnel from your arms and legs.' He felt confused, unable to comprehend that he had been wounded. 'Shock must have deadened your senses,' went on the woman. It was almost as if she could read his mind.

'Where am I?' he asked again. 'I need to get back to my unit.'

8

'All in good time.'

He glanced around the room and saw his tattered clothes piled on a chair, his red kerchief too. So they knew he was a POUM member. The woman noticed.

'The Nationalists came and went,' she said. 'They accused us of collaboration; they shot the padre and two teenage boys. Then something happened to disturb them so they moved on.' Her voice broke. 'At least our homes are still intact. We thought they would be razed to the ground.'

'And yet you took me in?'

'We're not broken that easily,' she replied with a tight smile. 'By the way, my name's Asunción. You haven't told me yours.'

'Esteban Morán,' he mumbled.

CHAPTER ONE

Autumn 1936

Maggie Morán rushed to greet the postman. Surely there would be a letter bearing a Spanish postmark today! She turned away disappointed when he handed her a bundle of brown envelopes. Her mother's voice reached her as she closed the front door.

'Maggie, where are you? Has my newspaper been delivered yet?'

'Yes, mother, I'll bring it up with your breakfast.'

'I don't want any breakfast.'

'You must eat.'

Maggie heaved a sigh. Katherine seldom left her room these days. She had never recovered from the death of her husband, Miguel, two years earlier. To make her more comfortable, Maggie had moved an armchair in there, along with a wireless set. She had also managed to put up a couple of shelves on which to house her mother's favourite books, and screwed in hooks so that photographs of Miguel looked down from all four walls.

She carried the breakfast tray upstairs and placed it on the table in the bay window, where her mother was sitting, staring out at the grey skyline.

'I've put your favourite marmalade on your toast, mother.'

'I told you, I'm not hungry.'

'Just try a piece with a nice cup of tea.'

Katherine didn't move. Her daughter gave a little shrug and turned back to the bed to tuck in the sheets and blankets and straighten the bedcover. 'I've got to go out now,' she said.

'What for?'

'For some groceries; we're nearly out of tea and sugar.'

'Well, don't be long, and don't forget to buy my favourite custard creams this time.'

'I won't.'

There was a dank November mist hovering in the air as Maggie made her way across Stanmore Common, prompting her to pull her scarf more tightly round her neck. A man walking a dog exchanged a cheery 'good morning' with her but, apart from him, there was no one about. She reached the local shops and lingered in front of the dress boutique to admire a skirt on display, before moving on to the pet emporium to watch two puppies frolicking in the window.

The grocers shop was further down the road. The doorbell tinkled as she went in. The proprietor, Mr Butler, who knew her well, greeted her. 'Morning, miss, what can I do for you on this dreary day?'

Maggie placed her order and waited while he patted out the butter and measured out the cheese.

'Shall I slice the ham thinly for you?'

'Yes please. Mother prefers it that way.'

'How is she these days?'

'Not very well,' replied Maggie. 'She misses my brother.'

'Have you heard from him?'

Maggie shook her head.

'Ah me, why do these young men do such reckless things?'

'That's what I keep asking myself. Even though we're half Spanish, I can't understand why Robert had to rush off and join the International Brigade.'

The grocer frowned as he continued to slice the ham. 'You ought to get out more, young lady. You shouldn't be stuck in that big house with just your mother for company. Why don't you find yourself a job in town?'

Maggie smiled at his concern. 'I can't do that,' she said. 'I can't leave mother. It's convenient being a free-lance translator working from home. It means I can keep an eye on her and do the work as well.' She gave a short laugh. 'Of course, it also means I'm always at her beck and call.'

'You should put your foot down.'

'That's easier said than done.'

Maggie glanced at her watch as she left the shop. She'd better hurry. Mother didn't like it if she took too long. Laden with two bags of groceries, she walked as fast as she could since, by now, the mist had changed to a steady drizzle. By the time she reached home, her hair was hanging lank to her shoulders. She let herself in and dumped the shopping bags on the kitchen table.

'I'm back, mother,' she called up the stairs.

There was no reply.

Maggie shrugged. She was probably having a little nap. She put the groceries away and decided that they could both do with a cup of tea. Placing the kettle on the hob, she lit the gas and went to the bottom of the stairs again.

'Mother, I'm back. I'll bring you up a cup of tea in a minute.'

There was still no reply.

A shiver of apprehension ran through her. It was unlike her mother to fall into a deep sleep during the day. Running upstairs she went into the bedroom. The room was empty, the breakfast tray untouched. Going back onto the landing, she saw that the bathroom door was half open. There was water on the floor.

With a pounding heart, Maggie pushed open the bathroom door and stopped on the threshold in horror. Her mother, still in her nightgown, was sprawled in the bath. Rose-coloured water slopped over the edge to form a puddle on the linoleum. One of Miguel's old cut-throat razors lay on the floor.

'No!'

Maggie yanked out the plug and, as the water began to recede, wrapped her arms around her mother's body, trying to haul her out. But she was a heavily-built woman and she sank back into the water.

'Mother,' she shrieked, but her mother's eyes remained closed as the blood continued to ooze from deep cuts in her wrists.

At last, she managed to get her out of the bath and lay her on the wet floor. Close to hysterics, she yelled, 'Mother, don't do this to me!'

Frantically, she felt for the pulse in her neck but there was no reassuring throb. In a desperate bid to bring life back to the inert figure, she slapped her face. There was no response. Why hadn't she guessed this could happen? Had she missed some sign earlier in the day?

Panic sent disjointed thoughts racing through her head. Was it *her* fault? Sinking to the floor beside the body, she reached for her mother's hand, squeezing it hard, willing a reaction from her. Yet as the minutes ticked past, she realised she needed to do something. Pressing her eyelids tightly shut, she tried to focus her thoughts. What would Robert do? Suddenly, overcome by nausea, she blinked open her eyes, and leaning over, vomited into the pink-stained bath.

Everything became a haze after that: the coatless dash across the Common in the rain; the distraught entry into Mr Butler's shop; the kindness of Mrs Butler when she heard what had happened; the way the couple had taken charge and called an ambulance. The police came as well and there was a lot of questioning going on. Mrs Butler insisted on helping her clear up the bathroom and tried to persuade her to stay with them overnight but she declined, preferring instead to remain at home.

More than anything, she needed to come to terms with her feelings. Mother and daughter had never been close and, since her husband's death, Katherine had seemed bent on making life difficult for her children. It was as if she blamed us, thought Maggie. She wondered whether she could have done more for her mother.

Over the next few days, Maggie was swamped by a mixture of emotions: guilt, pity, self recrimination. She hated herself for not having shed any tears but with urgent tasks building up, there was little time for grieving. After several more unsuccessful attempts to get in touch with her brother, she was forced to go ahead with the funeral without him. The arrangements were not as straight-forward as she would have hoped. First, there was the inquest, followed by a heated discussion with Father Rutherford of the Catholic church as to whether, due to the suicide, her mother could be buried in consecrated ground. Eventually, Maggie persuaded him that, due to her continuing grief over Miguel's demise, Katherine had been of unsound mind at the time of her death, and he agreed for her to be interred in the cemetery adjoining the church.

The week after the funeral, she decided that a visit to her mother's solicitor was overdue. After polite preliminaries, he dourly told her that she would need to contact her brother before the reading of the will.

'Why?' she asked.

The solicitor gave her a patronising smile, and taking off his spectacles, twirled them around between finger and thumb. 'These things are better handled by a man.'

Maggie frowned. 'That's ridiculous, there's no reason why I can't handle my mother's affairs.'

'Your brother is the senior twin.'

'Only by a matter of minutes!'

'Nonetheless …'

'I'm afraid I've lost contact with him.'

'Oh dear, that's a pity. Have you any idea of his whereabouts?'

'I know he's in Spain.'

'What on earth is he doing there?'

Maggie cleared her throat, trying to invent a feasible reason for Robert to abscond to Spain. 'He's travelling around,' she replied. 'After university he wanted a break before starting his career.'

'Ah yes, I remember, he got a First in Engineering, didn't he?'

Maggie nodded.

The solicitor put his spectacles back on and muttered, 'Spain, you say. Hmm, I can think of more agreeable places to visit, but I suppose your family's Spanish connections would draw him to explore the Hispanic territories. Does your brother speak Spanish?'

'Like a native,' she replied, thinking how well Robert would fit in over there with his dark complexion and arresting brown eyes.

'Indeed …' The solicitor pondered for a moment. 'Perhaps before we read the will you could go away and try to track him down through the authorities; the British Embassy in Madrid might know where he is.'

This arrangement suited Maggie. It gave her a reprieve; now she could put off making decisions about her own life for a little longer. She still needed time to put her thoughts in order.

The reprieve proved to be short-lived. She had done very little translation work over the past few months and the bills had started to mount up. She found out that her mother had been in the habit of shoving unwanted correspondence, mainly bills, into a drawer in her bureau. The discovery of a bundle of these sent Maggie hurrying back to the solicitor.

'What can I do?' she said. 'I can't pay them. Can you release some money in advance of the reading of the will?'

'I can't possibly do that,' he said rather smugly, 'But of course, there is the cottage in Devon …'

'What cottage?'

'The one your grandfather left you.'

'I don't understand.'

'It's a two-roomed stone cottage in the heart of the country. It may be a bit run-down but I dare say it would bring in enough to put you on your feet again.'

'Why was I never told about it?'

'You were under twenty-one when your grandfather died but I assumed your parents would have told you about it once you came of age.'

'They didn't,' snapped Maggie. She paused to think. 'Does this mean I can take possession of it straightaway?'

'I don't see why not.' He hesitated. 'I wonder if your brother knows about the villa your grandfather left him.'

'Is that in Devon too?'

'No, it's in Toledo.' He paused, then added, 'It's south of Madrid.'

'I know where it is,' retorted Maggie, more sharply than she had intended.

The solicitor pursed his lips, seeming almost to be about to reprimand her. 'Hmm…' he muttered. 'Maybe that's where he's gone.'

Maggie's heart lifted. 'Have you got the address?'

'Certainly.' The solicitor opened the file in front of him and carefully copied the address onto a piece of paper. 'Here you are. Maybe this will bring a good result.'

'Can you give me the address of the Devon property?'

'Certainly.' The solicitor reached for a second piece of paper and began writing. 'It's very remote,' he said.

'Is there a station nearby?'

'Not really, you'll need a car. Do you drive?'

Maggie gave a gulp of dismay. She had been amongst the first people to take the Driving Test after it was introduced two years earlier, an experience so nerve-racking that she had vowed never again to get behind a steering wheel. Her brother had been scornful but, of course, he had obtained his driving licence before the test was brought in. His teasing had always rankled.

'Yes, I do,' she managed to stutter.

The solicitor picked up on her nervousness. 'Well,' he said. 'You could go by train but driving down would give you more flexibility.'

'I'll bear that in mind,' she replied.

Two days later, after several practise runs, Maggie took courage and started on the drive down to Devon. Snow flurried against the windscreen, making the driving even more hazardous but necessity cast fear of handling the car out of her mind. She needed money; the cottage was her nest egg. But why hadn't her mother told her about it once she had come of age?

Before the trip, she wrote to Robert at the Toledo address and telephoned both the Foreign Office in London and the British Embassy in Madrid. There was no reply from Toledo and neither department was helpful. She enquired as to the current situation in Madrid after the Nationalists' thwarted attempt to seize power, only to be told that such information was confidential. She listened to the wireless but soon realised that events building in Germany under Hitler had supplanted news from Spain.

The cottage was not easily accessible. It was at the end of a rough track, bordered by fields. No doubt, it was idyllic in summer but in winter it was forbidding, and in the gloom of the late afternoon, rather spooky. Maggie parked the car as close to the property as possible and trudged the rest of the way up to the cottage. The keyhole was rusty, and at first she had difficulty in unlocking the door. It swung open eventually to reveal a narrow hallway with a room off each side. The light switch didn't work, but fortunately she had brought a torch with her. Taking the door on the right first, she went cautiously into the room. The floorboards creaked as she walked over and opened the wooden shutters. A thin ray of light penetrated the grimy window, revealing peeling wallpaper and scratched paintwork. An alcove off the room had served as a kitchen. It contained a chipped butler sink, a stained wooden draining board and a rusty range which clearly hadn't been used for years.

Retracing her steps, she went into the room opposite only to find it in exactly the same state of disrepair. The only difference here was the existence of an inglenook fireplace, dirty with ash and half-burnt logs. She recalled the solicitor's words: *It may be a bit run-down.* 'That's an understatement,' she muttered to herself, her spirits plummeting. How was she going to find a buyer for this dump? Filled with disappointment, she returned to the first room to close the shutters. A shuffling noise startled her. She spun around and saw a scruffily dressed man standing in the doorway.

'You startled me,' she gasped.

'Sorry miss.'

'Who are you?'

He shrugged but didn't give a direct answer, saying, 'I saw the door was open so I came to check up.'

It took Maggie a second to make out his strong West Country accent. Pulling herself together, she replied, 'I'm the owner, here on business.'

On hearing this, he doffed his cap and took a step towards her, asking, 'Are you thinking of moving in?'

'No, I shall be selling it although I can't see what business it is of yours.'

He rubbed a hand over the ginger stubble on his chin and grinned, revealing tobacco-stained teeth. 'Selling it? Now that *is* interesting. What price would you be asking?'

'I haven't decided yet.'

'Well, missie, what would you say if I made you an offer?' '

Maggie couldn't hide her astonishment. 'Are you serious? It would need some work done before you could move in.'

The man gave a snort. 'I wouldn't want to live here,' he started to say, then seemed to think better of explaining his reasons for wanting to buy the cottage. 'What d'you say? How much do you want for it? You can't expect much for a ruin like this.'

For a moment, Maggie was tempted to snatch a figure out of the air. Surely he couldn't be serious? Instead, she said, 'Why don't you make me an offer?'

His eyes narrowed. 'Umm, £150 would be generous.'

Maggie caught her breath. £150 would go a long way to settling the outstanding bills. But she could see that he was a wily old man and a sixth sense told her not to jump at his offer.

'I'll think about it,' she said. 'Give me your name and address and I'll contact you.'

'Have you got something to write on? he asked.

She handed him a slip of paper and a pen and watched him lean against the wall to write down the necessary details. After handing it back, he held out his hand for her to shake. It was large and calloused and dirty. Smothering her disgust, she shook his hand, flinching at its strength.

'I'll bid you good day,' he said. 'I hope you'll take my offer seriously. You won't get a better one. Take care on your way back along the lane. It's getting dark and there are a lot of pot holes.'

Backing to the door, he disappeared into the gloom. After a few minutes, she left the house, locking the door behind her. Feeling puzzled, she stood for a few minutes watching the man as he plodded across the field. Why was he interested in her derelict cottage? He looked like a penniless tramp.

She went back to the car and sat pondering on the incident. He had given her an address in Lapford. She decided to find somewhere to stay overnight to give herself time to think over his offer. Starting the engine, she reversed the car, taking a left turn at the end of the lane. She had noticed a pub on the road on her way to the cottage and decided that a chat with the landlord with a few oblique questions thrown in might prove informative. Country pub landlords always knew everything there was to know about the locals.

The landlord of the Smugglers Inn was no exception. A stocky man with a ruddy complexion and twinkling grey eyes, he greeted her cheerfully. 'What can I get you, young lady?'

This was the first time she had ever ventured into a pub on her own, and feeling rather daring, she ordered a shandy.

'Are you on holiday?' enquired her host as he pushed the drink across the bar towards her.

'I came to take a look around the area,' she replied.

'Thinking of moving down here, are you?'

'Not exactly.' She smiled, warming to his friendliness. 'As a matter of fact, I already own a house near here. I came to check on it.'

He looked surprised. 'You're a property owner, my word.'

She gave a little grimace. 'It isn't much. In fact, it's little more than a ruin. It's just along the road, not more than five hundred yards from here. You get to it via a dirt track.'

'Well, I'll be damned! You mean that cottage in Merlin Lane? Old Arthur Trevellan's been after it for years.'

'Arthur Trevellan?' gasped Maggie. 'Why I've just met him. Are you serious, does he really want to buy it? Only I thought … Well, to tell the truth he didn't look as if he had two pennies to rub together.'

The landlord threw back his head and laughed. 'That old bugger!' He cast her a quick glance and added, 'Excuse my French.'

Maggie continued to stare at him, her brows raised enquiringly.

'Old Trevellan's the wealthiest man in these parts; owns most of the land around here except for the strip in the middle, the bit where your property's situated … ' He gave another hearty chuckle. 'Thing is, that's the bit with the fresh water stream running through it.'

'I didn't see a stream,' interjected Maggie. 'Although I must admit that by the time I left it was too dark to explore.'

'It's at the rear of the cottage, almost hidden by the trees.' He leant across the bar and spoke confidentially. 'You're sitting on a little goldmine. If you play your cards right, you'll get a good price out of old Trevellan.'

Maggie took a sip of her shandy and said, 'He offered me £150.'

'Don't accept it. That piece of land is worth at least six times that amount to him.'

Maggie did a quick calculation. Nearly a thousand pounds? She blinked and asked, 'I can't drive home tonight. Do you know of a guest house near here?'

'You can stay here, we have a couple of rooms to let,' replied the landlord. 'And I tell you what, tomorrow morning, you can have a word with an auditor fellow I know. He'll advise you what to do.'

'Thank you very much,' said Maggie, feeling completely bemused by the turn of events. 'Can I get something to eat?'

'Certainly you can. Go and sit down over there and I'll get my missus to make up some sandwiches for you.'

CHAPTER TWO

The next few weeks flashed past. With the sale of the cottage at a good price, Maggie was able to settle the bills and still have a sizeable amount to put in the bank. This was fortunate since she had been too busy trying to discover Robert's whereabouts to do much translation work.

Her emotions were in turmoil. She missed her mother although she felt ashamed to admit to herself that Katherine's absence was more of a blessing than a sadness. Robert was constantly in her thoughts. She recalled the day of his departure for Spain: the fervour in his eyes, the spring in his step. He had kissed their mother dutifully, ignoring her pathetic pleas for him to change his mind: *Robert dear, who'll do the heavy chores? Who'll look after the garden?* Maggie couldn't remember his precise reply but she knew he had cleverly reassured Katherine that all would be well and that he would be home again in a few months' time.

His parting from her was different. They had hugged, she with tears streaming down her face, he with an expression of concern in his dark eyes.

'I have to go, Maggie, you do understand, don't you? I feel drawn there as if by an invisible thread.'

'But Robert, you're going into the unknown. You've only been to Madrid once in your life and that was long before the troubles began.'

'The Republican Government has created the Popular Army. They need recruits, I've got to enlist.'

'Please don't, Robert.'

He seemed not to hear her. 'I owe it to grandfather. He taught us the language, he showed us how to be Spanish.'

'No,' she implored. 'We were born and brought up in England.' She tossed her head. 'We're not Spanish, you and I, we're English.'

He had gripped her shoulders and insisted, 'You may be English but I'm not.'

With these words ringing in her ears, he had pivoted on his heel and left. She heaved a sigh. Robert, the great romantic! Her brother was the living image of their paternal grandfather, Esteban Morán, who had fled from Spain with his child bride, Estela, in 1875 after being hunted down by the Carlist Militia. She reflected on how they had settled in England with Esteban making a reasonable living as a wine importer. For business purposes, he had been forced to learn English, but Estela had never bothered and neither of them had made an effort to integrate into British society.

Maggie looked around her. Esteban had bought the house on Stanmore Common. She and Robert had grown up there. It was a rambling old place with wood-panelled rooms, high ceilings and small leaded windows. Difficult to heat in winter, it provided a cool haven during the summer months. The garden was big and mostly overgrown. Over the years, the orchard had degenerated into a wild wood, the vegetable garden had become a mass of brambles. She sighed, remembering how their grandmother had sent them out to pick apples and pears and collect the raspberries and gooseberries which grew so profusely. Estela would bottle the fruit and make delicious jam. But as she grew older, this enthusiasm for providing home produce for the family gradually lessened until she didn't even bother to chase the children out to forage. The unpicked fruit was left to rot.

Her mouth twitched with a hint of bitterness when she recalled how utterly involved in one another, their parents, Miguel and Katherine, had been. It was, thought Maggie, as if a whole generation had been missed out. It had been *Abuelo Esteban* who had welcomed them on their return from school, and *Abuela Estela* had always been ready with a glass of fresh lemonade and homemade cake. Their grandfather would recount stories of old Spain, relate anecdotes about the Spanish side of their family. Somehow, during his flight from Spain he had managed to smuggle out a number of Castellano story books, which he read to the children. He never spoke to them in English.

Only weeks after Esteban's death, followed almost immediately by that of Estela, Robert had gone off to university to do a civil engineering degree. Maggie herself had opted to study languages, travelling to London daily to attend a language college. She'd been desperately lonely. Her father, Miguel, who worked from home administering the wine importing business, was always busy in his study, and most days her mother would be in there with him, writing letters, reading or sewing. Gone were the days when she had her brother for company, sharing secrets and dreams, especially Robert's.

With these thoughts cavorting around her mind, Maggie threw herself into her translating work. There was an abundance of it now that it had been officially accepted that Spain was in the throes of civil war. What she learnt shocked her, giving her even more cause to worry about Robert. Each week, she telephoned the

Foreign Office for news, but they were unable to help her. She continued writing to both the villa in Toledo and the address on the outskirts of Madrid where Robert had stayed on his arrival in Spain, to no avail.

Reports on the Spanish conflict got relegated to the lesser columns of the newspapers when May saw the Coronation of King George VI, the destruction by fire of the Hindenburg airship, and the Chicago Memorial Day massacre. Worry about her brother consumed her. She could neither eat nor sleep. She started looking for a job in town but invariably withdrew her application once an interview appointment was granted. Somehow, making a commitment was out of the question. She instinctively knew that something else was waiting in the wings. Then one sleepless night she realised what it was: she was destined to go to Spain to look for Robert.

Once the decision was made, Maggie couldn't wait to get started. The first snag she encountered was her passport. It was out of date. Unwilling to wait for a postal renewal, she went up to London to renew it in person. The next trip was to see the solicitor so that he could take care of any bills which might crop up during her absence.

'Are you taking a holiday?' he asked.

'Yes,' she lied.

'How long will you be away, a week a fortnight?'

'I don't know. It's open-ended.'

'Hmm, where are you going? You ought to leave me a contact address.'

Maggie began to bristle. 'I can't, I shall be travelling around.'

'On your own?'

'Why do you assume I'm travelling alone?' she retorted.

This embarrassed him. 'Well ... I just thought ...' He changed the subject. 'Have you heard from your brother?'

26

This question made her blush. 'No.'

His heavy brows drew into a frown. 'You're not going to Spain, are you?'

'Of course not,' she stuttered. 'To start with I shall be stopping off in Paris.' To put an end to the interview, she picked up her handbag from the floor beside her chair and said, 'I'll have to go, I've got some shopping to do.'

The visit unsettled her. Maybe the solicitor was right. Surely it was madness to go voluntarily into a war zone. She had no idea of the regulations in force for tourists entering Spain. The journey would be long: train to Dover, ferry to Calais, train to Paris, from where she would be able to travel all the way to the French-Spanish border. The only advantage she had was her fluency in the Spanish language.

It was early summer and the trains and the ferry were crowded with holiday-makers. As if to justify her half lie, she decided to spend two days sightseeing in Paris, although her visit to the Nôtre Dame and the Eiffel Tower were marred by her impatience to get underway. On day three she paid her bill, left the hotel and started on her quest.

With her heart beating like a drum, she boarded the Biarritz train at Montparnasse. She had managed to get a couchette but she found to her dismay that her travelling companion was a businessman on his way to Bordeaux. At first, the idea of sharing a sleeping compartment with a man had appalled her but the guard on duty as good as told her to 'take it or leave it'. '*Mais, mademoiselle,*' he insisted impatiently. 'There's nothing I can do about it. In any case, there's an attendant on duty all night.' He shrugged his shoulders. '*Qu'est-ce que peut passer?*'

Yes, indeed, she thought, what could possibly happen with passengers crowding the corridors and the emergency cord within easy reach? Nonetheless, even with her doubts allayed, she hadn't slept because the man in the bunk below snored loudly.

When the glimmer of dawn pierced a crack in the blinds, she lifted herself onto one elbow and peeped out of the window. They had reached the Gasgoigne Gulf and the sea looked grey and calm. As she gazed out at it, the train took a bend in the track permitting an explosion of sunlight to reflect blindingly on the glassy water.

Her travelling companion grunted and came to life. He sat up, groaning when he bumped his head on the upper bunk. He stretched and yawned and asked conversationally, 'What time is it?'

Maggie's French was rusty but passable. 'Eight o'clock,' she replied. 'Did you sleep well?'

'Like a baby,' he replied jovially. 'Will you use the bathroom first, or shall I?'

'Please go ahead,' she said. With him out of the way, it would be easier to adjust her clothing and make herself presentable in the carriage rather than in the cramped bathroom. Besides, once washed and shaved, he might go in search of some breakfast in the dining compartment.

She guessed correctly and for the remainder of the journey as far as Bordeaux she was left alone. A feeling of loneliness swept over her. What was she doing? She had never before travelled abroad on her own. The only place she had visited was Normandy on a school trip, and of course there had been a flying visit to Madrid with her parents when she and Robert were little. She couldn't remember why their parents had taken them there. It had certainly not been a sightseeing trip; a visit to relatives maybe, although she couldn't remember meeting any of them.

To cheer herself up, she went in search of food. It was ten o'clock and she hadn't eaten since leaving Paris the day before. She soon found the dining compartment, where she chose a seat on the coast side of the train.

After ordering fresh croissants and coffee, she spent the next hour enjoying the view. It was spectacular. Being high season the beaches were packed, the promenade cafes populated. There was an atmosphere of total abandon. No doubt, by nightfall, the nightclubs would be full, lovers would be strolling along the sands under the stars and, in the casinos the lives of gamblers would be changed forever.

Arrival in Biarritz provided an insight into a world she had only previously witnessed on the cinema screen. The well-to-do descended from the train en masse; chic women dressed in the latest Paris fashions flourished long cigarette holders; precocious children ran hither and thither between stacked suitcases.

At last the frenzied expulsion of passengers was over. The platform was clear of luggage, a whistle blew, the engine belched out smoke and the train started moving. Maggie gave a little shudder. She was travelling into the unknown. Unknown? Not quite. She knew that Spain was in the middle of a civil war, she knew that Robert was in there fighting for a noble cause she couldn't comprehend. She knew that however scared she felt, she had to go and look for him.

Maggie returned to her compartment and tried to read her book but a mixture of excitement and apprehension kept her mind off the pages. The train slowed to a crawl as they neared the French-Spanish border and she pressed her nose to the window pane. Once the engine ground to a halt, the few remaining passengers got off. Maggie followed them. She glanced around, not knowing what to do until a big bearded man carrying a holdall cheerfully assured her that there was nothing to worry about.

'It's only a change of trains,' he explained. 'Wait here and I'll find out more.'

Feeling uneasy, she went to sit in the Waiting Room and became even more concerned when after an hour nothing had happened. Losing patience, she went to enquire at the ticket office but found it closed. She went out into the street but it was deserted. By now it was late afternoon and she began to panic. All at once, the big man came back.

'*Mujer*, come with me,' he called.

He was a forbidding figure: tall, heavily-built and scruffily dressed. Feeling intimidated, she pretended not to hear him. But he called her again and started striding towards her.

'It's no good staying here, *mujer*, they've stopped all the trains going across the border.'

'What?'

'They've stopped all connections.'

The colour drained from Maggie's cheeks. 'How can I get into Spain?' she gasped.

'Where are you heading?'

'Madrid. I thought I could get a train straight through from here.' Anxiety made her voice sound shrill.

'You'll have to cross the border on foot.'

'Oh God! Is it far?'

'A couple of miles or so but it's across country.' He glanced at her feet. 'It's a pity you're wearing those shoes. Still, it can't be helped. Come on I'll show you the way.'

He snatched up her suitcase and jumped down onto the railway line, walking along between the tracks for several yards. Maggie stumbled along behind him. Leaving the railway line, he led her up a steep slope to a rough path, which seemed to go on endlessly. He trudged on ahead of her and Maggie found herself panting as she tried to keep up with him. She almost panicked when he disappeared around a bend but on reaching the top of the hill, she found him waiting impatiently for her, her suitcase at his feet.

'That's Spain,' he grunted, pointing into the distance.

'It looks quite a long way off.'

'It's not too far. Where have you come from?'

'England.'

He chuckled and said, 'Well this is nothing compared to the distance you've travelled.' Then, looking puzzled, he added, 'At first, I thought you were Spanish.'

'I'm half Spanish,' she replied.

Picking up her suitcase again, he strode on still talking. 'Where did you learn the language?'

'From my grandparents. They came to live in England during the Carlist period.'

'That would account for some of the antiquated expressions you use.'

Maggie couldn't restrain a smile. 'Come to think of it, they were very old-fashioned, from another century.'

'What made you come here? It's not a safe place for tourists these days.'

'I'm not a tourist.'

By this time, the man was well ahead of her and conversation was impossible. She struggled along the stony track, afraid of twisting her ankle in her unsuitable shoes.

He stopped beside a stream and shouted, 'We're nearly there.'

To her dismay, he waded through it, stopping on the other side to look back at her, a scornful grin on his face. Maggie hesitated. The water ran clear and swift but she saw that for her it would be knee-deep. She didn't know what to do.

The man dropped her suitcase and his own hold-all onto the grass, and throwing back his head, let out a roar of laughter. 'Well, well, how are you going to get across?'

Maggie felt both furious and humiliated. This wasn't the way she had imagined she would arrive in Spain. She started to slip off her shoes but he waded back and swept her up in his arms. On the other side, he lowered her to her feet and said, 'Welcome to Spain.'

Flushed with embarrassment, she mumbled her thanks.

'It's not far to the next town. You can get the train from there. When we get to the road, just keep going.'

'Aren't you going that way?'

'I have business to attend to first,' he replied and without another word, he thrust her suitcase into her hand and made off in the opposite direction.

It took another thirty minutes to reach the town. Her feet were hurting and, despite his intimidating presence, she felt utterly lost without the man for company. The road was deserted but it occurred that it had been surprisingly easy to make the crossing from France. Surely there were border patrols in place but, looking back at the mountainous countryside, she could only imagine that her guide had been aware of their inspection schedules and knew when it was safe to cross.

She found the station quite easily and although she had hoped to go directly to Madrid, it seemed the only way was via Bilbao. Exhausted and hungry, she got on the train, sank into her seat and promptly fell asleep.

CHAPTER THREE

Something's wrong. The thought flashed across Maggie's mind as the train pulled into Bilbao Station. The sound of distant gunshots startled the passengers crowded together in the corridor, prompting them to turn to one another for reassurance.

'What's happening?' whispered a young mother standing beside Maggie, her voice trembling with alarm as she clutched her baby to her breast.

'I don't know,' answered Maggie, and alerted by the sound of footsteps, she peered through the window and saw the driver and guard running off through the ticket office. She tugged at the window's leather strap and leant out, quickly withdrawing her head when a shot rang out and a light bulb dangling from the platform ceiling shattered.

Passengers started to panic, jumping from the train and rushing for the exit. Maggie found herself being propelled along the corridor, followed by the woman with the baby. She scrambled down from the train, turning to help the woman, and together they dashed for cover, crouching behind a platform bench.

Spasmodic gunshots continued although the perpetrators of the shots were nowhere to be seen. Suddenly, an explosion rent the air. People were flung off their feet. Losing control, the young mother stood up, screaming. Responding to instinct, Maggie snatched the baby from her, folding her own body over it as she cowered on the floor. Secondary explosions pierced the air. Terrified for the woman's safety, Maggie shouted at her to take cover, tugging at her skirt, but she continued to stand transfixed, screaming in the midst of the mayhem.

All at once, the carriage nearest them shuddered. The windows blew outwards, showering glass and debris over the platform. Maggie curled her body around the baby, her bag slung across her head in an attempt to shield them both. She heard a thud and felt, rather than saw, the baby's mother fall backwards against the wall.

Like the tail-end of a firework display, mini explosions ricocheted along the platform, accompanied by the shrieks and moans of injured passengers. The nauseating smell of cordite and burning wood irritated her nostrils. With a trembling hand, Maggie tweaked back the baby's blanket. Its face was screwed up as it let out a wail. Her heart convulsed with relief: thank God the child was alive. She turned to check on the mother. The woman's body was slumped against the wall, blood seeping from a wound where a shard of glass had penetrated her chest. Her eyes stared wildly into space, her mouth gaped in mid-scream.

Bile rose to Maggie's throat as she took in the shambles around her. People were sprawled on the platform, rivulets of blood coursed along the ridged paving, those who had managed to scramble to their feet ran for the shelter of the waiting room, a carpet of broken glass crunching under their feet. Maggie fought to keep her head, waiting until she was certain the onslaught had subsided. Rising up from her crouched position, she stood trembling, her eyes smarting from the smoke, unable to focus properly. She looked from the woman's body to the crying baby nestled in her arms, trying to recall whether the woman had been accompanied. She thought not. There had been many women travelling alone with their children. Fleetingly, she wondered why they were going *into* the battle zone rather than *out* of it.

'Come with me, *mujer.*' A gruff voice brought her to her senses. Looking around, she was astounded to see the big man who had brought her across the border. Then, as now, he seemed a daunting figure, with thick unruly hair framing a weather-beaten face and full red lips disappearing into a greying beard.

When she didn't react, he said, 'You can't stay here, *mujer.*'

'What about the baby?'

'Bring him, can't you see? His mother's dead.'

Without waiting for her reply, he brushed slivers of glass from her suitcase and picking it up, strode ahead of her out of the station. The baby's cries were now a gentle whimper. Maggie shielded it with the blanket, but as she stumbled after the man, her arms began to ache. She had had no idea babies were so heavy. How old was it? Was it a boy or a girl? The nondescript colour of the blanket gave no suggestion as to the sex of the child.

Urging her to keep up with him, the man led the way through back streets. She was out of breath. He moved very fast, amazing for a man of his age. She guessed him to be in his mid-fifties or maybe older. He wore a leather jerkin over a dark long-sleeved shirt. His trousers were baggy, open sandals covered his feet. She glanced down at her own clothing: her jacket was blood-stained, her skirt torn at the hem.

Shivering with trepidation, she stumbled along behind the man, too terrified to let him out of her sight, yet afraid of where they might end up. A hundred yards or so further on, led into the doorway of a house.

'Where are we going?' she mumbled.

He placed a finger to his lips and gently rapped out a knocking rhythm on the door. A hushed voice reached

35

them through a speaker on the door frame. The man grunted a few words and the door creaked open.

A noise from the adjoining room startled Maggie into wakefulness, forcing her to face reality. What a lot had happened in twenty-four hours! With a shudder, she recalled the man who had rescued her, their covert entry into the house, the furore their arrival had caused, the concern for the baby. An elderly couple had taken charge, soothing her worries, putting her at her ease. The man was bent and grey, the woman thin and bird-like. She seemed almost too fragile to stand unaided. They did not ask her who she was and where she was travelling to. They simply took care of her, bathing a cut on her face and sending her to bed after a simple meal. These were Basque people, who spoke a language of their own. Clearly, the bearded man knew them well.

She got up and went to open the shutters. A stream of daylight revealed a sparsely furnished room. The old woman had left her a jug of water and a bowl on the dressing table. Maggie almost burst out laughing when the cracked mirror above the dressing table showed a face looking twice her age. Her dark hair and eyebrows were sprinkled with grey dust, streaks of dirt stained her cheeks. Some blood had seeped through the hastily applied sticking plaster covering the cut on her forehead.

She dipped her face into the cool refreshing water, dampening the front section of her hair so that when she had dried herself on the towel hanging on a rail by the wall, her reflection told her that she had partially returned to normal. With a rush of panic, she was reminded that she had given up her safe life in England to travel to war-torn Spain to search for her brother. In a few weeks' time she and Robert would be twenty-five. She frowned with determination. They would spend their birthday together. She had made up her mind about that.

36

The door opened and the old woman came in. 'Ah, you're awake. Did you have a good sleep?' she asked in Spanish.

'Yes, thank you.'

'Come and join us.'

'How's the baby, *señora*?' asked Maggie.

'Fast asleep. Would you like to see him?'

She raised her eyebrows. 'So it's a boy?'

The woman nodded and taking her hand, led her through the main room to a small alcove where the drawer from a dresser had been emptied out and placed on the floor. The baby looked peaceful in his makeshift cradle, his small mouth forming into a secretive smile as he sucked at his thumb in contented sleep.

'Has he been fed?' asked Maggie.

'Yes, my dear, don't worry. I've looked after him.'

'How old d'you think he is?'

The woman pursed her lips. 'About four months. He's healthy enough. How terrible that he will grow up not knowing his mother.'

'Is there anything amongst his clothing to show who he is, his name perhaps?'

'I'm afraid not.'

They went back to where the woman's husband and the bearded man were waiting. Maggie sat down on the sofa beside her hostess.

'*Señorita*, while you were asleep we talked about what we should do,' said the husband. When she remained silent, he went on. 'Later today our friend here will go back to the station and find out anything he can about the mother.'

'Isn't that dangerous?' gasped Maggie.

'We face danger every day.' He paused. 'Now, *señorita*, we should introduce ourselves. My name's Jesús Fajardo, my wife is Caridad and this is our good friend, Tomás Montalvo.'

Maggie nodded at each of them in turn, and addressing Tomás said, 'I can't thank you enough *señor*. I wouldn't have known where to go or what to do.'

The old man went on. 'What is your name, *señorita*?'

'Maggie Morán and I'm English.'

Caridad looked surprised. 'My dear, you look Spanish with your dark hair and eyes.'

'Why have you come here?' asked Jesús. 'Spain is in turmoil. This isn't a good time for an English woman to travel alone.'

Maggie could tell that Jesús' observation was made out of concern for her safety rather than criticism. Warming to their kindness, she told them about the recent death of her mother, going on to explain, 'When I went to see mother's solicitor, he insisted that as Robert is the eldest he must be present at the reading of the will. Without Robert - or at least his written consent - the will can't be read.'

'That's terrible,' said Caridad.

'Have you got a photo of your brother?' asked Tomás.

Maggie drew out a snapshot from her handbag and showed it to him. Tomás passed it over to the others. Caridad looked at it and said, 'He's very good-looking.' She glanced up at Maggie. 'I suppose there is a resemblance.'

Yes, thought Maggie, but Robert's far better looking than I am. She experienced a twinge of sibling envy. Was it fair that a man should be blessed with such an engaging personality, possess such perfect teeth and long eyelashes?

She felt herself blushing under their scrutiny and hastened to explain, 'We're twins.'

Tomás handed the photo back and asked, 'Do you know where he's staying?'

'I'm not sure. I have an address on the outskirts of Madrid but I don't think he's there any more because he never answers my letters.' Her spirits sank as the two men exchanged a meaningful glance. 'What is it?' she burst out.

'There's been bombing over the north of the city recently. It's not a good place to be.'

She felt panic rise, and raised her voice. 'I have to go and find out for myself. Besides, there is another possibility. Our grandfather left my brother a villa in Toledo.'

'Toledo eh?'

'Toledo is now a Nationalist stronghold.' Noticing Maggie's alarm, Tomás went on, '*Esté tranquilo, mujer,* I will help you find your brother.'

Maggie's eyes widened. 'Will you really?'

'I'll do my best, but you must be patient. First things first. I think we must all agree that the little one…' He nodded towards the sleeping baby. '…must take priority. I'll leave you now and, hopefully, when I return I'll have some news about his identity.'

Being left in the company of the old couple made Maggie feel uncomfortable. She made a valiant attempt to keep polite conversation going but, in the end, gave up. Jesús ignored the presence of the women and dozed off in his chair.

'I hope you like dance music,' said Caridad, going to an ancient gramophone player and putting on a record. Maggie couldn't get the image of the dead woman out of her mind, and to her, the lively Latin American melodies seemed inappropriate. She was glad when Caridad ran out of records. When the old woman settled herself in her chair to do some darning, Maggie took the opportunity to fetch her book and catch up with some reading.

As soon as Tomás came back Maggie sprang to her feet. 'What have you found out?'

He shrugged. 'Not much. The woman could have joined the train from any number of stations along the line.'

'Well then,' said Maggie. 'You can trace her back through those places. They were only small communities; someone will know who she is.'

'I doubt it.'

'Why?'

'Her body's been taken away.'

'To the morgue?'

Tomás gave a bitter laugh. 'The morgue? They don't bother with that these days. They'll have taken her straight to some communal burial place.'

Maggie was appalled. 'But that's barbaric! What about her husband?'

'She was wearing black, and for a young woman that probably means she was recently widowed.'

Caridad joined in. 'My dear, there are too many for the morgue. In the height of summer, they have to bury them as quickly as possible.'

'But she must have relatives somewhere,' protested Maggie, losing sight of the fact that she herself had no one other than Robert.

Maggie gazed from one to another of her companions. They seemed resigned to the situation. Anger surged through her. How could they stand by and let such things happen? A rush of fear brought back her brother's image. Things could be even worse in Madrid. No wonder she hadn't heard from Robert; the postal services must have been disrupted. How could he get in touch with her? Or - the dreadful alternative rose again - suppose he's dead! No…she couldn't let herself believe that. She balled her fists and turned away from the scrutiny of the others.

It was Caridad who brought them back to the most important issue. 'What are we going to do about the baby?' she asked.

On cue, the child let out a cry. He had been quiet during Tomás' absence but, clearly, he was accustomed to four-hourly feeds. Caridad disappeared into the kitchen and, this time, Maggie followed her. 'Can I help?'

The old woman moved swiftly, her arthritic fingers darting here and there as she placed a saucepan of milk on the hob. 'There's a bottle over there,' she said, nodding towards a corner cupboard. 'It needs washing.'

'Sterilising surely?' observed Maggie, placing a saucepan of water onto the hob next to the milk saucepan.

'I used it while you were asleep. It belongs to my daughter-in-law but her children are bigger now.'

'Does your son live here in Bilbao?' asked Maggie.

'He's in hiding.' Caridad wiped a tear from her cheek. 'Who knows whether we'll ever see him again.'

'What about your daughter-in-law?'

'She left Bilbao some time ago to stay with her family in Oviedo. She and the children will be safe there, but my son, who knows what will happen to him.'

Maggie felt moved to place an arm around the old woman's skinny shoulders but resisted the temptation. Maybe she wouldn't take kindly to her sympathy.

The water reached boiling point and Maggie carefully carried it to the tin container which served as a washing-up bowl. She poured in water and placed the old-fashioned curved baby bottle into it, together with the only teat available. It was discoloured and misshapen but it would have to do. Her knowledge of baby care was scant but she knew that, back at home in England, babies up to six months of age were either breast-fed or were given some kind of powdered milk. This baby was going to get boiled fresh milk and she wasn't even sure whether it was from a cow, a goat or a buffalo.

When the bottle was ready, she cast her mind back to a distant memory and tested the milk for temperature by dripping some onto the back of her hand. By the time, she returned to the other room, the baby was in full throttle. Tomás had picked him up and was making an attempt to quieten him by rocking him back and forth. Maggie's lips twitched in amusement. This giant of a man could not have handled the tiny bundle more delicately.

He handed the baby to Maggie, who gently pressed the teat to his mouth. The crying ceased at once as he hungrily gulped down the bottle's contents. Maggie looked up to see the other three occupants of the room smiling indulgently.

'Has he been changed?' she asked after he had finished his feed.

'*Pañales?*' cried the old woman, throwing up her hands. Darting into the adjoining room, she returned with a tattered piece of towelling.

It didn't look too clean but Maggie knew she couldn't refuse to use it. Once fed and changed, the infant was returned to his makeshift cradle where he soon fell asleep.

Tomás rubbed his hands together and said, 'We have to decide what to do about him.'

Maggie frowned. 'First of all, let's give him a name.'

Caridad nodded her head in agreement. 'It's disrespectful not to give him a name.'

This took a good ten minutes of intense discussion until they fixed on the name of Donato because it meant 'gift' in Latin.

More discussion followed and it was finally decided that when Maggie and Tomás moved on, Donato should stay with the Fajardo's until such time as they could contact their daughter-in-law. They were convinced she would be willing to look after him.

42

Maggie's arguments that they should approach the authorities about the child fell on deaf ears.

'He'll be put in some terrible orphanage, or end up with uncaring foster parents.'

'He'll be subjected to abuse and disease.'

Caridad wrung her hands, weeping. *'Pobre Donato niño, we can't let that happen.'*

With three pairs of judgemental eyes trained upon her, Maggie bowed to the inevitable. Clearly, they thought her hard-hearted and, she had to admit, that her affection for the tiny mite was growing by the hour. Could she allow Donato to be subjected to such unimaginable horrors?

It was agreed that she and Tomás should leave first thing in the morning, travelling to Burgos together. When he handed over some pesetas to Jesús, Maggie felt morally obliged to delve into her own purse. Even giving away a small amount could mean one day less in Madrid. On leaving home, she had allotted herself a certain sum of money and she had no idea how to get more from her bank account in England if she ran out. Her journey had already been delayed by several hours and now it seemed they would have to travel by bus and by foot before they could reach another station down the line where they could re-board the train.

Maggie was awoken in the morning by Caridad, who had got up early to feed Donato. Saying goodbye to the old couple and parting from Donato was more difficult than she could have imagined. Rescuing the baby had made a huge impression on her. She had read somewhere that if you saved someone's life you would forever be responsible for them. It was nonsense of course, but giving his soft cheek a farewell kiss tore at her heartstrings.

They had barely gone two miles when the air-raid started. Russian bombers flew in low over the city. Tomás pushed her into the shelter of a building, gripping her arm as she trembled uncontrollably beside him. The attack was brief but heavy and when they went back into the street, Maggie saw a huge column of smoke rise above the distant houses.

Tomás voiced her fears. 'That was close to where we were last night.'

'Donato?' she gasped.

He turned her to face him. 'You go on. The next station isn't far from here. I'm going back to find out if they're all right.'

Through chattering teeth, Maggie muttered, 'I'm coming with you.'

He gripped her arm. 'No, you go on.'

She shook away from him, forcing herself to regain control. 'I must find out whether they're safe.'

'I'll let you know. We'll meet up in Madrid, I promise.'

She shook her head vehemently and said firmly, 'I can't go on without knowing.'

He studied her for several seconds, then picked up her suitcase and strode back along the road. She followed close behind him, as always finding it difficult to match his stride.

They entered the city through a pall of dust and smoke and were forced to cover their noses and mouths with handkerchiefs to stop themselves from coughing. The bombing had been concentrated on the town centre. Buildings were burning fiercely with firemen, armed with hoses and buckets of water, trying to dowse the flames. Chaos reigned. Ambulance sirens screeched against the clamour of shrieks and moans. Helpers dug at the ruins, survivors sobbed close by. The road ahead was blocked but, undeterred, Tomás clambered over huge chunks of concrete. Maggie chased after him, ignoring the dangers, more afraid of being separated from him than from falling and hurting herself. At last they reached the house, or what remained of it.

'*Dios mio!*' Tomás stood surveying the devastation.

Maggie fought faintness as her gaze probed the ruins. No one could have survived this.

'They're all dead,' she gasped. 'That dear, sweet old couple and the baby.'

Then she heard a faint whimper. Was it possible that Donato was alive? Throwing caution to the winds, she dropped her bag and struggled across the bricks and beams, guided by the ever increasing sound of that tiny child's cry. She could see him, trapped in the rubble. A concrete beam had fallen across the drawer where he lay, wedged up at an angle by part of the wall which was still intact. Dust swirled around him, pieces of debris floated down.

She heard Tomás come up behind her as she crouched down to peer into the hole.

'*Mujer,* that beam could come crashing down any moment. Let me go to him.'

She waved him back. 'No, you're too big to squeeze in there. I'll go.'

A shower of masonry made them duck their heads.

'It's too risky,' he said, brushing dust from his hair and beard.

'I can do it,' she insisted.

This time, he didn't argue but stood back to give her sufficient room. Maggie took a deep breath, gearing herself up to crawl into the small gap in which Donato was trapped. She had never liked small spaces and this endeavour was testing her to the utmost. The beam was so low that she was obliged to slither rather than crawl and, at one point, she was afraid that her shoulders would not fit through. She withdrew and took off her jacket. Once again, she wriggled forward, stopping each time rubble showered down. The concrete beam gave a groan and she instinctively covered her head with her hands. But the beam did not shift and she inched her way further and further into the gap until she was within reach of the baby.

The drone of a drill shattered her concentration and she heard Tomás' expletive as he yelled to someone in the road to stop the drilling. Silence. Her heart beat fiercely against her ribcage, her breath came in short, sharp bursts. Donato had been showered with shards of masonry but, miraculously, nothing had fallen on his face. When he saw her, he stopped crying. It was almost as if he knew that the least movement or sound could bring the building crashing down on top of them. Reaching into the makeshift cradle, she cautiously pulled him out. He snuggled against her neck, his breath whispering into her ear. Wrapping his blanket firmly around him, she started inching her way back until something caught her gaze. The feeding bottle. She wriggled forward, snatched it up, and once again, began the difficult retreat, feeling her way by touch.

As she got closer to daylight, she called out, 'Tomás, take off my shoes.'

She heard his foot crunch on the rubble and felt his big hands slide her shoes off her feet. Freed of the encumbrance of footwear, she felt her way back with her toes. When at last she was able to stand up, she staggered across the ruins, stumbling over boulders and metal girders, oblivious to the abrasions to her feet. But all at once, the enormity of what she had done hit her. She felt her head begin to spin and, acting on instinct, she quickly passed the baby to Tomás before passing out.

She opened her eyes to see a young man crouching down next to her.

'Are you injured?' he asked.

She shook her head, a movement which almost cost her another bout of faintness. 'I'll be all right,' she whispered, then lifted her gaze to look around. 'Where's the baby?'

The man patted her shoulder reassuringly. 'He's quite safe, Your father's got him.'

Tomás, her father! Maggie nearly burst out laughing but quickly realised that the man's assumption was a logical one. He helped her to her feet and led her over the ruins to where Tomás was seated on a large piece of concrete, cradling Donato in his arms. He smiled at her and said, 'You did well. The baby's unharmed. It took courage to do what you did.'

Maggie gave an involuntary shudder, admitting to herself that had she had time to think about the consequences she might not have been so brave. She thanked the other man, who needed to get away now that she was with her 'father'. He clambered off over the ruins to join the rescue team.

Maggie sat down next to Tomás and took the baby from him. He picked up her shoes, bending to place them back on her feet. She looked down. Her stockings were in shreds, her feet were bleeding. There was a deep gash on the top of her instep, which needed to be cleaned and bandaged. Tomás took a grubby-looking handkerchief out of his pocket and tied it round her foot to restrict the bleeding.

'Can you get your shoes on?' he asked.

Tentatively, she slipped her left foot into her shoe. The sides scraped against the cuts but at least it fitted on. The right foot was difficult. The cuts and bruises were more serious and her foot was beginning to swell up. Wincing, she managed to force her foot into the shoe but, when she stood up and placed her full weight onto her foot, she could not hold back a yelp of pain.

'I'll help you,' said Tomás. 'We've got to get out of here. Those Ruskies might decide to come back. Besides, you're a foreigner and some highfaluting Nationalist officer might decide to take you in for questioning.'

'They can't do that, I've done nothing wrong,' she protested indignantly.

'I know that but they could question you, and it could take hours, even days, sorting things out. We can't afford that. Besides, they might take the baby away from you.'

Maggie considered his response. Surely, handing the baby over would be the sensible thing to do. Besides, suppose Jesus and Caridad had escaped, perhaps they hadn't been in the house. They could still take care of Donato. She realised the futility of this possibility. They would never have gone out without him.

'Maggie, we *have* to take him with us.' Tomas' voice jerked her back to reality.

'Yes, I know.'

What else could they do? She looked down at Donato's tiny face and experienced a tug of emotion. What had Caridad said? A cold, clinical orphanage, uncaring foster parents paid to take on unwanted children? She gave a mental shake of her head. She couldn't let that happen to Donato.

'Perhaps we could contact the Faraja's daughter-in-law in Oviedo,' she suggested.

Tomás uttered a snort of derision. 'Do you really think she'd welcome another mouth to feed with her husband away and three children of her own?'

Maggie winced again as she shifted from one foot to the other. 'What's the alternative?'

'There is none. We take him with us.'

She knew it was the only way and, given a choice, she also knew that she would have chosen that solution. It was fear that had made her have doubts. Tomás had said she was courageous. She shook her head as she faced up

48

to reality: she was a coward. Robert was the brave one, the twin who took risks, the twin who led the way.

CHAPTER FOUR

Italy - January 1937

'Hey, Palmiro, have you heard? We've been volunteered.'

'What are you talking about?'

'Our squad's going into the action. All leave's been cancelled. We're off to Spain.'

'You're joking?.' Palmiro frowned suspiciously as he scrutinised his companion's face. 'Is it true?' He was well used to Salvatore's practical jokes.

The other man nodded. 'You'd better let your family know you won't be home.'

Palmiro's frown deepened. 'They'll be devastated. It's my sister's wedding next week, she'll never forgive me if I miss it.'

Salvatore gave a laugh as he slapped Palmiro on the back. 'Never mind, my friend, you can be there for the christening.'

'What are you implying?'

'Nothing, calm down. Can't you take a joke?'

'It didn't sound like that to me.'

'Touchy, aren't we?'

Salvatore jumped back as Palmiro balled his fist and took aim.

'Oops!' he gasped as he narrowly avoided the punch. 'I think I'd better get out of here.'

Physically, the two men were not dissimilar. They were both typical southern Italians, stocky and dark-skinned and stood no more than five foot seven. But Palmiro knew that in a serious fight, Salvatore would come up the winner. He had no intention of putting this possibility to the test.

Left alone, he gathered his thoughts. Maybe it wasn't so bad. Since Abyssinia, his platoon had been kicking their heels waiting for something to happen. But it was bad luck about the wedding. Santina would be terribly disappointed, Eduardo would take it as a personal affront, his mother would wail in despair, and his father would be furious. It crossed his mind that he could abscond. Many conscripts did. There were plenty of places to hide out in his neck of the woods. But if you got caught, the consequences were unthinkable and, with the wedding arrangements in place, officialdom would soon track him down. He gave a mental shrug. There was no getting out of it.

Before the wedding date, he managed a day's leave, travelling home overnight and returning the next day. The family reacted as he had predicted: tears and hugs and beating of breasts. In a way, he was glad to get away from it. Heaven knows, being in the army had broadened his horizons. He now knew there was something beyond Calabria's dusty terrain, that in the big cities the oldest son did not automatically enter the priesthood, that nursing was not the only respectable job for a woman. He had learnt that it was acceptable for women to smoke and to eat in a restaurant on their own, although the latter were usually either American or British.

'How did it go?' asked Salvatore when he got back to the barracks.

'They weren't happy.'

'What did you expect?'

Palmiro shrugged. 'They've hired a photographer for the wedding so I'll see photos.'

Salvatore rubbed his hands together. 'Well, my friend, we're off tomorrow. Can't wait to see a bit of action.'

'Did you go home yesterday?'

'Briefly.'

Palmiro was not altogether comfortable about his friendship with Salvatore. The young man never took anything seriously and refused to reveal anything about his family. Knowing that he came from the back streets of Naples, Palmiro considered it prudent to curb his curiosity. Streetwise and cunning, Salvatore was not a man you could cross question. He knew everything that was going on, he knew how to break the rules without getting caught and, in a barrack room argument, he always came out on top with his quick-fire responses. Palmiro both liked him and hated him but he instinctively knew that it was better to be a friend of Salvatore's than an enemy.

Palmiro was forced to take to his bunk during the voyage from Genoa to Cadiz. His journey to Abyssinia had been marked by the same terrible sea-sickness. On each occasion, the sea had been smooth but the very suggestion of tidal movement sent his stomach into spasm. He was the only one in his squad to suffer and, as a consequence, he became the target for ridicule. After the initial tormenting, Salvatore came to his aid, sending his persecutors packing so that he could at least suffer in private. He wanted to die and began to regret not making off into the mountains of Calabria when he'd had the chance.

But the trip was short and recovery almost instant once his feet touched dry land. It was still winter but the climate was not dissimilar from that in the south of Italy so that, after the foggy dampness of five days spent in a camp north of Milan whilst waiting for the go-ahead to march to the coast and board ship, Cadiz seemed fairly amenable.

The men came up with endless theories as to what was in store for them. No information had been given out and, as Palmiro reminded himself, if they had been told where they were going and for what, there was no doubt the majority of them would not have been any the wiser. Unlike Abyssinia, this was not Mussolini making a conquest to colonise a country. This was a civil dispute within a foreign land and it puzzled him as to why they should be there.

However, it soon became clear that the Italians were not the only foreigners assisting the insurgents. Under Hitler, the Germans were sending aid to the Nationalists.

A month passed without action. The enlisted men slipped into holiday mood. The unusually mild January brought a feeling of well-being. It also brought the inhabitants out of their villages. The officers, too, relaxed their regimen, casting a blind eye as the men began fraternising with local girls. Palmiro found himself attracted to one of them.

Milagros was a small, dark girl with large brown eyes. Her hair hung to her waist in ringlets. She was exceptionally timid and blushed whenever anyone spoke to her. Even to his eighteen-year-old eyes she seemed extremely young. It was a child-like ingenuousness that put him at his ease, enabling him to try to overcome the language barrier and communicate with her. The other men managed to communicate in a jocular, more obvious way although there were one or two incidents where misunderstandings occurred and a girl would run away screaming out something about her *modestia*.

Strangely, it was this innocent encounter that gave Palmiro his first taste of war. Whenever the pair strolled beyond the village, Milagros' mother would insist that her little brother, Gualterio, went with them. This didn't bother Palmiro. He had no ulterior motives, and Gualterio was happy to trail along behind them, toeing a track of dust in and out of clumps of grass or aiming stones at iguanas as they slithered to safety in the cracks of walls. As they returned to the village a burst of gunfire shattered the quiet of the late afternoon.

'*Mi casa!*' screamed Milagros.

Before Palmiro could stop her, she sped towards the village. Instinctively, the young soldier snatched at Gualterio's arm, gripping him so tightly that the boy cried out. Astonished, he watched the girl run into a building. Seconds later, there was an explosion with bricks and mortar tossed into the air onto the narrow road. He stood frozen, still grasping the boy's arm. As the dust began to settle, he saw his companions running about in all directions, officers shouting commands. An old woman stood in shocked silence not ten feet away from him.

'Look after the boy,' he shouted in Italian, thrusting the child at her and running the rest of the way to the village.

The scene was catastrophic. Houses on both sides of the street had been destroyed, there were body parts strewn across the road, a river of blood streamed between the cobblestones. A toddler stood in the middle of the carnage, balled fists clutched to her open mouth, from which no sound came. A soldier whisked her away to safety while several others appeared from a house further along the road, prodding ahead of them three Republican prisoners forced to march with arms raised above their heads.

Palmiro jumped to his officer's command, taking over the escorting of the prisoners to the police station with its single cell. The captives were a scruffy threesome: unshaven and slovenly dressed. They refused to answer

54

when asked for their names, and pressure to clean up the mess left by the explosion and assist the injured took priority.

On returning to the scene of devastation, Palmiro joined his companions searching through the rubble for possible survivors. He tried to tell himself that Milagros had somehow escaped but, in his heart, he knew it was impossible. She had disappeared into the house only seconds before the explosion. He went down on his hands and knees, casting aside bricks and large pieces of concrete, coughing as the dust continued to rise, squinting to relieve the stinging at his eyes. Occasionally, the noise around him would rise in volume as if someone had switched on a wireless but, for most of the time, he was cocooned in his own private world.

Salvatore called out to him but he waved him away as he scrambled deeper into the ruins of Milagros' house. Then he saw her. She lay face up, eyes wide open, arms spread out as if welcoming death. A concrete pillar lay across her stomach; below it, her bare feet peeped out, the toes pointed as if she were dancing. Her pale blue flowered dress above the pillar was shredded and bloodied.

He turned his head away and vomited into the crater, choking for breath. After a few minutes the vomiting stopped and he sat down on a boulder to recover. Deliberately keeping his gaze away from the girl lying in the ruins, his mind flew back to his time in Abyssinia. He had seen no fighting there due to having been posted to the Ogaden Desert on road construction duties. It had been hard, gruelling work which bore little resemblance to soldiering. At the end of his term in East Africa, he had spent six months in Naples from where he had been able to go home on leave fairly frequently. He had seen nothing out of the ordinary, in fact life had been easy with his board and lodging taken care of and a gang of happy-go-lucky young men for companionship. He had been living in a dream world. This was the real world: harsh and cruel.

The mood in the camp changed. A solemn silence spread over the detachment. Even meal-times, usually lively events, were quiet. When Enrico got out his mouth organ and started playing, his companion nudged him in the ribs and he put the instrument away. The worst thing was when Palmiro was put on guard duty. The imprisoned men talked among themselves in a strange dialect he could not fathom. He wanted to demand information, ask them where they were from and why they had chosen this particular village to attack but he knew that even if he could have communicated with them, he would have found it impossible to stay rational. He hated them. They were murderers. They had cut short the life of a beautiful young girl. He had learnt through the rumours flying around that Milagros was only fourteen. He wondered what had happened to her little brother and whether her parents were still alive. He did not know who to ask. Perhaps Salvatore would be able to winkle out information.

Guard duty gave him time to think, and like a long watched pot of water heating on the stove his thoughts rose to boiling point. The prisoners slept for part of the night, but as there were no bunks in the cell they were clearly uncomfortable squatting against the wall. During the early hours, one of the men produced a set of five stones and they began flicking them across the concrete floor, chortling and goading one another. The seething in Palmiro's brain was impossible to restrain. Why were they so cheerful, so uncaring? Didn't they realise what they'd done? Dropping his rifle, he thrust an arm through the bars of the cell and snatched at the nearest man's shirt front, twisting it and tugging the man towards him so violently that his face crashed against the iron bars, making his nose bleed. Without considering the repercussions, Palmiro drove his fist into the man's cheek. There was a crack and both of them knew the cheek bone was broken. The man's companions jumped to his defence, wresting him from Palmiro's grasp. They shouted at him in their unintelligible dialect, making such a racket that another soldier on guard duty outside, came running in.

'You idiot!' he yelled when he saw what Palmiro had done. 'You'll be sent to the guardhouse for this.'

But Palmiro was beyond caring. Ignoring the soldier, he calmly wiped the victim's blood from his fist and resumed his duty position.

Two days in isolation were not so bad. When he was let out of the guardhouse, Salvatore greeted him with an amused grin. '*Benvenuto, amico*. What got into you?'

'I acted on impulse,' replied Palmiro. He had no intention of explaining the reasons for his actions. Revenge for the Neapolitan was provoked either by sex, money or territory. Salvatore would never have understood Palmiro's need for retribution for the life of an innocent young girl. He recalled his father's advice when he was called up. Drawing him into a fierce embrace, Gianni had mumbled, 'Take care *figliuolo*, don't be impetuous, curb your impatience.' His voice broke. 'I won't live forever and you're my only son. Some day soon, your mother and sisters will need you. Don't deliberately throw yourself into the firing line.' Wise words, which he had already disregarded.

'What's happening to the prisoners?' he asked.

'Oh they've been sent off to that camp up north in the Tierra Muerta.'

Palmiro bit back his anger. Those callous brutes were being let off lightly. They should have been put on trial and punished for what they had done. But he didn't have long to reflect on the injustice of it as the next day they were on the move.

Once again, they saw little action. Three Nationalist columns from the south, the west and the north-east joined up to converge on Malaga and by the time the Italians arrived, the last Republican defenders had fled along the coast towards Almeria. There followed a short lull after which news came through that they were heading northwards ready for a fresh assault on Madrid.

The change in climate from the clement south to the wintry conditions in the Jarama Valley were a shock to the troops, most of whom were southern Italians.

'This is it,' muttered Palmiro as they prepared for battle.

'We'll soon wipe them out,' retorted Salvatore. 'Those Republicans troops aren't equipped for serious fighting.'

'And we are?' countered Palmiro with a hint of sarcasm.

The next few hours were the worst in his life. Snow fell during the night and the ground was rapidly reduced to a sea of mud by the tramping soldiers. Palmiro found the noise deafening. It numbed his brain so that blindly following orders was his only recourse. His companions fell all around him. He lost sight of Salvatore early on. The enemy, familiar with the territory, appeared from nowhere. This wasn't real, this was a terrible nightmare.

An enemy infantryman ran towards him. With fixed bayonet Palmiro launched himself forward. The other fellow was young, no older than he was. Their gaze met and he saw his own fear reflected in the other man's eyes. Instinct told him that his opponent was not a born killer. But there was no going back. He caught sight of another soldier coming towards him. Gritting his teeth, he ran his bayonet through the infantryman ahead of him. There was a sickening squelch as the man was forced backwards into the mire. Closing his eyes, Palmiro wrenched the bayonet out of the body and turned to face the new threat.

Back at base camp, the men were subdued. The Nationalists had made big advances but the battle had been a bloody one. Palmiro was relieved to find Salvatore sitting on his bunk smoking. He accepted the cigarette his friend offered him, lit up and drew on it. They were strong French cigarettes, and he wondered how Salvatore had come by them.

'What's the date?' he asked.

'I think it's the eleventh.'

'My sister got married today.'

'I hope the weather was better there than here.'

'It's the first time I've missed a family celebration. I've been to all the baptisms, confirmations, weddings and funerals. I can't believe I've missed one of the most important of all.'

'Cheer up, *amico,* like I said, you'll be home for the christening.' He ducked as Palmiro jokingly threw a punch at him.

After a couple of weeks, they were on the march again, this time towards the Basque country. Their morale was boosted by the relatively easy capture of Brihuega, but the advance on Guadalajara, some thirty-four miles north of Madrid, was not so straight-forward since, although the Italian units had been augmented and Russian tanks and aircraft had also been deployed, the ferocity of the Republican counter-attack led to a Nationalist collapse.

The light-heartedness of the Italian troops dissipated as they were forced on yet again. It seemed to Palmiro that they were always on the march. The conditions were horrendous, the camps inadequate and their uniforms unsuitable for the cold, wet weather. A few men went down with pneumonia and, by the end of the month when they had almost reached Bilbao, they were in a sorry state.

Spring came suddenly, but despite the improvement this brought to their living conditions, the Italian troops felt tired and disillusioned. They complained loudly that this wasn't their fight and that it was time for them to go home. Palmiro did not verbalise his feelings like so many of his compatriots. While he was growing up, he had listened to the young people in his village praising the changes made by Mussolini: the improved train services, the wide *autostradas*, the financial benefits to women who produced large families. However, most of the villagers had never travelled further than ten miles from home and were clinging to the belief that fascism would bring a better future.

Since joining the army Palmiro had seen how different life was in the north of Italy, where families were smaller and had better living conditions. Why then, was Mussolini rewarding women in the south for augmenting the birth-rate? This contradiction left him feeling puzzled.

He possessed a questioning mind and although he agreed with his fellow soldiers that the Spanish war had nothing to do with Italy, he listened and watched and grew to admire the resistance put up by the Republican fighters, who were standing up to the oppression which he now realised had already taken hold in his own country. *El Generalisimo* and *Il Duce* were brother fascists. Mussolini was already a dictator; Franco had ambitions to achieve the same status. While he deplored the actions of the Republican terrorists in Cadiz, he came to recognise that their target had been the army not the villagers. Milagros had unfortunately been caught up in the crossfire.

There was talk of a siege on Bilbao and the word went round that this would not be the walkover it had been in other towns. Although not well armed, the Basques were proud and resilient; their army had withdrawn behind the 'Ring of Iron' which surrounded Bilbao. The advancing units knew they would put up a brave fight but after heavy bombing by the Germans, the towns of Durango and Guernica fell and with their 'Ring of Iron' breached, the Basque army abandoned the city leaving the Nationalists to move in almost unopposed.

The Italian units were camped south of Bilbao. They had a lot of idle time on their hands with short bursts of activity when called upon to suppress an uprising. These insurgents from the fragmented Basque army were ill equipped and easily put down. Generally speaking, the Italians were dispensed with immediately after the conflict but, on one occasion, Palmiro saw at first hand, the treatment meted out by the Nationalists. From a distance, he watched a score or so bedraggled men being frog-marched into the woods, followed by a volley of gunfire.

'What's happening?' he muttered to Salvatore.

His friend shrugged. 'They don't take prisoners.'

'What about that prison outside Cuenca?'

'That's for foreigners. They kill their own.'

Palmiro watched the soldiers march out of the copse and realised how blind he had been. This sort of thing had been happening all the way through yet he had refused to let himself accept it. He turned away in disgust.

The next day they were called to another outbreak on the outskirts of the city. It was a scary skirmish, dodging over bombsites and damaged buildings fighting an enemy who knew its way around the back alleys. Palmiro saw one of his companions go down but since that first encounter in Cadiz, he had become inured to losses in the squad. Another Italian soldier fell as he reached the

61

doorway of a derelict house, shot by a sniper from within the building. Cautiously Palmiro eased his way in, squinting to pierce the darkness after the bright sunlight outside. A bullet skimmed past him to embed itself in the woodwork close to his ear. He sensed rather than saw a movement to his right and swung round. The point of a bayonet clashed against his rifle, which he brought up fiercely, expecting to meet his maker. To his surprise, the other man's rifle clattered onto the tiled floor and an expletive rang out. Now that his eyes were attuned to the gloomy interior of the building, Palmiro saw what had happened: his opponent had caught his foot on a broken tile and lost his grip on his weapon.

The man regained his balance almost at once but it was too late. Palmiro moved further into the room, his rifle aimed at the man's head. The other man knew he had no chance. Their roles had been reversed. He threw back his head and laughed, a deep resounding, scornful laugh. '*Arriba Espana*' he shouted at the moment of death.

Time passed and skirmishes became more frequent as the Basques re-grouped for a counter attack. The bombing was stepped up and, each day, more and more civilians fled the city. With growing horror, Palmiro saw that they were treated no differently to the Republican defenders, shot down in the street, their bodies left to rot. Often, relatives tried to recover their loved ones but often they were too afraid to venture forth.

Then, one day towards the end of June, they were called upon to play escort to a handful of Basque prisoners. Palmiro deliberately closed his mind to the worst scenario. Until now, the Spanish themselves had been assigned to the firing squad. This time, one of the Italian officers was put in charge. To Palmiro's dismay, he was among the small unit ordered into the woods with the prisoners. They put up no resistance, standing in line, staring unwaveringly ahead. It was a terrible moment for Palmiro.

Back at camp, the men from the firing squad kept their thoughts to themselves, refusing to satisfy the curiosity of their companions and talk about the incident. Palmiro deliberately distanced himself from the others but Salvatore followed him to the edge of the camp.

'Want one?' Salvatore offered him a cigarette and, when Palmiro took it and lit up, he said scornfully, 'Do you really believe we Italians never did that in Abyssinia?' He took a long draw on his cigarette, squinting against the smoke as it spiralled into his face. 'Don't kid yourself, I saw it happen.'

Palmiro cast him a sharp look. 'How come? You were on road building with me.'

'I was over there months earlier than that. At the front.'

'You never said.'

'You never asked.'

'Why were you delegated to road building?'

Salvatore gave a shrug. 'A mishap.'

'What d'you mean?'

'Got into a fight, killed a fellow soldier.'

'By accident?'

'You could say that.' Salvatore dropped his cigarette stub and ground it into the earth with the heel of his boot. 'I lost my temper. They believed me when I said it was an accident, reassigned me. There was no proof one way or the other, you see."

'That's terrible!' Palmiro was genuinely shocked.

'What is? My reassignment or the killing?'

Palmiro refused to be drawn into stating an opinion. He flicked his cigarette stub away, and for something to say, muttered, 'I always knew you were hiding something.'

Salvatore's confession persuaded him to keep the thoughts he had been about to voice to himself. The courage of the condemned men had impressed him. They had been prepared for death, welcomed it. They hadn't cowered but had held their heads high and faced the firing squad without a flinch.

Salvatore seemed to read his mind. 'You'll get used to rough justice,' he said with a shrug and walked away.

But Palmiro did not get used to it. The memory of those brave Basques haunted him day and night. Since landing in Spain, he had witnessed much cruelty and bloodshed. Neither side seemed to have any regard for human life and in order to keep his sanity, he had been forced to harden his resolve and block out these atrocities. It was the small incidents like Milagros' death and the defiance on the faces of the prisoners facing the firing squad that played at his mind.

The next day the Italians were sent to check for guerrilla fighters. There were one or two discoveries but little of note. Palmiro brought up the rear and it was as they were leaving a small hamlet ten miles south of the city that he heard a cry. At first he thought it must be a bird trying to find its way out of a building. He stopped and listened. Another cry. This did not come from a feathered creature, this cry was human.

He went back to a row of derelict houses, stopping to listen now and again and, when he heard nothing further, he turned back to follow his companions. But the cry came again, closer this time and he knew he must investigate. Cautiously, he made his way through a doorway, listening for movement, his rifle ready. Alerted by a noise behind him, he half turned but the world went black and he slumped to the ground.

He came round after a few seconds, blinked and looked up hazily to see a giant of a man standing over him. The man toed his leg. 'On your feet! I can't kill a man while he's lying on the ground.'

With his heart racing, Palmiro staggered up, swaying unsteadily. Even standing up, the man towered above him. The rifle he had dropped was pointed at his chest. 'Italian, eh? Your bloody compatriots won't miss you till bed-time and by then, my friend, you'll be sleeping peacefully.'

As his vision cleared, Palmiro looked around in the futile hope that one of his companions would appear. He saw that debris covered the floor and every piece of furniture was broken save for a trundle bed in the corner. Then, he heard the cry again and a woman hurried in from the back of the house. She was carrying a baby, and she looked to be only slightly older than he was. Clearly, she was angry.

'Let him go, Tomás!' she shouted. The man ignored her. She rushed over. 'Without his rifle he can't harm us. Can't you see, he's all alone?'

'If I let him go, he'll be back here with reinforcements in next to no time.'

'Not if you tie him up and leave him to be found,' insisted the woman. 'He's only a young foot soldier.'

The man continued to argue. 'He had a gun and was going to use it.'

'How do you know that?'

'This is war, *mujer*,' scoffed the man.

'I can't let you shoot him.'

The man adjusted the rifle, saying, 'Killing him makes sense. That way, we can camp here for the night without worrying about him.'

'I won't stay if you kill him,' shrieked the woman. 'I'll take Donato and leave.'

'*Idiota!* You won't get far without me.'

'I won't stay,' she insisted and to demonstrate her determination, she pushed past the man to the door, stumbling on the rubble covering the floor.

Palmiro heaved a sigh of relief as the man lowered the rifle. 'Come back, *mujer,* there's some rope in the yard, go and fetch it.'

The woman gave a jubilant smile and carefully placed the baby on a blanket spread on an upturned stool. But she hesitated before doing the man's bidding.

'Promise...promise me you won't shoot him while I'm out of the room,' she mumbled. Pointing at the baby, she added, 'You wouldn't so something like that in front of Donato, would you?'

A grin spread across the man's face. 'Trust me, *mujer,* have I let you down so far?'

Reassured, the woman went out through the back of the house, swiftly returning with a length of thick cord. The man gave a grunt and snatched it from her, then pushing Palmiro back onto the bed, he set about tying him up.

'That'll have to do,' he muttered as he stomped out.

The woman waited until the man was out of earshot, then said, 'You'll be all right now. Don't worry, his bark's worse than his bite. His name's Tomás and I'm Maggie.'

'Thank you, Maggie,' mumbled Palmiro.

Casting him a sympathetic smile, the woman picked up the baby and left the room, leaving him to speculate on his destiny.

Palmiro slept little that night. Unable to move, he experienced excruciating cramp in his arms and legs. Also, by morning, his bladder was full to bursting. He called out but no one came and he began to wonder whether the couple had made off, leaving him to his fate. To suppress panic, he pondered on his captors, trying to imagine why they were still in the village when the rest of its inhabitants had fled. The man, Tomás, was years older than the woman and he thought they must be father and daughter. He felt puzzled. The man took little interest in

66

the child and the woman seemed ill-at-ease with it. Was the baby hers?

These riddles helped to keep his mind off the awful cramp in his legs until the door opened and the big man came in. The top buttons of his shirt were undone and Palmiro saw that he wore a red kerchief around his neck. So he was a member of POUM! The day before the kerchief had been hidden by his shirt collar. Palmiro sifted through the confusion of information he had accumulated over the previous months. POUM was the Workers Party of Marxist Unification, a far left-wing anti-Stalinist group in opposition to the fascist Francoists. Although fighting towards the same end, they were unpopular with the Republicans due to their leader, Andrés Nin's former affiliation with Trotsky. He realised that Tomás was a force to be reckoned with and decided to pretend he hadn't noticed.

'I've brought you something to eat. You can thank *her* for it,' said Tomás, nodding towards the doorway where the girl was hovering.

'For God's sake, loosen these ropes,' begged Palmiro.

'Too tight, are they?' sneered his captor.

Maggie rushed into the room. 'Tomás,' she cried. 'Untie him, can't you see he's in pain?'

She ran over to the bed and started loosening the bonds, pulling off Palmiro's boot and rubbing his feet to bring life back to them.

'I need to piss,' he hissed at the man.

Tomás pushed Maggie aside, untied the remaining knots, yanked the Italian to his feet and half dragged him outside.

When they returned, Maggie was sitting on the righted stool, dandling the baby on her knee. 'Donato is so happy this morning,' she announced. 'Look, he's beginning to recognise me.'

67

Palmiro smiled to himself. So he was right, the baby wasn't hers. He was used to babies. He came from a large family and had a multitude of nieces and nephews.

Maggie looked up and caught his gaze. 'Eat up,' she said, pointing to the food Tomás had brought in. 'You don't know when you'll get your next meal.'

A night's sleep seemed to have softened Tomás' attitude. 'We don't mean you any harm,' he said. 'So we've decided to tie you up again…' He gave a guttural laugh. '…but not so tightly this time. Then, we'll leave you here for your companions to find you.'

'They won't come back for me,' protested Palmiro.

'Maybe they won't, but another squad will find you before long.'

'No!' protested Palmiro. 'If the Republicans get here first, they'll kill me.'

'Don't worry, those *maldito* Nationalists are swarming all over the place.'

'No!' This time Palmiro shrieked his protest. 'It's not like that. I don't want to go back to my unit.'

Tomás' heavy brows drew together. Then his lip curled. 'Don't tell me you're a deserter!'

'No!' shrieked Palmiro even louder, his Spanish becoming ever more fractured. 'You don't understand. I can't stand what the Nationalists are doing.'

'It's a soldier's duty to obey orders whatever he thinks.'

Palmiro looked from one to the other of the pair and saw suspicion in the man's eyes, sympathy in the woman's.

Reaching for the rope, Tomás started to push Palmiro back onto the bed.

'Stop!' cried Maggie. 'Listen to what he has to say.'

'We haven't time.'

'Yes we have.'

Palmiro studied them, wondering whether he had read Tomás accurately. And the woman, where did her allegiance lie?

He took a deep breath and announced, 'I want to go to Madrid and join forces with the International Brigade.'

CHAPTER FIVE

Maggie's heart leapt. If this young Italian knew the whereabouts of the International Brigade, he could lead her to Robert.

'What's your name?' she asked.

'Palmiro Aiello,' he replied holding out his hand to shake hers.

Tomás stepped between them. 'Don't listen to him; he just wants to make his escape.'

'That's not true,' stammered Palmiro in his halting Spanish. 'I have a mother and father in Calabria, sisters and nieces and nephews. I want to survive. Why should I be used as battle fodder for those fascist brutes?'

Tomás gave a snort of disbelief. 'If you're so keen to survive, why do you want to join the International Brigade?'

Palmiro looked crestfallen. There was no answer to that.

'Let's take him with us, Tomás,' begged Maggie.

'He'll lead us into a trap.'

Palmiro turned his gaze on Maggie, his dark brown eyes pleading. 'I say he comes with us, he'll give Donato more protection,' she insisted.

Tomás shrugged his massive shoulders. 'Be it on your own head.' Pointing at Palmiro, he grunted, 'And you, my young fellow, one step out of line and I'll shoot you. Maggie, feed the child before we go. I shall be in the back room if you should need me.'

After Tomás had departed, Maggie smiled at Palmiro. 'Tomás takes a bit of getting used to but he's been very kind to me. We only met two days ago.'

Two days ago! Was it possible? So much had happened in such a short time. With a shudder, she remembered the elderly couple who had sheltered them and who had offered to care for the orphaned child. Pushing these thoughts aside, Maggie went to prepare Donato's bottle. She was grateful to Tomás for having foraged out a supply of evaporated milk for the baby. When she returned she found Palmiro sitting on the bed staring at a snapshot.

'Is that your girlfriend?' she asked.

He shook his head. 'It's my youngest sister. She got married a few weeks ago and I wasn't there.'

'May I have a look?'

He handed over the dog-eared photo, which showed a dark-haired girl, smiling at the camera. 'She's pretty,' murmured Maggie, handing it back.

'Two of my sisters are widows,' explained Palmiro.

Maggie looked shocked. 'How awful!'

'The oldest one lost her husband in Abyssinia, the next from youngest lost hers from diphtheria.'

'Have they got children?'

'Two each.'

'Luckily, my other brothers-in-law are there for them. It's hard to make a living but they help one another. We're family,' he continued with a shrug. 'It's normal.'

Their conversation was cut short by Tomás who threw a bundle of clothes at Palmiro. 'Put these on, they should fit you.'

The Italian blinked and held up the civilian suit and shirt. 'Thanks, they look the right size.' Getting to his feet, he looked pointedly at Maggie, who took the hint and left the room so that he could change his clothes in private.

Tomás called her back in and she found him standing in front of the fireplace, stoking Palmiro's smouldering uniform with a stick. When it had burnt almost to ashes, he said, 'All set.' Gripping the Italian's arm, he went on, 'No tricks, you can make yourself useful by guiding us past the Italian encampments.'

The Italian looked even younger in civilian clothes. 'How do I look?' he asked, shuffling his feet and colouring a little.

'Very smart,' replied Maggie.

Thus it was that a young couple with a baby and the baby's grandfather made their way safely through the Italian line towards Burgos. It was hard going for Maggie since Donato was unwilling to be carried by either of the men. She struggled on, her feet still painful from the abrasions she'd suffered when she'd rescued the baby. Palmiro carried her suitcase, leaving Tomás with his own hold-all, in which he'd hidden the Italian's revolver, the rifle having been abandoned because it was too conspicuous. He had also extracted a knife and a water bottle from Palmiro's equipment.

That night they found shelter in a barn, milk from a cow for the baby and six eggs, which they managed to cook over a fire in Palmiro's army mess tin. Maggie fretted over the cleanliness of the baby's bottle. There was no way of sterilising it and she wasn't certain that milk directly from the cow was what you were supposed to give babies. At home in England, such practice would have been unthinkable. However, Donato sucked happily at his bottle and seemed content. Because everything had been lost in the Bilbao bombing she was obliged to make do with articles of her own underwear to serve as nappies, tearing slips, knickers and blouses into triangles so that she could at least ring the changes, washing the baby and the garments in any stretch of water they came across. It was unsatisfactory without the necessary hot water and soap. But here, Palmiro came to the rescue. Amongst his equipment, he had a small cake of soap. It was coarse stuff but Maggie was grateful to make use of it. At least, it meant that both Donato and his clothes smelt clean.

She was relieved that he was still too young for solid food. This would have proved a real difficulty since the three of them were obliged to eat whatever they could find, either from abandoned houses they came across en route or by picking vegetables and fruit from the fields.

They were about half way to Burgos when a bus came along. This welcome sight made Maggie realise that civilisation had not completely broken down. Tomás signalled and the bus pulled up. They climbed aboard and a man gave up his seat for her. Despite the windows being open, the air inside was stale. The vehicle jolted along the uneven road bumping the standing passengers against one another. Donato started crying until the man seated next to Maggie began making faces at him. He looked like a farm labourer and smelt awful but Maggie smiled gratefully at him for entertaining the baby.

From time to time, the bus stopped to let people on and off until eventually they reached the bus terminal in Burgos.

'We should be able to get a train from here,' said Tomás.

For the first time since Maggie had arrived in Spain, everything seemed normal. People were going about their business apparently untroubled. Tomás explained that this was because in the previous October *El Generalissimo* had set himself up in the city as Head of State.

'D'you mean the recognised Head of State?'

'Hardly,' scoffed Tomás. 'The Republicans will never accept him.'

They found lodgings for the night, sharing supper with the host family, who although amiable enough, seemed

73

unwilling to discuss anything other than the price of food and the weather.

The next day dawned hot and humid. In the north, the temperature had been pleasant but the further south they went, the warmer it became. The baby suffered from both heat and nappy rash and Maggie took the opportunity to ask the wife of the proprietor where she could purchase nappies and a few summer clothes for Donato.

The woman threw up her hands. 'Dios Santo!' she exclaimed. 'Such things are not easy to come by these days.' She tilted her head thoughtfully. 'I have an idea. Melisa Juréz miscarried last month, maybe she will let you have some clothes.'

'Oh no!' cried Maggie in horror. 'Don't ask her; that would be too cruel.'

The woman patted her arm. 'Leave it to me, my dear.'

Later that morning, the woman came back armed with baby garments and nappies. Maggie was reluctant to accept them but after the trouble the woman had taken, she felt it would be churlish to refuse. On inspection, she realised the clothes were not new, the nappies were thin and discoloured from frequent washing. Clearly, they were second or even third hand. The woman also provided her with another feeding bottle and a bowl and spoon and pointed out where she could buy evaporated milk, which she could dilute with water for the baby.

During their stay in Burgos, Tomás kept a sharp eye on Palmiro but it became apparent that the young soldier had no intention of returning to his detachment.

Tomas began to warm to him. 'You realise what will happen if you're caught, don't you?' he said, drawing a hand across his neck in a dramatic gesture.

The young man nodded. 'I'll take my chances.'

Despite his softening attitude, Tomás was still a little suspicious of Palmiro. 'Don't get too friendly with him,' he advised Maggie. 'We still don't know whether we can trust him.'

Maggie disagreed. The more she saw of the Italian, the more she liked him. Whenever Tomás left them alone, they would exchange stories about their lives. She told him about Robert and he promised that when he joined the International Brigade he would look out for him.

They left Burgos the following afternoon and caught the train to Madrid. It was crowded but Tomás managed to find a seat for Maggie. The journey gave her time to reflect on the past few days. She realised she knew nothing about Tomás. They had met under extraordinary circumstances, the events that followed had been so swift and unexpected that she had not had time to discover who he was and why he was travelling to Madrid. She had told him her reasons, but he had never offered information about himself. Throughout the time they had spent together she had trusted him without question. Now, it began to bother her.

Five hours later, the train pulled into Madrid. There was a frantic scramble as passengers fought their way off the train. Tomás advised Maggie to wait until most people had left. But Maggie was troubled. It was late afternoon and they had no lodgings booked. She was concerned for Donato. The baby had not settled during the journey. He had grizzled and refused his feed. When she mentioned it to Tomás he brushed her aside with, 'He didn't like the train.'

But Maggie didn't believe him. Most babies enjoyed the rocking rhythm of a train. Besides, from the very first moment she had cared for him Donato had obligingly drained his bottle to the last drop. He had always looked healthy and bright-eyed but now his cheeks were flushed.

They were the last to leave the train, and it seemed a long walk to the end of the platform. As they came out of Chamartin Railway Station into the stifling heat of Calle Agustin de Foxá, she almost stumbled. Palmiro placed his arm under her elbow, his brows raised in concern.

'Let me carry the baby for a while,' he said.

When Maggie passed the infant over Tomás looked alarmed. 'Hand the child back at once,' he ordered.

Maggie looked astonished and Palmiro said indignantly, 'Did you think I was going to run off with him?'

Tomás glowered at him but didn't take the matter any further, leaving the other two to follow him across the road.

'Where are we going?' asked Maggie. 'Only…'

'Trust me,' retorted Tomás. 'Have I let you down yet?'

The younger pair exchanged a glance and obediently kept up with him as he made his way through the crowded streets. He turned off the main road and led them through quiet alleyways, stopping at last at an insignificant looking café with a few shabby tables and chairs on the sidewalk beneath a faded awning.

'We'll eat here,' he told them.

Maggie started to protest. 'Shouldn't we find somewhere to stay first?'

'Don't worry, I know a place. It's not far away.'

A large plate of paella and a carafe of red wine restored Tomás' good humour and the three of them exchanged generalities, teasing Palmiro when he made a mistake in his Spanish. The baby slept throughout their meal but, before leaving, Maggie asked for some boiled water so that she could make up a bottle for him with the evaporated milk.

When she found it difficult to wake him up, she grew anxious. 'What's the matter with him?'

'He's not hungry,' said Tomás.

But when the baby woke up and started screaming, he too began to look concerned. 'We'd better leave,' he said, calling the waiter for the bill.

'I haven't much money,' mumbled Palmiro, looking embarrassed.

Tomas waved his apology aside. '*No problema.*'

'But…' Still embarrassed, Palmiro hastened to promise to repay him. 'Thank you so much,' he said.

'*De nada.*'

Maggie dug out some pesetas from her purse and slid them across the table, but Tomás pushed them back at her. She was too upset about Donato to insist. Snatching them up, she shoved them back into her purse and left the café, rocking the baby in her arms.

The others joined her outside. The shrieking child spurred Tomás on and Maggie found it difficult to keep up with him. At last, they turned into a small cobbled street in the old quarter populated by a selection of seedy-looking boarding houses. Tomás walked up and down inspecting them from outside, then having made his selection, he left Maggie and Palmiro and disappeared inside, reappearing a few minutes later.

'I've managed to get two adjacent rooms plus a cot for the baby,' he said.

That night Maggie got very little sleep. Donato screamed non-stop. She paced the floor, rocking him in her arms, afraid that he would wake the rest of the paying guests, but most of all, she was afraid that there was something seriously wrong with him.

Tomás knocked at her door. 'He must be hungry,' he said.

'He's been fed,' she replied tearfully.

'Then, he must need a nappy change?'

Maggie shook her head.

Palmiro poked his head round the door. 'He's teething,' he announced. 'Look at his flushed cheeks. Here, let me have him.' Taking Donato from her, he gave the baby his little finger to bite on and gently rocked him to sleep. Handing him back to Maggie, he said, 'He should be all right now.'

'How did you learn so much about babies?' asked Maggie.

'I've got four nieces and nephews,' he explained. 'And numerous cousins, you pick up hints with so many squawking infants around the place.'

Tomás had already disappeared back to bed and as Palmiro turned to leave, Maggie caught his hand. 'Thank you so much,' she said, planting an impulsive kiss on the young man's cheek.

He blushed and backed out of the door, closing it quietly behind him.

Maggie was relieved to learn that Donato's distress was due to teething, a symptom which would pass with time. She had been afraid he had caught some dreadful disease from the feeding bottles. However, it seemed he had a strong constitution.

After Palmiro had gone, she climbed into bed and spent a restless night, waking in the morning still feeling tired. It was a shock when she discovered that the other two were not in their room. Leaving the baby asleep, she went downstairs to look for the proprietor.

'Si?' The woman was busy cleaning the reception area and didn't seem too pleased about the interruption.

'Have you seen my companions?' she asked.

Barely pausing in her work, the woman replied, 'They left over an hour ago.'

'They've gone?'

'That's what I said.' She turned away and continued her sweeping.

'Did they say when they'd be back?'

She shrugged. 'The big man paid for both rooms before they left.'

Maggie was dumbfounded. Tomás had abandoned her! He had left her with a baby that didn't belong to her and made off. She could not believe he would do such a thing. She ran up the three flights of stairs and flung herself onto the bed in tears.

At last, she dried her eyes and took stock. She had come to Madrid to look for Robert and that was exactly what she was going to do. Tidying herself up, she turned her attention to Donato, who had woken up and was showing signs of hunger. That meant another trip downstairs to plead with the unfriendly landlady for the use of her cooking facilities to make up Donato's bottle.

By the time she got back upstairs again, the baby was yelling loudly but the feed quietened him. Following Palmiro's instructions, she burped him over her shoulder before changing his nappy. Collecting up her belongings, she squashed them into her suitcase and struggled downstairs with baby and luggage.

The proprietor was nowhere to be seen. She rang the bell on the reception desk and waited. After ten minutes and several more presses on the bell, the woman shuffled out from one of the rooms off the hallway.

'*Sí?*'

'I've got to go out. Could I leave my suitcase here for a couple of hours?'

The woman frowned. 'We don't like things cluttering up the hall,' she grumbled, then shrugged and said, 'All right but collect it by mid-day.'

'Of course. Is there a taxi rank nearby?'

'Down the road, first left.'

Maggie shifted Donato to her other arm. Her back was aching but at least now she didn't have to worry about the suitcase. She left the house and made her way to the taxi rank where she hailed a cab.

'Where to?'

'The British Embassy,' she replied.

When the taxi dropped her off in Calle Fernando el Santo, Maggie saw with dismay that there was a long line of people stretching from inside the Embassy gate along the pavement. As she joined the end of the queue, Donato let out a cry, reminding her of what she planned to do. Her thoughts during the previous sleepless night had been centred upon Donato's destiny. She had wavered from one proposal to another, settling in the early hours on what must surely be the most practical: she would hand him over to the Embassy. At the same time, she would make enquiries about Robert. *Yes,* she told herself, *this was the sensible route to take.* This way she could kill two birds with one stone!

The woman in front of her turned and smiled at the baby. 'What a delightful child!' she said in English. 'I expect you're anxious to get him safely home to England.'

'No...no, actually, I'm here to find out about my brother,' muttered Maggie.

She was reluctant to be drawn into a conversation with a total stranger, but the woman persisted. 'You ought to get out while you still can. Most British nationals can't wait to leave Madrid. The bombing's escalating and who knows how long the Republicans can hold out against the Nationalists.'

'We'll take our chances,' replied Maggie.

The woman frowned. 'You *are* in English, aren't you?'

Maggie bristled under the woman's scrutiny. She wanted to tell her to mind her own business but the prospect of having a row with someone in a situation from which she couldn't get away prevented her. 'Yes, I'm English,' she replied coolly.

'What's happened to your brother?'

Can't she take a hint? thought Maggie. 'He's disappeared and I'm trying to trace him.'

At that moment, the queue moved forward and Maggie hoped the interruption would discourage the woman from further questions. She felt ill at ease and was still battling with her conscience about what to do with Donato. Shifting him from one arm to the other, she felt his soft breath on her cheek and experienced an overwhelming surge of affection.

The woman seemed unaware of Maggie's rejection. 'He must be heavy. Would you like me to hold him for a little while?'

'It's quite all right,' replied Maggie, straightening her shoulders and trying to flex her arm under the baby's weight.

'This is going to take ages...' said the woman. '...what with the Ambassador and most of his staff moving to Hendaye...'

'I don't understand,' gasped Maggie.

'Didn't you know? They moved out last year, leaving only the vice-Consul and a skeleton staff to deal...' She swept out an expressive arm. '...to deal with all this.'

'Are there queues like this every day?' asked Maggie.

'Yes, and it's going to get worse.'

Maggie had considered giving up and returning the following day but this news made her change her mind. She decided that, however long it took, she would wait. It was over an hour before she reached the entrance to the Embassy, giving her plenty of time to reflect that, despite her earlier misgivings at finding that Tomás and Palmiro had left the *pension*, it was extremely unlikely they had abandoned her. It was more likely that Tomás had dragged Palmiro off on some errand and they would return to the *pension* later. She chided herself: why hadn't she left them a note telling them where she had gone?

Donato fell asleep in her arms and seemed to grow heavier as the minutes ticked past. Once inside the Embassy grounds, Maggie was able to admire the building, this occupation taking her mind off the discomfort of carrying the baby. She recalled having read that the grandiose palace had once belonged to the Marquis of Alava. Now its walls had lost their paint and the surrounding garden was overgrown. How sad that it had been allowed to become so run-down! The line shuffled forward and, at last, she found herself in Reception. The place was buzzing with activity.

'Sign in here please,' instructed an orderly. Balancing Donato on her hip and with her bag swinging from her free arm, she wrote her name and her Stanmore address.

After a short wait, a tall man in a pin-striped suit with a starched shirt and stiff collar made his way through the crowds and spoke to her, introducing himself as Charles Patterson, Personal Assistant to the vice-Consul. She followed him to his office, where he gestured to a chair in front of his desk before going to sit down opposite her.

'Well...' He glanced at the name on a piece of paper in front of him. 'er...Mrs Morán, I assume you and the child want to get out of Spain as soon as possible.' He made a steeple with long sinewy fingers and leant towards her. 'You realise it's not easy and there could be a long wait.'

'I haven't come for that,' replied Maggie.

'Oh?' He straightened up and raised an eyebrow in surprise. 'Then, what can I do for you?'

'I only arrived in Spain a few days ago - to look for my brother,' explained Maggie. 'He came to Madrid last year and I haven't heard from him since before Christmas.' Patterson continued to regard her without comment. Was it her imagination or was he eyeing her suspiciously? She found herself clutching Donato in a defensive hold.

'What's your brother's name?'

'Robert Morán.'

'Was he staying in Madrid?'

'He was to start with and I've been writing to him from England, but he doesn't reply to my letters.'

'Where exactly was he staying?'

'On the outskirts, in Alcobendas, with a family.'

'Have you been to see these people?'

'Not yet, I wrote to them but they didn't reply either.'

'Maybe they've moved from Alcobendas.' He paused for thought. 'Umm, but I think this would be your best starting point. Why don't you go and see them. If they've left, a neighbour might be able to tell you where they've gone.' He glanced at his watch. 'Of course, I could check our records to see whether your brother registered with the Embassy on his arrival but that would take time and, as you can see, the staff are already over-stretched.'

'Oh please...that would be help...ful.' The words died on Maggie's lips as Donato started to wriggle on her lap and she caught a glint of curiosity in Charles Patterson's eye. Was he wondering about the baby? Would he have noticed that she and Robert shared the same surname? What if he asked whether she was married?

Focusing on the baby, he asked with feigned joviality, 'What a handsome little chap! How old is he?'

'Er...four months.' Why did she feel guilty? After all, Donato had been foisted on her accidentally; she hadn't kidnapped him. She tried to draw the conversation back to Robert. 'Please check the records so that I'll at least know he got here safely.'

'Have you got a photograph of your brother?'

Still struggling to cover her confusion, Maggie delved into her handbag for Robert's photo and handed it over. Patterson took it and asked, 'You did say your brother, not your brother-in-law?' So he *had* noticed the surname.

'Robert's my brother.'

83

His brow wrinkled. 'Morán? I take it that you have Spanish connections. Could your brother have contacted your relatives?'

Maggie shook her head. 'We've lost touch with the Spanish side of the family.'

'Why did he come to Spain?'

Maggie did not know how to answer. Did the British look kindly on the International Brigade? Before she left England wireless reports had indicated a neutral approach from the British Government but it could be different here in Spain. She decided to play it safe. 'He told me he wanted to explore the country our grandparents told us about,' she replied. She could always mention the International Brigade later when she had figured out the official ruling on the situation.

Charles Patterson pressed the intercom and asked a typist to check the records. Turning to Maggie he asked, 'Is your husband with you?'

'No, I'm travelling alone.'

He frowned. 'Isn't that a little foolhardy, Mrs...Morán...?'

Maggie tried not to react but she felt the colour rise to her cheeks. Patterson went on, 'Madrid isn't the safest place in the world these days, especially for a woman with a baby. Where's your husband?'

Maggie knew she was getting into deep water. 'I'm...I'm not married.'

Patterson shifted his gaze to the blotter in front of him. 'Hmm, I see.'

Now's the time to explain about Donato, she thought, surely the Consulate would be able to take the baby off her hands and send him to England where he could be fostered. Swallowing her earlier defensiveness, she started to speak but, at that moment, the typist came back into the room.

'Well, Miss Jenkins, did you find anything? asked Charles Patterson.

'There's nothing on file, sir,' volunteered the girl. Maggie's eyes widened. Surely there'd be a record of her telephone calls and her written enquiries? 'Of course,' went on the typist, 'I could look in the older files down in the basement.'

Patterson shook his head. 'That won't be necessary, Miss Jenkins.' He turned to explain to Maggie. 'During the present conflict, we keep all records of registered British nationals to hand, so if your brother did register, his file won't have been stowed away in the archives...' Heaving a sigh, he went on, '...so er...Miss Morán, unfortunately I can't help you. We will, of course, make further enquiries and if we hear anything we'll let you know.'

Donato chose this moment to wake up and fill his nappy. Maggie gulped, 'I'm so sorry; I changed him before I came out.'

Looking uncomfortable, Patterson waved off her apology. 'No matter,' he said with a grimace of distaste and, picking up a pen, asked, 'Where are you staying?'

'Calle San Nicolas,' she said. 'But…but I can't remember the name of the *pension*.' She got up to leave, regretting having mentioned the name of the street.

To her dismay, Patterson hadn't finished with her. 'Are you sure you're managing all right with the baby?' he asked.

'He's fine, everything's fine, really, don't worry about us,' she replied quickly, raking her mind for an excuse to curtail the interview.

'That isn't your child, is it?'

His words threw Maggie into turmoil. When she'd arrived at the Embassy, she'd made up her mind to explain everything in order to rid herself of the responsibility of caring for Donato, and concentrate instead on the real reason she had come to Spain. Looking down, she met the baby's trusting gaze and realised that, with his dark complexion and big brown eyes, he looked typically Spanish. If she handed him over, the Consulate might pass him on to the Spanish authorities. Caridad's words came back: *He'll be put in some terrible orphanage; he'll end up with cruel, uncaring foster parents; he'll be exposed to abuse and disease.*

'I'm...I'm looking after him for...for someone. He's my landlady's sister's baby.' This explanation would surely be untraceable. 'I...I must go now, they're expecting me.'

Charles Patterson reached for the intercom again and spoke into it, 'Miss Jenkins, please ask Mr Bennett to come up.'

A young man came into the room and approached the desk. Patterson scribbled something on a piece of paper and handed it to him, reminding Maggie of a scene from 'Tosca' where Scarpia betrays the lovers. She shook her head to rid her mind of this absurdity.

Patterson pushed back his chair and stood up, advancing from behind the desk in order to shake hands with Maggie. 'It's been nice meeting you,' he said. 'We're always here to help British citizens, you know.'

On reaching the reception area the young man escorting her seemed embarrassed. 'Shall I take the baby for a moment while you sign yourself out?' he suggested.

'I can manage, thank you,' she replied sharply. Juggling the baby, her handbag and the pen she scribbled her signature where it was required.

'Allow me to accompany you to the gate, Miss Morán.'

'There's no need.'

He smiled and said by way of explanation, 'We finish interviewing ex-patriots at mid-day and the gate's locked, so I shall have to see you out.'

When he opened the gate, Maggie went to go through but, at that moment, the young man put out his hand to stroke Donato's head. Maggie recalled the note Charles Patterson had passed him, and panicked. Had he been instructed to snatch the baby? Acting instinctively, she swung her bag in Bennett's face and slipped through the gate, pushing aside the disgruntled gathering of people loitering outside.

A taxi drove past and she hailed it, wrenching open the door and flinging herself and Donato inside. The last thing she saw was the young man's astounded expression as he clutched a hand to his cheek and shouted something at her.

'Where to?' asked the cabbie.

'Anywhere,' she shouted back. 'Just drive.'

CHAPTER SIX

Half an hour later, Maggie rushed into the *pension,* Donato in her arms. Tomás and Palmiro were waiting for her in the lobby. They jumped to their feet and Palmiro took the baby from her while Tomás led her to a chair.

'What's the matter?' he asked. 'You're shaking like a leaf.'

'I've had a terrible time,' she gasped.

'What happened?'

She started to babble on about Patterson and Bennett until Tomás grew impatient and interrupted her. 'You're not making sense, *mujer.*'

Palmiro tried to soothe the situation. Jiggling the baby on his knee, he said, 'Calm down, Maggie. Start from the beginning and tell us what happened.'

She stifled a sob and looked gratefully at the young Italian. Lacing and unlacing her fingers in her lap, she recounted her interview with the vice-Consul's assistant.

'Did you enquire about your brother?' asked Palmiro.

'Yes, but they have no record of him.'

'That doesn't surprise me,' said Tomás.

All at once, Maggie recalled her consternation when she had discovered that Tomás had paid for the room and then vanished. She turned on him accusingly, 'Where did you disappear to? I thought you'd gone off without me.'

At this, Tomás threw back his leonine head and let out a roar of laughter. 'Until you and the child are settled you're my responsibility.'

'Why?'

'Because that is what Jesús and Caridad would expect.'

Maggie looked surprised, but at the same time, she experienced a warm feeling. Going back to the interview, she said, 'I thought that Bennett fellow had been told to take Donato away from me but, looking back, I think he was just trying to be friendly.'

'Yesterday you couldn't wait to hand him over to the authorities,' scoffed Tomás.

'I know,' gulped Maggie. 'But everything's changed. I can't let them take him away.'

'Don't worry, *nena,* the Consulate staff have got better things to do.'

'But … but I told Patterson where I was staying.'

'They aren't going to bother about one Spanish orphan when the country is swarming with them. How did you escape?'

'I hit Bennett in the face with my handbag,' she whispered. 'Then I did a bunk.'

Tomás gave another hearty laugh. 'I wish I'd been there to see that.'

Seeing the funny side of it, Maggie gave an embarrassed giggle. 'I feel terrible. Suppose I gave him a black eye!'

The proprietor barged in. 'It's time you lot left,' she said. 'If you stay here any longer, I shall have to charge you for another night.'

Tomás glowered at her. 'Don't be so pushy, *mujer,* we'll leave when we're good and ready.'

Maggie could see that the woman was intimidated but she stood her ground. 'I've got more people coming to take these rooms later today so you'd better leave now. I need to clean up.'

To mollify her, Maggie said, 'Don't worry, *señora,* we're just leaving. Where's my suitcase?'

'It was in the way so I've put it round the back,' retorted the woman, disappearing to retrieve the offending article.

'Where are we going to stay? asked Maggie, beginning to panic.

'Don't worry, Tomás has found you some accommodation,' replied Palmiro.

'That's wonderful.'

'Don't get too excited before you've seen it,' growled Tomás. Going to the door, he added, 'I'll be back to pick you up in twenty minutes. Make sure you're ready.'

The accommodation Tomás had found her was worse than Maggie could have imagined. She reflected that the cottage in Devon would have been more habitable. The rooms were in a run-down area of the city which, in earlier months, had suffered bomb damage. The building stood more or less intact between two derelict houses. The lower apartments looked uncared for, with broken windows and patched-up doors. There were slates off the roof and the windows of the upper storeys were mostly boarded up.

Tomás pushed open the front door and led her into a gloomy hallway. The staircase was in a state of disrepair and looked unsafe with its cracked stair treads and wobbly banister rail. When they reached the top floor, Maggie stopped in the doorway and stared in dismay. The room was large and square but there was hardly any furniture: a double bed, a sofa and a chest of drawers. An alcove housed an electric cooker, which was thick with grease. The french window led onto a narrow balcony overlooking the bombsite. To her relief, the windows were still intact although there was a crack here and there.

90

Palmiro stepped out onto the balcony, heard it creak and jumped back inside.

'Don't go out there,' he warned Maggie.

'Where's the bathroom?' she asked.

'One flight down. You'll have to share it with the occupant of the rooms below,.' Tomás informed her.

She bit her lip. 'What about bedding, a cot for Donato?'

'All in good time,' he snapped.

Maggie couldn't hide her consternation. Shifting the baby from one hip to the other, she announced, 'We can't stay here.'

'Where else are you going to spend the night?'

'I'll find a bed and breakfast.'

'You'll be lucky to find anything around here. Besides, I've paid a month's rent in advance.'

Maggie looked furious. 'Why didn't you ask me first?' she screeched. 'Don't I have a say in the matter?'

'You didn't do too well went you went off to the Embassy on your own,' came Tomás' retort.

Palmiro intervened. 'Just a minute, Tomás, you can't blame Maggie for what happened at the Embassy. It sounds to me as if the vice-Consul was totally unsympathetic to her enquiry. As for the man who led her to the gate, Maggie wasn't to know whether he intended taking Donato away from her.'

Tomás raised his eyebrows in surprise. This was the longest speech Palmiro had ever made and, even though he spoke in fractured Spanish, he managed to make his point loud and clear.

To the surprise of his listeners, he went on, 'By the way, Tomás, you know why Maggie came here, you know what I want to do; if you don't mind me asking, what are you up to in Madrid?'

There was a long silence. Maggie held her breath. She had to admire the young Italian. She wasn't sure she

91

would have dared to aim such a direct question at the big man.

At last Tomás replied. 'I can't tell you. I would if I could but it's far better that you don't know.' For a moment, she was afraid Palmiro was going to insist, but he must have thought better of it. Tomás went to the door. 'I'm going out to fetch a few necessities,' he said.

'Just a minute,' called out Maggie. 'You've fixed me and the baby up but what about you and Palmiro?'

'*No problema*.' He stopped and wagged a finger at her, seemingly having forgotten their altercation. 'Listen, *nena*, you concern yourself with looking after the little one and forget about us.'

It wasn't until after Tomás had left that Maggie realised how tired she was. It had been a long, eventful day. Looking round the room with its peeling paintwork and scuffed furniture made her heart sink.

Palmiro's gaze followed hers. 'It isn't much, is it?' he said. 'But at least, it's summer so you won't have to worry about being cold.'

'I hope it doesn't rain,' muttered Maggie, looking up at a dark stain on the ceiling. She straightened her shoulders. 'Never mind, I'll just have to make the best of it.'

'What are you going to do about finding your brother?'

'I'll follow the only lead I've got.'

'What's that?'

'The people he stayed with when he first came over here.' She sighed. 'It's just that now I've got Donato to look after…'

'I'll help you out.'

'That's kind of you, Palmiro, but how can you? You're going off to join the International Brigade?'

'It will take time to find out where to enlist, and besides, I'll get leave sometimes.'

Maggie gave his hand a squeeze. 'You're a good friend, Palmiro, but I'm worried about you. I wish you wouldn't join up.'

'I want to,' he replied.

'Aren't you afraid the Military Police might catch up with you?'

He shrugged. 'I'll have to take my chances.'

At this moment, Donato decided he was hungry again. Opening his mouth, he gave a loud yell. 'He wants his bottle. How am I going to feed him with nothing to boil water up in?' gasped Maggie.

'Don't worry,' said Palmiro. 'I think there's someone in on the floor below. I heard music when we passed the door. I'll run downstairs and borrow a kettle.'

By the time Tomás returned, thanks to the loan of a saucepan from the tenant downstairs, the baby had been fed.

'I've managed to find a few things for you,' said Tomás, dumping a cardboard box on the floor and emptying out the contents. 'There's a few provisions: powdered milk, coffee and bread.' He looked triumphant. 'Plus sausage, eggs and a little oil, and…' He flourished a plate in the air. '…some cooking utensils.'

'Thank you,' said Maggie.

'What's more, I managed to get hold of a Moses basket and a pram. They're downstairs in the hall. Of course, they'll need a good clean.'

Maggie couldn't believe her ears. 'Tomás, you're a miracle worker,' she cried.

'Now the child's asleep, you'd better start cooking,' said Tomás.

'Not until I've cleaned the stove.'

93

'Oh God! Women!' With a long-suffering sigh, he delved deeper into the cardboard box and brought out a scrubbing brush and some soap.

His exasperation was expressed in jest and Maggie realised, from the smell of cognac on his breath, that he had been at the bottle. Thankfully, imbibing alcohol didn't make Tomás' belligerent, on the contrary, it sweetened his disposition.

Once Tomás had given the cooker a thorough clean, Maggie prepared a simple meal, which they ate squashed up together on the sagging sofa, their plates balanced on their knees.

'That was good,' said Palmiro, mopping up his plate with a last morsel of bread.

Maggie glanced towards the window. 'It's getting dark,' she said. 'Where are you two sleeping tonight?'

'Don't worry about us,' replied Tomás. 'I've got contacts here. We'll find somewhere to bed down for the night.' He pulled himself to his feet and winked at Palmiro. 'Come on, *Italiano*, let's leave the lady to get her beauty sleep.' He turned to Maggie. 'I'll be back first thing in the morning.'

'What about you, Palmiro?' asked Maggie.

'Thanks to Tomás I shall be off to contact the International Brigade. Don't worry, I haven't forgotten about your brother. I'll ask around as soon as I get the chance.'

Maggie sprang to her feet. 'Thanks, Palmiro. Thank you both for all you've done for me…' She waved a hand at the sleeping baby. '…for both of us.'

It was only after the pair had departed that she again felt the weight of responsibility. What did she know about looking after a baby? She began to regret not having taken the opportunity to leave Donato at the Embassy.

94

As evening shadows settled into night, the sound of music floated up from the room below. Whilst the others were with her she hadn't noticed it and now, in her loneliness, she strained her ears to hear it, finding the melodies reassuring. There was someone else in the house. She was not completely alone.

A terrible weariness came over her as she set about making up the bed with the sheets and blanket Tomás had provided. She deliberately left Donato's bed-time feed until the last minute in the hope that he would sleep through till morning. However, she was not destined for a peaceful night. At two o'clock, lightning flashed across the room through the unscreened window followed by a loud clap of thunder. Disorientated, she thought for a moment that it was an air-raid. She had been too tired to close the shutters before falling into bed and now they were rattling against the window frame. Running across the room in bare feet, she struggled to reach for the window catch as the wind caught the rain-lashed window and blew it open. It flapped against the wall, defying her attempts to reach it and, forgetting Palmiro's warning not to go onto the balcony, she stepped outside.

There was another blinding flash of lightning. She stood, transfixed, gazing out at the spectacular scene in front of her. Ruined buildings took on the shape of a film set, stark and unreal against the night sky. Another deafening thunder clap woke the baby; the window banged open and shut, its pane shattering into the room; a roof tile plunged past her. Maggie felt the balcony creak and leapt back just in time to see part of its masonry crash to the ground.

Frozen in shock, she clutched her arms about her, shivering in her thin night-dress. Donato's shrieks brought her to life. Swivelling around, she ran across the splintered glass, panicking that the shards had showered the Moses basket, reminding her of the terrifying crawl through the ruins to rescue him. To her relief, Donato's cradle was clear of debris. She picked him up and rocked him, whispering reassuring words in Spanish until his cries died away and she was able to put him down again.

Another flash of lightning lit the room for several seconds but the thunder clap that followed seemed more distant and she realised the storm was abating. As calm settled over the room, she felt a stab of pain, and looking down, was surprised to see a trail of blood from the window to where she stood. Both her feet were bleeding, new more serious cuts and abrasions replacing the now healing wounds from several days ago. Sinking onto the bed, she buried her head in her hands and wept.

CHAPTER SEVEN

'*Qué chingados!* Tomás stopped in astonishment when he came into the room.

Maggie was on her hands and knees sweeping up glass with an old dust pan and brush she had found in a cupboard on the landing. She had torn up a cotton skirt to wind round her feet, but blood was seeping through the makeshift bandages.

Palmiro, entering behind Tomás, rushed over and helped her to her feet. 'Let me do that,' he said, leading her to the sofa. She cried out with every step.

Tomás strode across the room. The now pane-less french window hung on its hinges, letting in a stream of sunlight to reveal the devastation. A puddle of water rippled on the floor beneath a stretch of sagging plaster dangling from the ceiling. The wall was stained, the wallpaper bloated.

He turned back and stared at Maggie. She met his gaze with dull eyes. 'It was the storm! Tomás, this place is awful. Part of the balcony has collapsed too. Honestly, we can't live here.'

Ignoring her lament, he crouched down in front of her and gently unwound the bandages. 'Tch, these cuts are deep, I'm going to have to get you to the hospital.'

Maggie looked alarmed. 'What about Donato?'

'Palmiro can stay here and look after him. You don't mind, do you, *Italiano?*'

'Of course not.'

'I've already prepared his feed,' said Maggie as the big man lifted her up in his arms and carried her to the door. 'You just need to warm his bottle. Can you manage?'

Palmiro grinned. 'If you only knew how many times I've watched my sisters do it,' he said.

As Tomás carried her down the stairs, he joked, 'You seem to have a talent for injuring your feet, *nena*.'

When they reached the next landing, the door to the apartment was open. A young girl stood there. 'What's happened?' she asked. Tomás quickly explained. 'I'll go and keep Palmiro company,' she said, hurrying upstairs.

'What's that all about?' grumbled Maggie. 'How does she know Palmiro?'

'They met yesterday when he went to borrow the kettle. I think we might have a budding romance here,' explained Tomás, giving a wink.

'But she only looks about sixteen.'

'Young love, eh!'

They reached the ground floor and he lowered her gently to her feet while he unlocked the main door.

'How are we going to get there,' she asked. 'You can't possibly carry me all the way.'

'My push bike's outside.'

'Your bike!' croaked Maggie. 'I can barely walk, let alone ride a bike.'

'I'll do the cycling, you'll ride cross bar.'

Maggie's laughed. 'You're not serious?' But her laughter died when she saw the bike leaning up against the wall of the house.

'It's the only way I can get you to hospital,' retorted Tomás. Before she could stop him, he hoisted her up onto the cross bar then swung his leg over the bike. 'Don't worry, *mujer*, just keep still.'

Thus began the most bizarre bike ride of Maggie's life. The journey was both painful and precarious. Clearly, Tomás was familiar with the area because he rode through the back streets without bothering to check for directions, cleverly avoiding pot holes and rubble littering the street and making detours around bombsites. They reached the hospital to find the waiting room packed.

Tomás surprised her by saying, 'It's not too bad today.'

'But, Tomás, we'll be here for hours,' she protested. 'I can't leave Palmiro in charge of Donato for that long.'

'*No problema*, Rosario is there too.'

'Rosario?'

'The girl from downstairs. Besides, they get through very quickly, you'll see. You should see what it's like when they're really busy.'

She started to protest again but Tomás' bushy brows drew together impatiently. 'Stop fussing.'

Recognising the warning signs, she looked at him nervously and decided it would be prudent to keep her qualms to herself. Her feet were painful, especially when the queue moved forwards and she had to place her full weight on them. The waiting room was chaotic with screaming children and hysterical mothers. After an hour, Tomás found her a chair, which she sank into with a sigh of relief. He had told her there were glass splinters embedded in the soles of her feet and she began to worry. Suppose she couldn't walk for days? How would she be able to cope with Donato? With these fears running through her mind, she found it difficult to hold back tears and turned her head away from Tomás, afraid that he might notice and think her stupid. Her thoughts wandered to the house on the Common. She had been safe there. How could she have been foolish enough to come to Spain in the middle of a civil war? How could she ever find Robert in the midst of this chaos?

Another hour passed before her name was called. Tomás helped her to a cubicle where a nurse unwound the soaked bandages and examined her feet. She pursed her lips and said, 'I can't attend to this myself, you'll need to see the doctor,' before disappearing to check on the next patient.

Yet another hour passed. Maggie felt panic rise. She couldn't stop thinking about Donato. How were Palmiro and Rosario coping? Would Palmiro know how to change the baby's nappy? At last the doctor came. He was tall and thin and very solemn. 'Your left foot will soon heal,' he assured her. 'But there are still several pieces of glass in the right foot and one of them is rather deep. Do you want me to get them out now or would you rather wait for a general anaesthetic?'

Maggie gave a gulp. 'Do it now,' she muttered, fighting back the bile rising to her throat.

The doctor left the cubicle, reappearing with the nurse. 'Hold the patient very still,' he told her. Giving Maggie a grave glance, he said, 'Are you sure you wouldn't prefer to wait, this could be painful.'

'Just get on with it,' snapped Maggie, closing her eyes in readiness.

The return journey was a nightmare. Maggie was in agony. Both feet were heavily bandaged and every bump in the road sent pain shooting through them. She held the handlebars so tightly that her knuckles shone white and, from time to time, despite the painkillers the doctor had given her, she came close to passing out. Although it was now late afternoon, the heat was unbearable and to add to her discomfort, the bicycle wheels sent dust spiralling into the air, drying her throat and making her eyes itch.

She could feel Tomás' breath hot on her neck as, from the seat behind her, he pushed the pedals as fast as he could. His arms, encircling her body to steer the bike, gave off a sweaty odour.

When they reached the house, he lifted her off the bike, and said, 'Are you all right?'

She nodded, unable to speak and, to her surprise, she thought she caught a glance of respect from the big man. He carried her upstairs, and on reaching the top landing, kicked open the door to the room. This startled Rosario, who was sitting on the sofa, nursing Donato. Palmiro was nowhere to be seen. The young girl got up and came to greet them.

'How are you? I hope it wasn't too painful.'

'It wasn't too bad,' lied Maggie as Tomás lowered her onto the sofa. 'Has Donato been good?'

Losing her shyness, Rosario said, 'Oh yes, he's a beautiful baby. You are *so* lucky.'

Me? Lucky! thought Maggie. It had never crossed her mind that she was lucky. Most of her life had been humdrum and, now that she had found the courage to take events into her own hands, she seemed to have met with nothing but bad luck.

'Where's Palmiro?'

'He's gone out to do some shopping. Now listen, you're not to do anything, just rest with your feet up.'

Maggie experienced a stab of conscience, recalling her off-hand attitude towards the girl on their departure for the hospital earlier in the day. 'Thank you very much for looking after Donato,' she said. 'He seems to have taken to you. Is there any chance you could help me out during the next few days?'

Rosario's eyes lit up. 'I would love to.'

A warm feeling rushed through Maggie, but it was a feeling mixed with envy. The girl was slight and pretty with long wavy hair and enormous hazel eyes. She could not be more than sixteen or seventeen. She raked a hand through her own mop of dark hair, feeling old and frumpy. Here she was at twenty-four, no family apart from Robert, few friends, and what was worse, she had never had a proper boyfriend. She burst into tears.

Rosario immediately placed Donato in his cot and ran over to her. 'Oh dear,' she said. 'You've had a terrible shock, no wonder you're upset.'

Drawing a handkerchief out of her pocket, she handed it to Maggie, who sniffed into it, beginning to smile through her tears. 'You're very kind,' she said.

'To tell the truth,' replied Rosario. 'It's been lonely here on my own.'

'On your own?'

The girl didn't have time to reply because Tomás broke in. 'I'll get that window fixed for you, Maggie, we can't have the bats flying in here during the night and getting tangled up in your hair.'

'Bats!'

'Only joking, *mujer.*'

Chuckling, he headed for the door and lumbered down the stairs.

'Is he your father?' asked Rosario.

It was Maggie's turn to chuckle. 'I've only know him for a few days,' she explained, and went on to tell Rosario about her journey across Spain with the baby she had rescued.

'You've been so brave,' gasped the young girl.

'Who's brave?' Palmiro came into the room armed with a few provisions.

'Maggie is.'

'Don't I know it?' said Palmiro. 'She saved my life. Tomás would have shot me.'

Maggie blushed. 'It wouldn't have come to that,' she protested. 'As I've told you before, Tomás' bark is worse than his bite.'

During the days that followed, Maggie grew to rely on Rosario's help. The young girl was willing to do anything: shopping, washing or cleaning. She learnt that Rosario had been living in the apartment downstairs since her parents had been killed in an air raid.

'Have you no other family?' asked Maggie.

'I've got a brother, Luis, but he's in Barcelona.'

'Why?' asked Maggie cautiously, wondering which side he was on. She had learnt that in Spain you could never be certain of a person's political leanings.

Rosario looked surprised. 'He's fighting for the Republicans. Who can blame him when the Nationalists were responsible for our parents' death?' She frowned and went on bitterly, 'What irony, when they were in favour of Franco!'

As her feet began to heal, Maggie started to take back responsibility for caring for Donato. She noticed that Rosario seemed upset and realised that the young girl had a natural aptitude with babies and clearly didn't want to relinquish looking after him. An idea dawned. When Tomás called on her one day, she voiced her plans.

'About Rosario…' she began.

'What about her?'

'I've thought of a way of helping her and earning some money myself.'

'Oh yes.' Tomás didn't sound interested. He was in the kitchen area inspecting the groceries Rosario had managed to purchase.

Maggie hobbled across the room. 'Are you going to listen to my idea or not?'

'Go on.'

Maggie felt annoyed. Tomás was still only half listening. He seemed more intent on finding something to eat, and she realised that until his hunger had been assuaged, he wasn't going to take any interest in what she had to say. Stifling her impatience, she set about cooking some spaghetti topped with beef tomatoes and cheese.

The meal restored his good humour and when he smacked his lips and settled down on the sofa, she broached the subject again. Donato distracted her this time, and she was obliged to prepare his feed. Thus, it was later in the evening before she was able to tell him about her plan.

As she put the sleeping baby in his cradle, Tomás got up to leave.

'Don't go yet,' she cried.

He yawned and started to stand up. 'I've got an early start in the morning.'

Pushing him back onto the sofa, she insisted on sharing her idea with him. 'Once my feet are better - and it won't be long now, I'm going to suggest that Donato and I move in downstairs with Rosario.'

'Why would you want to do that? Surely you're better off up here on your own?' He got to his feet and started lumbering towards the door.

Maggie got there first, barring his way and frowning impatiently. 'Listen, Tomás, you haven't heard the rest of my plan.'

He grinned with amusement at her insistence. 'Come on, tell me. What is this plan of yours?'

'Well ... Rosario could look after Donato while I look for work, teaching English. Once I've made some contacts, I can use the upstairs room as a classroom. It's perfect.'

'Have you spoken to Rosario about this?'

'Not yet, but I'm sure she'll agree. She's got no commitments ... '

'How do you know that?'

'We had a long talk the other day. She's lonely and she'll welcome my company.'

'Well ... ' said Tomás cautiously. 'I suppose it could work.'

Maggie's eyes lit up. 'Besides, with Rosario looking after Donato, I can devote more time to searching for Robert and … '

'Aren't you shelving responsibility?' Tomás' tone startled Maggie.

'What d'you mean?'

'You took on the task of caring for the child.'

Maggie felt her cheeks redden. 'Cast your mind back,' she snapped. 'I was the one who wanted to follow the official route and give him up for adoption; it was you and the Fajardo's who stopped me.'

'Yes, Maggie, but you were the one who ran away from the Embassy when you thought they were trying to take him away from you; now you're trying to dump him on somebody else.'

She stared at the big man in stunned silence. His words made her feel cruel and uncaring. 'That's not true,' she gasped, finding her voice again. 'Don't you see, everything will fall into place if Rosario agrees.'

Tomás looked thoughtful. 'I suppose so,' he admitted in the end.

He got up to leave but she tugged at his sleeve. 'Surely you didn't mean what you said?'

He gave a careless shrug and Maggie surmised that although he seemed to regret his thoughtless indictment, he was unwilling to take back his words.

Maggie was right about Rosario. She was only too willing to fall in with the suggestion of shared accommodation, and within a couple of weeks, things were looking up. Tomás repaired the broken window pane, and provided additional furniture for the upstairs room while Maggie and Donato moved downstairs with Rosario.

Palmiro called in frequently. He had approached the International Brigade and was waiting to hear back from them. It soon became clear to Maggie that Rosario and the Italian were becoming fond of one another. She watched their budding romance with interest until, one day, she overheard them discussing Palmiro's plans to enlist.

'I don't want you to go,' sighed Rosario. 'Can't you stay in Madrid and find work here?'

'I couldn't live with myself if I did that,' he replied. 'After what I've seen, I feel duty-bound to fight these usurpers.'

'My brother thinks the war could go on for years.'

Palmiro shook his head. 'It won't. Volunteers from all over the world are joining the fight. We'll knock them out soon, just you wait and see.'

Rosario was still doubtful. 'I don't want you to go. I would rather you went home to Italy.' A wistful look came into her eyes. 'At least I'd know you'd be safe there.'

'What chance would I have of seeing you if I went home?'

'You could come back after the war.'

'No,' said Palmiro determinedly. 'I can't go home.'

As she eaves-dropped, Maggie realised that he hadn't told Rosario about deserting from his unit. Until then, it had not occurred to her how this could affect his longed-for return to his own country. The next day, he turned up looking very serious. 'My papers have come through and my uniform,' he said.

Rosario made no attempt to hide her distress. Running across the room, she threw her arms around Palmiro's neck and sobbed, 'When do you have to go?'

'The day after tomorrow.'

'Where will they send you?'

'I don't know.'

Several weeks passed and once Maggie's feet had begun to heal, she was able to take Donato out in the old pram Tomás had provided. She enjoyed exploring the city.

Abuelo Esteban had told her so much about Madrid that she felt as though she already knew it.

Meandering through the streets gave her time to reflect on how much her life had changed in a short period of time. Only a year ago she had been living in the dark old house on Stanmore Common with Robert and her mother. Robert's surprise decision to leave for Spain had been a blow to both women, but with hindsight, she realised she should have seen it coming. He had long been searching for a cause to fight for.

When she got back to the apartment, Rosario noticed her pensive mood. 'A penny for your thoughts?' she said.

'I was daydreaming.'

'Are you feeling homesick?'

Maggie shook her head. 'There's nothing for me in England.'

'How did you learn to speak Spanish so fluently, Maggie?'

'Robert and I were brought up by our Spanish grandparents and they always spoke to us in Spanish,' explained Maggie. 'They were forced to leave Spain during the earlier troubles.'

'How did they manage to make a living in England?'

'My grandfather set up a wine importing business - he still had contacts in Spain. The business passed to my father.'

'Do your parents live in England?'

'No, both my parents and my grandparents are dead.'

'So you're an orphan like me.'

Maggie's mouth twitched into a half smile. She had never thought of herself as an orphan. Donato was an orphan, so was Rosario, but she wasn't sure that a grown woman qualified as an orphan. 'I suppose I am,' she conceded at last.

'It must have been hard for your grandparents when they arrived in England.'

107

'It was. My grandmother, Estela, never came to terms with living there. I once asked her why she hadn't learnt English. Do you know what she replied? She said "There's no need, my child, your grandfather and I will be going back to Spain one day." Of course, it didn't happen,' finished Maggie with a sigh.

'What were your parents like?'

'My mother was English, but Robert and I didn't see much of either our mother or father. They were always working.'

'How sad! You must have had a lonely childhood. What brought you over here?'

'My brother came over to join the Republican Militia. Both my mother and I tried to stop him…' She sighed. '…but Robert is pig-headed, he always does exactly what he wants to do.'

'How does Donato fit in?' asked Rosario. 'I know he's not your child. Are you looking after him for someone else?'

Maggie hesitated before replying. Until now, she had only given Rosario the briefest version of her history. How much should she tell her? Was it safe to confide in a young girl she hardly knew? Her thoughts flew back to how close she'd been to handing Donato over to the authorities. The Embassy visit had knocked all her good intentions on the head. Donato was hers to take care of whatever the future held. Could confiding in Rosario jeopardise his safety?

'As I told you before, he's an orphan I've been asked to take care of,' she replied.

Rosario accepted this explanation with a shrug, and focused her interest on Robert.

'Palmiro told me you went to the Embassy for news of your brother.'

Maggie shuddered. 'What a disaster that was! They weren't a bit interested in his plight. They're too busy

108

trying to get British nationals out of the country before things get any worse.'

As she uttered the words, Maggie realised how naive she had been. Why would the Vice-Consul be interested in helping people coming into a war zone when they were doing their utmost to get people out?

To further satisfy Rosario's curiosity, she went on, 'Robert was captivated by Esteban's anecdotes about old Spain; then, at University, he became involved with the Marxist movement. When he ranted on about communes and a fair share for all, mother and I didn't take much notice of him. We were used to his outlandish ideas. But as the Nationalists began to take hold under Franco, Robert became even more obsessed.' She shook her head at the recollection. 'I still didn't think he'd act on his beliefs. I should have known. He always claimed he felt more Spanish than English.'

The following week, with Rosario's agreement, Maggie began putting her plans into action. When Tomás called in she greeted him enthusiastically.

'*Hola* Tomás, just wait until you see the schoolroom. I've given it a clean and now you've provided furniture, all I need is some stationery. Can you help?'

'I'll do my best,' he said. 'But where are you going to find pupils?'

'Rosario will help me. She's going to get in touch with some old school friends.'

'Will they be able to afford the lessons? You don't want to end up doing this for nothing.'

'I won't be charging very much at first, but once the word gets around I'll be able to put my fees up.'

Tomás looked sceptical. 'I wish you luck,' he said.

CHAPTER EIGHT

Palmiro made his departure with a heavy heart. It had been difficult saying goodbye to his friends, especially Rosario.

'I'll come back, God willing,' he said.

Rosario gave a little shudder. 'Take care,' she whispered.

She held him so tightly that he found it difficult to breathe. Then Donato hiccupped, breaking the tension, making them all laugh and giving him the opportunity to turn his attention to the others. He hugged them all in turn, kissed the baby, and hurried from the room, loping downstairs two at a time. The parting had been more difficult than he could have imagined. Even the big man had seemed sorry to see him go.

It had been Tomás who had told him how to get to the recruitment centre. He discovered that he was something of a misfit. Most of the recruits were either English, French or Polish. He had scant knowledge of any of these languages, added to which they seemed suspicious of him due to the number of Italian soldiers who were fighting on the Nationalist side. During the waiting period, he felt ambivalent: wanting to get going yet reluctant to distance himself from his newfound friends. Once the call came, he found himself included in a battalion destined for Brunete where the Republicans were trying to cut off the Nationalists' siege of Madrid from the West. His companions were a mixed bunch, mostly French. Maggie's plea to keep a look out for her brother played at his mind. It seemed an impossible task even though he discovered that there were a number of Englishmen in his unit.

He soon realised that Mussolini's army issue uniform and weapons, although inadequate, were superior to those issued by the International Brigade. However, there was a good atmosphere among the volunteers. They were optimistic, whereas the Italian conscripts, who had been sent to fight a war which they felt had nothing to do with them, were resentful and complaining. It was true that some of the younger volunteers soon lost their zest for adventure when faced with the realities of combat but, to counteract this, there were many men dedicated to resolving the situation in Spain and bringing an end to the civil war.

He heard through the grapevine that the foreign brigades had grown enormously, with volunteers coming from as far away as South America. Until joining up, he had been ignorant of the hard-line politics sweeping through Europe. Here, talking with men from different countries, he learnt that a European war was inevitable. It was simply a question of which country swung which way. He hoped Italy would not be involved but he knew Mussolini favoured Hitler and that it was only his depleted army resources, a result of Italian participation in Abyssinia and Spain that was holding him back. Through his better informed companions, Palmiro's eyes were further opened to the consequences of a Fascist Europe.

He wondered what had happened to his companions in the Italian Army. Had Salvatore got himself killed yet? Was Enrico still playing his mouth organ at meal times? He tried not to let his mind wander towards home. No doubt Salvatore was right and his sister, Santina, was pregnant by now. He asked around about Robert Morán, but he always met with a shaking of heads.

Because of the mix of nationalities, it took longer for friendships to be forged. Spanish was the common language but he soon found that apart from the South Americans very few of the volunteers spoke more than a smattering of Spanish whereas he had picked up quite a lot along the way, especially since leaving the Army and he often found himself playing interpreter. He steadfastly avoided questions about his own background.

A month after volunteering, he was given weekend leave. He caught the train into Madrid and found his way to Maggie and Rosario's lodging. It was late afternoon by the time he arrived and he was surprised to meet a pair of chattering teenagers coming down the stairs towards him. He allowed them to pass, smiling at their giggles as they left the house. On reaching the third floor, he met Maggie with the baby in her arms.

Her eyes lit up. 'Palmiro! How wonderful! I didn't expect to see you so soon.'

He dumped his kitbag on the floor and took Donato from her, grinning when the baby snatched at his little finger and tried to put it in his mouth.

'He's grown.'

'Babies grow very quickly during the first year,' said Maggie knowledgeably. She had heard a mother say this while queuing for a bus on her way home from college some years earlier.

'He's a handsome boy.'

Rosario heard them talking and rushed out to greet him, blushing deeply. Taking the hint, Maggie took the baby back from him and went upstairs, leaving the couple staring at one another.

Palmiro held out his arms and Rosario rushed into them.

Two hours later, the three of them sat cross-legged on the floor eating paella, the ingredients for which Rosario had somehow managed to get from the neighbours, who were only too ready to donate provisions for a member of the International Brigade.

Palmiro felt deliriously happy. Although it had been a hot day, the evening air was fresh with a light breeze blowing in through the open window. The food tasted delicious, the Rioja, drunk from tumblers, intoxicating. He couldn't take his gaze off Rosario. After a glass of wine, her initial reserve evaporated and she told him how awful it was when she lost her parents, talking animatedly about the difference her friendship with Maggie had made to her life.

She enthused about Donato. 'He's the sweetest child I've ever seen. I take him out every day.'

Maggie joined in with her enthusiasm. 'He's advanced for his age,' she said.

He found it amusing. It was almost as if Donato had two mothers, such was their pride in him.

'Any news of Robert?' asked Maggie eagerly.

Palmiro shook his head, knowing that she had deliberately held back from questioning him. He wished he had good news for her. 'I haven't met many English people.' Maggie bit her lip and lowered her gaze, and to ease her discomfort, he asked, 'How are the English lessons going? Were those your pupils I saw coming downstairs when I arrived?'

Maggie nodded. 'A lot's happened in four weeks. The lessons are going well.'

He eyed her with admiration. 'Well done!'

'My friends have passed the word around,' said Rosario. 'They've told me that Maggie is a really good teacher.'

'How's Tomás?' asked Palmiro.

The girls exchanged a glance. 'He's disappeared,' said Maggie.

'Disappeared?'

'It was just after you left,' Maggie went on to explain. 'One night he turned up saying he would be away for a day or two. He seemed tired and agitated so I sent him upstairs to take a nap in the schoolroom and, in the morning, he'd gone.'

'Didn't he say where he was going?'

'No.'

Palmiro shrugged. 'You know what he's like; he'll turn up again.'

When Rosario went to make coffee, he watched her every move with an unguarded gaze. She was so graceful, her waist so tiny, her feet so small. He wanted to protect her, couldn't imagine how she could cope all alone in the world with her brother far away in Barcelona and her parents dead. Thank goodness Maggie was there to look after her! He saw the English girl as a mature woman. He knew she was in her mid-twenties and in his eyes, this made her responsible and wise.

'Tell me about this school of yours, Maggie?' he said.

'Rosario helped me by putting the word about. Despite all that's happened, there are still a lot of wealthy families in Madrid and it's surprising how many young people want to learn English. I suppose because it's an international language and women are becoming more emancipated now.'

Palmiro nodded in agreement although he couldn't imagine why such lively young girls would be interested in learning a foreign language. The young women in his village took in laundry, did a bit of dressmaking or entered into domestic service. None of these occupations required a foreign language and he couldn't imagine that it would be any different in Spain. As for furthering their education, the girls from his neck of the woods spent their spare time gathered in groups, self-consciously flirting with the local boys who hadn't yet been drafted.

During the journey back to his unit, Palmiro couldn't get the image of Rosario out of his mind. She was exquisite, like the china doll his sister, Santina, had once owned. He understood by the way she talked that she had led a privileged life. She spoke of her parents with gentle affection and he had the feeling that despite the lapse of months since their deaths, she had not yet allowed herself to mourn for them. Mention of her brother brought a sparkle to her eyes and he wondered why the young man had not yet found a way of getting her to Barcelona. Was it possible that he thought she was safer in Madrid? Whatever the circumstances, he was glad that Maggie had taken Rosario under her wing. She had looked after Donato so competently, she would know how to care for his Rosario. With a start, it dawned on him that he already felt possessive of her.

He was surprised that Tomás had disappeared. The fatherly figure had seemed like a rock. His knowledge of Madrid, his useful contacts and his ability to get hold the most unusual objects, had led both Palmiro himself and Maggie to lean on him. He brushed aside the disturbing possibility that Tomás was on the run. No, thought Palmiro, the likelihood was that the old fool had gone on a bender and was still recovering in some seedy back street slum. He felt sure Tomás would be back with Maggie by the time he managed another weekend leave.

Soothed by the rhythm of the train, he closed his eyes and gave verse to delightful images of Rosario, not knowing months would pass before he would get another chance to see her.

After Palmiro had left Rosario seemed thoughtful. Maggie discreetly left her alone but during the course of the evening when the two young women were quietly listening to the wireless with Donato asleep she started talking about him, saying how nice he was and how much they would miss him.

'D'you think he'll settle in Madrid after the War, Maggie?' she said.

'He might want to go home to Italy. It's only natural.'

'But there's nothing to stop him coming back again, is there?'

Maggie cast Rosario an amused smile. 'I suppose if there was something or someone here to draw him back, he would.'

This brought a blush to the teenager's cheeks and she hurriedly turned her attention to Donato, saying, 'He's waking up. I think he'll need changing.'

Things had calmed down in the city, bringing people out of their homes. This encouraged Maggie and Rosario to venture further afield as often as possible. The baby was putting on weight and doing well despite the inexperience of his carers. Neither Maggie nor Rosario knew anything about babies but somehow maternal instinct kicked in.

Thanks to Rosario's contacts, Maggie's language classes were doing well. The schools had closed for the long summer break and many of the more well-to-do parents were keen for their children to catch up with their education since schooling had been fragmentary during the earlier part of the year due to the heavy bombing and an exodus of teachers from the city. These pupils, mostly girls, provided Maggie with a reasonable income.

The day-to-day need for survival gave Maggie little chance to pursue her enquiries about Robert, but she hadn't lost sight of her quest and she was getting impatient until, at last, eagerness and anxiety persuaded her to resume her search for her brother. By now, the bombing had eased, her feet had healed and she had managed to put a little money aside for emergencies. Her only concern was that Tomás had still not put in an appearance.

Leaving Donato in Rosario's charge, she took the decision to visit the people with whom Robert had lodged on his arrival in Spain. Feeling excited yet nervous, she set off for Atocha Station. What would these people be like? Would they lead her to Robert? Suppose Robert was still living there? Of course, that begged the question: why hadn't he replied to her letters? But since arriving in Spain she had learnt that nothing worked normally. Possibly the mail had not been getting through.

She found herself in a district, which due to its proximity to Barajas Airport, had given rise to a number of hastily constructed apartment buildings, which dwarfed the original older houses. The streets were almost deserted as the September heat bore down, and she wished she hadn't bothered to bring a cardigan. She knew the address and the name of the people she was seeking, but now she was close to her destination, she realised that she had no idea which way to go.

She approached an old woman, who was hobbling along the road carrying a shopping basket but the woman drew away, hurrying off without a word. The same thing happened at her next try: a mother and child this time. The child hopped up and down, sucking her thumb but the mother shook her head and rushed off, pulling her daughter after her. Maggie felt puzzled.

On her arrival in Spain, she had realised that her Madrid accent coupled with her olive complexion, thick dark hair and brown eyes had disguised her Anglo-Saxon origins. She had often pondered on how strange it was that neither she nor her brother bore any resemblance to their blond blue-eyed English mother. At school in England, their foreign looks had marked them out as different. Why then, did the people here eye her with mistrust? She caught a glance of herself in a shop window

117

and stopped. What she saw was a smartly dressed young woman with hair tied up in a chignon, leather handbag and high-heeled shoes. The penny dropped. She was too chic for these people. They saw her not as a foreigner but as a possible Nationalist sympathiser. She was learning fast that suspicion and betrayal were rife in Spain. With a glimpse back into her memory, she recalled her grandfather describing the conditions from which he and her grandmother had fled during the last century. The full extent of their plight became clear. How sad and terrified Esteban and Estela must have been when they were forced to leave their family and friends and set up home in a foreign country! She recalled *Abuelo* explaining how they had set foot on English soil not knowing a word of the language.

She stared into the shop window. Her appearance was all wrong. How could she have made such a foolish mistake? Determined to put things right, she headed for the nearest open space, a run-down patch of grass with one wooden bench under a tree. Pulling out the comb which held her hair in place, she let her hair fall to her shoulders, running her fingers through it to make it appear dishevelled. Her skirt was straight and mid-calf length with a kick pleat at the back. She scooped up some dust from the ground and rubbed it over the material. It's a pity, she thought, but needs must. The shoes and bag were a problem: too smart by far. She had to tone down her appearance if she were not to alarm Robert's friends. Then she had an idea. Every town in Spain had a market. Where better to find shoes which would be more suitable for her purpose? It meant parting with a few pesetas, but it couldn't be helped.

She headed for the centre of town until a babble of voices told her she had located the market. Pushing her way through shoppers, she searched for footwear only to find that most of the stalls sold food or kitchen utensils.

However, she came across a stall selling cheap canvas bags, and purchasing the largest one she could find she was able to fit her own leather handbag inside it. The shoes were still a problem.

Glancing up, she met the gaze of a teenager. The girl was staring at her high-heeled shoes with obvious envy. She was wearing a pair of scuffed brown brogues. Taking into account that the girl was about the same height as she was, Maggie made an instant decision.

'Do you like them?' she asked, pointing at the shoes.

The girl nodded shyly.

'You can have them.'

The girl took a step backwards, shaking her head.

'I mean it. Give me your shoes and you can have these in exchange.'

The girl's mouth dropped open. Still backing away, she gave a negative wave, but. Maggie caught hold of her sleeve. 'Come on,' she said. 'I'm in a hurry and I can't walk properly in these. Take them and let me have yours.'

The temptation was too great. Slipping off her own shoes, the girl watched apprehensively while Maggie took off her high heels. The exchange was swift. Without giving Maggie a chance to change her mind, the girl ran off barefoot with the high heels dangling from her hand, clearly not caring whether they fitted or not.

Maggie slipped her feet into the brogues. They were a little big and she realised there was a hole in the sole of one of them but she felt confident now that she blended in with the rest of the community.

Leaving the market place, she sought a likely passer-by from whom to ask the way and, this time, after a lot of umming and ahhing and scratching of head, the old man she'd approached, sucked at his pipe and pointed her in the right direction.

The address she was seeking turned out to be in a new apartment block on the edge of town. She climbed the five flights of stairs to the top floor, stopping outside the door to regain her breath. Her knock was answered by: '*Quien es?*'

'I would like to speak with Señora Gonzales?'

Again: '*Quien es?*'

Maggie took a deep breath. 'My name's Maggie Morán.'

This proved to be the 'open sesame'. The door flew open to reveal a middle-aged woman with her hair scrunched back in an untidy knot.

'*Qué sorpresa!* Come in *Señorita.*' Clearly the woman had recognised her name.

The warm greeting heartened Maggie, raising her hopes. Señora Gonzales led her into a rather untidy room off the corridor. Hastily untying the apron tied around her waist, she explained that she had been doing some housework.

'I hope my visit isn't inconvenient,' apologised Maggie. 'I should have let you know I was coming.'

'*No problema, Señorita.* Would you like some coffee?'

Without waiting for a reply, the woman disappeared from the room, leaving Maggie to take in her surroundings. The room gave off an aura of gloom. It was crammed with heavy, old-fashioned furniture, the sofa was threadbare as was the rug which was half rolled up in front of the fireplace. There was a broom leaning up against the wall and a feather duster on the floor beside it. The wooden shutters were only slightly open but Maggie could see that the french window led onto a narrow balcony.

Señora Gonzales reappeared, carrying a tray with a coffee pot and two cups on it. She brushed aside a magazine from a low table and put the tray down.

'Please excuse the mess,' she said, unfurling the rolled-up rug with the toe of one foot whilst trying to conceal a used breakfast bowl behind a large ornament with her hand. Having succeeded in this manoeuvre she hurried over to the window to open the shutters, allowing more light into the room. Maggie noticed that she had changed her blouse and combed her hair, even applied a little lipstick.

'The coffee will be ready in a minute,' she said, sitting down opposite Maggie and folding her hands on her lap.

Maggie was about to speak when Señora Gonzales lifted her eyebrows and said earnestly, 'How's your brother?'

Maggie's spirits plummeted. 'I haven't seen him,' she said. 'I came here to find him.'

The woman's hand flew to her mouth. 'I had no idea. I thought you would be the one to know his whereabouts.'

'No,' said Maggie, shaking her head. 'I came here to ask *you* that question.'

Señora Gonzales looked disconcerted. 'Oh dear,' she mumbled.

Maggie struggled to hide her disappointment. 'When was the last time you saw him?'

'Six weeks ago to the day.' When Maggie raised a surprised eyebrow, Señora Gonzales went on, 'It was my granddaughter's birthday, you see.'

'Could he have gone to Toledo?' Maggie knew this would have been impossible since it was unlikely that Robert knew about the villa his grandparents had bequeathed him.

'Toledo? He wouldn't have gone there.'

'Do you know where he *was* going?'

Señora Gonzales shook her head. 'He wouldn't say.'

Maggie frowned thoughtfully. 'Six weeks ago. Let me see…' She recalled that Palmiro had been sent to Brunete by his detachment. Could Robert have gone there too?

But Señora Gonzales volunteered information that dispelled that theory. 'Your brother joined a POUM detachment.'

'What? But Robert came here to join the International Brigades.'

'Robert?' The woman looked momentarily puzzled, then she smiled in comprehension. 'He calls himself Esteban now. Didn't you know?'

No, thought Maggie angrily, it seemed there were a lot of things she didn't know. 'Tell me about his connection with POUM.'

'It's a small far-left guerrilla group fighting on the fringes...'

'I know what it is,' snapped Maggie. Señora Gonzales stiffened, prompting Maggie to offer an apology. 'I'm sorry, I didn't mean to speak so sharply.'

The woman leant forward and touched her hand. '*De nada*. You must be very concerned about him.' She poured the coffee. 'But don't worry, I'm sure he can take care of himself.'

All at once, Maggie could no longer control her emotions. Bursting into tears, she said, 'Why didn't he reply to my letters?'

Señora Gonzales nearly dropped the coffee pot. 'What? That can't be right. He wrote to you every week. Why, I posted the letters myself!'

'I didn't receive any of them. Did Robert get *my* letters?'

'He received one just after he arrived.'

'Only one? But I wrote at least half a dozen,' gasped Maggie. Her mind was in a whirl. If Robert had only received her first letter, then he couldn't know their mother was dead.

'It's the postal services, nothing works properly any more,' said Señora Gonzales. 'Look, my dear, my husband will make some enquiries. As soon as he gets home, we'll ask him, but I'm afraid he doesn't get in until well after eight.'

'Oh dear, I was planning to go back to Madrid tonight. Do the trains run late?'

Señora Gonzales looked alarmed. 'You can't travel at night, my dear.'

'Is there a hotel nearby?' asked Maggie, doing a quick mental calculation of the amount of pesetas she had left in her purse.

'Hotel? What are you thinking of? You must stay with us.'

'Are you sure? I don't want to cause you any inconvenience.'

'*No problema.*' Handing her a cup of coffee, the woman said with a smile, 'Let's drop the formalities. My name's Elvira and my husband is Paco.'

Maggie felt comforted by Elvira's friendliness and it wasn't long before she found herself telling her about her mother's death and the chain of events it had set in motion.

'You see, the solicitor said he needs Robert's signature in order to release money from our mother's legacy. Luckily, he told me about the cottage in Devon. Without selling it I would have been in deep financial trouble.'

'How did she die?' asked Elvira.

Impulsively, Maggie opened her heart to her companion. 'It was awful. She ... she committed suicide.'

Elvira looked horrified. 'You poor child,' she cried, moving closer and putting her arm around Maggie's shoulders. 'Whatever made her do such a terrible thing?'

Maggie hesitated. How could she explain to this kind-hearted woman that her mother had been totally obsessed with her husband, that she had never had any time for her

123

children, that after Miguel's death, she had gone into deep mourning, refusing to do anything around the house and expecting her daughter to wait on her hand and foot?

Luckily, she was saved from further questions by the arrival of Paco, who turned out to be a burly man with a gruff but friendly manner. At first, he seemed unwilling to be drawn into Maggie's quest, but in response to his wife's insistence, he eventually promised that first thing next morning he would make enquiries through his contacts.

'I must say,' he said, taking a long drag on his foul-smelling cigarette. 'It never occurred to us that anything was wrong because Esteban didn't seem to notice that you didn't write to him.'

On seeing the hurt in Maggie's eyes, Elvira hastily tried to soften her husband's lack of discretion. 'Of course, he often mentioned you, my dear. Clearly he's very fond of you.'

That night, Maggie slept fitfully in the bed which she guessed Robert must have occupied during his stay with the Gonzales.. She woke up in the morning, startled into life by a dream in which her brother was lying wounded on a deserted battlefield. Over breakfast with Paco and Elvira she listened with trepidation to the newscaster's spiel about the previous day's events, thankful when there was no mention of overnight fighting.

Paco kept his promise and before going to work he made enquiries with his contacts, who were more up-to-date than he was, on the location of the various POUM brigades.

'I'm sorry, Maggie...' said Elvira when Paco explained that no one knew anything. '...but POUM members move around a lot, you know. I promise that if anything turns up we'll let you know straightaway.'

Maggie left the Gonzales' no wiser now than she had been when she arrived. Elvira insisted on giving her lunch and afterwards she made her way to the station, her vision blurred by the tears that insisted on welling up.

As she trudged the half mile home from Atocha Station, her mood lifted: soon she would see Donato and Rosario again, and who knows, she thought, what tomorrow will turn up. She was still determined about one thing: she and Robert would spend their twenty-fifth birthday together.

CHAPTER NINE

Maggie arrived home to a warm welcome. Rosario was relieved to see her and Donato gurgled happily when she took him in her arms.

'We've been worried about you, Maggie,' said Rosario.

'We?'

'Yes, Tomás is back. He's staying in the schoolroom; I hope you don't mind.'

'Of course I don't. Did he say where he'd been?'

Rosario shook her head. Handing Donato back to Rosario Maggie ran upstairs and knocked on the door of the upstairs room. She heard a shuffling before the door was opened by only a chink. Tomás' bearded face appeared. When he saw her, he opened the door fully, and she saw that he wore only a grubby vest and thick cord trousers held up by a piece of string. He looked like a tramp and was clearly the worse for wear. With a lopsided grin, he waved her inside.

'The wanderer returns,' he chuckled.

'Me or you?'

'Both. How did your trip go? Did you learn anything?'

'Only that my brother left the Gonzales' weeks ago and they have no idea where he is now.'

'So he joined one of the International Brigades?'

Maggie shook her head. 'He enlisted with a different organisation. It's called POUM.'

Tomás' face clouded. 'Are you sure?'

She nodded.

'Do you know that POUM is a left-wing party outlawed by all the other organisations?'

'What does that matter? They're all fighting for the same cause.'

Tomás' heavy brows drew together. She couldn't understand why he was angry and, in a bid to gain time to think, she allowed her gaze to travel around the room until it fastened on the chair in the corner. There was a red kerchief hanging over the back of it. Paco had told her that POUM had no official uniform, their badge of membership was the red kerchief. Why hadn't she guessed? Of course, Tomás had been wearing a red kerchief when she'd first bumped into him on the train journey. He too must be a member of POUM.

She was about to challenge him, when he said, 'POUM's disorganised, the men receive no formal training, their equipment is out of date...'

'What are you trying to tell me?' she demanded.

Tomás took hold of her arm. 'I might be able to find your brother but, if I do, you must persuade him to leave Spain with you.'

'Hmm, fat chance! Robert won't do what I tell him.'

Tomás looked puzzled. 'In that case, why are you so keen to find him?'

'I've got news for him, family news. Our mother died and I need to tell him about the reading of her will.'

His grip tightened on her arm. 'Promise me, you'll leave Spain once I've contacted your brother.' The urgency in his voice alarmed her.

Standing her ground, she demanded, 'Who are you to tell me what to do?'

Tomás twisted her around to face him. '*Mujer,* you know nothing. You haven't seen the atrocities being carried out in the name of freedom.'

'What about the bombing in Bilbao?'

'Huh, that? You haven't seen what happens on the battlefields.'

Maggie felt a shiver of dread run through her. Suppose Robert was injured or dead! 'That gives me even more reason to stay on,' she protested.

Tomás must have sensed her qualms because he let go of her arm, saying, 'What are we arguing about? Let's decide what to do once I've found your brother.'

'Now you're talking sense,' retorted Maggie.

His frown returned. 'You must leave whether your brother goes with you or not. It would be easier for you to slip out of the country on your own.'

'I can't go without Donato.'

'Rosario will take care of him.'

'No!' Maggie shook her head vehemently. 'She's waiting for a call from Luis. He will want her to go and join him in Barcelona.'

'That won't happen. Barcelona's in chaos.'

The thought of leaving Donato behind filled Maggie with panic. She tried to conjure up valid reasons for not leaving Spain. 'Rosario's too young to take charge of a baby.'

Tomás' mouth curled into a sneer. 'You left him in her care while you went off for two days,' he retorted.

'That was only temporary.' She crossed the room and snatched up the red kerchief, dangling it in front of him. 'You're a member of POUM too.'

He flinched, surprised that she understood the significance of the kerchief. Speaking more quietly, he said, 'Sit down and listen to me.'

His calmer tone persuaded Maggie to do as he asked. She perched stiffly on the edge of a chair and waited for him to explain.

'POUM is in the throes of being disbanded. Our leader, Andrés Nin, was executed in July. Since then, there's been no order or discipline; numbers are shrinking, and as I said, our equipment is obsolete, make-do weaponry and so forth. We're not only fighting fascism but we're up against the Republican Army as well. POUM members are being rounded up and imprisoned. Do you want that for your brother?'

Maggie stared up at Tomás wide-eyed. 'Of course I don't, but how can I get him to leave when I don't know where he is?'

'I'll try to find him and bring him here.'

'You mean, you really do know where he might be?'

'I've got a pretty shrewd idea, but I'm not making any promises.' He crouched down on his haunches in front of her. 'Let's say three weeks. If I haven't found him in three weeks time, promise me you'll leave without him.'

'Not without Donato,' she snapped.

'We'll see about that. Would you agree if I found the child a good home?'

Maggie lowered her head into her hands. She needed to think. What Tomás said made sense. With luck he might track Robert down, but she wasn't so sure about giving up Donato. How could she part from the baby she'd grown to love? On the other hand, maybe his home was here in Spain with people of his own kind. Giving a hard swallow, she raised her head to look directly into the big man's eyes and nodded in agreement.

Rosario looked up in alarm when she saw how upset Maggie was.

'What happened for goodness sake?'

Between sobs, Maggie relayed the gist of her conversation with Tomás, finishing with, 'I don't think I can leave without Donato. I'm too attached to him.'

'Maybe Tomás *will* be able to find a good home for him. He's got lots of contacts.'

'Locate Robert, bring him back here, find a home for Donato. In three weeks! It's impossible.'

'I can look after Donato until Tomás finds a suitable family to take care of him.'

'But Rosario, Luis could send for you at any time'

The girl shook her head. 'I don't think he'll send for me yet. Things are bad in Barcelona.' Maggie was surprised. She hadn't realised the teenager was aware of the Catalan situation. She was even more surprised when Rosario went on, 'Besides, I'd like to be here for Palmiro when he comes back on leave. Trust Tomás, he knows best.'

Maggie smiled and kissed the teenager lightly on the cheek. 'Thank you, Rosario, thank you for making me see sense.'

But she hadn't seen sense. The more she thought about Tomás' dismissal of her, the more determined she was to stay. She would use the big man to find her brother but she knew that she could never persuade Robert to leave the country. Why, he'd even chosen to call himself Esteban! Meeting the Gonzales couple, spending time with Rosario, encountering the young Italian deserter who was risking all for a cause he believed in had fired her own ideals. She was beginning to understand why her brother had come to Spain.

Tomás joined them for supper that evening. Taking advantage of his affable mood, Maggie fired questions at him, never suggesting that she disagreed with his actions.

'When are you leaving?'

'Tonight.'

'You're not travelling on that bike, I hope?'

He laughed at her joke and said, 'I've got a lorry parked out at the back.'

So he had transport. 'Are you going alone?'

Tomás raised his eyebrows. 'Why all the questions?'

'I'm interested, that's all. Besides, I want to know how you intend to bring my brother back to Madrid.'

Tomás gave a huge guffaw. 'I see, so your brother's a lily-livered Englishman! Can't make it without suitable transport.'

Biting back a sharp riposte, Maggie responded with a smile, 'That's unfair.'

'Huh. So I mustn't do an Englishman an injustice.' Tomás seemed intent on rubbing her up the wrong way.

'You forget, he's half Spanish.'

'That's right.'

Maggie dug a hand into her pocket and handed Tomás a photograph of Robert. 'Here, take this.'

Tomás looked at it and raised his gaze to study her. 'I'd know him anywhere. The likeness is remarkable.'

'We're twins and...' She gave a shy smile. '...we planned to spend our twenty-fifth birthday together.'

'So?'

'Our birthday's in a few days time.'

Tomás heavy brows drew together. 'Is it *that* important to you?'

'Of course it is,' butted in Rosario. 'Twins have a special bond and they like to celebrate the occasion together.'

To break the tension, Maggie asked, 'How long do you think you'll be away?'

'For as long as it takes.'

Smothering her disappointment regarding the likelihood of sharing her birthday celebrations with Robert, she said, 'Thank you for doing this for me, Tomás.'

After he had left the room, Rosario could no longer restrain her excitement. 'Isn't he wonderful? You were so lucky to meet Tomás on the train.'

'Yes I was.'

The girl sighed. 'I wish Luis would come back to Madrid.'

'Have you got a photograph of him?'

131

'Yes of course.' Rosario reached for her bag, took out a snapshot and handed it to Maggie.

'He looks about the same size as Robert. Have you got any of his clothes here?'

Rosario looked startled. 'Yes, but why? Oh I see, you want to give Tomás some spare clothes in case your brother needs them.' She smiled. 'I'm sure I can find some. Come and have a look.'

Maggie followed Rosario into the bedroom and waited while she pulled a battered suitcase down from the top of the wardrobe. The girl spread the clothes out on the bed so that Maggie could pick some out. She chose carefully, settling for a faded shirt, a dark grey sweater and a pair of worn looking trousers.

'Can I have these?' she asked.

'Of course,' replied Rosario. 'But those trousers and that shirt are old, why not take these for your brother? She held up a pair of cord trousers with braces attached.

'No, these will do, but perhaps I could have the braces.' she pointed. 'That cap too?'

'Take them,' said Rosario, smiling when Maggie rammed the cap on her head.

'How do I look?'

'You look good but will the cap be big enough for your brother?'

'Oh yes, 'I'm sure it will be just fine.'

Maggie glanced at herself in the mirror, grinning with satisfaction at the image grinning back at her. Her plan was taking shape. Luis' old trousers might be a bit long but the braces would help and she could roll up the bottoms. The cap was perfect for hiding her hair. Next, on the pretext of going out for some fresh air, she sneaked around to the back of the building and found Tomás' lorry parked behind a shed out of sight of the road. In order to smuggle out the borrowed clothes, she had stuffed them into the canvas bag she had got from the market a couple of days earlier.

Panic kept her awake for most of the night. She got up while it was still dark and crept out of the house, leaving some money and a note for Rosario, explaining her departure. She hoped the girl would not be too upset that she had not confided in her.

The first rays of dawn had appeared by the time she reached the road. To her relief the lorry was still there. It was a tarpaulin-covered vehicle, easy to hide in. She clambered aboard and quickly changed into Luis' clothes, stuffing her own into the bag along with a flask of water and a packet of dry biscuits, which she had taken from the kitchen cupboard. Hopefully, these would keep her going until they reached their destination.

Using the bag as a pillow, she curled up on the floor of the lorry and waited for Tomás to arrive. Nervous exhaustion made her nod off and she woke up with a start when the engine grunted into life. They were off! For a dreadful moment, she wondered whether she had picked the right vehicle. Suppose this belonged to someone else and she was being driven to god knows where! She was tempted to draw back the curtain separating the driver's cabin from the back of the lorry to check, but thought better of it. It wouldn't do for Tomás to discover her and turf her out onto the street. After several bumpy miles when they had left the city far behind, she heard Tomás' gravel-like voice break into song and sighed with relief as she snuggled down on a pile of rags, her head cushioned on the canvas bag.

Maggie woke up with a start, momentarily forgetting where she was. The lorry was at a standstill. She held her breath, expecting Tomás to draw back the tarpaulin curtain and find her. Then she realised that instead of daylight, the lorry was parked in semi darkness. Muttered

133

voices reached her. Someone was giving orders. She drew back into the void as the tarpaulin was pulled aside. Curling herself into a ball, she folded her arms over her head to hide her face. No one noticed her. Peeping out through her fingers she saw that the lorry was parked in a warehouse. Several men were lifting heavy boxes into the vehicle, pushing them back as far as they would go. She wanted to scream out to stop them, but knew she couldn't.

There was a length of wood along the side of the lorry and when the men went away for more boxes, she pulled it clear and rammed it across the width of the vehicle. With her bag jammed in beside it, the plank formed a wedge, giving her sufficient room to stay squeezed up behind the driver's seat. She hoped they didn't pile in too many boxes. It was a vain hope. The boxes kept coming. She cowered in the corner of the lorry, too terrified to reveal herself.

'That's enough,' someone shouted.

Surely now they would find her! The tarpaulin on the opposite side of the lorry was hitched back and one of the men began roping the boxes together. 'There's room for two more here,' he called out.

Maggie drew her knees up to her chest as two more boxes were shunted into the lorry next to her. Holding her breath she sat with her arms wrapped around her knees waiting to be discovered. Then she heard Tomás grunt a few words before climbing into the driver's seat. He started the engine and reversed the lorry.

The wheels jolted over rocky ground. Maggie's heart pounded. Clearly they were well into the countryside. Soon, she would find Robert. But it wasn't long before she realised that she had to stretch her legs. She looked up at the boxes piled above her and almost wept in despair. Suppose one of them toppled on top of her. She could only guess at their contents: guns and ammunition! There was only one thing she could do.

Reaching up, she pulled at the tarpaulin curtain and called out Tomás' name, but due to the noise of the engine and his own bellowing chant, he didn't hear her. In desperation, she rammed her flask into the small of his back. This had the desired effect. With a screech of brakes, the lorry stopped, dislodging some of the boxes. Luckily, the rope held them in place.

Tomás swivelled around to face her. 'What the hell!' Reaching out, he grabbed her by the arm and hauled her through the curtain into the driver's cabin.

'I'm sorry, I'm sorry,' she stuttered, tears streaming down her cheeks.

Bringing up his large, calloused hand, he slapped her across the face, making her teeth rattle as she fell back against the seat.

'*Idiota!* he shouted. 'What the devil did you think you were doing?'

'I … I wanted to help you find Robert.'

'The front line's no place for a woman like you … an Englishwoman! Have you any idea of what you'll find when you get there? Besides, your pathetic *English* brother is probably dead.'

'Don't say that,' shrieked Maggie.

'If he's alive and as brave as you think he is, he won't thank you for making this journey. You have no idea, *mujer*. You were shocked in Bilbao but just wait until you see how POUM members live. Your brother and his companions are living in dug-outs like animals, they drink river water, they eat whatever they can scratch together from the land around them. All that, besides fighting an unseen enemy: hunted down by the Nationalists, hounded by the International Brigades.'

She cowered away as his tirade went on and on. All at once, he stopped ranting and jumped down from the lorry. Striding around to her side, he opened the passenger door and pulled her out. She fell heavily to the ground, looking up at him, too terrified to move. Yanking her to her feet, he pushed her onto a boulder by the side of the road and, producing a flask from his pocket, he uncorked it and handed it to her.

'Drink!'

Maggie put the flask to her lips and took a sip, recognising cognac. She recalled giggling when Palmiro had taken his first taste of cognac, choking and spluttering afterwards.

'Don't play the little lady with me. Drink some more!'

Again she put the flask to her lips and this time took a large swallow. It took her breath away but she felt better. Tomás snatched the flask and took a swig himself as he paced up and down, mumbling curses under his breath.

Having come to a decision, he stopped pacing and glowered down at her. 'You'll have to come with me. Get in. I'll drop you off near Tres Lomas.'

As she clambered in, she could hear him rearranging the boxes in the back, still muttering to himself. Joining her in the front cabin, he grumbled, 'We could have got two more in.'

As they drove along, Maggie found her confidence returning. 'What's in those boxes?' she asked.

'Never you mind.'

'I want to know.'

'Huh!'

'They're full of ammunition, aren't they?'

'What d'you think?' He frowned as he manouevred the vehicle around a large pot-hole, then added, 'You could have got us killed. If any of those boxes had become dislodged, we would have been blown up.'

'I'm so sorry,' she whispered.

Tomás drove on. Maggie hardly dared to look at him. To stop her legs from trembling, she sat with her hands firmly clasped in her lap, pressing on her knees until they hurt.

'Where did you get those clothes?' asked Tomás after a long silence.

'From Rosario, they belong to her brother.'

'Is she in on this conspiracy?'

'No!' retorted Maggie. 'She had no idea I was going to do this. I left her a note. She thinks I was going to give you the clothes for Robert.'

Tomás cast her an even angrier glance. 'So you think she's too young to look after the kid when you leave Spain but it's all right to keep dumping him on her when the mood takes you.'

Maggie resented his accusation. 'That's not fair!' she protested.

He drove on in silence, a silence that Maggie was too scared to break. As it began to grow dark, he veered off the road onto a narrow track, pulling to a halt in a dip in the hillside. Jumping down from the lorry, he trudged up to a cave about one hundred metres further on. It was well hidden by trees. Maggie scrambled out of the lorry and followed him. She found him bending over some packages in the entrance to the cave and as she approached, he looked up and pointed inside.

'There's your lodgings for the night, *mujer*, make the most of it, you might not have such luxury tomorrow night.'

Maggie was exhausted, but she was also hungry and when Tomás lit a fire and produced some chorizo she knew she wouldn't be able to sleep until she had satisfied her hunger. He handed her a plate of beans and a beaker of rough red wine. She scoffed down both in record time. After that, she slept soundly, waking to the sound of the lorry's engine. Panic-stricken, she leapt to her feet and rushed to the entrance of the cave, afraid that Tomás was leaving without her. Her fears were unfounded. He was standing in front of the vehicle with his head under the bonnet.

Maggie heaved a sigh of relief, realising how much she had come to rely on this remarkable man with his coarse manners. He must have sensed her presence because he looked up and gave her a wave, calling out, 'Breakfast soon.'

She took the opportunity to complete her ablutions in private, thankful that he was busy with the vehicle. By the time she had finished, he was on his way up the hill to the cave.

It didn't take him long to get a fire going. She drank the strong, sugarless coffee he had prepared, chomping hungrily into the crusty roll which went with it.

After they had finished eating, Tomás killed the fire and packed up their things, and they were soon on their way. It wasn't long before he was airing his lungs again, and to Maggie's surprise, she found his voice quite pleasant. There were questions she wanted to ask him, but instead she spent her time gazing out of the window at the deserted landscape. Three hours later, he brought the lorry to a stop at a cross-road.

'This is where we part company,' he told her.

'What do you mean?' cried Maggie in panic. 'You can't leave me here. I thought you were taking me to Tres Lomas.'

He pointed at the track ahead. 'Follow that road and you'll eventually get there. Go to the hospital and ask for Raul. He'll look after you.'

'What about finding Robert?'

'I've got a delivery to make, but Raul may know where to look.'

'Will he take me there?'

'He's mad if he does.'

Maggie felt excitement rise. 'Thank you Tomás. I'll pay Raul, I'll do anything.' Reaching up, she planted a kiss on the big man's bearded cheek.

'You've got a long walk ahead of you, *nena*, you'd better get going,' he said gruffly.

Maggie smiled to herself. She could tell he'd been touched by her show of affection. 'How far is it?' she asked.

'About eight kilometres.' He glanced down at her feet. 'I hope those boots are sturdy. The terrain's quite rough.'

'I'll be all right,' she replied with more conviction than she felt.

She scrambled out of the vehicle and started to walk away but Tomás called out to her. 'Listen, *mujer*, I'll try and arrange to pick you up in a couple of days time. Meanwhile, take these!'

Maggie retraced her steps, wondering what he intended to give her. He climbed down from the lorry and thrust a flask and a couple of rolls into her hand. 'Be warned, if you see anybody on the road, hide in the shrubbery.' Clamping his large calloused hand on her shoulder, he gave her a gentle shake. 'D'you hear me? Run and hide but if necessary, use this.'

Maggie flinched as he held out a small leather holster. 'I can't take that,' she protested. 'Why, I've never handled a gun in my life.'

'Take it! It could save your life.'

She shook her head. 'I don't want it.'

'So you'd rather be picked up, raped or shot…'

'That wouldn't happen, I'm a foreigner.'

'Do you really think those Nationalist pigs will stop and ask to see your passport? Take it, *mujer,'* sneered Tomás.

Maggie could see there was no point in protesting. Cautiously, she took the revolver, holding it at arms-length. 'I don't know how to use it.'

'Tomás gave a raucous laugh. 'It's not dangerous while you've got the safety catch on.' He took it back from her. 'Here, look!'

After taking a glance around to make certain there was no one within earshot, he released the safety catch and took aim at a tree. The bark around it shattered.

Startled by the loud report, Maggie blinked and shrank away. 'I don't want it.'

Pulling her by the wrist, Tomás insisted on giving her a crash course on its use. Releasing the safety catch, he forced her to have a go, and after several attempts, she found that it was not as difficult as she had thought. She didn't want to take the gun but the look on Tomás' face warned her not to argue.

'You might thank me for it one day,' growled Tomás as he climbed back into the lorry. 'Now get going if you want to get there before dark.'

Maggie stood transfixed as she watched him drive away. The revolver felt hot in her hand. Until recently, the only time she had seen a gun was on a cinema screen. Since arriving in Spain, she had seen many but they had been in the hands of soldiers, not civilians like her. With a shudder, she shoved it back into its holster and put it into her canvas bag.

Feeling terribly alone, she swivelled around and stared at the deserted landscape. The distant mountains seemed like an insurmountable wall, the road ahead stretched endlessly to the horizon. Her heart thumped and her mouth felt dry. She began to panic. What if she got lost? What if, as Tomás had suggested, she were to be attacked? Surely he would not have left her to fend for herself if there was real danger lurking in the undergrowth!

He had said Tres Lomas was eight kilometres away. She had to believe him. The scrub-land on either side of the road was scorched and yellow after the August heat, and although with the approach of autumn, the temperature was lower, it was still exhausting having to trudge along under the mid-day sun on a road strewn with potholes. She toed a stone, sending a shower of dust up into the air and startling a rabbit out of its hiding place.

To keep her mind occupied, she made plans for the joint birthday celebrations. Hopefully, Robert would be able to get away from the front line to spend that special day with her. Suddenly, the clatter of hooves jolted her back to reality. Remembering Tomás warning, she threw herself into a dried-up ditch by the roadside. Peeping up from her hiding place, she was relieved to see that the clattering she had heard was being made by a donkey and its master who were coming over the brow of the hill. She clambered out of the ditch and continued along the road, nodding a greeting to the wrinkle-faced peasant as he passed her. This encounter served to make her quicken her pace. It wouldn't do to dawdle. The sooner she got to Tres Lomas the better.

CHAPTER TEN

Dusk was falling by the time Maggie reached the town. She felt exhausted after the bumpy ride in Tomás' lorry and the long walk along the uneven road. Much to her relief she met no one else en route and now that she had reached the town, Tomás' precautions seemed alarmist.

She made for the hospital, which turned out to be a one storey, whitewashed building, badly in need of renovation. She went inside but found the reception area deserted. A buzzer with a notice inviting visitors to ring for attention was sited in the middle of the counter. She pressed it. Nothing happened. After ten minutes, she decided to go in search of life.

A pair of swing doors led through to a corridor. Paint was peeling off its walls, mould had gathered around cornices and the floor was stained with … blood? Maggie gave an involuntary shudder and continued on her way. The doors to the wards were closed but a small window at the top of each one gave on to the interior.

Maggie stopped and peered through one of the doors. What she saw shocked her. Narrow beds placed side by side barely left room for a nurse or doctor to attend to patients. She pushed open the door and went in. The smell of antiseptic and human detritus was overpowering. A low rumble made her turn her head. In the nearest bed a heavily bandaged man reached out a hand, moaning as he did so.

Maggie spun around and fled, colliding at the door with a young man.

'What are you doing here?' he demanded. 'The wards are out of bounds to visitors.'

'Just … just looking for somebody.'

'You should go to Reception.'

'I did, but there's no one there.'

'You should have waited.'

'I did wait,' protested Maggie. 'But when no one came, I decided to look for someone to help me.'

'Who are you looking for?'

'Raul.'

The young man frowned. 'Who *are* you?'

For a moment, Maggie felt unnerved. The man seemed defensive and she could not imagine why. All she'd done was stray into the corridor leading to the wards. In an English hospital she would not have been met with such hostility.

She drew in her breath and said, 'My name's Maggie Morán and I've come here to look for my brother. I was told to ask for Raul.'

'I'm Raul.'

Covering her surprise, Maggie said with a smile. 'Then, perhaps you can help me.'

The man's frown deepened. Reaching out, he whipped the cap from her head so that her hair fell to her shoulders. 'That's better, now I can see you're a woman. What's your brother's name?'

'Robert Morán.'

'Robert? That's an English name…Morán? Let me see, there's Esteban … '

'Yes, that's him,' cried Maggie, fairly hopping up and down with excitement. 'He likes to be called Esteban. Do you know him?'

'Our paths may have crossed once or twice, although I'm not sure I can be of much help. He could be

143

anywhere. Those renegade fighters are dug in all over the region. They're difficult to pin down.' Maggie couldn't hide her dismay. Taking pity on her, he smiled and said, 'Look, I'll be finished in half a hour. Meet me in the bar down the road. You can't miss it. Tell the bartender you're a friend of mine. I'll join you there as soon as I can.'

Maggie waited for over an hour. It was beginning to get dark and she wondered whether Raul had changed his mind and decided that reuniting her with Robert was none of his business. She whiled away the time by studying the pictures on the walls. There were photographs of bull fights, matadors in their suits of lights, as well as flamenco dancers clashing their castanets. She began to fret about finding accommodation for the night and was just about to ask the barman whether he knew of a cheap hotel when Raul walked into the bar.

He gave her a wave and went to the bar to order before joining her at the table. The barman came over with a tray on which there were two short drinks and two coffees.

'I hope you like Queimada,' said Raul.

'I've never tried it,' she said, warming to her companion, who during their time apart, seemed to have softened his attitude towards her.

He smiled. 'It's from my part of the country.'

'Where's that?'

'Galicia, in the north.'

'Why did you leave Galicia?'

'I had to when Franco moved in.' Nodding at the drink, he touched her hand which was resting on the table. 'Go on, try it.'

Too late Maggie remembered that, apart from the rolls Tomás had given her, she hadn't eaten for hours. The strong liquid went straight to her head and made her choke. Through the tears it brought to her eyes, she saw that Raul was grinning in amusement. '*Aqua!*' he called to the bartender, who rushed over, looking equally entertained.

'You should have warned me,' protested Maggie after she had partially recovered.

'Would you like another one?'

At first she thought Raul was serious, then realised he was teasing her.

'No, coffee will do.'

'Have you eaten?'

'No.'

'Neither have I. Will you trust me to order something for you?'

'I'm not sure,' she replied, matching his mood of levity.

'Alfonso!' he called. 'Bring us a *tortilla* and salad and some nice crusty bread.'

Maggie was relieved. Clearly, Raul had a quirky sense of humour. She noticed there were bloodstains on his shirt front and wondered whether he had been in the operating theatre. Judging by what she had seen in the ward, she could imagine the dreadful operations he might have witnessed.

'Are you a doctor?'

'Not yet. I was half way through my studies when the war broke out. I hope to resume them once it's all over. Tell me, have you recently come over from England?'

Without going into detail, she explained how her brother had left for Spain a year earlier and how, after the death of their mother, she had decided to come and look for him, adding that she wanted them to spend their twenty-fifth birthday together.

'That's some adventure,' said Raul when she had finished.

Their omelette arrived and they both attacked it ferociously. Half way through, he asked, 'How did you get to Tres Lomas?'

'Tomás Montalvo brought me.'

Raul raised a surprised eyebrow. 'That old scoundrel! I'm astounded he agreed to that.'

Maggie gave a self-conscious laugh. 'He didn't. I stowed away in his lorry. He was furious when he found me.'

Raul let out a hearty chuckle, causing several drinkers to turn and stare at them. 'Well, I must say,' he said. 'For a gentle *señorita inglesa* you've got guts. Where are you going to stay tonight?'

Maggie blushed. 'I don't know.'

'It's a bit late to find anywhere, but I can offer you a broom cupboard if you're not too fussy about size.'

'A broom cupboard?'

'Yes, it's the hospital linen store. There's a camp bed in there. You're welcome to sleep there tonight.'

'Suppose someone finds me!' gasped Maggie.

He shook his head. 'They won't. And tomorrow I'll fix you up with a room somewhere in town.' He got to his feet and held out his hand. 'Come on, let's go.'

'But I haven't paid,' she protested.

'Don't worry, I've put it on the tab.'

They left the bar and walked back to the hospital where Raul led her along the corridor to a small windowless room. It was, as he had described, the size of a broom cupboard but there were some shelves along one wall piled high with bed linen. Raul pulled a folded canvas bed out from a corner of the room and put it up for her before handing her a sheet, a pillow and a hospital issue blanket.

'I think that will do you for tonight, Señorita Morán.'

'Maggie, please.'

'What a strange name.'

146

'It's short for Margaret.'

'I would never have guessed.'

'My second name is Estela after my grandmother.'

'Your brother prefers his Spanish name, what about you?'

'I'll stick to Maggie.'

'Goodnight Maggie, I'll come back for you in the morning. … Oh, and by the way, the lavatory is down the hall. Try not to let anybody spot you sneaking along there.'

Next morning, Maggie woke up feeling refreshed. After having spent the previous night sleeping in a cave on the hard ground, the camp bed had seemed like luxury. She was ready and waiting by the tie Raul arrived.

'Well,' he said. 'You look better this morning. Did you sleep well?'

'Very well.'

'Were you disturbed?'

She smiled. 'No one came in here.'

'I have to check in for work in an hour's time but you'll be pleased to know that I've found you some accommodation.'

'That was quick.'

'I don't waste time,' he grinned. 'Gather your things together and I'll take you there.'

The accommodation proved to be in a backstreet hotel not far from the hospital. It was rather shabby but clean.

'When can you take me to my brother?' asked Maggie.

Raul looked taken aback. 'I didn't promise anything.'

'But I thought…'

He grinned at her. 'Look, Maggie, my shift starts in five minutes. We'll talk about it later.'

'What am I going to do with myself all day?' muttered Maggie, almost to herself.

'Take a look around town, not that there's much to see. Tres Lomas is little more than a village.'

He left then, leaving her to ponder on what she was doing in a town she didn't want to be in. All at once, she felt angry. On the road with Tomás there had been hope, the encounter with Raul had produced more hope, now it seemed she would have to bide her time. Her grandparents had always called her a patient little thing in contrast to her impetuous brother. She now realised that her own spontaneity had been overshadowed by Robert's more extrovert personality. But things had changed, *she* had changed. She had reached the point where she couldn't bear having to wait. She resolved to call in at the hospital later in the day and try to persuade Raul to take her to see Robert. At home in England, she would have been shocked by such audacity but here, in Spain, it seemed that rules were meant to be broken.

At two o'clock she made her way to the hospital and found Raul outside, smoking. He looked pleased to see her.

'Have you explored the town, Maggie?'

'There wasn't much to explore.'

He stubbed out his cigarette. 'I have to get back. I only popped out for a cigarette. As usual, we're short-staffed.'

'When do you get off?' she asked.

'Who knows. I might have to stay on for another shift.'

'You work too hard,' she said.

'We all do.'

'Do you think you'll be called out today?'

'You can never tell.'

She stepped closer to him. 'If you do, can I come out with you?'

He frowned. 'I don't know about that. We see some terrible sights. How would you cope?'

148

'I'll be all right,' she rushed to assure him. 'I once took a First Aid Course.'

He threw back his head and laughed. 'And that qualifies you to come with me to the front line, does it?'

Maggie stiffened, and he noticed.

'I'm sorry, Maggie. Look, I have to get back now. I'll be in touch later.'

Maggie watched him lope away, noticing how tall he was, how broad his shoulders were. Even though she felt disappointed at his rather offhand attitude, she couldn't help admitting to herself that she liked the way his brows drew together in a straight line when he puzzled over something and the way he touched her hand in a bid to lend reassurance.

With a sigh she turned to go back into town, but hesitated and went instead to sit under the large pine tree in front of the hospital. She was impatient to see her brother for two reasons: apart from making certain that he was all right, she had begun to fret about leaving Donato with Rosario. She felt guilty for having rushed off without saying goodbye. Suppose the girl got fed up with baby-minding and decided to hand Donato over to the authorities!

A shout startled her. Raul came running across the grass waving his arms. He stopped in front of her and said, 'Come on, now's your chance. We've been called out and I think the emergency is close to where your brother is camped. I hope you're not squeamish.'

Taking her hand, he dragged her across the grass to where a nurse was already climbing into an ambulance.

'What made you change your mind?' she gasped.

'We need all the help we can get. Like I said, we're short-staffed.'

She found herself squashed in the front seat between Raul and the nurse, who gave her a nod of greeting as the vehicle jerked into life. They came upon the camp suddenly. There were people milling about in what seemed to Maggie to be total confusion. She looked for her brother but couldn't see him. Suppose he was one of the injured! Her heart beat fiercely as she jumped down from the ambulance and followed Raul and the nurse into the midst of the mayhem.

'How many?' asked Raul.

'One dead, two wounded.'

Before Maggie could ask who had died, the leader said, 'That poor French sod bought it. Died instantly.'

'Let's see to the other two,' said Raul, while the nurse opened up her First Aid kit and started giving morphine to one of the injured.

Maggie shrank back as she saw the horrific wound the young man had suffered. He moaned as Raul applied pressure to his leg to stop the bleeding. She turned away, sickened by what she saw, and at the same time, ashamed by her reaction and by the relief she felt that Robert wasn't one of the wounded men. Under normal circumstances she would have questioned those around her, asked them whether they knew her brother but the appalling sight she was witnessing made her curb her tongue.

It was Raul who supplied the information. 'No one knows where your brother is, Maggie, but he's well-known to them and they think he's somewhere in this area.

'Will you drive me out here again.'

'We'll have to see.'

'Thanks, Raul,' she muttered as they climbed back into the ambulance with the nurse remaining in the rear with the wounded men.

It was while they were driving along an open stretch of road that the attack came. There was a loud explosion.

Both Maggie and Raul ducked their heads with Raul instinctively slamming his foot down on the brake pedal.

'Are you all right?' he asked, pulling himself up to look through the shattered windscreen.

'I think so,' she said, brushing slivers of glass off her clothing. 'Oh! You're injured.'

'It's nothing.'

Blood was gushing from a wound in Raul's right arm.

Maggie gave a gasp, her eyes widening in alarm as the image of her mother's limp body sprang to mind. Once again, she could see the pink-stained bath, the wet floor, the blood seeping from Katherine's slashed wrists. Whatever happened, she mustn't lose her nerve. Pulling aside the dividing curtain, she called out, 'Raul's been injured.'

'How bad?' asked the nurse.

'He's taken a bullet to his upper arm.'

Raul gave a moan and muttered, 'I'm all right.'

'I can't leave these men,' said the nurse, addressing Maggie. '*You'll* have to do something.'

'Tell...tell me what to do,' stammered Maggie.

'Tourniquet it. You'll find another First Aid Kit under the front seat. There's a strap in there, use it.' She disappeared behind the curtain and Maggie could hear her attending to one of the injured men.

She was close to panic but when Raul's eyes started to glaze over, she dived down into the foot-well to retrieve the box. Wrapping a piece of bandage around the wound, she pulled the tourniquet strap as tight as she could. Raul's face was devoid of colour but the seat and the steering wheel were covered with blood. His eyes flickered open. 'Change places with me and drive.' She could hardly make out his words.

There was no time to think because more bullets ricocheted along the side of the vehicle. Maggie jumped down from the passenger side and hurried round to yank

151

open the driver's door, ducking her head as she ran. By the time she had climbed in, Raul had somehow managed to move over to the passenger seat and was leaning his head on the headrest.

'Drive!' he ordered her.

Shifting the ambulance into gear, Maggie jolted the vehicle forwards, narrowly missing a pothole. More shots careened along the road, persuading her that it would be better for them to take their chances on the road than be a sitting target for a sniper's bullet. Ramming her foot down on the accelerator, she drove on while the wind whistled through the shattered windscreen, bringing tears to her eyes. But it wasn't long before they had out-distanced their attackers and she was able to slow down.

Raul opened his eyes. 'Well done!' he mumbled and promptly passed out.

It was getting dark by the time Maggie drove the ambulance into the hospital yard. During the rest of the journey Raul had slipped in and out of consciousness. Several orderlies rushed out with stretchers for the wounded men and, at the mention of Raul's name, another two came out to help him.

'Is he going to be all right?' she asked.

One of the men turned and gave her a smile. 'He should be, thanks to whoever applied the tourniquet; without it he would have bled to death.' Maggie heaved a sigh of relief but she didn't mention that she had been the one to apply the tourniquet. 'Go home and get some rest, *señorita*, you look tired.'

'Thank you, I will,' she replied.

Back at the hotel, she kicked off her shoes and threw herself onto the bed, fully clothed. It was completely dark by the time she woke up. The events of the day seemed like a bad dream, but as soon as she realised that the bad dream had in fact been real, she leapt off the bed and ran

152

into the bathroom to wash her face. She glanced at her watch and saw that it was nearly ten o'clock. How could she have slept for so long? She had to go and check on Raul. He would think her uncaring if she didn't pay him a visit, she told herself, deliberately casting aside her own desire to see him again.

She combed her hair and changed into the skirt and blouse she had stuffed into the canvas bag. Back at the hospital, she found Raul sitting in a chair with his arm in a sling. He looked much better than when she had last seen him.

'*Holá* Maggie!' he said. 'Are you rested?'

'I'm fine, how are you?'

'Much better, thanks to you. If you hadn't driven us back I would have been a gonner.'

She grinned. 'Me too, I suspect.'

It was his turn to grin. 'You're probably right.'

When she started to leave, Raul surprised her. 'If we don't find your brother in time for your birthday, we'll still celebrate it, Maggie.'

Maggie's brows shot up. 'It's not *that* important,' she mumbled. 'After all, twenty-five is not a special birthday, not like twenty-one.'

'How did you and your brother celebrate your twenty-first birthday?'

'We didn't. Our family wasn't the party-going kind. Robert…' She unconsciously reverted to her brother's old name. '…and I went to the pictures and his current girlfriend came along too.' She gave a snort. 'He's never without a girl hanging on his arm.'

'What about you? Any boyfriends?'

Maggie laughed self-consciously. 'Fat chance with mother around.'

'Bad as that, huh?'

Covered with embarrassment, Maggie stuttered, 'Oh no, I didn't mean…I was only too willing to look after her.'

'Time you got back into bed, my friend.' One of Raul's nursing companions appeared in the doorway.

'I'll say good-bye then,' said Maggie, getting up and edging towards the door.

'Don't I get a good-bye kiss?'

Maggie blushed. 'Of course,' she said and went back to give Raul a peck on each cheek, Spanish fashion.

'You smell nice,' he said.

'Lavender soap,' she replied, feeling surprised.

He laughed. 'We only get carbolic in here.'

'Rubbish!' laughed a young nurse, who had joined them. 'He's only kidding.'

'I'll stop by and see you tomorrow,' said Maggie.

'*Hasta mañana*,' replied Raul.

'*Hasta luego*,' she smiled back.

CHAPTER ELEVEN

Maggie left the hospital in a daze. What had Raul said: *We'll still celebrate your birthday*? Did he mean it? Somehow, with those words ringing in her ears, finding her brother in time didn't seem quite so important.

She returned to the hotel, had a light supper in the restaurant and, on finding that for once there was hot water, she took a leisurely bath and went to bed to sleep until eight the next morning. She awoke with a feeling of well-being. Even the photograph that Rosario had taken of Donato only a few days before her departure from Madrid failed to re-evoke her desire to get back to him.

She spent a quiet day looking around the small town. A detective story picked up in a second-hand bookshop helped her pass the time. It was an Agatha Christie translated into Spanish and sometimes the poor translation made her laugh out loud. In the early afternoon she went to the hospital only to find that Raul had been discharged.

'Where is he?' she asked the young nurse, who was in the process of preparing his room for another patient.

'He's gone back to his lodgings.'

'Oh…do you think he'd mind if I called on him?'

'I should think he'd be pleased,' smiled the girl. 'He wanted to come back to work but of course they wouldn't let him. I think he could do with a bit of company.'

'Where are his lodgings?'

'He's got a room in the men's quarters, number fourteen.'

'Would I be allowed in there?'

The nurse laughed. 'Who's going to stop you?' she said, and from the window, she pointed out a row of pre-fabricated buildings. 'He'll be there unless, of course, he's playing hooky.'

'*Gracias.*'

'*Buena suerte!*'

Feeling a rush of colour to her cheeks, Maggie made a hasty departure. Had the nurse guessed how she felt about Raul? She had barely had time to figure out how she felt herself. Suppose other people guessed before she did.

She made her way across the hospital courtyard half hoping that, as the nurse had suggested, Raul might be playing hooky. She was about to knock on the door of number fourteen when it opened and she found herself face to face with one of the nurses.

'I'm so sorry.'

For a moment Maggie thought she had got the wrong room, but the girl asked, 'Are you looking for Raul?'

'Yes…but if it's not convenient…'

'Maggie!' Covered by embarrassment, Maggie hesitated, but Raul's tone was welcoming and gave her no opportunity to change her mind or to think up an excuse for a quick getaway. 'Maribel's just going, aren't you?'

The other girl grinned. 'I suppose I am.'

'Don't let me chase you away,' said Maggie.

'Don't worry, I was leaving anyway. Now it's up to you to keep this rascal in order.'

The door closed behind her and Maggie found herself alone with Raul. He was stretched out on a chair with his legs propped up on a footstool. His right arm was supported in a sling.

'Come and sit down next to me,' he said, patting the chair on his left.

She walked across the room and sat down. 'How are you feeling?'

'Much better. I'll be as right as rain in a few days time.'

'You mustn't overdo it.'

He laughed. 'You sound like my mother.'

'Oh…oh. I didn't mean to.'

'What are we going to do about your birthday?'

'I was so hoping Esteban would be here,' she said, using the name her brother now preferred.

'There's little hope of that,' said Raul. 'But we could have a party.'

'A party? But I don't know anybody.'

'I do.'

'But they'd be your friends not mine or my brother's.'

'Don't worry, they snatch at any opportunity to have a party. It helps to relieve the tension. Shall we go and have something to eat in the canteen?'

'Isn't it against the rules for outsiders to eat at the hospital?'

He grinned. 'I'll vouch for you.'

That night, Maggie slept soundly but she woke up with a feeling of disappointment. Her dream of spending her birthday with her brother had not materialised but she reminded herself that he was, after all, fighting on the front line. Their birthday was unimportant to him. He probably wouldn't even remember it. But the belief that they would spend their twenty-fifth birthday together had meant a lot to her, sustaining her through the trials of the journey to Madrid and the stowaway trip in Tomás lorry.

She spent most of the day in her hotel room composing a letter to Esteban - trying to get used to his new name - in the hope that she could somehow get it to him. Late in the afternoon, Raul telephoned her. 'You must come over to the hospital this evening, Maggie. We can have something to eat together.'

'I don't feel like celebrating,' she replied.

'I'll expect you at eight o'clock,' he insisted and put the phone down, giving her no chance to protest.

She went to his chalet just before eight, determined to cut the evening as short as possible. Giving a rap on the door, she expected Raul to open it. Instead, Maribel invited her in. The place was in semi-darkness and it was several seconds before she realised that the room was full of people.

'*Feliz cumpleaños!* Everyone sang out the birthday song, leaving Maggie open-mouthed.

Raul strode across the room and drew her in. 'We couldn't let you spend your birthday all alone, now could we?'

Somebody poured wine while Raul introduced her to the assembled company. They were all from the hospital and she wondered how they had managed to get time off.

Raul explained: 'Things have been quiet today so we've been able to relax a bit. No doubt, things will hot up again soon.' He laughed. 'We have to make the most of any spare time we have and enjoy ourselves.'

Much to Maggie's surprise, food and music had also been organised, and despite his wounded arm, Raul was able to join in with the dancing, albeit awkwardly. The evening flew past and when the others started to leave, Maggie got ready to go with them.

'Don't go, Maggie.'

'It's late. You should get some rest.'

'Stay a while longer.'

She dropped the cardigan she was holding and went to sit down next to him. 'How's the injury after all that activity?'

He slipped his arm out of the sling. 'I don't really need this. It's just for show.'

158

He placed his other arm around her shoulders and drew her close.

'Be careful!'

'Who me or you?'

Before she could stop him, he had pressed his mouth over hers. Maggie felt overwhelmed. She was a twenty-five-year-old innocent. It both irked and frightened her. What she felt for this man was different to anything she had felt before. Back home in England she would have expected to date a man over a period of time before making any sort of commitment. But things moved more swiftly than she could have imagined and, although she knew that alcohol was influencing her responses, she also knew that she couldn't refuse this good-looking Spaniard..

Bright sunlight woke Maggie next morning. She blinked, remembering, as she recognised Raul standing at the end of the bed with a mug of coffee in his hand.

'Did you sleep well?' he asked.

'Like a baby.'

'Me too. I had to get up early because I've got to report in for work this morning.'

'Already?'

'Yes, I can do light duties, but they won't allow me to drive.' He placed the coffee mug on the bedside table, and leaning over, kissed her gently. He hadn't shaved and she felt his prickly bristles on her cheek. 'Sorry,' he apologised, putting a hand to his chin. 'I'm going to shave when I get to the hospital. You'll have to make your own way back to the hotel, I'm afraid.'

'Thank you for last night…I mean the party and everything,' said Maggie.

'It was my pleasure.' He looked concerned. 'You haven't got any regrets have you, I mean…'

She blushed. 'None at all.'

'I'll phone you about meeting up tonight.'

He backed to the door, opened it and, with a wave, disappeared through it.

Maggie picked up the coffee mug, sipping from it now and again. Her eyes glazed over as she relived the previous evening and its incredible outcome. She felt that she should be suffering some kind of remorse but she wasn't. In a moment of revelation, she saw again the intimate looks that had so often passed between her parents. Yes, she thought, Miguel and Katherine had been truly in love, a love that had lasted their entire lives. No wonder her mother went to pieces when Miguel died!

Draining her coffee cup, she got out of bed and started to get dressed. There was a rap at the door. Had Raul come back? A second rap told her it was urgent. She went to open it.

'Maggie, you must come. They need another ambulance driver. Ramon is off sick and there's an emergency down in one of the villages. Come quickly!' Maribel could barely get the words out.

Maggie clapped a hand to her mouth. Drive the ambulance again? Was she up to it?

'Come on, Maggie!'

Maribel gave her no time to consider refusal. Taking her by the arm, she dragged her to the waiting vehicle.

Maggie climbed into the ambulance, astounded to find Raul already waiting for her in the front passenger seat.

'What are you doing here?'

'I've come to navigate.'

'You're not well enough.'

'Shut up, Maggie, and get going,' retorted Raul.

It was a bumpy ride and Maggie was forced to keep her attention on the road ahead. She wanted to question Raul, to ask him where they were heading but she knew that if she lost concentration, even for a second, the vehicle could veer off the road.

Once they were on their way, he provided information. 'We've got to pick up a pregnant woman in an outlying village; she's suffering from pre-eclampsia.'

'What's that?'

'A serious condition in pregnancy. She and the baby could die.'

'Oh dear, I hope we'll be in time,' gasped Maggie, stepping on the gas.

'Hey, go easy! You don't want to run us off the road.'

They reached the village and climbed out of the ambulance. A group of women dressed in black greeted them. They were wringing their hands and weeping. 'You're too late,' explained one of them. 'Fatima's dead.'

'And the baby?' asked Raul.

The woman shook her head.

Maggie felt close to tears. If only she had driven faster, an extra five or ten minutes might have made all the difference. The woman went on: 'She went into convulsions. It's unlikely you could have done anything.'

'Why are they all dressed in black?' Maggie whispered to Raul. 'I can't believe they're all widows.'

'The Nationalists shot most of the men from this village some months ago,' he replied, adding with a sigh. 'I'll have to help them bury the woman.'

'How can you with your arm still not properly healed?'

'There's no one else to do it.'

'I'll help you.'

He cast her a sidelong glance. 'Perhaps you could.'

They each collected a spade from one of the women and walked to the edge of the village where Raul chose a spot for the grave. It wasn't long before some of the women began helping with the digging.

'Go back to the vehicle, Maggie,' said Raul. 'Sort out some medical supplies to leave with these people.'

Maggie trudged back to the ambulance, feeling puzzled when she saw that the back door of the vehicle was ajar. She pulled the door open but a slight rustling sound made her hesitate. It was dark inside but she detected a movement. 'Who's there?'

There was no answer. She gave a swallow and leant inside. To her surprise her hand made contact with a small leg. She gave it a gentle tug. A little girl wriggled towards her. She was white-faced and trembling.

Maggie stared at the child, noticing her dirt-streaked cheeks and her red-rimmed eyes.

'What were you doing in there?' she demanded.

'We meant no harm. Don't send us away,' begged the child.

Maggie's voice rose in surprise. 'Are there more of you? How many?'

'Just me and my brother.'

'Where are your parents?' She realised at once how stupid that sounded. Clearly, their father must have perished with the rest of the men from the village. 'I meant…your mother?'

'She died when the soldiers came.'

Maggie stifled an involuntary sob. 'You're orphans?' she gasped, momentarily unable to take in the state of affairs. 'Er…' Her hesitation alarmed the little girl, who drew back into the ambulance.

Hastening to ease the situation, Maggie reached into the vehicle and encouraged the child to approach her. 'Get down here and stand beside me; I won't hurt you,' she said quietly. After a moment, the little girl did as she was told. The boy, who Maggie could now see, was a few years younger, edged closer to the opening, giving her the opportunity to lift him down to stand beside his sister.

'Don't be afraid,' she said to them. 'Can you tell me your names?'

The girl spoke up. 'Eva.'

Maggie turned to the little boy. 'And your name?' In contrast to his sister, he gazed fixedly ahead, showing neither fear nor interest. Swiftly, she scrutinised their appearance. The girl wore a tattered summer dress and scuffed sandals; the boy's trousers were torn and his grubby shirt hung out of the waistband. He also wore sandals but the toes had been cut out of his, presumably to allow for growth. His toes were filthy. His face was thinner than his sister's.

The little boy didn't reply but continued to stare at her in an unsettling way.

'He doesn't talk,' volunteered Eva. She hesitated. 'His name's Fabio.'

Maggie held out her hand to him and although he didn't back away, he made no effort to touch her. She frowned at the girl. 'Why doesn't he talk?'

'He hasn't talked since…since the soldiers…' Her mumbled words became incomprehensible as she lowered her gaze, shuffling the dusty ground with the toe of her shoe.

Oh God, thought Maggie, what am I going to do? 'I'm afraid you can't stay here.' She crouched down to their level and smiled in an attempt to soften the refusal.

'Take us with you into the town.'

Maggie shook her head. 'I can't do that.' The pair stood hand-in-hand staring at her disconcertingly. She went on, 'Who's going to look after you if I take you into town?'

Glancing over her shoulder, she saw that Raul was erecting a cross on the grave. One way or the other, she needed to act quickly.

'Who's been looking after you since your mother died?'

'No one.'

Maggie couldn't believe her ears. 'Surely someone in the village has been taking care of you, an aunt, a cousin, maybe?'

The girl shook her head.

Maggie bit her lip. 'I can't take you with me,' she said, going on to explain. 'It's just not possible. For a start, I don't live in the town. I'm from Madrid.'

The little girl came to life. Clutching at Maggie's skirt, she implored, 'Please, please, you must; we can't stay here, we'll starve.'

'No you won't, the villagers won't let that happen.'

Tears welled in Eva's eyes as she again pulled at Maggie's skirt. 'Pleeese…'

The plight of the pathetic pair tugged at her heartstrings. Would it be so bad if she took them into town. Someone there might take them in. She hesitated uncertainly. Another glance over her shoulder told her that Raul and the others were coming back.

'Quick, get back in the ambulance,' she said. 'And keep very quiet.'

The children scrambled up into the vehicle, crawling to the far end. *What have I done?* thought Maggie, realising as Raul joined her, that the die was cast. There was no longer time to change her mind. He looked exhausted as he mopped his forehead, wiping away perspiration.

'Have you sorted out the medical supplies?' he asked.

She could see he was wondering why she hadn't completed the task. 'I was just going to.'

'I'll help you.'

'There's no need, Raul, I'll do it. You look tired. Get in the front and wait for me.'

'Hurry up, we'd better get going if we're to reach Tres Lomas before dark.' He studied her face and frowned. 'What's wrong?'

'Nothing. I…I just feel a bit sad about what happened to that poor woman.'

He shrugged and went to sit in the front while she collected some supplies, handing them to a woman who was waiting. The woman thanked her and Maggie waved to a group of villagers watching from a distance. Then she climbed into the vehicle and started the engine. She felt anxious, afraid that a noise from the rear might alert Raul to the stowaways. During the drive she had plenty of time to think about the consequences of her impulsive action. Who would look after the children? Would there be a family in Tres Lomas willing to take on a pair of traumatized orphans? She felt sick with worry and was aware that Raul kept giving her covert glances. Clearly, he knew something had upset her.

Thankfully, it was dark by the time they reached the hospital. Raul got out first and went inside, giving Maggie the chance to check on the children. Had she not known that they were hiding there when she opened the back door of the ambulance she would have concluded that the vehicle was empty.

'Quickly,' she whispered. 'You must be quiet. I'll take you to where I'm staying.'

That was a rash decision. How was she going to smuggle them upstairs to her room? The children complied without question. Hand-in-hand, they followed her across the car park and into the street. She walked quickly, forcing them to run in order to keep up with her. Luck was with them. There was no one on duty at the hotel so she ushered them upstairs without being seen.

'You'll have to be ever so quiet,' she warned them, adding jokily. 'Otherwise the hotel owner will know I've brought someone in with me and throw us out.'

For the first time, Eva smiled. 'We'll be like tiny mice,' she whispered.

Once they were settled, Maggie said, 'I'm going to the shops to get something to eat. I won't be long but I'll have to leave you here on your own for a little while.'

Eva's smile was replaced by a look of anxiety. 'You will come back?'

'Of course. I'm trusting you to be very good.'

Eva grinned and pointing to her little brother said, 'He's ever so good.'

'How old are you, Eva?'

'Nine, nearly ten.'

'And Fabio?'

'He's seven.'

She left them then, running down the stairs noiselessly, hoping she wouldn't meet anybody on her way out. She found a grocers shop just closing up for the night and hurriedly purchased some chorizo, cheese, and some fruit and salad. Back in her room, when she produced the food the children ate ravenously, stuffing it into their mouths as if afraid she would take it away from them. She tried to draw the little boy out of his shell but whenever she addressed him, he stared at her in silence.

'Does he talk to you?' she asked Eva.

Eva shook her head. 'He used to be a chatterbox but he doesn't anymore.'

'Has anybody tried to encourage him?'

Again Eva shook her head.

Maggie studied the pair. Eva was a pretty girl with softly waving hair and a sweet expression. Her brother was small for his age, or at least Maggie thought he was. She really didn't have much experience with children so she knew her judgement was unsound.

After they had eaten, she managed to smuggle them along to the bathroom without being seen. She washed their hands and faces, then led them back to the room and put them to bed, settling herself in the armchair with a blanket over her knees. The armchair was old and creaky. It squeaked every time she moved but at least the children were too tired for this to disturb them. They slept long and deeply, waking at nine thirty the following morning.

She fed them each a roll and butter. They only had water to drink but this didn't seem to worry them. She was surprised they didn't ask her where they were going to live. She wondered whether they thought the hotel was her home. After all, it was unlikely they had ever been in a hotel before. She decided to leave them in the room while she went in search of Raul. She *had* to tell him about the children. He would be angry, he would probably never speak to her again, let alone help her. She hadn't a clue as to how she would cope. Tomás was supposed to come back and collect her. What would he say when she introduced two additional children? This thought prompted the realisation that she was assuming Eva and Fabio would come with her to Madrid. How would Rosario feel about two extra mouths to feed? And the flat! How would they manage? They were cramped enough already.

'I have to go out,' she said. 'But I'll be back, it's just that I have to see somebody.'

Eva looked suspicious. 'Not a policeman?'

Maggie laughed. 'Of course not. Don't worry, no one knows you're here.'

She left them then to make her way to the hospital. During his break, Raul came out to see her. He looked rested and greeted her warmly. They went to sit under the tree in the courtyard, enjoying the mid-morning sun. Raul lit up a cigarette.

'How's my little English nurse?' he joked.

'Very well,' she replied.

'You drove the ambulance just fine, Maggie. Well done!'

She glanced down at her feet, fiddling with the edge of her cardigan. 'I have something to tell you.'

167

He placed a finger under her chin and turned her to face him. 'You look serious. What is it?'

She didn't know how to break the news and ended up blurting it out. 'I picked up two orphans yesterday.'

'What d'you mean?'

'I picked them up from the village and brought them back here.'

'How?'

'I hid them in the back of the ambulance.'

'What? Maggie, you must be mad.'

'I know I shouldn't have but they seemed so forlorn and they had no one to look after them. The boy's traumatized. He can't speak.'

'What d'you mean?'

'He's mute, but I'm sure it's only temporary.'

'How do you know that?'

'Eva told me he hasn't spoken since their mother was killed. They've been looking after themselves since then.'

'And you fell for it?'

Maggie felt her cheeks redden. 'She was telling the truth.'

'Really!' Raul's sarcasm resonated. 'Maggie, you've come from a country where everything is organised properly, where rules and regulations exist. You're in Spain now, in the middle of a civil war. You can't take anything at face value. I guarantee Eva's lying. Those villagers are like gypsies, they'll say anything to gain sympathy.'

Could Raul be right? Could Eva be taking her for a ride? The image of the pathetic pair rose in Maggie's mind. She shunted aside misgivings. Those children were in genuine distress. Eva was terrified and Fabio hadn't uttered a single sound since she had found them. No seven-year-old could keep that up for so long.

Yet Raul's serious expression unnerved her as he asked, 'Where are they now?'

'In my hotel room.'

'Don't tell me the proprietor let them stay there?'

'I smuggled them in.'

'You seem to be very good at smuggling,' snapped Raul. 'First Tomás' truck and now this!'

'That's unfair.'

He glanced at his watch. 'I get off in a hour's time. I'll come and see them for myself. In the meantime, I'll try and figure out a way of getting them back to their village.'

'They're not going back,' shouted Maggie. 'Can't you find a nice family who'll have them, here in the town?'

'I might be able to find someone to take the girl but…'

Maggie's jaw tightened. 'They mustn't be separated.'

'No one would take on a mute orphan…' His eyebrows drew together. '…a child who can't or won't speak. You say he's traumatized. How d'you know that? He might have been born dumb, he might be retarded.'

'Rubbish! Anybody can see he's in shock.'

'All the more reason for him to return to the place he knows.'

Maggie stared defiantly into his eyes. 'There's only one solution. I'll take them back to Madrid with me.'

Raul gave a raucous laugh. 'You'll do what? What makes you think Tomás will agree to transport them there?'

She twisted away from him. 'Don't worry, I'll convince him.'

'I doubt that.'

With these words, Raul got up, stubbed out his cigarette and strode off. Maggie was close to tears as she walked back to the hotel. What had possessed her to do such an impulsive thing? She had said confidently that Tomás would agree, but in her heart she wasn't so sure. Tomás could be very pig-headed and they certainly hadn't parted on the best of terms two days ago. Suppose he

169

refused! Could she bring herself to let Raul take them back to the village? At the entrance to the hotel, she straightened her shoulders and tried to put on a brave face. She mustn't let those poor little orphans sense her uncertainty.

Raul didn't arrive until two and a half hours later. During this time, Maggie tried to entertain the children by telling them some of the stories *Abuelo* had recounted to her during her childhood. They were fascinated, just as she and her brother had been. On seeing Raul, Eva and Fabio got to their feet and moved away. They held hands and stared at him with wide eyes.

'Well,' said Raul. 'I've arranged to take them back to their village tomorrow. '

Eva's eyes grew wider and she gripped her brother's hand more tightly. Instinctively, Maggie went to stand beside them, putting a hand around the little girl's shoulder. 'You can't do that.'

Raul began to get angry. 'There's no other way.'

'Can't you see, they're traumatized. God knows what will happen to them if they go back. Fabio will probably never speak again.'

Raul took a step closer, making the children shrink back even more. 'There's no other way,' he repeated.

Maggie tried persuasion. 'Please, Raul, let them stay with me at least until Tomás gets back.'

'That's another thing. He's coming to pick you up tomorrow morning.'

'There you are, then. Problem solved. I'll get Tomás to take us all back to Madrid.'

Raul again stepped forward. 'I'll take them now. They can sleep at the hospital for tonight.'

'No!' Maggie hastily moved to shield the children with her body. 'You're not taking them.'

Raul's anger boiled over. 'You're mad, Maggie, utterly mad.'

'At least, they can stay here with me tonight.'

This suggestion seemed to ease the situation, and on reflection, Maggie could only guess that Raul imagined this semi-concession on her part would turn the end result in his favour.

'All right. I'll be back tomorrow morning at ten o'clock. Make sure you're ready to leave. Tomás hates being kept waiting. I'll make the other arrangements when you've gone.'

With a rush of warmth towards Raul, she realised he had worded this carefully in order not to distress the children, fooling them into believing that she had won the argument. And she *would* win it because she had made up her mind that she wasn't going to give up that easily. She would win both Raul and Tomás round.

CHAPTER TWELVE

The confrontation with Tomás was even worse than Maggie had expected. She met up with him outside the hospital, having left Eva and Fabio back at the hotel.

He was adamant. 'Two more orphans? Out of the question.'

'But Tomás,' pleaded Maggie. 'They've no one to look after them.'

'Raul says that someone in their village will take care of them.'

'They won't. The poor little things have been abandoned. I can't imagine how they've survived up to now.'

'What about Donato? What about Rosario? You wouldn't be able to gallivant off to visit your brother leaving her with three children to look after.'

'I won't be visiting him. He'll come to see me.'

This seemed unlikely but Maggie felt it gave strength to her argument.

'You're asking the impossible, *mujer*. Have you talked to your brother about this?'

'Of course not, I haven't met up with him yet but I'm sure he'd support me.'

Tomás gave a gruff laugh. 'I doubt that. Besides, can you afford to keep them?'

'I'll give more lessons, find an extra job.'

'Find a job? Doing what?'

'Why are you so opposed to this? You were the one who insisted we take Donato with us.'

'That was different. You had a duty towards him after what happened to the Fajardo's.'

'I can't see any difference.'

'Stop being obstinate, *mujer*, they're not coming and that's an end to it.'

Tomás turned on his heels and strode off.

Raul joined her. 'I told you, didn't I?'

'I'm not giving up yet.'

'I've arranged to take them back to their village tomorrow morning and there's a room for them at the hospital tonight.'

'They won't need it, we're leaving this afternoon.' Raul raised his eyebrows as Tomás marched past them. 'Where's he off to?' asked Maggie.

'He's going to join an old drinking buddy. They get drunk every time he comes here. You won't get away today if he spends too much time with him.'

'Oh dear,' wailed Maggie.

She went back to her hotel, purchasing some provisions and a notepad and pencils on the way. Drawing kept the children busy for an hour but, clearly, they were tired of being cooped up in the room. Eventually, she took the risk of allowing them out onto the balcony in order to get a breath of fresh air, but she warned Eva not to talk to her little brother while they were out there. As for Fabio, like a little shadow, he continued to follow his sister wherever she went: across the room, onto the balcony, back again.

It was late afternoon when Tomás' vehicle drew to a halt outside the hotel. From the balcony, she could hear his strident voice cajoling the proprietor to let him in.

That's it, thought Maggie, Raul was right, Tomás is too drunk to drive us back to Madrid today. Hushing the children, she ran downstairs to see if she could pacify the proprietor. It turned out there was no need. It seemed, he too, was one of Tomás' old drinking buddies.

'Are you ready, *nena*?' Tomás called out amiably when he saw her.

'You're in no fit state to drive,' she countered.

He flung out his arms. 'That's where you're wrong. We're going to drive all night if necessary. I want to be back in Madrid by the morning.'

Maggie was in a quandary. At home in England, she would never have considered getting into a car with someone as drunk as Tomás. But as Raul had pointed out earlier, this was Spain where neither rules nor commonsense existed.

Raul turned up at that moment. He had a grin on his face as he said to Tomás, 'I see you had a good time, old fella.'

Tomás slapped him on the back, almost knocking Raul off his feet. 'The best,' he said. His eyes widened as he looked beyond Raul and Maggie. 'And what have we here?'

Maggie looked back over her shoulder. Eva and Fabio stood hand-in-hand at the bottom of the stairs. The proprietor looked astonished. 'Where the devil did they come from?'

Maggie made a snap decision. Without replying to the man she gave Eva a gentle push. 'Quickly, Eva, get in.'

The little girl reacted instantly. Pulling her brother after her, she clambered into the back of Tomás' lorry.

Tomás rolled from side to side, barely keeping his footing. 'Hey, what's this?' he demanded.

'We're ready to leave, Tomás,' smiled Maggie. 'Don't you remember, you promised to take these two with us.'

'Did I?'

Raul's grin broadened. 'How do you do it?' he mouthed at her.

For an instant, Maggie had a moment of trepidation as Tomás seemed to sober up. Then he shouted, 'Why not? The more the merrier. Come on, *nena*, get your things together and we'll get going.'

Maggie flew upstairs to collect her belongings, shoving them into the hold-all, and quickly checking the room to make sure she hadn't forgotten anything. The proprietor stood at the foot of the stairs, barring her way, but she had the money ready for him. Shoving it into his hand, she just had time, to give Raul a wave before climbing into the cabin of the lorry beside Tomás.

'God help you!' laughed Raul as Tomás put the vehicle into gear and started to drive off. He called out something else, but the engine was too noisy for her to catch his farewell words.

It was a terrible journey. Despite Tomás' intention of driving all night, this didn't happen. After a few kilometres, he braked abruptly and said, 'I'm going to take a nap. Wake me in a couple of hours.'

Maggie also decided to take a rest. She climbed into the back of the lorry with the children and the three of them curled up together. Eva and Fabio slept but although Maggie closed her eyes, she couldn't stop worrying about the rest of the journey. From experience, she knew that once sober, Tomás' attitude towards the children could change. What if he refused to continue? What if he insisted on taking them back to Tres Lomas? Also, it had now hit her that Rosario might not be pleased to see them. On the other hand, it would be good for Donato to have other children around him. At last she dozed off, waking up with a jolt when the vehicle started moving. She crawled to the dividing curtain and pulled it aside.

175

'Do you want to come in the front?' asked Tomás. 'Or are you going to stay back there with your two urchins?'

'I'd better stay here for a while,' she said. But it wasn't long before the jolting of the vehicle persuaded her to join Tomás in the front. Fortunately, the children slept on, unfazed by the bumpy ride.

They pulled into Madrid in the morning. By then, travel sickness had rid Maggie of her misgivings. All she wanted was to get out of the vehicle. The children woke up and Eva started crying.

'What's the matter?' Maggie asked her.

'Fabio's been sick.'

So the bumpy ride had upset the children as well.

'You'll have to clean it up,' snapped Tomás.

Tomás drove the lorry to the back of the apartment block, braked sharply and jumped out. Pulling aside the tarpaulin, he uttered an expletive and held his nose. 'That kid's in a mess,' he said.

Maggie joined him. She helped the children out of the lorry, realising at once that Fabio was, indeed, in a mess. But he looked so distraught that, without thinking, she picked him up and carried him at arms-length into the house. Eva followed, dragging the hold-all behind her. Rosario heard them and raced to the top of the stairs.

'Maggie, at last!' She stopped in her tracks when she saw the child in Maggie's arms. 'Who…who's that?'

Eva appeared next to Maggie and Rosario gasped a second time.

'I'll explain,' said Maggie. 'Once I've got these two upstairs, and cleaned up,' she added.

'Of course.'

Rosario went back into the apartment, holding the door open for them. Maggie lowered the little boy onto the sofa. He smelled awful, his face was white and he looked even more frightened than before. Eva dropped the hold-all and went over to him.

176

'It's all right, Fabio,' she whispered, keeping her distance from his soiled clothing. 'These people are our friends.'

Rosario still looked astounded. Maggie didn't explain, but asked, 'Where's Donato?'

'In the bedroom taking his mid-morning nap.'

Maggie ran in there, stopping beside his cot to experience a rush of love as she looked down at the sleeping baby. Rosario joined her.

'He's grown.'

'In three days?'

'I can see a difference in him. Has he been good, Rosario?'

Rosario smiled. 'No trouble at all.'

'Has anything happened since I've been away?'

'Nothing, but Maggie, who are these children?'

Maggie took her hands. 'Please don't be angry with me. I couldn't leave them. They're orphans.'

'You've taken charge of them?'

'Temporarily.' She felt it best not to enlighten Rosario just yet as to the true circumstances.

At that moment Eva appeared in the doorway. 'Fabio's been sick again,' she said.

'I'm coming.'

'I'll get a bowl and some water,' said Rosario. 'But I don't know what we are going to do about clothes. Has he brought any spares with him?'

Maggie shook her head. 'They've only got what they're standing up in, I'm afraid.'

'Oh well,' said Rosario pragmatically. 'We'll think of something.'

Once again it was Tomás who came to the rescue. After Maggie had cleaned out his truck, his attitude softened, and on seeing the plight of the children, he hurried off to

177

one of his black market sources, returning soon afterwards with a few clothes.

Eva was quite excited at having a different dress to wear. Her little brother stood passively by while she took off his soiled clothes and put the new ones on. Maggie felt distressed by his lack of emotion. She kept wondering what was going on in his head. Was he re-living the moment of their mother's death? Was he able to remember anything at all?

Rosario prepared a simple meal for them all, after which they put the children to bed with Maggie and Rosario doubling up in Rosario's single bed in Donato's room.

'I'm sorry, Rosario,' whispered Maggie as she switched off the bedside lamp. 'I shouldn't burden you like this.'

'You had no choice,' replied Rosario. 'My only worry is how we are going to afford the extra food. They look as if they need feeding up, poor little mites.'

'We'll manage,' said Maggie. 'I'll do extra teaching and I'll look for some translation work. I'm sure I shall be able to find some.'

'You haven't mentioned Robert,' said Rosario. 'Did you find him?'

'No,' whispered Maggie. 'But Raul said…'

'Raul?'

'I met him at the hospital in Tres Lomas.'

With that, she yawned and turned on her side, falling asleep immediately and leaving Rosario still wondering what had happened during the trip.

The next day Maggie woke up to find Rosario giving the children breakfast. Sleepily she shuffled round the table to sit down between the two children. To her surprise, she saw that Fabio was busy with a pencil and paper, drawing a picture. Her heart missed a beat when she saw that it featured guns and bodies lying on the ground. But what

178

surprised her most of all, was the skill of the little boy's sketching. She was about to make a comment when Eva said, 'I had a lovely dream last night. I dreamt me and Fabio were in a garden with a prince and…'

Maggie listened to the little girl's version of a story she had told them back in the hotel two days earlier. *Gracias Abuelo,* she murmured to her defunct grandfather.

Through her musings, she heard Eva say, 'I knew you wouldn't turn us away.'

Maggie raised her eyebrows. 'Did you? How was that?'

'You see, I knew you were kind, like that man Jacinta found on the hillside.'

'What man? Was he a soldier?'

Eva wrinkled her nose. 'He wasn't one of the nasty ones. He was wounded and Asunción made him better.' She stared directly at Maggie. 'He looked just like you.'

'What?' Maggie twisted around to face Eva, causing her to edge away, muttering, 'I…I'm sorry.' Fabio on the other side of his sister, clung to her arm in alarm.

Rosario, who had come into the room carrying Donato, frowned at Maggie. 'What's the matter? You're frightening the children.'

Maggie clapped a hand to her mouth and tried to rectify the situation. 'It's…it's just something Eva said,' she stuttered.

Eva burst into tears. 'I didn't mean…'

Maggie put her arm around the little girl. 'It's all right, you haven't done anything wrong. I was just surprised about the man you said looked like me.'

At these words, it was Rosario's turn to look surprised. 'Robert?'

'I don't know,' said Maggie. 'Eva, do you know the man's name?'

'I can't remember.'

'Try to remember.'

'It was a long time ago.'

'How long?' she demanded.

'I don't know. It was just after the nasty soldiers left. Everything was so awful.'

Rosario stepped in. 'Maggie, I think you should leave it for now. Can't you see you're upsetting Eva.'

Maggie got up and paced up and down. 'I'm sorry,' she said. 'It's just that...to think I was in the village where Robert had been.'

'You don't know for sure. It seems like a rather strange coincidence,' said Rosario, trying to be practical.

'Coincidences happen and the village is in the right area. Raul says Robert's squad is somewhere around there.'

'Here, take Donato,' said Rosario. 'He's been pining for you. You can give him his feed.'

This dispelled the tension and soon Eva and Fabio were playing together in the corner of the room. Maggie experienced a surge of anguish as she watched them, ashamed of her outburst. However, she felt convinced that the injured man was her brother and she intended to question Eva further.

She felt troubled. Out of the blue her hopes had been raised only to be dashed by the unreliable memory of a nine-year-old. Eva had said the soldier was not one of the nasty men; that must mean he was a member of one of the International Brigades because the villagers were certainly republicans. But she had learnt that Robert had joined up with POUM and she wasn't sure how the villagers viewed this renegade group. However, there really wasn't time to worry about her brother's whereabouts. Her most pressing concern was finding more work. Rosario got in touch with her friends to let them know she was back and that English lessons could resume, but Maggie knew this would not bring in enough money. She needed to find a more reliable source of income. She decided to contact the British Library. Much to her surprise, the receptionist was only too pleased to hear from her.

'We're looking for an English translator,' she said. 'Our regular person has gone back home. The work is a bit erratic but the pay's not bad.'

'Is it technical?' asked Maggie.

'Only occasionally, most of the work is fairly straightforward.'

'In that case, I'll be happy to do it.'

'Have you got a typewriter?'

Maggie gulped back her dismay. This was the first hurdle. Should she tell the truth and risk losing the job or should be lie and somehow hope that Tomás would come up trumps again? She decided on the second option.

'Yes, of course. When can I start?'

'Come back this afternoon for a translation test and we can go from there.'

The trial proved simple enough and much to her relief Maggie found herself with a free-lance job which looked to be ongoing. She arrived home with an armful of folders.

'But you haven't got a typewriter,' Rosario reminded her.

'I know, but Tomás has promised to look out for one for me. In the meantime, I can start by writing the work out by hand.'

'I don't know how you're going to manage.' Rosario bit her lip. 'You haven't got a very extensive dictionary or any other reference books.'

'There's always the library,' laughed Maggie. 'They can hardly refuse me their facilities. I expect they'll let me borrow the books I need.'

'I hope so.'

Eventually, Tomás managed to secure an old Remington typewriter. It had been dumped on a heap of rubbish and was in need of repair. Maggie cleaned it up but couldn't do much about the lower case 'e' which frequently stuck. She hoped her employers wouldn't be too fussy about presentation as long as she got the translation accurate.

Despite the overcrowding, the occupants of the tiny apartment settled down well. At first, Eva and Fabio were at first as good as gold, but gradually the little girl became restless. Fabio wasn't great company. Most of the time, he would sit in the corner staring into space, which worried Maggie. Would he never come out of his shell? She wondered whether she should take him to see a doctor, but this would cost money and involve a lot of questions, which she wouldn't know how to answer.

She knew that Rosario was finding it difficult to keep the children entertained now that Donato was also sitting up and demanding attention. She felt guilty for not being able to help but money needed to be earned and she had no choice other than to spend time upstairs in the schoolroom, teaching or working on her translations. Tempers were beginning to fray and Maggie knew that they would have to find more spacious accommodation before too long. Then they had a visitor.

CHAPTER THIRTEEN

Palmiro's heart thumped against his ribcage as he hurried along the street. He knew there had been air raids during his absence and he prayed that Rosario and her companions were safe. He was in need of some respite. The Brunete campaign had been tough with a discouraging defeat by the Nationalists. The casualties had been shocking and he himself had narrowly escaped injury when he had pulled a wounded companion out of the line of fire. The poor sod had died anyway. Although it was months since the Guadarrama battle and he had spent the rest of the time dealing with minor skirmishes, Palmiro still had nightmares about those dreadful July days.

It was a pleasant October afternoon. The heat of summer had gone, replaced by a gentle warmth and the special luminosity of autumn. I hope they're in, he thought as he turned the corner and saw, with relief, the battle-scarred building. Seeing it with fresh eyes, he realised just how run-down it was. He pushed open the outer door and went inside, stopping for several minutes to brush down his uniform and polish first one boot and then the other against the back of his trousers. He wanted to surprise Rosario, but above all, he wanted to present himself looking smart.

He could hear a young child's voice as he reached the top of the stairs, and for one ridiculous moment, imagined it was Donato. As he went to knock on the apartment door, he came face to face with a little girl. On seeing him, she shrank back before turning on her heel and running to Rosario for protection.

'Palmiro!' Rosario's face lit up. 'How wonderful!'

Easing the scared child away from her, she ran over to Palmiro, stopping abruptly in front of him, not knowing what to do. He stared back at her, feeling awkward. But the pleasure of seeing her and the joy in her eyes soon dispelled his embarrassment and, dropping his kitbag, he took her in his arms. Over Rosario's head, he saw the little girl run to the corner where a small boy was squatting on the floor. She sank down next to him.

'Who are they?' he whispered.

Rosario gave a giggle and whispered back, 'Our family's grown since you went away. These two have had a bad experience and they're frightened of anyone in uniform.' Taking his hand, she led him over to the children. 'This is Eva and her little brother, Fabio.'

Palmiro grinned. Eva momentarily shrank back but, when she saw Rosario's encouraging smile, she tentatively took his outstretched hand and did a little curtsey.

'She's sweet,' he said. 'Where did you find them?'

'They're Maggie's waifs. She brought them back from Tres Lomas.'

'Has she found her brother?'

Rosario shook her head. 'Not yet. Have *you* heard anything?'

'No. The recruits are mainly English but no one has heard of Robert Morán.'

At that moment, Maggie came down from the top floor. 'Hello Palmiro,' she cried. 'You've been granted leave!'

'Only a couple of days,' he said. 'But I may be billeted in Madrid soon.'

'That would be good,' said Rosario. 'You could stay with us.'

184

She realised immediately how impossible that would be and giggled with embarrassment.

'Maybe we can find somewhere bigger,' said Maggie. 'I'll get on to Tomás again. He promised to look around for us. Palmiro's arrival might spur him on.'

'But what about tonight?' said Rosario.

'Don't worry,' replied Palmiro. 'I dare say I could kip down with one of my mates.'

'We won't hear of it,' said Maggie. 'We'll borrow some bedding and you can sleep upstairs in the schoolroom.'

'How is everything, the lessons I mean?'

'Good, I've got some translation work too.'

'How long have Eva and Fabio been here?'

'Not long, I found them…' She laughed. 'Actually they found me when I went out in the ambulance with Raul.'

'Raul?'

'It's a long story. I'll tell you all about it over supper.'

Tomás joined them for the meal, bringing with him several bottles of rough red wine, which he consumed lustily. After the children had gone to bed, the four gathered together by the open window to enjoy the balmy evening. They exchanged anecdotes and discussed the latest news, with Tomás doing most of the talking. He only kept quiet when Palmiro described the Brunete battle.

'The losses were terrible,' said the young man. 'The heat was unbearable, even I found it heavy-going and I'm used to soaring temperatures. I can't imagine how your fellow-countrymen coped, Maggie. Some of them were from Scotland.'

Maggie gave an involuntary shudder. 'It can be very chilly up there.'

'They should never have gone in,' said Tomás. 'They were ill-prepared.'

185

'We didn't know the Nationalist contingent was so big,' said Palmiro. He gave a shake of his head. 'I've never seen anything like it.'

Rosario moved them on to Maggie's story, which the English girl told, making light of her part in driving the ambulance and saving Raul from losing too much blood.

'Raul?' said Palmiro. 'His name keeps cropping up. Who is he?'

'Well, he's a half-trained doctor working at the hospital in Tres Lomas. He's very brave, goes out on dangerous missions.'

Tomás roared with laughter. 'She's sweet on him,' he chuckled.

'No I'm not!' protested Maggie, her cheeks beginning to redden, but it was no good, the others had decided she had fallen in love and no amount of denial would rid them of their belief.

'Have you any idea where Robert is?' asked Palmiro.

'Raul…' Again Maggie blushed. '…he thinks Robert's in that area, and after what Eva told me…'

Tomás looked up sharply. 'What did she tell you?'

'She said a wounded freedom fighter was nursed back to health in their village just after the Nationalists had left. She can't remember his name but I think it might have been my brother.'

Tomás gave a snort of disbelief. 'Out of all the freedom fighters roaming the countryside, do you really think this one could be your brother?'

'It's possible. I'm hoping she'll remember his name.'

'Vain hope, *mujer*.'

Palmiro smiled fondly as Rosario jumped to Maggie's defence. 'It's more than likely because Eva said he looked like Maggie.'

'Hmm.' Tomás clearly didn't think much of the nine-year-old's story. 'She was probably imagining it.'

186

Tomás' sneer brought the evening to an end. When he got up to leave, the others decided it was time for bed. Maggie discreetly went to the bathroom to give Palmiro and Rosario a few moments to themselves.

The next couple of days passed swiftly. Palmiro was grateful when Maggie took charge of the children, leaving him time to be with Rosario. They went for walks, strolling hand-in-hand in Parque de Ritiro. They sat down opposite the statue of Alfonso XII to soak up the autumn sun, quietly watching passers-by: women pushing prams, old men shuffling along chatting to one another. But they knew that this peaceful scene masked hidden tension, especially when from time to time, someone would cock an ear skywards as if listening for the sound of enemy aircraft.

By mutual consent, they tried to avoid streets where buildings had been badly damaged or where there were barricades, persuading themselves that life was normal. But Palmiro knew that life was far from normal. Not only was he in the middle of a civil war in a foreign country but he was falling in love with a girl, who in ordinary circumstances would be far removed from his world. The more Rosario talked about her life before the war, the more he understood the differences between them.

Sighing wistfully, she said, 'I didn't realise how lucky I was, my parents were well off. We lacked for nothing. My brother was doing well at the university and I was happy at school. We played tennis, went swimming, danced…oh, how we danced.'

'Ballroom dancing?' asked Palmiro. He had never tried it but he knew that in Milan there were a lot of dance halls. Some of his fellow soldiers had gone dancing while they were billeted up there. Although they invited him, he hadn't joined them. In his eyes, ballroom

187

dancing was the province of the wealthy, such as Rosario's family.

'Yes, and Flamenco as well. I took lessons. I'll teach you one day.'

He laughed. 'I've got two left feet.'

'I had singing lessons too, and I played the piano.'

Palmiro gave a swallow. What chance did he stand with a girl like Rosario? How would she fit in if he took her to meet his family? Even during these difficult times, she still managed to dress smartly. His sisters had never been able to afford clothes like Rosario's. He heaved an inward sigh. She was too good for the likes of him. Yet as he looked at her, he couldn't imagine life without her. In the trenches, it was Rosario's image that kept him going. Even in his darkest hour when he had seriously considered going AWOL yet again, her smiling face, her lilting voice had somehow persuaded him to do the right thing and stay put.

Her voice penetrated his musing. 'Once things get back to normal…'

'Things will never get back to normal,' he grunted.

She eyed him sharply, her optimism contrasting with his gloom. 'Yes they will.'

He changed the subject. 'Have you heard from your brother?'

'He sends me money but he doesn't write much. I've no idea what he's doing. He's supposed to send for me…' She stole a glance at Palmiro. '…but I'm not sure I want to leave Madrid.'

Palmiro experienced a warm glow. She really liked him, but when she asked him to tell her about his home and family, the warm glow changed to panic.

'There's nothing to tell.'

'It must be fun being part of a big family.'

He tried to put her off. 'Big families aren't that wonderful; you never get any time to yourself, you have to share everything.'

'I wouldn't mind that.'

'I bet you would,' he said, recalling the day his cousin borrowed his favourite Roberto Murolo record, then accidentally sat on it. He'd promised to replace it but that had never happened.

'How many sisters have you got?'

'Four. The youngest one got married earlier this year. I couldn't go to the wedding because I was already in Spain.'

'That's a shame.'

'Santina was very upset.'

'What about the others?'

'Two are widows.'

'Oh dear,' gasped Rosario.

'They lost their husbands in North Africa.'

'That's terrible.'

He shrugged, recalling the number of young black-clad mothers in his village. 'These things happen,' he said.

'Tell me about the place you live in.'

'There were always festivals in the village. You know what we Italians are like.'

'Yes,' she sighed. 'The Spanish and the Italians are very much alike.' She looked at her watch. 'We'd better get back. Maggie will be run off her feet with those children.'

Palmiro was relieved to get off the subject of his village. 'Do you think Fabio will ever speak again?' he asked as they headed for the park gate.

'I don't know.' replied Rosario, shaking her head sadly. 'According to his sister he hasn't uttered a word since their mother was killed.' She reached for Palmiro's hand. 'Come on, we'd better hurry.'

189

Palmiro followed her along the road, away from the untouched area to where bombed buildings and piles of rubble reminded him that they were in a city torn apart by war. Yes, he thought, in a few hours time his leave would come to an end and the reality of the battlefield would obliterate everything else. He frowned, not quite everything: he would still have the memory of a wonderful hour in the park with Rosario.

CHAPTER FOURTEEN

In the end it was Raul who solved the problem of accommodation. He arrived out of the blue in early November. Maggie had given up hope of hearing from him again. Due to her ever pressing concerns about their daily existence, she had even given up badgering Tomás about continuing the search for Robert. Tomás had been right, of course, how could she possibly leave Rosario to look after three young children while she went off on a wild goose chase? And now, with the passing of time, she had to admit to herself that it was extremely unlikely that the freedom fighter Eva had told her about was her brother.

Palmiro had been gone for nearly a month, although he kept in touch with Rosario through the military postal service. This had made Raul's lack of contact seem even worse. She thought about him a lot. Their parting had been cut short. They hadn't even said 'goodbye' properly. She could hardly believe their night together had really happened. Had he actually made love to her? The following day he had seemed like a stranger.

His surprise arrival threw her emotions into turmoil. She was in the apartment alone when he knocked at the door. Thinking it was probably Tomás, she didn't look up from her typewriter but called out, 'Come in, the door's open.'

'Well, aren't you going to say 'hello' to me?' said a voice from the doorway.

191

'Raul!' A blush crept over her face when she saw him. She could hardly bring herself to speak. If only he had given her some warning! She quickly regained her composure, and getting up from her desk, hurried over to greet him. 'What a lovely surprise!'

'They sent me off on a break; said I'd been putting in too many hours, that I needed some rest.'

'And you decided to come to Madrid.' Secretly she hoped it was her presence that had drawn him there.

He laughed. 'I've found myself a bolt-hole.'

'A bolt-hole? Here in Madrid?'

'A friend has lent me an apartment to use whenever I want to.'

'You'll share with him.'

'With *her*,' he corrected. Maggie's spirits sank. This wasn't what she wanted to hear. Then Raul went on, 'Rochelle's the daughter of a family friend and she's left for an indefinite stay in France. I've got the run of the place.'

'That's great,' said Maggie, hoping her relief wasn't making her too enthusiastic.

Raul looked around. 'So this is where you live. You seem a bit over-crowded.'

'We are now, with Eva and Fabio.'

'So they're still with you,' he chuckled.

'Of course.'

'How do you manage?'

It was Maggie's turn to laugh. 'With difficulty,' she admitted.

'Where is everybody?'

'Rosario's taken the children to the park for the afternoon, and as for Tomás, we don't know where he is. It's anybody's guess. No doubt he'll turn up soon.' Privately, she was convinced he had gone on one of his benders.

192

All at once, Raul's mood changed. 'Why are we talking like passing acquaintances?'

Before she had time to resist, he pulled her into his arms and kissed her. As usual, his touch was enough to melt her reservations and, for a few moments, she allowed herself to be lulled into acquiescence. But as they drew apart, she couldn't stop herself from wondering whether he *really* cared for her. If he did, why hadn't he written or phoned up over the past few months? As if reading her mind, he supplied the answer to her unspoken question.

'We've been run off our feet at the hospital. You've no idea how bad it's been. I've been thinking about you a lot; I wanted to write but there wasn't time. And then the telephone service broke down.' He paused to draw breath. 'Did you write to me?'

Maggie started guiltily. 'Only once but when I didn't…'

At that moment, Rosario arrived back with the children. On seeing Raul she hesitated in the doorway. Maggie rushed over and drew her in.

'Rosario, this is Raul,' she said, feeling herself blush as she said his name.

'I've heard a lot about you, Raul,' said Rosario, kissing him on both cheeks in the customary manner.

'Favourable or unfavourable?' he joked.

'Favourable of course.'

Raul turned his attention to the children. 'Eva and Fabio look well. Has the boy spoken yet?'

Maggie shook her head. 'They're fine but they get bored. It's all right when the weather's good and they can go out, but on rainy days it's so cramped in here.'

He gestured to the typewriter. 'I see you're working.'

'Yes, I give English lessons and I'm doing some translation work.'

Raul threw out an arm. 'How can you work in here, with all this going on?'

'Normally I don't. I work upstairs in the schoolroom, but it's unheated and with winter coming I don't know how long my students will be prepared to put up with the cold. I've asked Tomás to find somewhere else for us but I think he's fed up with me. After all, I've been a burden to him ever since I arrived in Spain.'

'Maybe I can help.'

Maggie didn't have a chance to follow this up because she could see that Rosario needed her assistance with preparing Donato's bottle and seeing to the children's meal. She left Raul with Eva and Fabio and, from the kitchen, she could hear him trying to entertain them.

When she went back into the room, he was squatting on the floor with them, throwing dice. He looked up and studied Donato who was pointing at him from Maggie's arms. 'He's a fine little lad,' said Raul. 'He seems to like you. Maybe you have a way with babies.'

Maggie laughed. 'I don't think so,' she said. 'It's just that I've been thrown into it.'

'Where did you find him?'

Maggie proceeded to describe the eventful life Donato had had so far, making light of her part in his rescue.

Raul stared fixedly at her. 'He looks well on it but, Maggie, where do you go from here?'

'I don't know. I live from day to day. It's the only way.'

'What about finding your brother?'

'I haven't given up on him,' Maggie replied curtly. 'I'll start looking for him again soon.'

She wanted him to stop questioning her but he persisted. 'What's going to happen to these children when things get too difficult and you decide to go home?'

'I'd never abandon them,' she protested angrily. 'They're like my own.'

'Will you settle here in Spain?'

'If necessary.' She didn't want to think about the future and she hated Raul for bringing up these problems. Realising she had spoken rather brusquely, she softened her tone. 'We'll be all right once we find better accommodation. Something will turn up.'

'Well,' said Raul. 'I might be able to help.'

Maggie's eyes widened. 'How?'

They were interrupted by Donato giving a huge burp, which made Eva giggle and even brought the hint of a smile to Fabio's face. 'I'll tell you later,' said Raul.

Rosario, discreet as ever, took charge of the children after the meal. She usually read them a bed-time story, in the hope that this would bring Fabio out of his shell.

Left alone, Raul said, 'Come back with me tonight, Maggie, I'd like to show you the apartment I'm staying in.'

Maggie wasn't sure it a good idea. She was still uncertain about his feelings for her. He seemed to swing hot and cold. Then he smiled his disarming smile and she found herself agreeing.

When Rosario came back into the room, she said hesitantly, 'Do you mind if I go out with Raul tonight?' Rushing on with, 'Of course, if you don't want me to, I won't go.'

If Rosario suffered any disquiet, she kept it to herself. 'Go ahead,' she said.

'I won't be late back.'

'Take all the time you need. I shall go to bed early so I'll see you in the morning.' She pressed a light kiss on Maggie's cheek and waved her away. 'Off you go.'

It was a chilly evening, with a fine mist obscuring the streets. 'Is it far from here?' asked Maggie.

'About twenty minutes.'

'How did you get to Madrid?'

'A friend dropped me off on his way to Toledo.'

They rounded a corner and Raul stopped. 'This is the building. What do you think?'

'It looks very grand.'

'Rochelle's grandfather left it to her but she prefers living in France, especially these days.'

'Why doesn't she sell it?'

Raul gave a chuckle. 'Who's interested in buying property in Madrid under the present circumstances.'

'I didn't think of that.'

He took her hand. 'Come on.'

The apartment was on the second floor. The sturdy oak door with it's ornate panelling was a far cry from the utilitarian entrance to the apartment she shared with Rosario and the children. Raul unlocked it and ushered her inside.

Maggie was impressed. Since her arrival in Spain she had only visited unpretentious households: the Fajardo's and the Gonzales had been families of modest means. She wondered about Raul's own family. Were they well off or were they working class people? He led her through to a comfortable lounge, and before switching on the light, went across to close the shutters against the night.

'This is a splendid room,' he said. 'It gets the sun all day long.'

He showed her the rest of the apartment with its well equipped kitchen, two bathrooms and two bedrooms, plus a small box room and a study.

'If only we had somewhere like this!' cried Maggie.

Raul grinned. 'You can move in here if you like.'

'Move in here?'

'Why not? I shall only need it once in a while. Rochelle's asked me to keep an eye on the place. She said I can do what I like with it.'

'But won't she want to come back one day?'

Raul shook his head. 'She prefers living in France with her French relatives. There's nothing to keep her in Madrid. No doubt she'll put it on the market if it's still standing once things get back to normal.'

'What about the rent? An apartment like this must cost the earth.'

'Rochelle left it up to me and I won't charge you. As far as she's concerned the place will remain empty except when I use it. What d'you say?'

'I'll have to ask Rosario but I'm sure she'll agree.' She twirled around still unable to believe her luck. 'The children will be so happy here. They'll have a bedroom to themselves, Rosario and I can share…' She turned to face him. '…of course when you come back, you will take over the main bedroom. It's your right.'

Raul burst out laughing. 'The box room will be fine for me.' Taking her by the hand, he led her to the kitchen where he pulled the cork on a bottle of Rioja, pouring two generous glasses.

Maggie took the drink from him and, as usual, took too large a gulp. Feeling slightly giddy, she remembered that she hadn't had much to eat all day. When he led her back to the living room she was glad of his support. He nudged her down into the sofa, brushing his lips against her hairline and whispering endearments.

Dusk was falling, and the room was filled with shadows. Only the glow from the early appearance of the waxing moon gave light. From an adjacent apartment the sound of a strumming guitar caressed the air. Raul took the wine glass from her hand and placed it on the coffee table, urging her back against the cushions and kissing her fiercely, bruising her mouth. His hands began to explore her body until she felt she must yield to the sensations he aroused in her. He had made love to her before and it had been wonderful, but this time it was different: special.

197

'Stay the night, *mi tesoro*,' he whispered.

She tried unsuccessfully to push him away. 'What about Rosario?'

'You heard what she said, *I'll see you in the morning* And remember, we've only got a couple of days. I have to leave the day after tomorrow.'

Maggie's heart raced. Spend a night in a luxury apartment with an attractive Spaniard. How could she refuse?

Christmas came, followed by the New Year celebrations. But with uncertainty hanging over the city, 1938 didn't augur well. Maggie and Rosario tried to make the festival of the Three Kings on sixth January as festive as possible. Rosario even managed to find some bonbons, and some balloons for the children to play with.

They were much more comfortable in the new apartment and, on the whole, life was easier. But despite this, a cloud hung over them for, although Rosario tried to hide her concern, Maggie knew how worried she was since Palmiro's letters had become less frequent. She tried to cheer her up but the rumours filtering through were not encouraging. To make matters worse, Rosario's brother, Luis, had not been in contact for weeks.

When Raul managed visits during January and February, Maggie's happiness knew no bounds, but guilt plagued her. Was it fair to be so happy when Rosario was so depressed?

During these visits, Rosario behaved with her customary discretion, keeping the children amused and sending them to bed early in order to leave the amorous pair time to themselves. This added to Maggie's guilt. Maggie told herself that their affair was nobody's business but hers and Raul's, but she hated flying in the face of Rosario's beliefs. The girl had been brought up in a strict

Catholic family and Maggie knew it could not be easy for her to turn a blind eye to the situation.

She also fretted about getting pregnant and although Raul took precautions, she knew these were not full-proof. She suffered pangs of conscience, knowing that her grandparents would have been horrified at what she was doing, and she determinedly pushed aside the stories of hell and damnation which had been drummed into her schoolgirl brain at the convent she had attended. Chastity made no sense in this mad world in which she found herself.

The children had settled down well, obediently keeping quiet when students came. Maggie's translating work continued and, for a while, life was tranquil.

Donato was now about a year old, and as they had no idea of his date of birth, they agreed to celebrate his birthday on seventeenth of February. Maggie baked a cake and Rosario managed to buy a couple of new toys in the market. Even though Eva and Fabio were excited, the little boy still refused to speak.

It was while they were celebrating that Eva said, 'I've remembered the name of that soldier.'

A hush fell over the gathering.

'What soldier?' asked Maggie.

'The one Jacinta found.'

'What was it?' Maggie held her breath, not daring to hope.

'Esteban.'

'Are you sure?'

Remembering she still had a snapshot of Robert in her purse, Maggie rushed from the room to fetch it. 'Is this the man?' she said, showing it to Eva.

By now, the little girl was more interested in the promised birthday cake than in looking at a crumpled photograph of a stranger. She wrinkled her nose and muttered, 'I'm not sure, but I think so.'

199

Maggie's heart gave a somersault. If she could persuade Raul to take her back to the village someone might remember her brother and know where he had moved on to. She bit back the urge to question the little girl, saying, 'Thank you Eva, now, let's cut the birthday cake.'

Rosario brought up the subject after the children had gone to bed. 'You *must* follow it up, Maggie. Who knows, it could be your brother. You must go back with Raul next time he comes here.' She giggled and gave Maggie a sly glance. 'I'm sure he'll be only too happy to do you a favour.'

'What do you mean?' Maggie burst out, the colour rising to her cheeks.

'Well,' said Rosario. 'It's obvious you two like one another a lot.'

Maggie's blush deepened. 'I don't know about that, but I do know that I can't leave you with three children to look after.'

'I can manage.'

Maggie continued her protestation, realising that she was on safer ground now. 'I don't think so. It would be different if Tomás was around. I wish he'd come back.'

Maggie was restless over the next couple of weeks. Communication was unreliable and no one knew for sure what was happening but Eva's announcement had given her renewed hope of finding Robert. She questioned the little girl again until Rosario intervened. 'Don't badger her, Maggie, clearly, she can't tell you anything more.'

'I suppose not.'

'You must do what I suggested and go back to Tres Lomas with Raul.'

Maggie smiled fondly at Rosario. The girl was only seventeen yet she was mature beyond her years. She hoped that things would eventually work out for her and Palmiro. They deserved some happiness.

Raul didn't return until the middle of March. Once the greetings were over, she lost no time in telling him about Eva's pronouncement.

He swiftly dampened her spirits. 'If he was once there - and it's a big *if* - it's unlikely he's still there. Besides, the child could be talking about anybody.'

'But she says his name was Esteban.'

'It's not an uncommon name. I wouldn't put too much importance on the ramblings of a little girl.'

'But it's Robert's second name,' insisted Maggie. 'Why, you knew him by that name. He always wanted to be called Esteban. It's what our grandfather was called.'

'Don't get carried away, Maggie.'

'I'm not. I really think it was Robert. After all Eva said he looked like me. Everyone says we're very much alike. Please take me to Tres Lomas with you so that I can check it out. It will only be for a few days.'

Raul looked startled. 'How will you get back to Madrid? Tomás has disappeared and I can't guarantee finding time to drive you.'

'Something will turn up. It always does. Rosario says she will take charge of the children.' Maggie could hardly believe her own words. What was she thinking? She could easily find herself left high and dry in Tres Lomas.

Raul shook his head. 'It's a silly idea, Maggie. It will only turn out to be another wild goose chase. Don't think I've forgotten about your brother. I've been keeping a look out, asking questions but, so far, there's no sign of him.'

Maggie felt for his hand. 'Please Raul.'

Raul remained silent for a moment. 'All right, but don't blame me if you find yourself stranded there. Things are more dangerous now. There have been skirmishes on the outskirts of town. My friend's coming back from Toledo to collect me tomorrow so you'd better get your things together.' He furrowed his brow. 'You'd better bring your British passport. '

Maggie lost no time in collecting together a few spare clothes. Just before leaving, she opened a drawer in the dressing table to take out her passport, and as she went to close it, she saw the gun half hidden under a pile of handkerchiefs. She had completely forgotten about it and chided herself for not having found a safer hiding place for it. Hastily, she shoved it back where it had been.

The proprietor of the hotel greeted Maggie as if she were a long-lost friend. '*Hola Senorita, como está*. It's good to see you.'

She realised this was because of the over generous tip she had given him on her hasty retreat from Tres Lomas previously. On this occasion, he offered her a better room, one which overlooked a small courtyard encircled by trees at the rear of the premises. Spring was fast approaching and she was pleased to have a glimpse of greenery, something she missed in the built-up area of Madrid where she was now living. It struck her that the shrubbery surrounding the house on the common back home in England would be coming to life. Despite its overgrown condition, in the spring, the large garden always surprised her. Trees and bushes burst forth with buds almost overnight, filling her with hope that life would improve. She sighed wistfully, recognising that this was the very first time since arriving in Spain she had given a thought to the house on the common. The sigh brought a shudder. Over the winter the empty house would have become even more cold and hostile. She didn't regret leaving.

This time she had brought a few extra clothes with her, just in case she had to spend a week or two in Tres Lomas. Raul went directly to the hospital to take up his duties, and as it was a pleasant afternoon, Maggie went for a walk along one of the three hills between which the small town was situated.

There was no one about, but as she reached the steeper slope towards the top of the hill, she thought she heard a footstep behind her. Turning around, she saw there was no one there. Again it came. This time she was certain. Swivelling around, she came face to face with a teenage boy. He frowned, furrowing dark brows above deep-set eyes. Without warning, he ran up, snatched her purse and started off down the hill. Maggie acted on instinctively.

'Come back, thief!' she shouted, giving chase.

The boy glanced back over his shoulder and gave an impudent laugh. But his impudence cost him his liberty as he caught his foot on an uneven paving slab and tripped. Before he had time to regain his feet Maggie launched herself at him.

'Got you!' she yelled, snatching back her purse and grasping him firmly by the arm.

The boy glared at her. 'What are you going to do now?' he grunted.

What indeed? thought Maggie. Should she march him to the Police Station or should she let him go? There was a third choice, which she decided was probably the best one.

'Where do you live?' she asked.

'It's none of your business.' He followed this with a string of obscenities, many of which were new to her.

'Come on,' she said. 'Show me.'

He stood up, apparently having decided to humour her. She was a little surprised at how tall he was, almost her height. Previously, he had been on the lower section of the slope and had not appeared quite so intimidating. Now she realised that if he wanted to, he could easily overpower her.

'Well,' she said. 'Lead the way. I don't think your mother will be pleased to learn you've been thieving.'

As she spoke it occurred to her that the boy could be a gypsy whose mother would encourage him to steal. He noticed her hesitation, and before she could stop him, shook off her hand and ran down the hill to disappear into an alleyway.

Maggie stared after him, knowing that it would be useless to follow. The incident had shaken her and she decided to return to the hotel. But there had been something about the boy that puzzled her. Despite his audacity, there was a hint of vulnerability about him.

The next day when she met up with Raul she had put the incident out of her mind. There was something more exciting to think about: Raul informed her he would take her to Eva's village so that she could question Asunción, the woman the little girl had told her about. He led her to a rusty Ford truck sporting a sign on it's side, which read, '*Arnaldo Mendes - Verduleria*'.

'Where did you manage to find this?' asked Maggie, laughing as she climbed into the passenger seat. Brushing aside some straw, she wrinkled her nose. 'It smells of rotting vegetables.'

Raul grinned. 'Arnaldo's a friend of mine. He's lent it to me before. I'm afraid he doesn't clean out his truck very often.'

The drive was not a comfortable one. The suspension was non-existent, the once dark green leather seats were split where the springs had pushed through and the mud-speckled windscreen looked as if it could shatter at any moment. But after a couple of hours they arrived at the outskirts of the village without incident. As they approached, Maggie saw several women working in the

204

fields. It was arduous work, more suited to men than women but she knew that the only males living there were young boys, some of whom were also helping.

Raul drew to a halt in the centre of the village and they climbed out. An elderly woman approached them. She was bent almost double and walked with the aid of a stick. '*Buenos días*,' she said.

'Good morning, *Senora*,' said Raul. 'How are things with you?'

The woman gave a toothless smile. 'We struggle on,' she said. 'Although I'm not much good these days with my arthritic legs. How can I help you?'

'We've come to see a woman called Asunción. Do you know her?'

'Know her? She's my daughter-in-law. She's working in the fields today.'

'Is your granddaughter around?' asked Maggie.

'Jacinta? She's in the schoolroom.'

So, thought Maggie, they do at least have a school here. 'Is there any chance we can speak to them?' she said.

'They'll be home at mid-day for something to eat. You can see them then. Can I offer you coffee?'

'That would be very nice,' smiled Maggie.

Raul and Maggie followed the old woman into one of the cottages lining the main street. Inside, despite the brightness of the spring morning, it was dark and damp. Maggie gave a little shudder as she glanced around the room. It was sparsely furnished and she realised that even their first home in Madrid with its draughty windows and peeling paintwork was more habitable than this.

The woman busied herself preparing coffee, apologising for the chipped cups in which she served it. 'The soldiers smashed everything in sight,' she explained. 'They left us with barely anything. We would all be dead if they hadn't been threatened by the arrival of the others.'

'The others?' echoed Maggie.

205

'Yes, the Republican Militia. They drove the Francoists out.'

Maggie felt moved to touch the woman's blue-veined hand. 'You must have suffered terribly,' she whispered.

At that moment, a young girl burst into the house. '*Abuela*,' she started to say, then stopped abruptly, drawing back into the doorway when she saw the visitors.

'Come in, my dear,' said her grandmother. 'These people have come to talk to you and your mother.'

'Who are they?' The girl looked nervous as she sat down on one of the wooden chairs and dumped her school books on the table.

The door opened again and a woman appeared. 'What have we here?' she gasped on seeing a room full of people.

'Come, come, Asunción,' said the old woman. 'These people would like to talk to you.'

'To me? Who are they?'

Raul got to his feet and gestured to Asunción to take a seat. He waited while her mother-in-law poured more coffee.

'You may recognise me, *señora*, I drive an ambulance. I came six months ago when the unfortunate woman died in childbirth.'

'Yes, I remember you, but who's she?' She pointed at Maggie.

Maggie waited while Raul introduced her. She sensed antagonism but hoped the woman would turn out to be helpful.

'The *señorita* would like to ask you about a freedom fighter from POUM who we believe you nursed back to health about a year ago.'

'Esteban Morán,' cried Asunción, her face lighting up. 'I remember him well. He was a charming young man.'

Maggie leant forward, her excitement spilling over. 'He's my brother,' she gasped.

206

The woman immediately turned her attention to Maggie. 'Why,' she said. 'I should have known. You look just like him.'

'So I'm told. We're twins,' she explained. 'Was my brother badly injured when Jacinta found him?'

'Nothing life-threatening but he had some nasty shrapnel wounds and was suffering from shock. The wounds took time to heal. What's happened to him? Is he all right?'

'We don't know. That's why we're here. We hoped you would have some idea of where he went when he left the village.'

'That was a year ago.'

'I know.'

'POUM has been disbanded since then. There are splinter groups but they're unofficial and they're being hounded by both the Nationalists and the Republicans.'

Maggie's heart sank. What had her brother got himself into? 'Did he say where he was going?'

'I think he was going to the Ebro area, but *Señorita,* that was months ago. He could be anywhere now.'

There seemed very little to add after that and Maggie couldn't wait to leave the cottage. But Raul had something else on his mind and she was angered when he said, 'Two children smuggled their way into our ambulance that day last September.'

'Eva and Fabio Pizarro? Are they safe? We were told they had been fostered out,' said Asunción.

Maggie cast a furious glance in Raul's direction as he went on, 'Have they a got any relatives here?'

'A great uncle. He was looking after them until they ran away.'

Maggie could barely breathe as she waited for Raul's reply.

'Why did they run away if their uncle was caring for them?'

'Hmm,' grunted Asunción. 'A lot of good he was, drunk half the time, asleep the rest of the time. He only escaped the Nationalists because he was snoozing somewhere up there in the hills. Missed it all, he did. He can hardly look after himself, let alone a pair of traumatized children. Running away was the best thing they could have done.'

'Is there no one else in the village who could take care of them?'

Asunción looked embarrassed. 'The truth is we are all so busy. The girl would probably be all right but the boy means trouble. He was always playing up. The uncle couldn't handle him.'

'He's perfectly good now,' cried Maggie, immediately wishing she had kept her mouth shut.

'Has he started to talk?'

'Not yet, he just sticks close to his sister, follows her around wherever she goes.'

'I understand they've gone to live in Madrid. Are you looking after them?'

Maggie was about to say 'yes' but Raul forestalled her. '*Señora,* do you think their uncle would have them back?'

The old woman gave a mirthless chortle. 'That old fart, why he was relieved to see the back of them. I don't fancy their chances if they come back here.'

Raul frowned. 'What do you mean? Surely he wouldn't maltreat them!'

'It depends what you call maltreat. He certainly wouldn't bother with them.'

Maggie listened with growing alarm until, all at once, her indignation bubbled over. 'Well,' she said. 'Eva and Fabio are perfectly happy now. They must stay where they are.' With that, she got to her feet and thanked the women for their help, obliging Raul to follow suit.

When they got outside, he turned on her. 'What were doing in there? I'd almost got the women to take them back.'

'Take them back, that's the last thing they wanted.'

'You saw how embarrassed Asunción was, she was on the point of giving in.'

'I doubt that. Besides, I never asked you to do that,' retorted Maggie, almost in tears. 'I've never once suggested that Rosario and I can't cope with those children. You had no right to interfere.'

Maggie remained silent on the journey back to Tres Lomas. Inside she was seething. She had persuaded Raul to take her to the village to seek news of her brother but it had never occurred to her that he would use the visit as an excuse to return Eva and Fabio to their previous life.

Raul took her silence for disappointment. 'I warned you,' he said. 'A year is a long time and, in any case, clearly Esteban didn't give them a definite destination. Probably he was thinking of their safety. It's better if the villagers are ignorant of what's going on.'

'Asunción said all his companions were killed. That must have been terrible for him.' An idea suddenly occurred to her but she didn't voice it. Could Robert have gone back to England? She discarded the idea at once. Of course, he wouldn't have left Spain.

'Where do you go from here?' asked Raul.

'I…I don't know.'

'You're still angry with me about the children, aren't you?'

'Can you blame me?'

'I was thinking of you. You're burdened with so much and yet you still want to look for Esteban. Maggie, you're trying to do the impossible.'

'No, I'm not.' A frown contorted her features as she turned on him. 'I'm managing perfectly well. Even though

209

I have to go back to Madrid to check on Rosario and the children...' She thrust out her chin. '...I'll be back in Tres Lomas to continue my search before you know it. I'm never giving up.'

'I don't doubt your determination but...'

'No buts. If *you* won't help me, I'll find someone who will.'

'I never said I wouldn't help you,' protested Raul angrily.

They slipped into silence, then Raul spoke as if there had been no dissension between them. 'Maggie, why don't you move in with me for the rest of your stay?'

Taken by surprise, she gasped, 'Are you allowed to have overnight visitors?'

'Who's to know?'

Maggie couldn't help smiling to herself. Despite their disagreement Raul still wanted her around. He put a hand on her knee. 'Say yes, Maggie.'

She made a swift decision. It would, after all, save her some money. 'All right,' she said, 'I'll move my things in tomorrow if you're sure about it.'

He stopped the truck and leaning over, kissed her firmly on the mouth, then tucking a lock of her hair behind her ear, he said, 'I've never been more certain about anything.'

The next few days passed in a dream for Maggie. As Raul was unable to find anybody willing to give her a lift back to Madrid, she was obliged to stay on. She wondered wistfully whether he was deliberately putting off her departure. Neither of them brought up the subject of the children and she hoped her outburst had put paid to Raul's idea of returning them to their village.

Despite Raul's long shifts they managed to spend time together but things changed on the fourth day. After work, he came hurrying in with some exciting news.

'Maggie, I think I've located your brother. A couple of wounded men arrived this afternoon. One of them, an Englishman, knows Esteban.'

Maggie eyes gleamed with excitement. 'What did he say?' she gasped, clutching Raul's hands.

'He says he's with a renegade POUM group not far from here. They're carrying out subversive operations, sabotaging roads, blowing up bridges.'

Maggie frowned and tightened her grip on Raul's hands. 'That sounds terribly dangerous.'

'All warfare is dangerous,' said Raul.

'When can you take me to see him?'

Raul shook his head. 'I can't, I'm not allowed to venture into those areas except in an emergency. But I may be able to get a message to him.'

'That's no good. If we delay, his squad may move on. You said yourself that the POUM are always on the move.'

Raul frowned and shrugged his shoulders. 'It's the best I can come up with at the moment.'

'Let me speak to the patient concerned.'

'It won't do any good. For one thing, he's quite ill, slips in and out of consciousness.'

By now, Maggie was determined to get her own way. 'Why can't you borrow Arnoldo's truck like you did before?'

'This is different, Maggie. Esteban's squad are carrying out dangerous manoeuvres. You can't go there on a whim.'

'On a whim!' Maggie was lost for words. How dare Raul treat her quest to find her brother so lightly!

Realising his mistake, Raul tried to rectify the situation. 'I didn't mean finding your brother isn't important, but I can't flout hospital rules just when I feel like it.'

'Huh!' Closing in on him, Maggie balled her fist. 'You were only too ready to flout the rules about not allowing visitors to share your accommodation; you were prepared to go back to the village when you thought there was a chance of returning Eva and Fabio to their uncle but...'

Raul gave a snort of exasperation. 'That's unfair. I knew nothing about their uncle before we went there. Listen, Maggie,' he said earnestly. 'Going into the fighting zone is a different matter. No sane individual ventures there unless they have to.'

'*I* have to,' insisted Maggie.

Raul couldn't suppress his anger. 'Well, you'll just have to find somebody else to take you.'

Before she could retaliate, he snatched up his jacket and marched off, leaving her staring after him.

As she watched him go, Maggie thrust a knuckled fist into her mouth. She felt hollow inside. The thrill of learning the whereabouts of her brother was totally eradicated by the row. How badly she had handled things! Of course, Raul didn't want to risk escorting her into a war zone. Why should he? It wasn't *his* brother they were looking for. The tears spilled over as she wondered what to do next, chiding herself for the harsh words she had uttered as she recalled Raul's kindness towards her. Would he ever speak to her again? Throwing herself down onto the bed, she howled with frustration.

CHAPTER FIFTEEN

Later in the day, Maggie went out. The sun was shining, and after an hour of wallowing in regret and self-recrimination, she decided that a dose of fresh air was what she needed. Her footsteps took her towards the hospital. Perhaps she would bump into Raul on one of his cigarette breaks. She knew he always went to sit beneath the large tree outside the hospital, and she might get a chance to say how sorry she was. She hung around for longer than she should have done, reluctant to leave.

Just as she was about to give up, Raul appeared, but it wasn't to take a cigarette break. He came out escorted by one of the nurses. After assisting a young man into the ambulance, the nurse went back into the hospital, leaving Raul to settle the patient. As Raul climbed into the driving seat, he turned and caught sight of Maggie. She ran over to him.

'You never give up, do you?' he scowled. 'Hop in but promise me you'll do exactly what I tell you to.'

'Thanks Raul,' replied Maggie, clambering in before he had time to change his mind.

'I'll be in and out of the camp very quickly. There'll hardly be time to look for Esteban,' he said as he started the engine.

'I can look for him while you're checking your patient is all right,' insisted Maggie.

The patient, overhearing their conversation, tweaked back the dividing curtain. 'So you're Esteban's sister?' he said in English.

Maggie smiled back at him over her shoulder. 'Yes, do you know my brother well?'

'He's one of the best,' replied the young man. 'He's fearless, he laughs in the face of danger.'

Maggie gave a swallow. That sounded like Robert. 'Has he mentioned me?' she asked.

'Many times, but he believes you're back home in England. He's going to be very surprised. You took a risk coming over to Spain.'

'I had to find Robert.' Because the man was English she found herself referring to her brother by his given name.

'Robert? Oh I see. D'you know, I took him for a Spaniard until he mentioned you. I can't believe he's English. You look like him but you seem very different.' He gave a chuckle. 'Except of course that you're both prepared to take risks.'

'Oh, I'm not like my brother,' protested Maggie. 'When we were growing up, he was always the one in the forefront. I always took a back seat.' She began to get a crick in her neck, and without thinking, clambered into the back of the ambulance to be with the patient. 'What's your name?'

'Peter Knowles.' He held out a hand, wincing from his shoulder injury.

'Maggie Morán. What made you join POUM?

'It was by accident. I was studying Spanish at the university in Barcelona when things started warming up; then, one thing led to another.'

'Do you regret it? I mean, now that you've been wounded and you know how bad things are?'

'Sometimes. But this war won't last forever and...'

Chatting to Peter helped pass the time until Raul called out, 'Nearly there, Maggie, you'd better get back here.'

The ambulance came to a halt in a dell. Half a dozen people rushed out, brandishing guns. They were wearing dark clothing and had smeared their faces with charcoal so that the whites of their eyes gleamed. She could hear distant gunfire and saw a spiral of smoke rise above the hillside.

She clambered out and helped Raul lead Peter Knowles to join his comrades.

'He's not fit to fight,' Raul explained to the woman who rushed out to look after him. 'We wanted him to stay in the hospital but he insisted on reporting back here.'

Maggie scanned the faces of the group for signs of her brother. Then she saw him. At first, he didn't notice her and she realised that she would be the last person he would expect to see.

'Robert!' she shouted.

He recognised her voice, and stopped in his tracks to stare in disbelief. 'Maggie!'

Dropping his weapon, he rushed over, picked her up and swung her round as if she were a doll. His pleasure at seeing her made her forget her anger at him for not bothering to contact her over the past months. In fact, it was some time before she remembered that he didn't know about the death of their mother. She decided to put off giving him that news until later.

Raul came over to join them and the two men shook hands. 'I'm afraid this will be a very short reunion,' he said. 'We can't stay. I've got to be back in Tres Lomas by tonight.'

'I'm staying,' said Maggie firmly. She was still standing arm-in-arm with her brother.

Raul stared from one to the other. 'Two peas in a pod; are you coming, Maggie?'

215

She shook her head. 'Not yet. I want to stay here at least for tonight.'

'It's dangerous, Maggie. You don't belong here.'

'My brother will take care of me.'

'Of course I will,' confirmed her twin. 'Don't make a big issue of it.'

But Raul persisted. 'How will you get back to Tres Lomas?'

'I'll worry about that tomorrow.'

'You could be stuck here for days.'

'I'll take my chances.'

Her brother grinned. 'My sister's a determined little minx. She must stay, Raul, we've got a lot to catch up on.'

'How will she get back?' persisted Raul.

'Don't worry, someone will drive her.'

Raul frowned but, realising he had lost the argument, he started back to the ambulance, saying, 'Take care.'

Maggie called to him. 'Raul, thank you so much for bringing me here. You've helped me a lot since Tomás dumped me at your doorstep back in September.'

She watched him drive off, experiencing a sense of loss. But her brother didn't give her time to ponder as he introduced her to his companions.

'Look everybody,' he announced. 'This is my sister. She's come here to rescue me from you lot because she believes you're a bad influence on me.' They all laughed, making Maggie feel rather foolish. He went on, 'Make her comfortable. Who's prepared to give up their bed for the night? Oh no, forget that…' He held up a negating hand. 'It's down to me, isn't it? This means I shall have to sleep out in the open.'

Maggie's eyes widened although she didn't say anything because she was uncertain as to whether he was teasing her or not. She glanced around, noting that they were a mixed bunch of nationalities, whose common language seemed to be English.

216

Shyly, Maggie greeted them one by one. When Robert introduced the only two women in the group, he said, 'This is Abril from Andalucia and Dolores, who hails from the Catalan area. Abril does the cooking. You see, women aren't supposed to fight…' He winked. '…but that doesn't stop Dolores.'

As darkness descended, the gunfire ceased and the atmosphere became more relaxed. Maggie watched Abril prepare the meal. It was quite a feat considering she had to cater for a dozen people with only a few primitive cooking utensils. She expected Dolores to offer assistance but it seemed that she was more at home cleaning weapons than sharing in the culinary duties.

Maggie offered help. 'Can I do anything?' she said.

Abril shook her head. 'Go and talk to Esteban, you must have plenty to catch up on.'

Maggie made a mental note to refer to her brother by his Spanish name in future. He seemed to have forsaken his English roots; besides, when speaking English he now had a marked Spanish accent.

Leaving Abril to her tasks, Maggie went in search of her brother. The time had come to tell him about their mother, a moment she had been dreading. She found him seated on a boulder smoking and sat down next to him. The night had brought a drop in the temperature and she wrapped her arms about her body, wishing she'd brought warmer clothes with her. On the distant mountains snow glistened under a starry sky, beneath her feet, the ground was iron-hard. She pulled the sleeves of her cardigan down to cover her hands, blowing on her fingertips in a bid to warm them.

Feeling puzzled that her brother had shown so little curiosity as to how she had found him, she asked, 'Don't you want to know how I got here?'

'Raul brought you.'

Maggie couldn't hide her irritation. 'And how did I get to know Raul?'

He stubbed out his cigarette, looking surprised by her display of intolerance. 'I don't know, why don't you tell me?'

Maggie frowned. He may be calling himself Esteban she thought, but he's still the same old Robert: wrapped up in himself, not interested in other people. She studied his profile as he lit up another cigarette, thinking sadly that after all, he was her only living relative, all she had in the world.

'How did you manage to get away from the she wolf?' he asked.

Maggie stiffened and said tightly, 'If you mean mother…'

'Of course I mean mother.'

She got up and walked away a few paces. He followed and stood behind her.

'I was coming to that,' she said.

'Well?'

With tears in her eyes, Maggie turned round to face him and, with the words tumbling out unimpeded, she described what had happened. As she did so, the image of Katherine's inert body, the blood-stained bathroom, the desperate race across the Common to Mr Butler's shop came rushing back and she found herself shaking uncontrollably. On reflection, she realised it would have been more sensible to pick up the phone and call for an ambulance herself but, at the time, she'd needed reinforcements, someone else to take charge. Her brother stared at her dumbstruck. Then, he placed an arm around her shoulders.

'It must have been terrible for you, *hermanita*. Suicide!'

For some time, they stood together in silence staring out into the gathering dusk, each of them stunned by the dreadful reality of their mother's death. The dark clouds parted to reveal a pale moon and, for a moment, it was as if the past terrible year had been nothing more than a dreadful dream. Maggie felt her brother's arm tighten around her and knew that he was experiencing the same emotions. She snuggled into his embrace, feeling closer to him at that moment than she had for many years.

'Grub's up!' one of the English speaking members called out, breaking the spell.

Robert took her hand. 'Come on, you'll feel better when we've eaten.'

The meal was a simple affair comprising chorizo and beans washed down with a beaker of coarse red wine. Maggie, who had been brought up on her grandmother's paella, tortilla and other classic Spanish food, found this peasant fare bland. Even in the restricted conditions she and Rosario were constrained to suffer in Madrid, the meals were tasty. Reminded of this, her thoughts once again turned to Donato. She missed him, longed to see his smile and hug him; when he reached out to clutch her forefinger, he was so strong. Despite the dreadful experiences of his young life, he was clearly a healthy baby. She thought about Eva and Fabio and wondered how Rosario was coping.

After the meal, one of the Spaniards got out a guitar and starting strumming. Then much to Maggie's surprise Dolores ran into the centre of the group and started dancing. Instead of the combat trousers and jacket she had been wearing earlier, she was dressed in a colourful gypsy skirt and blouse and wore a sequinned head-dress to hold back her waist-length black hair. Her dark eyes flashed as she expertly handled a pair of castanets and, in the firelight's glow, Maggie felt herself transported to the Spain her grandparents had so often told her about.

She exchanged a glance with her brother and he winked at her, a conspiratorial wink reminding her of the

219

old Robert from their childhood days. When he switched his gaze to the dancer his demeanour changed, and she instinctively knew that he and Dolores were more than comrades in arms. A surge of jealousy coursed through her, so fierce that it made the colour rush to her cheeks. Turning her face away so that the others would not see, she experienced yet another emotion: shame. Of course, Esteban, as he now called himself, would have found himself a woman!

When it grew dark, the men started drinking and joking: crude jokes, which Dolores and Abril laughed at although Maggie herself could not understand them. She was tired and longed to go to sleep but it was midnight before anybody slipped away. At last, Esteban showed her the sleeping quarters: an unconventional cave-like arrangement in the side of the hill.

'Where will you sleep?' she asked with feigned innocence, knowing that her brother would have no problem finding a bed for the night.

Breakfast consisted of strong black coffee, hard dry biscuits and a selection of fruit. Maggie felt mesmerized by the activity around her. People were coming and going and one man, in particular - someone she hadn't seen before - was shouting orders in a guttural voice. It soon became clear that he was in charge and she couldn't imagine why she hadn't noticed him the evening before. She felt intimidated by his dark, unshaven features and hooded eyes bridged by heavy brows.

All at once he noticed her. '*Quien es esta mujer?*'

'It's all right, Felix,' said Esteban, hurrying over to Maggie. 'This is my little sister. She's come a long way to find me, England in fact.' He spoke as if England was on the other side of the world, a place in which he had never set foot. So much for Tomás' advice to persuade him to return home, thought Maggie, and why does he insist on calling me his *little* sister?

The man's expression changed. Spreading his arms wide, he strode over to her and wrapped her in a bear-like hug, squeezing the life out of her. '*Bien venido, nena,* welcome to our humble abode!' He smelt of stale tobacco and sweat.

'*Gracias,*' she stammered once she had managed to get her breath back. However, she sensed that despite his words of welcome, he was a little annoyed at finding a stranger in their midst. She understood. This was a fighting unit, hangers-on were not welcome.

She wasn't able to talk to her brother alone again until the following evening because the men were kept busy cleaning their weapons and training. Some were out on reconnaissance, Esteban amongst them. He returned at suppertime and she was able to spend a little time with him. Remembering that she hadn't told him about the villa in Toledo, she said, 'Did you know that *Abuelo* left you a property here in Spain?'

He frowned. 'What are you talking about?'

Maggie delved into her pocket and drew out the piece of paper with the Toledo address on it. 'Here's the address.'

Taking it from her, he stared at it. Then he looked up. 'I didn't know anything about this.'

'Neither did I. He left me a cottage in Devon. I was able to sell it at a good price; that's how I got the money to come here.'

Esteban grinned and pocketed the slip of paper. 'You never know, it might come in handy one day.'

'By the way, I met Asunción and Jacinta,' she said.

'Who?'

'The people who nursed you back to health over a year ago. That's how I found you.'

'I'd rather forget about them,' he grunted.

221

'But they helped you.'

His eyes clouded. 'That wasn't a good time,' he said. 'I lost my closest friends.'

'I'm sorry.'

In a bid to appease her, he said, 'Tell me about Tomás. How did you meet up with that old rascal?'

Summarizing the story, Maggie told her brother about her adventures since her arrival in Spain.

He was astonished. 'I never thought you had it in you,' he said, squeezing her hand. 'Who's looking after those orphans you've collected?'

Maggie explained about Rosario but when he asked her what she intended to do in the future, she was at a loss. 'I honestly don't know. When I came out here, I had no intention of staying for longer than a week or two or at least until I found you.'

'Well, you've found me now, so I suppose you'll go home.'

Maggie looked aghast. 'I can't leave the children,' she cried.

'What about this other girl, Rosario? Can't she take care of them?'

'She's only seventeen and apart from the meagre amount her brother sends her each month, she has no other income. I'm the breadwinner.'

'I can't believe my ears,' gasped Esteban. 'My timid little sister, the breadwinner.'

There it was again, the reference to his *little* sister. She felt annoyed. 'I must go tomorrow or the next day. I can't leave poor Rosario alone for much longer.'

'I can't guarantee driving you back to Tres Lomas until later in the week. For one thing, while Felix is snooping around, I can't risk borrowing a vehicle. You'll have to stay here for a bit longer.'

'I can't.' All of a sudden, she wished she had heeded Raul's words and left with him. She was a misfit here.

222

Everybody had their daily duties, she had nothing to do. She felt useless. Even Abril wouldn't let her help with the cooking. That night, she sobbed herself to sleep, wishing she was in Raul's arms in his comfortable cabin instead of lying alone on a lumpy mattress in a murky cave.

The next day brought Maggie to the reality of war. Towards evening, just as it was getting dark, there was a loud explosion.

'Don't worry,' grinned her brother. 'That was one of ours. A contingent to the east blew up part of the railway line. There's a battalion of Nationalists being despatched westward. With any luck, they'll have been en route.'

'What?' shouted Maggie 'They blew up the railway line while the troops were travelling on it!'

'Don't be so sensitive, *hermanita*,' retorted Esteban. 'These things…'

His words were lost as gunfire broke out. The group took up strategic positions and Maggie found herself being shoved into a cave. Dolores pushed her deeper inside. 'Keep out of sight,' she muttered. 'Don't come out until someone comes to get you.'

Maggie sank down onto the uneven floor, finding herself in total darkness. Dolores had confiscated the kerosene lamp she had snatched up on entering the cave. She could hear gunfire but couldn't tell how far away it was. Trembling in the darkness, she reached out her hand to touch the wall, seeking reassurance. It was cold and jagged. Memories of her crawl through the ruins to rescue Donato came flooding back. But this was worse. In Bilbao, she had at least had the benefit of daylight, here there was nothing but darkness. She began to panic, could hardly breathe.

All at once a sound startled her. 'It's me, Maggie,' said a voice in English.

223

A match flickered and for several seconds, she was able to pick out Peter, who was lying on a make-shift mattress close by.

'I'm so glad you're here,' she gasped, comforted by the knowledge that she wasn't alone.

'I hope they don't shoot directly into here,' muttered Peter.

'So do I,' replied Maggie.

But it was only when a flare lit up the entrance to the cave that she realised what Peter had been worried about. To the left of them stood a stack of wooden cases. Maggie shivered. Hadn't Raul mentioned that the group were planning to blow up a strategic bridge currently held by Francoists? The boxes were similar to those transported by Tomás. They contained dynamite.

Shock, fear and cold combined to make Maggie shiver uncontrollably. Raul and Tomás were right. A soft English woman wasn't cut out for this kind of life. The noise was deafening. To combat her fear, Maggie tried to steel herself to think of pleasant things; it was better to die with nostalgic memories in her head than give in to sheer terror. Silently, she prayed that Robert would be all right. Like a cat, he had nine lives, didn't he?

She forced herself to think about Raul, to conjure up his face. He was the most attractive man she had ever met. She reminded herself that at college she had not had much luck with boyfriends. Her peers had disregarded parental advice about not smoking, consuming alcohol and staying out late. Maggie, on the other hand, had always respected her father's rules and, as a consequence, she had been on the edge of the group, the goodie-goodie who wouldn't say boo to a goose.

All at once, she heard a whistle followed by a deafening explosion, amplified by the hollowness of the cave. Shrapnel ricocheted along the floor. Then silence. Maggie found herself shivering with both fear and chill as she waited for the detonation which must surely follow. Nothing happened. She remembered Peter and called out, 'Are you all right?'

There was no reply. Sick with panic, she called again but he didn't reply. On hands and knees, she crawled blindly across the rubble-strewn ground until her hand came into contact with Peter's leg. He didn't move at her touch. She felt along his body until her fingers felt a warm stickiness.

'Peter,' she whispered. 'Are you all right?' But she knew instinctively that he would not reply. She folded her arms about her trembling body in an endeavour to combat hysteria and, slowly, despite the ringing in her ears, she realised that the gunfire had stopped. Unable to bear staying in the cave any longer, she groped her way along the jagged wall to the entrance.

As her eyes became accustomed to the fading daylight, she saw people running hither and thither shouting although she couldn't make out what they were saying. An inert body barred her exit. The man's eyes stared boldly up at her. She saw that her only resort was to step over him. With bile rising to her throat, she gave a gulp and picked her way between the injured. Smoke rose from burning shrubbery, the odour of cordite assailed her nostrils, burning her eyelids.

Someone shouted at her. 'Get the First Aid kit.'

She had noticed where it was kept the day before and ran obediently to fetch it. Dolores snatched it from her. 'Hold his arms down,' she said, nodding at an injured man, who was stretched out among the debris. 'I have to dress his head wound.'

Maggie knelt down beside the man and pressed on his upper arms, averting her gaze as Dolores applied a dressing. She felt nausea rising but being useful helped her control it.

'You can let go now,' barked Dolores.

'Peter's dead,' Maggie managed to mutter.

Dolores looked surprised. 'In the cave?'

'A piece of shrapnel hit him.'

Dolores touched her arm in a kindly gesture before going to the aid of another victim. The leader, Felix, was among the casualties and Maggie heard a voice she recognised shouting out orders. Her brother had taken charge. Someone was radioing to the hospital at Tres Lomas and Maggie guessed that Raul would soon be on his way. She prayed that he would arrive safely.

It was several hours before order was restored. The wounded were attended to and the dead were hastily prepared for burial. The remaining members regrouped to talk over their situation. Maggie sat on the periphery, listening. She was numb with shock and, although she had wrapped her jacket tightly around her, she couldn't stop shivering and was thankful when Abril dished out hot soup.

Cries and moans came from the cave where Dolores administered to the wounded as best she could. When, from time to time, she came out of the cave, Maggie was able to study her in the glow of the lantern she carried. She was undoubtedly a handsome woman, with strong features and a commanding manner. Her gaze swept past Maggie to rest on her Robert's face. She smiled at him, a haughty, challenging smile.

Raul arrived in the small hours. He had brought one of the nurses with him. Several men helped lift the wounded men, including Felix, into the ambulance and the nurse climbed in to sit between the stretchers.

'Come on Maggie,' said Raul. 'I expect you've seen enough.'

She nodded, hesitating only to give her brother a brief hug and extracting a promise from him that he would visit her in Madrid before too long.

'How will you get there?' she asked.

'I'll purloin one of the motor bikes.' He wrinkled his nose in the engaging manner she remembered so well and whispered, 'Felix won't be here to stop me.'

As she got into the vehicle, she looked back and saw him place his arm around Dolores' waist, drawing her close. Maggie raised her arm to wave, then let it drop when the couple turned away. Her twin had already put her out of his mind.

CHAPTER SIXTEEN

The drive back to Tres Lomas gave Maggie time to dwell on what had happened. She had come to Spain to find her brother and she had succeeded. He was alive and well, he had been delighted to see her, but something had changed. She realised now how much she used to rely on him for advice and support. He was her twin, her other half. But since coming to Spain, he was no longer hers, he belonged to a voluptuous gypsy, who laid claim to him with a flash of her eyes. Jealousy drove a knife into Maggie's heart and she longed to point out to her brother that this was not what their grandparents had envisaged for their only grandson. They would have been shocked to find Robert involved with such a woman.

Even the warmth of Raul's presence beside her in the ambulance, couldn't dispel Maggie's despair, especially when Raul gave her some bad news. 'Tomás has been arrested,' he said.

'What?'

'He was arrested last week and taken to Montjuic.'

Maggie felt a cold chill run through her. She had heard terrible rumours about what occurred at the Baroque-style castle overlooking Barcelona. 'I thought it was in Republican hands,' she murmured.

'The Nationalists have snatched it back,' replied Raul calmly.

Her voice trembled as she asked, 'What will happen to him? Do the Republicans attempt rescues?'

'Sometimes, but old Montalvo's not popular with the International Brigades. A gun-runner for POUM! They don't like that.'

Maggie felt stunned. She knew how fractious Tomás could be, how he was able to antagonise people with his erratic behaviour and brusque manner, but she harboured a fondness for him. She had a lot to thank him for. If he hadn't guided her across the border from France, she would have been forced to give up her search for her brother before it had even started. And there were many other occasions when he had helped her.

She voiced her indignation. 'Why would they be against him when they're all fighting on the same side?'

Raul cast her an ironic smile. 'You don't understand the Spanish psyche.'

'I'm beginning to realise that,' she groaned.

He tried to lighten her mood by asking: 'Why does your brother insist on calling himself Esteban? He could easily convert Robert to Roberto?'

Maggie laughed. 'Esteban was our grandfather's name. Robert idolised him, that's why he's adopted his name.'

They arrived back at the hospital in Tres Lomas to discover that one of the injured men had lost his battle for life. The other two were transferred to a ward, with Felix protesting that he wasn't injured badly enough to warrant a stay in hospital.

'With a leg wound like that you're going nowhere,' rejoined Raul.

This reminded Maggie that her brother was now in charge of the squad. She gave a shudder, wishing she could persuade him to return home. A terrible defencelessness coursed through her: what she was doing in this hostile country?

Raul snapped her out of her negative mood. 'We'll go out and have a special dinner tonight,' he said. When she looked surprised, he said, 'How long have you been in Spain?'

'Nearly a year.'

'And at last you've found your brother. I think that calls for a celebration, don't you?'

Maggie wasn't so sure. After the terrible events she had just witnessed, it didn't feel right to carry on as normal, let alone go out of their way to enjoy themselves.

'I'm awfully tired,' she said.

But Raul would not be put off. Giving her a hug, he said. 'Go back to my place and take a nap. I've got things to do in the hospital but I'll pick you up at nine o'clock. We'll go to Pablo's.'

Maggie gave a guilty giggle. 'I'm afraid I moved my stuff out of your place after that row we had.'

Unperturbed, he raised a quizzical eyebrow. 'Well, go and collect it. And remember, be ready at nine o'clock.'

He left her then, striding across the car park to the hospital entrance, leaving Maggie feeling rather foolish as she made her way to the hotel. Turning the corner, she caught sight of a fleeting figure, and instinctively stopped and stared. Were her eyes deceiving her or was that the boy she had met on her walk up the hill? She ran to the end of the road and was just in time to see him disappear around another corner. Was he stalking her? And if so, why? The other day he had been only too ready to make his escape after she had thwarted his attempted robbery. There was no chance of catching up with him now, so clutching her purse tightly she continued on to the hotel.

She sat down on the edge of the bed and thought about Raul. His presence sent her pulse racing; she felt herself blushing each time he spoke to her. It was only in the darkness when he took her to bed that she lost the embarrassment that dogged her during daylight hours. She let her mind wander, anticipating the joy of his embrace, the pleasure of hearing his whispered words of love. Did he mean them or was he simply playing with her? The mere possibility, brought a rush of heat to her cheeks.

The town hall clock struck the half hour, drawing her out of retrospection. Her emotions were in turmoil and she wished she had a woman friend in whom she could confide. Rosario was too young, and besides, she already knew the girl's response. Deeply religious, Rosario would never countenance sex before marriage.

At a quarter past eight she went to the bathroom and, given the shortage of hot water, washed as best she could. After applying a little make-up, she packed a few things into a small bag and left the hotel.

Rounding the corner at the end of the road, she came face-to-face with the mysterious boy. She tried to dodge out of his way, but he spread his arms and shook his head.

'What d'you want?' she demanded.

'I'm not going to steal from you.'

'What is it then?'

He replied with a question. 'Are you from Madrid?'

'Yes, but what has that got to do with you?'

'Are you going back there?'

'Yes.'

'Take me with you.'

Maggie was rendered speechless.

'Please,' he begged. 'I can't pay you but I'll do anything, work for you…I can turn my hand to anything. I'm strong - look!' He rolled up his sleeve to show her his biceps.

Despite her agitation, this brought a smile to her lips. 'I can see you're very strong,' she said. 'But I can't take you back with me. It's not up to me. I have to beg a lift to Madrid myself.'

'You could smuggle me into the vehicle with you.'

Maggie frowned. Had he heard about Eva and Fabio? Did he know she had already done a bit of human cargo smuggling?

'I have to go,' she said brusquely. 'I'm expected at the hospital.'

'I'll find you again,' he said, adopting a menacing tone. 'I know where you're staying.'

At that moment a man and a woman came into view. The boy looked over his shoulder and decided it was time to go. 'I'll be back,' he called as he sped off in the opposite direction.

Maggie heaved a grateful sigh as the couple walked past her, but the encounter had unnerved her; her heart pounded, her legs felt weak. What did he mean, he knew where she was staying? She wondered whether she ought to tell Raul, but the whole scenario seemed ridiculous and she didn't want him to think she was scared. She decided to put the incident out of her mind and increased her pace so that she quickly reached the more populated area of the town where she felt safer.

Raul was waiting for her on the steps of his cabin. 'Where have you been?' he asked, taking her hand and leading her inside. 'I've poured you a glass of Rioja.'

'I overslept,' she lied.

They sat down opposite one another, and again, she felt the familiar reddening of her cheeks as he looked into her eyes.

'Do we eat at once?' he asked. 'Or…?'

He didn't give her the chance to make the choice. Taking the glass of wine out of her hand, he pulled her over to the bed. 'Let's eat later.'

By the time they arrived at Pablo's it was ten thirty. The noisy hub-bub in Spanish restaurants was alien to Maggie. At home in England, whenever she had eaten out, there was always a subdued hush. She smiled to herself as she reflected that the English preferred to make themselves inconspicuous unlike the Spanish who liked to make their presence felt.

'I think you should go back to Madrid as soon as possible, Maggie,' said Raul. She looked at him sharply. Only a day ago, she couldn't wait to get back to be with Rosario and the children but the romantic evening they were having had changed that. For one horrible moment, she thought he might be trying to get rid of her? But then he went on, 'The Nationalists have made big advances. Tres Lomas could be next in the line of fire.'

'Surely they wouldn't attack the town? I can understand them wanting to get a foothold in some of the larger cities, but Tres Lomas isn't that important, is it?'

'Strategically, it sits on their route towards Catalonia. Besides, there are rumours that Franco has recruited more foreign help from the air; which gives the Nationalists the upper hand. They could start bombing the town.'

Maggie felt a shiver of fear. An air attack could expose her brother's group to even more danger. How could they defend themselves from low flying bombers?

'I want to stay,' she said. 'I can help, I can drive the ambulance. I've proved that.'

Raul touched her hand as she jabbed the prongs of a fork onto the paper tablecloth on the marble-topped table, tearing the paper and making a squeaking noise. 'I know, but you're needed in Madrid,' he insisted. 'Rosario can't manage without you for much longer.'

Maggie withdrew her hand and put the fork down. Lowering her gaze, she tried to despatch the demons. What Raul had said made sense, yet she didn't want to be separated from either Raul or her brother. Madrid was only a few kilometres away but in the present circumstances it felt like the other side of the world.

'You must leave tomorrow, Maggie.'

She shook her head. 'Not yet. I want to stay a bit longer, a few more days won't make any difference.'

Looking deep into her eyes, he reached for her hands again. 'You *must* go.'

She heaved a resigned sigh. It was no good arguing with him. 'Will you drive me back?'

'I can't, but Arnaldo Mendes will. He's a good friend of mine and I've already had a word with him. He's got some business to do in Madrid, and he says he'll take you.'

They walked back to Raul's cabin but when they reached the door, Maggie was seized by the need to be on her own. She knew that if she stayed the night she would end up begging Raul to let her stay on, and pride wouldn't let that happen.

'I think I'd better go back to the hotel,' she said.

When he didn't object the feeling of distrust returned. She couldn't fathom him. Earlier in the evening, their lovemaking had been wonderful; he had whispered endearments in her ear, been gentle, yet passionate.

'I'll walk you back,' he said.

'There's no need, I'll be all right on my own.'

He seemed uncertain, but her aloofness must have transmitted itself to him and he didn't insist. It was only when she turned the corner off the main road that she remembered the mysterious boy and realised that had she told Raul about him, he would have insisted on escorting her. She increased her pace, her gaze darting from left to right as she hurried along. The nearer she got to the hotel, the more her heart galloped. But she encountered no one.

Running upstairs to her room, she unlocked the door and threw herself onto the bed. What a strange and unexpected evening it had turned out to be! But Raul was right: her place was with Rosario and the children. Risking her neck in the face of an air attack was foolhardy.

Maggie woke up to the drone of aircraft. She had never heard anything like it. The planes sounded as if they were skimming the roof tops. The explosions were deafening. She leapt out of bed, flung on some clothes and raced downstairs to where the proprietor and his wife were making their way to a dugout shelter in the garden. As they hurried round to the back of the property, she caught sight of a now familiar figure. The mysterious boy was taking cover in a shop doorway.

Without thinking, she beckoned to him. 'Come into the shelter with us.'

The boy hesitated but the whine of circling aircraft grew louder and he followed her into the dugout.

'What's he doing here?' The proprietor's wife didn't sound pleased. 'That kid's always hanging around. Hasn't he got a home to go to?'

Maggie looked at the boy and guessed that he was probably homeless. A teen-age boy living on the street, she thought. How old was he: fifteen or sixteen? Did he have a job or was he surviving on what he could steal?

The four of them huddled in the confined space for more than an hour as the bombardment grew more intense. Smoke filled her nostrils and she began to worry when the old proprietor started to cave in under his barking cough.

'Pack it in, Laszlo,' snapped his unfeeling wife.

But the man continued to wheeze and cough until Maggie felt constrained to cover her ears. She knew there was nothing they could do for him. He needed to get out into the fresh air away from the suffocating stink of the underground shelter. She found herself uttering a prayer to the Virgin Mary, begging her to save the hospital from being hit, praying that Raul would have time to get to a shelter.

When at last the onslaught ended, she left the others and ran all the way back to the hospital. The town was

235

barely recognisable. Whole buildings had vanished and those that remained were obscured in a cloud of dust and smoke. She could taste the cordite and began to wonder whether, if she stayed longer, she would get used to the smells and tastes of Spain at war.

Fires had sprung up everywhere. She could feel the heat on her face as she skirted the worst hit areas. She snatched a handkerchief from her pocket to hold across her nose to stave off the stench.

The hospital had been partially hit. Patients in wheelchairs and on gurneys had been wheeled out into the car park where the harassed nursing staff were administering help. Maggie scoured the faces for Raul. At last she saw him. Skipping across lumps of concrete and debris, she ran over to him.

'Raul, can I help?' she shouted above the mayhem.

He waved her away. 'Get out of Tres Lomas now, Maggie, before they come back. Go and find Arnaldo. His truck's parked over that way...' He pointed in the direction from which she had come. 'He'll be expecting you.'

Raul turned back to the patient he was tending and Maggie saw that she had no alternative but to do what he told her. At least, she knew that for the moment he was safe. She spun on her heel and was astonished to see that the boy had followed her. He stood somewhat apart, staring at the chaos.

'Come on,' she called to him. 'You'd better get away from here. There's nothing either of us can do. They don't need onlookers.'

They hurried back the way they had come, ignoring the cries and shouts of shocked people emerging onto the street. When she became confused in the labyrinth of ruined buildings, the boy took charge. 'This way.'

Maggie followed him as he led her to an area of the town she had not visited before. They both saw the truck at the same time. Maggie recognised it as the greengrocer's vehicle Raul had used previously. The boy broke into a run. 'Look, there's Arnaldo.'

He stopped short. Arnaldo appeared to be getting into his truck. His upper body was draped over the driver's seat, his legs were dangling loosely on the running board. Maggie could see blood trickling down the side of his face and there were strafe marks along the outside of the truck.

'Don't go near him,' she shouted. But the boy disregarded her and on reaching the vehicle, he sent the old man's body flopping to the ground with nothing more than a gentle push.

'He's dead.' The boy's voice was matter of fact, as if seeing a dead body was an everyday occurrence.

'Come away,' called Maggie, ramming her fist into her mouth to stem nausea.

The boy ignored her. Shoving the old man's body out of the way with his foot, he climbed into the truck, and much to Maggie's alarm, started the engine.

'Look out!' she yelled as he bunny-hopped the vehicle a few yards along the road. He managed to brake as Maggie rushed across the road and yanked open the driver's door.

'It's all right, the engine isn't damaged,' he told her.

'Move over, you little idiot.' She pushed the boy over to the passenger seat, and clambered into the vehicle, shifting it into gear, desperation spurring her on as the whine of aircraft filled the skies once more.

They reached the outskirts of Madrid by mid-morning with Maggie driving the vehicle haphazardly Her main worry was that the truck would suffer a puncture or that they would run out of gas before they reached their destination.

They only exchanged a few words on the journey because Maggie needed to concentrate on her driving. She did ask the boy what his name was.

'Ángel,' he replied.

Maggie couldn't suppress a smile of amusement. What an inappropriate name for such a ragamuffin!

It was only when they stopped round the corner from the apartment block that she took stock of their appearance. She was covered in dust, her knees were grazed where she had scrambled over masonry and the hem of her skirt was torn. She realised that most of her belongings were still in the hotel although, even in her haste, she had remembered to pick up her purse and passport when she ran for shelter. She glanced at the boy and saw that, despite having managed to inveigle a lift to Madrid, his attitude was hostile, his features fixed in a sullen frown. She wondered what Rosario would think if she saw him.

She turned to him and said, 'What are you going to do now that you've got here?'

'I don't know.'

'Do you know anybody in Madrid?'

He shook his head.

'Have you ever been here before?'

Again, he shook his head.

'Why did you want to come here?'

Then he grinned. 'To make my fortune.'

'What?' Did he think he was Dick Whittington? She smothered a smirk and said, 'You must have had some sort of plan.'

He shrugged. 'I'll make out.'

'Have you got any money?' He rattled the change in his pocket.

'Show me.' He stuck his hand in his pocket and brought out some coins. 'Is that all? Here.' She opened her purse and gave him a handful of pesetas. 'Go and find

238

yourself a cheap boarding house for the night. Tomorrow, you'll have to look for a job.'

'Can't I stay with you tonight? I'll pay you.'

Maggie laughed. 'What! With the money I've just given you?'

He looked a bit sheepish. 'I'll work for you. I can turn my hand to anything.'

'No thank you. Off you go. You got your lift into Madrid, now be on your way. I don't want to keep bumping into you.'

The scowl came back but he didn't argue. Pushing open the door of the truck, he clambered out and, with his hands thrust deep into his trouser pockets, swaggered off down the street.

Maggie waited until he was out of sight before leaving the vehicle and heading for the apartment. She didn't want the boy knowing which building she lived in. Upstairs, she got a warm welcome. Rosario rushed over to give her a hug, as did Eva. Even Fabio smiled. As for Donato, he held out his arms for her and gurgled happily.

'Maggie, you look dreadful, what happened?' cried Rosario.

Breathlessly, Maggie described the journey home, omitting the incident with the boy.

'So the owner of the truck is dead?'

'I'm afraid so.'

'It must have been terrible for you.' She paused anxiously. 'Did you find your brother?'

'Yes.'

'Was he well?'

Maggie nodded but, all at once, she was overcome with exhaustion. Flopping down into a chair, she burst into tears and, between sobs, gave Rosario a garbled version of her time at the camp with Robert.

'Oh Maggie, how awful! You must have been shocked. Why, those freedom fighters are so brave.' She gave a shudder and whispered, 'I suppose Luis must be in the thick of it too.'

This brought another bout of sobbing from both girls until one of the children demanded their attention. Drying their tears, Rosario asked, 'Did you see much of Raul?'

'Yes, but we had a few disagreements.'

'That's love for you,' giggled Rosario, making Maggie blush.

'Any news from Palmiro?'

'No, nor have we heard from Tomás.'

Maggie bit her lip. 'Raul believes he's been arrested. He's promised to let me know if he hears anything.'

'I shall pray for him tonight,' said Rosario quietly.

Maggie spent the rest of the day with the children. She took them to the park and played ball with Eva and Fabio. The little boy seemed more settled now and she hoped he would begin to talk. He certainly knew how to express himself on paper, astounding both Maggie and Rosario with his sketches. They always depicted scenes of carnage: guns and swords and dead bodies lying on the ground. She tried to persuade him to draw something else.

'Why don't you do a picture of your sister. I'm sure she'd like that,' she suggested. But the little boy ignored her and continued to record his bad memories.

It was while they were playing in the park that she thought she spotted Ángel. Fabio threw the ball into the trees and Maggie ran to look for it. As she got there a figure she thought she recognised dashed away. Was the boy watching them? She quickly dismissed the idea because it was a sunny day and there were a lot of mothers and children taking the air. It could have been anybody.

After their evening meal, the business of getting the children to bed took up a lot of time. Maggie felt exhausted. She had been woken up in the middle of the night, had driven over rough ground in an unfamiliar vehicle for several hours, now she was ready to sleep in her own bed.

'I'll put the rubbish out before bed,' said Rosario, but when Fabio wandered into the room, she put the garbage bag down by the front door and went to him.

Maggie picked it up. 'I'll do it. I've got to move the truck to somewhere more convenient anyway.'

Leaving the apartment, she ran across the road to tip the garbage into the bin. She went to the truck, realising that such a scruffy vehicle looked out of place in a residential area. As she climbed into the driver's cabin she couldn't help thinking about Arnaldo, feeling guilty for having abandoned his body on the street. She wondered whether Raul had discovered what had happened to him.

She drove the vehicle a few streets further away to where it would be less conspicuous, but had some difficulty parking it, mounting the pavement in order to fit it in between two commercial vans. There was a grunt from the back of the truck. Alarmed, she swivelled round and saw Ángel's startled face looking up at her. He was half hidden by the tarpaulin and she would never have seen him had she not woken him up by jolting the truck up the kerb. Sheepishly, he rubbed a fist over his eyes and muttered, 'Hello, Maggie.'

CHAPTER SEVENTEEN

It was months since Palmiro had been in Madrid. He snatched every spare moment to write to Rosario, using a mixture of Italian and Spanish. She replied in her impeccable handwriting, sometimes using words he couldn't understand. He puzzled over these for days until, finally, he felt compelled to call on one of his Spanish companions for help. This resulted in a lot of teasing from the members of the squad, leaving him the choice of taking offence or joining in with the general badinage. He chose the latter.

He thought about Salvatore and hoped that he had survived the ferocious battles that had been taking place around Burgos. Some nights he lay awake imagining coming face-to-face with his friend in combat. What would happen now they were fighting on opposing sides? Sometimes he had nightmares, waking in a sweat because in his dream he was part of a firing squad assigned to shoot his erstwhile friend.

He managed to find a way of sending the occasional letter home, not mentioning his change of allegiance. In darker moments, he pined for his family, especially his mother. A shudder of dread would course through him when he pictured his father. An admirer of Mussolini, Luigi Aiello would be shocked to learn that his son had switched sides. In his father's eyes, Palmiro knew that he would forever be a deserter.

On one occasion, when he was curled up under a tarpaulin hooked over the branches of a tree, feeling low, a friendly voice called to him in English.

'Hey *Italiano,* what's the matter? Stop mooning over yon girl and come and join us by the fire.'

He looked up to see the affable grin of a ginger-haired Scotsman. Angus MacKay had only joined the squad recently but his larger-than-life personality had quickly won over the friendship of his companions.

Palmiro reluctantly left his makeshift shelter and joined the others. They were mostly English or French and they were telling jokes. His English was fragmentary but he joined in the hearty laugher not understanding everything. This proved to be the start of a enduring friendship with Angus, parallel to the friendship he had shared with Salvatore.

Over time, Palmiro discovered that there was more to Angus than a jocular personality. The twenty-six-year-old had travelled extensively, spending a lot of time in Italy and he spoke some Italian. He had been to Calabria and seemed instinctively to understand the problem of the young Italian's conflicting loyalties. They carried on a conversation in a mixture of English and Italian.

'There's no going back now,' Angus pointed out. 'Aye man, you've burnt your bridges. But maybe after this awful mess has been cleared up, your auld man will come to understand why you deserted.'

Palmiro shook his head. 'I doubt it.'

Angus drew on his cigarette. 'Why *did* you change sides?'

Palmiro gave a snort of derision. 'I didn't like the stories I heard. Too many Fascist big men all over Europe tramping on the little man. I couldn't stand the cruelty doled out by the Nationalists against their own people. Little did I know that the same treatment would be doled out by the Republicans.'

'If you feel like that, man, you'd better quit now. Find a way to go home and sort it out with your auld pa.' He sucked in his breath and added, 'Or is there something else?'

Palmiro felt the colour rise to his cheeks. 'There wasn't to start with. I honestly believed I was doing the right thing. Now…well there is another reason.'

'Rosario?' Before the young Italian could answer, Angus launched into a quotation:

O, my luve is like a red, red rose,
That's newly sprung in June.

Palmiro could barely understand the words so strong was Angus' accent but he knew instinctively that he was referring to Rosario. He was covered with embarrassment.

'Rabbie Burns,' explained Angus, although the name meant nothing to his companion. 'Well, are you serious about your Rosario?'

Palmiro nodded.

'She won't leave Spain,' warned Angus.

Palmiro frowned, recalling that he had on one occasion, shown the Scotsman one of Rosario's letters. 'How d'you know?'

'She's very young and didn't you say she was planning to join her brother in Barcelona? She won't leave without him.'

Palmiro felt crushed by Angus' logic. 'Who's to say what she'll do. In any case, maybe I'll stay here after the war.'

Although the possibility had been playing on Palmiro's mind for some time, this was the first time he had voiced it. Would it be so bad? Their two cultures were not so far apart. He could study the language properly, get a job and marry Rosario. She had only just turned eighteen, but did that matter? After all, his parents had married at eighteen and two of his sisters were mothers before their nineteenth birthdays. Later, when things settled down, he could take Rosario back to Calabria to visit his family. He was sure his mother and sisters would welcome him back even if his father refused to speak to him.

He offered Angus another cigarette and lit one for himself. In an endeavour to change the subject, he asked, 'What's it like in Scotland?'

Angus chuckled. 'Cold and wet mostly. Aye man, I'm a highland lad, at least I was until I became an international nomad. But Scotland is the most beautiful place on earth.'

'Then why did you leave?'

The Scotsman blew a smoke ring into the air. 'Family matters.'

'What d'you mean?'

'My brother's the laird, I'm the black sheep.'

'What's a laird?'

'A kind of lord of the manor.'

'And a black sheep?'

'The bad apple, the rebel.'

'Oh I see. We have something in common then.'

'Aye, it would seem so.'

'What did you do that was so bad?'

Angus sucked in his breath. 'It was clan trouble.'

Palmiro wanted to question him further but his companion was not to be drawn. The two men fell silent until there was an unexpected call to arms. It seemed they were on the move again. Rumours suggested they were travelling to the Aragon province. Palmiro tried to visualize the map. Would they pass through Madrid? Would he get the chance to see Rosario?

CHAPTER EIGHTEEN

'What are you doing here?' gasped Maggie once she had recovered from her surprise at finding Ángel in the back of the truck.

He backed away from her, mumbling, 'I meant no offence; I had nowhere else to sleep.'

'I gave you money, why didn't you find yourself some lodgings?'

'I tried but they wouldn't take me in.'

'I don't believe you. You spent the money on something else, didn't you, gambling or drink?'

He looked indignant. 'I had to get something to eat.'

'You would have got quite a feast with all those pesetas.'

'Money doesn't go far these days.'

'What do you know about it?'

He stuck out a belligerent chin. 'I've been fending for myself for long enough.'

'Perhaps you had better tell me about it,' retorted Maggie getting out of the truck and going round to release the rear flap. She grabbed Ángel's jacket and hauled him out, angry with him and with herself for not anticipating this eventuality. He made no attempt to wriggle free but stood docilely on the kerb, looking down at the ground between his feet.

Relenting, she said, 'Come on, you can stay with us tonight but first thing tomorrow morning, you must go and look for lodgings? You'll have to find work too. What jobs are you able to do?'

His gaze darted away and then back to her. 'Anything I can find.'

She shrugged and said, 'Let's get home. We can talk about this later.'

Striding ahead of him, she half hoped he would decide to make off, but he didn't. She was puzzled because his initial bravado seemed to have dissipated and she began to wonder whether he was younger than she had at first thought.

'How old are you?' She tossed the question at him as they got closer to the apartment.

'Fourteen.'

The hesitancy of his reply made her turn and study him. Again, he lowered his gaze. She stopped in her tracks and grasped his arm. 'Your real age?'

He muttered something incomprehensible, so she gave him a shake.

'Twelve.'

Twelve! And she had originally taken him for sixteen. She felt guilty. Despite the eventful day, her main preoccupation had been Raul's safety. Even the joy of seeing Rosario and the children again couldn't dispel her worries. With her mind on other things, she had assumed, wrongly, that the boy was old enough to look after himself.

She hurried ahead of him into the apartment building, mounting the stairs without knowing what she was doing. The boy followed at her heels. Uninvited questions coursed through her mind. What had induced her to bring him back with her? She could so easily have shoved him out of the truck and driven off without him. Tres Lomas was his home. He didn't know Madrid; a country boy, he would be totally lost in a big city.

Unlocking the apartment door, she whispered, 'Be quiet, Ángel, they're all asleep.'

'Who lives here?' he whispered back.

'My family.' The words slipped out instinctively and it was only afterwards that she realised she did, indeed, now have a family to care for.

She showed him where the kitchen and bathroom were, insisting that he should have a wash before bed. Leaving him in the bathroom, she went to make up the bed in the box room, the bed which Raul sometimes used during his visits to Madrid. She moved on tiptoe, not wanting to wake Rosario. The next morning would be time enough to break the news about their latest lodger.

It was after midnight by the time she got to bed. The day had been eventful but despite her tiredness, she couldn't sleep. Lying next to Rosario in the big double bed, images of the devastation in Tres Lomas rose to haunt her. Had Raul survived the second air attack? She wished now she had ignored his orders to leave; surely even without medical knowledge she could have been useful. At last exhaustion claimed her and she fell asleep to be woken the next morning by Rosario bringing her a cup of coffee. She gave an inward sigh. If only she could have a nice cup of breakfast tea, something she hadn't had since leaving England.

'What time is it?' she asked, rolling over onto her back without sitting up.

'Nine o'clock. I didn't want to wake you from such a deep sleep.'

All at once, Maggie remembered Àngel. Sitting up with a jerk, she snapped, 'Where are the children?'

Rosario looked taken aback. 'They're playing in the other room. Why?'

'I must get up.'

'What's the hurry? You should give yourself a day's rest before starting work.'

'It's not that,' cried Maggie, leaping out of bed and almost knocking the coffee cup out of Rosario's hand.

She left Rosario staring after her open-mouthed as she raced to the box room. Stopping outside, she calmed herself and opened the door. Ángel was still asleep. Closing the door quietly, she retreated, gearing herself up to tell Rosario about her midnight adventures.

Under the circumstances, Rosario took the news very well. After the initial shock, she said half-joking, 'Don't go away again, Maggie, we can't have any more orphans living here.'

Three quarters of an hour later, Ángel wandered into the living room. Maggie was washed and dressed and waiting for him. The women had decided not to introduce the boy to the children until they knew more about him and Rosario had taken them out so that Maggie could question him further.

He still seemed sleepy so she gave him some breakfast, hoping this would bring him to life. He munched away at his roll, sitting on the edge of the sofa as if he had never seen such sophisticated furniture before. Maggie began to wonder whether he was, in fact, a gypsy who had become separated from his clan.

'Where do you come from, Ángel?' she asked. 'I mean where have you been living?'

To her relief, he began to open up.

'In an empty house,' he said.

'With your parents?'

He shook his head. 'They've gone.'

'Where have they gone?'

He shrugged. 'Who knows?'

'Why didn't you go with them?'

'They didn't want me.'

'I can't believe that.'

'You don't understand,' he said.

249

Maggie began to feel exasperated. 'Explain!' she snapped.

'There are so many of us; they said I should be able to look after myself.' He thrust out his chin. 'And I can.'

'I don't know about that,' retorted Maggie. 'You would have been sleeping rough if I hadn't found you.'

'I was all right in the truck.'

'Why did you want to come to Madrid?'

'I felt like it.'

'Why? Did you think there would be more opportunities for thieving?' Although he didn't answer, he had the grace to blush. 'How long have you been on your own?'

'About a year.'

'Have you been to school?'

'A bit. Not lately.'

'Can you read and write?'

'A bit.'

Maggie was shaken to the core. Such a boy would not have slipped through the net back in England. He would have been put into a home long ago. All at once, she felt incredibly sorry for him and had to restrain the urge to move over to the sofa to give him a hug. After losing contact with her brother, she had spent many months feeling isolated from the rest of the world. How must this twelve-year-old boy feel? Even if he was a wandering gypsy, he would be used to having a lot of people around him. She wrinkled her brow. What could he have done to make them abandon him?

Commonsense told her that she mustn't allow herself to be fooled by the boy. He said he was twelve but maybe he had lied. He was certainly big for twelve. To curb her sympathy, she got up briskly and told him to go and get washed.

'Take off those awful clothes,' she said. 'And put on the dressing gown hanging behind the door in the bedroom. I'll get you some clean clothes when I go out.'

It meant spending money but there was no alternative. What a pity Tomás wasn't around to help out. She bit her lip, wondering what had happened to the big man. She knew he was a gun-runner and that he took risks, but he seemed strong, invincible; she couldn't imagine him being caught and imprisoned. Raul had said he could be executed without trial. What a terrible fate for such a colourful character! She shivered and pushed the possibility out of her mind. From leading a lonely life, she now found herself with an accumulation of people to worry about.

By the time Rosario and the children returned, Maggie had calmed down.

She introduced Ángel to everyone, explaining to him that Fabio was shy and didn't speak.

'He used to talk,' said Eva defensively. 'But he stopped when our mother died.'

Ángel stared at one and then the other, looking overwhelmed. Maggie studied him covertly, realising that his behaviour suggested he had told the truth about his age. But she still didn't trust him. Taking Rosario aside, she explained how she had met him, omitting the bit about him trying to snatch her purse.

'He can't stay here,' said Rosario. 'We're struggling already.'

'I know,' agreed Maggie. 'But how can I turn him away? He's only twelve.'

'Twelve?' Rosario was astounded. She bit her lip, her brow creased. 'All the same, he can't expect to stay here. Ask Raul to take him back next time he comes.'

Maggie nodded in agreement but she doubted whether Ángel would take kindly to that suggestion. 'How much money have we got left?' she asked.

'Not much,' replied Rosario. 'But this arrived for you today.' Picking up a large envelope she handed it to Maggie, who tore it open.

'Translation work. Thank goodness! Listen, Rosario, I'll have to leave you to look after the children while I get down to this translating. The sooner I get it done, the sooner I get paid. But next time you go out, can you pick up a few clothes in the market for Ángel? And keep a close eye on him.'

'Don't you trust him?' asked Rosario nervously.

'Of course I trust him,' replied Maggie, crossing her fingers behind her back.

Maggie got the work done in a couple of days and took it back to the Library.

The receptionist was surprised. 'That was quick,' she said. 'Thank you, I'll pass it on to the librarian.'

Maggie hesitated. 'Umm…'

'The girl raised an enquiring eyebrow. 'Was there something else?'

'Have you any more work for me?'

'Not at the moment. We'll be in touch.'

Maggie started to go to the door, then returned to the desk. 'I suppose you couldn't pay me straightaway, could you?'

'I'll have to see,' said the receptionist. 'We usually pay monthly.'

Maggie gave a swallow. 'I know, but I'm a bit short of money at the moment and…'

The girl reached for the intercom. 'I'll find out,' she said with a smile. Covered with embarrassment, Maggie listened to her speak into the intercom until she replaced the receiver and said, 'The principal's coming down to see you, Miss Morán, please wait over there.'

After fifteen minutes, an elderly, round-shouldered man appeared. He wore a stern expression and didn't bother to introduce himself before saying, 'Ah, Miss Morán, I understand you want to be paid rightaway. This is most irregular, you know. We normally pay our translators at the end of the month.' He cleared his throat. 'However, we've made an exception in your case.'

Feeling her cheeks redden, Maggie mumbled her thanks, regretting having made the request, yet knowing this was a lifeline for Rosario and the children.

Handing her a brown envelope, the principal peered at her through his thick-lenses spectacles. 'If we're satisfied with your work, there'll be plenty more for you in the coming weeks.'

Maggie thanked him again and made her escape.

A few days later, Maggie got a call from the Library.

'Someone will deliver the next lot of work to you personally,' the secretary informed her. 'Will this afternoon be convenient?'

'I'd rather come and pick it up myself,' said Maggie.

'It's a complicated piece of work. My colleague, Harry Fforbes, wants to explain it to you himself.'

Maggie recoiled. The last thing she wanted was her new employer coming to the apartment. 'Can't he explain it to me at the library?'

The secretary sounded impatient. 'Apparently not. Mr Fforbes says he'll be along at two thirty this afternoon.' She paused. 'Is there a problem?'

'Of course not,' replied Maggie uncertainly.

After replacing the receiver she began to panic. It was vital that no one in authority should find out about the children. If she shut them away in the bedroom while her visitor was present, they might make a noise. She pondered on the problem. She could always say she was looking after them for a friend. But she wasn't a very good liar. With a sigh, she fell back on the only alternative: Rosario would have to take them out to the park, Ángel as well. In the event, the boy proved difficult.

'I don't want to go to the park,' he grumbled. 'It's going to rain.'

Maggie glanced out of the window. He was right. Heavy clouds were looming and the wind had picked up.

'Please come,' said Rosario. 'Fabio wants to play with you.'

'No he doesn't. He never opens his mouth and he's too small to kick a football around. Look what happened yesterday, he ran away crying when the ball hit his leg.'

Rosario tried to reason with him but it soon became clear that he had no intention of going to the park. She got the other children ready, and Maggie watched her carry Donato down the stairs to where his pram stood in the corner of the hallway. Eva and Fabio followed her.

Maggie turned to Ángel. 'You'll have to stay in the bedroom when my visitor arrives. Don't forget, you're not supposed to be here. No one must find out about you.'

Ángel frowned. 'I don't want to stay in there.'

'It won't be for long.'

'Why can't I stay in here with you?'

Maggie began to lose patience. 'Because I say so,' she snapped, taking him firmly by the arm and pushing him towards the bedroom.

A knock at the door made her more insistent but the argument had now turned into a battle of wills. Maggie knew there was no way she could force Ángel out of the room. Letting go of his arm, she pointed to a chair by the window. 'Go and sit over there and keep quiet.'

After smoothing a hand down her skirt and checking her appearance in the hall mirror, she went to open the door. To her surprise, the man standing on the doorstep was not the principal. Instead, a tall fair-haired man who looked to be in his late twenties or early thirties greeted her with a friendly smile.

'Miss Morán?'

Ignoring her look of surprise, the young man shook her hand, saying, 'I'm Harry Fforbes from the British Library.'

Maggie quickly regained her composure. 'Please come in.'

She led him to the table where they each pulled out a chair and sat down. 'We're very pleased with your work, you know,' he said, removing his glasses and giving them a rub with a handkerchief before placing them back on his nose.

Warming to him, Maggie smiled and said, 'I do my best.'

'I've brought this piece over personally because, as you'll see, it's handwritten…' He flashed her a grin. 'My handwriting isn't very good.'

Maggie smiled politely and said, 'I'm sure I'll be able to decipher it.'

'Shall we go through it together?'

Ángel chose this moment to squash a fly against the wall with the flat of his hand. 'Ouch!', he said. 'That hurt.'

Maggie frowned at him and, hoping her visitor's command of the language wasn't very good, she reprimanded Ángel in Spanish. The boy pulled a face and scraped his chair round to face the window. Turning back to Harry Fforbes, she apologised in English.

'It's quite all right,' he replied.

But after that, Maggie found it difficult to concentrate. Tension made her aware of other sounds in the room: the ticking clock, the creaky floorboard from the flat above, and then, the sound of rain lashing against the window pane.

'I told you it was going to rain,' said Ángel triumphantly. 'You shouldn't have sent the others out.'

Maggie swivelled round to face him. 'Be quiet, Ángel.' Again, she offered her visitor an apology. 'I'm terribly sorry. Shall we continue?'

Thankfully, the boy kept quiet while they went through the next couple of pages. Then all at once, he jumped to his feet and scuffed his way across the floor, leaving the room with the door wide open. Maggie went over to close it.

'Look,' said her visitor, getting to his feet. 'I can see this isn't a convenient time for you, maybe...'

'It's perfectly all right,' retorted Maggie, panicking at the possibility that Harry Fforbes might lose patience and decide to place the work elsewhere. 'It's just that the boy can be a bit awkward sometimes.'

'I hope you don't mind me asking, but is he a relation of yours?'

This was the question Maggie had been dreading. How could she explain away such a badly behaved child? 'Of course not. He's the son of a friend, staying with me for a few days,' she said.

Harry's mouth twitched into a smile. 'I see.'

Maggie knew she was failing in her endeavour to brush over Ángel's presence. 'Please sit down, now he's gone we can carry on.'

Harry Fforbes shook his head. 'Look, you've got a few pages to carry on with, why not come to the Library tomorrow. I'll purloin an empty office for us to use. I should explain that I'm only here temporarily so I haven't been assigned a permanent desk.'

Maggie heaved an inward sigh of relief. 'All right, I'll make a start on the first pages straightaway, and I'll come and pick up the rest tomorrow. Would two thirty be convenient?'

'Of course.' He picked up the folder containing the remaining work and went to the door, where he hesitated and, with a tentative smile, asked, 'Er...are you free to have a drink with me this evening, Miss Morán?' Maggie was taken aback and didn't know what to say. At her lack of response, he frowned and said, 'I'm sorry. I've embarrassed you. I can see you don't want to.'

Maggie fought to regain her composure. Studying him properly for the first time, she realised how pleasant he was. Maybe meeting him for a drink would gain her a few 'brownie' points after her earlier rudeness.

'It wasn't that…'

'I took you by surprise.'

'Yes, I'm afraid you did.' She smiled and added, 'Yes, Mr Fforbes, I'd like to have a drink with you.'

He smiled back. 'In that case, I'll pick you up at eight o'clock.'

Maggie shook her head. 'No, I'll meet you somewhere.'

'I don't know this area very well. Can you suggest a place?'

Maggie thought quickly. 'El Bar de los Marineros, it's just around the corner from here.'

She heard the main entrance door slam, and guessing it was the others coming home, she was relieved when Harry murmured, 'Until this evening then.' Turning, he ran down the stairs, passing Rosario and the children on the way, as she knew he would.

CHAPTER NINETEEN

Maggie felt nervous as she walked towards 'El Bar de los Marineros'. She kept asking herself why she had agreed to meet Harry. She had, after all, already arranged to see him to discuss the translation work at the British Library the following day. Besides, Rosario's look of disapproval as she left the apartment hadn't gone unnoticed. She knew that Rosario's strict Catholic upbringing made it difficult for her to accept Raul's overnight visits; now to make matters worse, in the young girl's eyes, she was two-timing him.

It's only a drink, she reminded herself, not a date. But still, as she approached the bar, she deliberately slowed her pace. At the entrance, she had a change of heart and, turning on her heel, she began to retrace her steps, telling herself that she would apologise the next day, explain that something unforeseen had cropped up.

'Maggie!' She stopped short and turned around. Harry Fforbes was hurrying towards her. 'Where are you going?' he asked.

'I...I...' She didn't know what to say. Any excuse would sound lame.

'Come on,' he said. 'Let's go inside.'

An explosion of light and noise greeted them as Harry pushed open the door of the bar. Someone was playing a guitar and as the Flamenco music gained momentum, it occurred to Maggie that, if it weren't for the blacked-out windows, no one would know Spain was in the middle of a civil war. Harry found them a table and ordered two San Miguels.

'I didn't expect it to be so crowded,' said Maggie.

'Don't worry, the place will clear when they all go home for dinner.'

Maggie glanced around. It was obvious that most of the drinkers had come there straight from work. Harry was probably right. Most of them would leave soon.

They exchanged generalities and Maggie couldn't help warming to the young man. He wasn't wearing his glasses, and as she covertly studied him over her drink, she realised that he was very attractive. He had an engaging smile and his grey eyes twinkled when he laughed. She couldn't help comparing him to Raul; Harry was much more reserved but he had a quiet confidence about him which inspired trust.

She asked him what was happening back home in London. 'What stance does the Government take regarding Hitler?' she asked. 'I mean, with Neville Chamberlain as Prime Minister do you think peace is assured?'

'Let's hope so.' Harry's reply was guarded and Maggie felt that he had little faith in a peaceful outcome to the situation in Europe.

The bar began to empty and Harry asked her the question she wanted to avoid. 'What brought you to Spain, Maggie?'

She looked down and fiddled with the stained beer mat on the table in front of her. 'I came to find my brother.'

'Did you find him?'

'Yes…but...'

'But?'

She looked up and met Harry's gaze, once again wishing she hadn't agreed to meet him. How much should she tell him about Robert? Would he disapprove of her brother's allegiance to POUM? She didn't know what Harry's position was at the British Library; he could be an important official for all she knew.

'I met up with him on one occasion,' she replied, adding quickly. 'What are you doing here?'

'Me? I'm attached to the British Library. I've been sent here to check things out, to find out whether we should keep the library open during the hostilities.'

Maggie's heart contracted. 'You're a diplomat, part of the Embassy?' she muttered.

He laughed. 'I've got diplomatic status and the Foreign Office did fund my trip.'

'So you are an official?'

Harry's grey eyes narrowed. 'What's troubling you, Maggie?'

Pushing back her chair, she snatched up her handbag and stood up. 'Look at the time, I've got to go.'

'We've only been here a short while.'

'I may be needed at home.'

Harry reached out his hand and plucked at her sleeve. 'Sit down and tell me what's wrong.'

'Nothing's wrong.' She edged away, clutching her bag protectively in front of her.

He got to his feet. 'I'll walk you home.'

'There's no need.'

He spoke quietly but his voice was firm as he repeated, 'I'll walk you home.'

All at once, Maggie was overcome by a terrible debility. Her head began to swim and her legs started to tremble. The guitar melody, a lament now, was drowned out by a thumping at her temples, the colourful bull fighting posters on the walls began to revolve around her. She put a hand on the back of the chair to steady herself.

'Are you all right?' Harry's concerned voice reached her through a haze.

'No, I don't think I am.' She sat down again, and resting her arms on the table, lowered her head onto them.

Harry placed a hand on her shoulder. 'I'll get a doctor.'

She lifted her head and said, 'No, please don't do that, I'm all right.'

Recovering, she looked up at him, ashamed of her moment of vulnerability. She had never fainted, not even when she had found her mother's body, not even when she had been obliged to fix the tourniquet strap on Raul's arm.

Harry didn't look convinced and she realised that her face was probably devoid of colour. He called to the waiter to bring a cognac, then encouraged her to drink it.

The waiter went away and observed them anxiously from behind the bar. After a few minutes, he came over again, and said, 'Is the *señorita* feeling better now?'

Maggie forced a smile. 'I'm fine, thank you, just over-tired.'

Twenty minutes later, they left the bar, Maggie having given up hope of walking home on her own. Besides, she had to admit to herself, she wanted Harry to accompany her. He took her arm, matching his own longer stride to her shorter one. At the entrance to the building, she stopped.

'Thank you, Harry, I'll be all right from here. I'll see you tomorrow as we arranged.'

He shook his head, a concerned frown furrowing his brow. 'No, I insist on seeing you to your door.'

Maggie could see there was no arguing with him. Reluctantly, she bowed to the inevitable, praying Rosario would have got the children into bed by the time they reached the apartment. At the door, he didn't give her time to fumble for her key but rang the bell. Rosario answered the door.

261

'What's wrong?' she gasped on noticing Maggie's pale face.

'Thank you, Harry, I'm very grateful to you,' mumbled Maggie, urging him to leave.

But Harry wasn't so easily dismissed. 'May I come in?' he asked, addressing Rosario.

The young girl opened the door wider and he led Maggie to the sofa.

'What happened?' asked Rosario.

Maggie waved away her alarm. 'I had a fainting fit. I've been overdoing things lately. I'm all right now.'

Eva chose this moment to come into the room. 'Can I have a drink of water?' she said.

Harry looked up and asked, 'Who's this young lady? I didn't know you had a family, Maggie.'

Before Maggie had a chance to concoct an explanation, Rosario said impulsively, 'Eva's an orphan we're looking after.'

Harry narrowed his eyes as he said in Spanish, 'What about the boy I saw this afternoon?' Maggie realised that he was almost as fluent in the language as she was.

Rosario blushed and mumbled, 'He's just a friend.'

Maggie felt desperate. She could see that Harry's curiosity had been aroused and she prayed that none of the other children would wake up.

Then Eva said innocently, 'I think Donato needs changing; he smells horrible.'

Harry raised an eyebrow. 'You've got a baby as well?'

Rosario looked disconcerted while Eva, realising she had said something she shouldn't have said, reached for Maggie's hand, saying, 'I'm sorry, Maggie.'

She pulled the little girl to her. 'It's all right, Eva, you've done nothing wrong. Go back to bed, there's a good girl.'

Reassured, Eva took the glass of water Rosario had fetched for her and left the room. After she'd gone, Harry turned to Maggie and said in English, 'I think you had better tell me what's going on?'

'Nothing's going on. They're here temporarily.'

'But if the girl's an orphan…? And what about the baby? Are they related?'

Maggie shook her head. 'I told you, it's a temporary arrangement.'

Suddenly, Harry's voice took on a sterner tone. 'Stop trying to pull the wool over my eyes. I can tell there's something wrong,' he said in English.

Despite her scant knowledge of English, Rosario had understood the gist of the conversation. 'Maggie,' she said. 'For God's sake, tell him.'

Maggie had never heard Rosario speak so forcefully. Until now, she herself had been the driving force, the one to come up with ideas, and she had to admit, the one to land them in the trouble they were now in. She summed up the alternatives. If she declined to explain perhaps Harry would leave. She could see he was losing patience. But suppose curiosity or conscience prompted him to go to the authorities! A heavy silence hung over the room, broken only when Rosario said, 'I'd better go and change Donato.'

With tears in her own eyes, Maggie looked into Harry's honest grey ones and decided to trust him. 'It's a long story,' she whispered.

Smiling, he sat down beside her and took her hand, squeezing it gently. 'I've got all the time in the world.'

By the time Rosario re-joined them, Maggie had spilled out the whole story, making light of her relationship with Raul. Harry seemed speechless at first, then he said, 'Maggie, it seems you're trying to be nursemaid to the whole of Spain.'

She bit her lip, tittering self-consciously. 'That wasn't what I meant to do. When I came out here I intended to find my brother and persuade him to return to England with me.' She fiddled with the button of her cardigan. 'Of course, I knew he wouldn't, but I felt I had to try. I needed to see him again.'

'Of course you did.' Harry wrinkled his forehead. 'This Tomás, what's happened to him?'

'We don't know. We're hoping he got away somehow. He's very resourceful.'

'He sounds it.'

Maggie gave a little shiver and murmured pleadingly, 'You're not going to tell the authorities, are you?'

'Of course not, but listen Maggie, you'll have to make some decisions. The Nationalists will make a strike for Madrid again very soon. The city's already under siege. If Franco tightens his hold on the outskirts, nothing will get through: There will be no food, no medical supplies, no petrol. There'll be a shortage of everything.'

'Food's already scarce,' said Maggie.

'You haven't experienced anything yet. I would advise both you and Rosario to get out of Madrid before it's too late.'

'Are *you* leaving?' asked Maggie with a touch of defiance.

'My stay here is only temporary. Once my assignment is finished, we'll probably close the Library and leave.'

Maggie was dismayed. Despite having witnessed fighting at first hand, she couldn't believe that Madrid would be taken. Most of the time, everything seemed perfectly normal. It was true that there were shortages: queues for bread, rationing of milk. Their daily diet was monotonous but so far they had got by. But what if the British Library no longer needed her services? The call for private English lessons had fallen off recently and she had begun to rely on her income from translating.

Harry noticed her lapse into silence. 'Don't worry,' he said. 'They allow foreigners to travel and I'm sure we could find a way to help Rosario.' He ran a hand through his hair, making it stand up in a quiff. 'But those children will have to go into a home. They wouldn't be allowed out.'

'I can't leave them behind,' burst out Maggie, while Rosario moved closer to her, also looking alarmed.

Harry rose to his feet. 'I can see I've shocked you. Think about what I said and don't forget what happened in other cities Franco took.' At the door, he turned. 'I'll see you at the British Library tomorrow, Maggie.'

Letting himself out, he left the two women looking after him in stunned silence.

Following a restless night, Maggie woke up to find the children already breakfasted and dressed. After Eva and Fabio's initial timidity, the sister and brother were opening up. Although Fabio still didn't speak, he would shriek loudly and stamp his feet, pretending to be a soldier. Donato too was lively. Having learnt to walk, he toddled after the other children, waving his chubby arms and gurgling happily. Ángel had not changed. He was as surly as ever and Maggie was obliged to keep a wary eye on him.

Rosario joined her in the living room. 'The children need new clothes,' she said. 'Donato has grown out of everything and Fabio's trousers are almost threadbare.'

'I'll give you some more money once the Library have paid me for this latest translating job,' replied Maggie.

For once, Rosario displayed her temper. 'That isn't the point. Where am I going to buy new clothes? Money's only part of the problem.' She lowered her voice. 'Maybe Señor Fforbes was right, maybe we ought to get out of Madrid.'

Maggie cast her a glance, seeing what a strain the young girl was under. She wished Tomás would return. She couldn't bring herself to believe that the big man was still under arrest, or worse, dead. She had begun to realise how much she had come to rely on him.

'Raul might be able to pick up some clothes for them,' she said, but she knew she was clutching at straws.

'And when do you think he'll get here?' demanded Rosario.

'I...I don't know.'

Rosario stomped out of the room, leaving Maggie feeling helpless. She took the mug of coffee Rosario had made for her and shut herself away in the study in order to concentrate on the translation work. The work puzzled her. It was not what she had been used to and she wanted to ask Harry about it. She had mixed feelings about seeing him again. The previous evening had been an embarrassment, the outcome totally unexpected, and she now regretted having confided in him.

In the afternoon, she went to the Library where he greeted her formally. 'This way, Miss Morán, I've got everything ready for you.' Once they were out of earshot of the librarian, he asked, 'How are you today?'

'Fine thank you.'

'Fully recovered?'

She stiffened. 'Of course. Shall we get to work?'

Picking up on her restraint, he played along and settled down to his explanations without making any further personal remarks. When they'd finished, they shook hands at the door with Harry sounding very official as he told her not to hesitate to contact him if she had any problems with the translation work. 'Do you need a lift home?' he asked. 'I can easily purloin one of the official pool cars. There's one parked across the road.'

'No thank you, I've got some errands to do en route.' As she was about to walk away, she turned and said, 'Your Spanish is almost as fluent as mine, why do you need a translator?'

With a smile he replied, 'You flatter me. I'm not nearly as good as you are. Besides, you've got the responsibility of all those children, so why ask such a question? You need the extra money, don't you?'

Taken aback, Maggie blinked. 'Are you giving me the work out of charity?'

He gave a brusque laugh, and taking her arm, drew her back into the doorway. 'Don't be absurd. I gave you this work because you're an excellent translator.'

Maggie gulped back her embarrassment. Why was she being so touchy with him? She shook off his hand. 'I must go. I'll get the work done as soon as I can and I'll let you know when it's finished.'

As she left the building she realised how tired she was. Poor diet and overwork were taking their toll. It was only when she started walking that she appreciated how heavy her bag was. The folder containing the paperwork Harry had given her was bulky and kept slipping from under her arm. Buses didn't run in the direction of home and she wished now she had accepted Harry's offer of a lift. But it was too late. When she looked back, he had already disappeared from the lobby.

There were a lot of people about, everyone hurrying in different directions intent on reaching their destination. She pushed past mothers with prams and youngsters on bicycles. There were queues outside most of the food shops, reminding her that they too were low on basic supplies. Rosario had mentioned they were nearly out of flour and potatoes. That meant a tedious shopping trek, waiting at queue after queue for several hours. This task fell to the teenager because she, herself, couldn't spare time from her translation work. No wonder Rosario was short-tempered these days. With a shudder of guilt, Maggie admitted to herself that she had been selfish to load such heavy responsibility onto young shoulders.

Trying to keep tabs on Ángel was proving difficult. The boy would vanish from the apartment for hours at a time, returning late in the afternoon looking pleased with himself. When Maggie asked him where he had been, he would shrug and say, 'out and about.' But she guessed he was pilfering and on more than one occasion she had smelled cigarette smoke on his clothing. She knew she ought to challenge him but with so many other problems taking up her time, she chose to ignore it. Then, one day, he rushed into the apartment, shouting, 'Where are the keys to the truck?'

Maggie clapped a hand to her mouth. 'Oh God! I forgot all about the truck.'

'I've found somewhere to keep it,' said Ángel triumphantly.

'What d'you mean?'

He frowned at her impatiently. 'The truck! You can't leave it where it is. Either someone will make off with it or the police will cart it away.'

This possibility hadn't occurred to Maggie and she realised that Ángel was clearly more streetwise than she was.

'What d'you mean, you've found somewhere to keep it? We can't afford to pay for garage space.'

He tapped the side of his nose. 'Trust me. Come on, I'll show you.'

He ran off, urging her to follow, looking annoyed when she failed to keep up with him. He led her to an abandoned house closed in behind a wrought-iron gate. Stopping in front of the gate, he pointed at a single storey building adjacent to the house. 'There you are!' Enthusiasm lit up his eyes. 'It's perfect; no one will be able to see it.'

'That would be trespassing.'

He looked exasperated. 'Who cares? You want to hold on to the truck, don't you? It might come in useful one day.' He ran ahead of her and rattled the gate. 'Look, there's no one living here. The house has probably been condemned.'

Maggie ran a hand through her hair while she tried to think properly. The roof of the house had caved in, bricks from a chimney stack littered the lawn, the ground floor windows were boarded up. Ángel was right, the house was more than likely scheduled for demolition, and the work had probably been put on hold for the time being.

'Is that outbuilding safe?' she muttered under her breath.

Ángel grinned. 'Safe as houses.' Then he laughed loudly at his own pun, showing a side she hadn't seen before. 'Come on,' he insisted. 'I'll open the gate for you.'

Before she could stop him he had shinned over the top of the gate and opened it from the other side. Casting a furtive glance over her shoulder, Maggie joined him. Ángel raced ahead of her up to the sturdily built outbuilding, wedging open the double wooden doors to reveal a large empty space, clearly adequate enough for the truck. It seemed too good to be true.

'What d'you think?' he asked, his brow furrowed in hopeful enquiry.

Maggie bit her lip. 'Well…'

'Come on,' he said. 'Let's go and get the truck now.'

Maggie summed up the advantages, and all at once, the disadvantages disappeared. What had she got to lose? The truck wasn't hers anyway.

'All right,' she said, casting aside her remaining misgivings.

Maggie and Ángel arrived home after moving the truck to find that Harry had arrived with more work for her. He was squatting on the floor playing with Eva and Fabio, and it seemed he was a natural with children. She felt touched to see the kindness with which he treated them.

269

She was surprised, too, to find that he had brought presents: a doll for Eva, a toy engine for Fabio and a teddy bear for Donato. She wondered where he had found such luxuries.

'*Buenos días!*' he said, getting to his feet.

His greeting was formal but the smile in his eyes was not, and Maggie knew it was up to her to set the *modus operandi* in place. The way they addressed one another from now on would be enduring.

She smiled. 'Hello Harry.'

'Hello Maggie.'

At that moment, Ángel scurried into the bedroom but Harry called him back. 'Here, I've brought you a book,' he said.

'I can't read English.'

'It's in Spanish.'

'Oh.' Begrudgingly, Ángel snatched the book from Harry's hand, saying, 'I don't read much.'

'It's more of a comic book,' said Harry. 'Lot's of pictures.'

At this, Ángel's eyes lit up and he ran back into the bedroom, clutching the book.

'Well,' said Maggie, once the bedroom door had shut. 'You seem to have hit the right note there! By the way, was my translation satisfactory?'

'Yes thank you. but I'd like to talk to you privately, Maggie. Is there somewhere we could go.'

'There's my study, but it's a bit of a squash.'

'Lead on,' he said. 'I'm sure we'll both fit in.'

She felt embarrassed taking him into the cramped room with its over-sized mahogany desk, its piles of books and files and the trundle bed under the window. 'I haven't tidied up for ages,' she apologised. 'Please take a seat where you can find space.'

When he took the only chair, she went to close the door, returning to sit down on the edge of the bed, her hands folded in her lap. 'What was wrong with the translation?' she demanded.

'Nothing.'

'Then why do you need to speak to me privately?'

'I have a proposal for you?' Maggie flinched. This sounded ominous. He went on, 'I haven't been entirely truthful with you. The Foreign Office sent me over here to do some undercover research. With fascism rampant in a large part of Western Europe and communism threatening from the East, the British Government need inside information…'

Maggie's eyes widened. 'You're a spy!'

He looked amused. 'I wouldn't put it quite like that.'

'Then how would you put it?'

'I'm an under-cover agent, ferreting out useful information, that's all.'

Maggie suppressed a smile. 'I'd call that spying.'

'Call it what you like, but to the world in general I'm a librarian.'

'And how do you convey the information back to your bosses in London?'

'Through the diplomatic bag of course.'

'Why are you telling me all this?'

'Because, Maggie, I need your help.'

She threw back her head and laughed. 'How can I possibly help you?'

'You can, more than you realise.'

Maggie couldn't believe he was serious. Surely he was playing an elaborate joke on her.

'Look, Harry,' she said, rather more haughtily than she intended, 'Let's stop this nonsense. You go off and play your silly little spy games and I'll continue making the occasional translation for you.'

Harry's expression changed. His eyes grew hard and his mouth tightened. 'This isn't a game, Maggie. I…we really do need your help. You're in the perfect position to listen out for information and feed it back to me and, what's more to the point, you're in the perfect position to tackle the transcriptions.'

'What d'you mean?'

'Encoding.'

'What?'

'Encoding, it's not difficult. You'd have to sign the Official Secrets Act, of course.'

From the other room, a shriek rang out from Fabio. Maggie recognised his unique means of expressing himself and hoped he wasn't being too rough with Donato. She heard Rosario call out to him when the baby started crying.

'I ought to go and see what's going on,' she said, getting to her feet.

'Sit down, Maggie, Rosario is perfectly capable of handling the children.'

His firm tone prompted her to obey. She sat down again and waited for him to speak.

'Listen carefully. I propose to continue giving you translation work, but in with it, there'll be the occasional encoding job. You'll have to keep it from the others. No one must know what you're doing. I imagine this will be quite easy since Rosario is busy with the children and they wouldn't be interested anyway. You'll be well compensated for your work and protected should things flare up here in Madrid.' He leant towards her. 'Maggie, I'm giving you the chance to get out of Madrid when the time comes without the hassle you had to get here in the first place.'

'Suppose I don't want to leave Madrid?'

'You will when the street fighting starts, when both sides begin firing indiscriminately…'

Maggie's mind was in a whirl. 'Stop it,' she broke in. 'I don't want to hear any more. Before you go any further, the answer's 'no'.'

Harry drew back and rubbed his hands together. 'I see. Well, in that case, this conversation never took place, but if you have a change of heart you know where to find me.' He stood up. 'You ought to think about the children, Maggie.'

'I am thinking about them,' she said, also getting to her feet.

'Despite your refusal to help, I'm relying on you not to mention our conversation to anybody.'

'You can be sure of that,' she replied acidly.

They went back into the other room, and after saying goodbye to the children, Harry took his leave. Maggie saw him to the door, closing it firmly behind him and pressing her back against it. What was he up to? She wished fervently that she had never set eyes on him.

'What was that all about?' asked Rosario when she went back to join the others.

'Oh, just some special translation work he wants me to do but I refused it.'

'Why?'

'It was a bit technical. I'm not up to that.'

'Are you sure? You really shouldn't turn down money.'

'I'm the wage-earner here,' snapped Maggie. 'It's up to me to decide what I can or can't do.'

'Sorry,' murmured Rosario, turning away looking hurt.

Despite her days being fully occupied, Maggie's thoughts often drifted to the two people she cared for most. It was now April and there was no word from her brother. She deliberately closed her mind to what could happen to him. She had come to Spain to seek him out only to find a changed twin, a man who called himself Esteban, who lived recklessly with a woman who looked like a gypsy.

Raul had kept in touch although it was several weeks since she had seen him. He sent her news from the front

273

but, as time passed, she began to wonder whether the wonderful lovemaking episodes they had shared had been a figment of her imagination. Why didn't he take time off to visit her? Had he found himself a girlfriend at the hospital? There were plenty of pretty nurses to choose from.

Then, at the beginning of May, he turned up. He greeted her as if no time had passed, folding her in his arms in a warm hug. Rosario seemed pleased to see him, blushing under his flattering remarks about her hair; she had recently had it cut. The children were a little shy at first but Ángel took to him at once, clearly impressed at meeting someone who was frequently at the front line.

'How long can you stay?' asked Maggie.

'Only two days.' He grinned at her. 'I need pampering, someone to hold my hand and comfort me. It's been a difficult couple of months.'

'I dare say I can manage that.' She searched his face. 'Any news of my brother?'

Raul shook his head. 'His squad moved north-east and we lost all contact with them. I'm surprised he hasn't tried to reach you. He's got your address, hasn't he?'

She brushed off Raul's comment. 'He's too busy fighting the cause.' Secretly she was more worried than ever. Going north-east meant going into a troubled area.

'Tomás is back,' said Raul. 'The prison changed hands again and he got away. I expect you'll see something of him soon.'

Rosario looked relieved. 'I like him,' she said. 'I'm so glad he escaped.'

'What about your Italian friend?'

Rosario's face clouded. 'Palmiro? I haven't heard anything from him for ages.'

Maggie cast her a glance, feeling sorry for her. She wished she had more patience; sometimes these days the

274

daily struggle made her speak to the young girl more sharply than she meant to.

The two days flew past. Raul rested for most of the time although he did allow Ángel to take him to the lock-up to see the truck. When they came back, Maggie said, 'I feel terrible trespassing like that, and the truck isn't even ours. How dreadful that poor Arnaldo died so horribly.'

'He must have died immediately the bullet hit him,' said Raul. 'And I've no doubt he would be pleased to know that his truck is being put to good use. However, I think you should paint over his name on the side of it. Ángel could do that for you.'

'Oh yeah,' said Ángel eagerly.

Raul talked to the boy quite a lot, describing things that Maggie thought unsuitable for a twelve-year-old to know, but she soon realised that Ángel was probably more worldly-wise than she herself was.

At night, she and Raul shared the trundle bed, a bit of a squash, leaving her exhausted the next morning when she was obliged to get up and work while Raul slept on. He left in the evening of the second day. Maggie went out into the hallway with him, where he gave her a lingering kiss. She watched him lope down the stairs, stopping at the bottom to give her a final wave.

Returning to the apartment, she shut herself away in the study, needing time on her own to think. Somehow their lovemaking had not felt the same this time, and instinctively she knew it was she who had changed, not Raul. Sitting on the bed in the gathering darkness, she saw for the first time, that a metamorphosis had taken place. Her brother's disappearance into the battle zone without a word had sealed his separation from her. A wild and beautiful gypsy woman had stolen Robert away, changing his name and eroding his sibling loyalty. He wasn't interested in his timid sister nagging him to leave the country he loved.

275

As for Raul, wonderful though meeting him had seemed, he was in truth merely the link to her twin and since this link was no longer necessary, he was no longer important to her. Besides, she was convinced that Raul had never been serious about their relationship. She felt sure he was sleeping with other women. There were nurses at the hospital who would be willing; she had seen the way they looked at him. She frowned, realising with surprise that she didn't mind, and decided that next time she saw him she would tell him it was over between them.

Then there was Harry and, not for the first time, she wished she hadn't become involved with him. Before meeting him her emotions had been steady, now she didn't know where she stood.

Her conscience stabbed her. It had been Raul who had made it possible to see her brother, it had been Raul who had provided her and the children with a decent place to live. No doubt, he was under the impression that nothing had changed between them. How could she refuse him? Clenching her fists she realised that a sacrifice had to be made. She was indebted to Raul and she ought to honour her debt even if it meant soliciting herself in lieu of rent. What choice did she have?

She stood up and straightened her shoulders. The men in her life meant nothing. The important thing was her responsibility towards the children. From now on, she would look out only for them. Rosario was right. They needed money and she had the means to get it. Tomorrow, she would go and see Harry Fforbes. She would take advantage of any opportunity that came her way.

CHAPTER TWENTY

The next morning, Maggie telephoned Harry to make an appointment to see him. He suggested 'El Bar de los Marineros' and seemed pleased about her call.

'This afternoon at four o'clock,' she suggested, and he agreed.

They ordered coffees and chose a table in a quiet corner. The waiter remembered her from their previous visit. 'Are you feeling better, *señorita?*' he asked.

'Yes thank you.' She blushed, recalling the occasion. Since then, apart from feeling tired, she had felt fine.

'Have you changed your mind?' asked Harry without preamble.

'Maybe, but I need to know more about the project before I commit myself.'

'That's understandable, fire away!'

She glanced furtively over her shoulder. The other tables were unoccupied, the barman was busy polishing glasses, the owner was seated at the rear of the bar, his head bowed over what looked to be a bookkeeping ledger.

'Is it safe to talk here?' she muttered, half covering her mouth with her hand.

Harry raised an amused eyebrow, and she stared back at him through narrowed eyes finding it impossible to believe that he was involved in an undercover operation. He looked so ordinary, so respectably English. During her years at the London language college in Holborn she had observed endless young men dressed exactly like him, all going about their nine-to-five jobs.

Still speaking quietly, Maggie said, 'How dangerous is it going to be?'

'It's not dangerous at all.'

'It must be if it's undercover.'

Harry leant back in his chair and stretched out his legs, clasping his hands behind his head. 'Well, I suppose there's an element of risk but nothing to speak of. And it's very well paid.' He mumbled a sum that astonished her but she tried not to show her surprise.

'What would you expect me to do?'

He dragged back his legs and rested his elbows on the table, leaning forward so that their foreheads were almost touching. 'Listen to people talking, in queues, in shops, anywhere public. Are you a churchgoer?'

Surprised, Maggie shook her head. 'Not really. We were brought up as Catholics and our grandparents made us attend Sunday Mass, but our parents weren't very religious. When we got older, it was left up to us.'

Harry reached for her hand. 'I want you to start going to Mass again.'

'Rosario goes every Sunday, and sometimes during the week.'

'Then go with her. Mingle with other women, chat to them if possible.'

'That's easier said than done.'

'Why?'

'We can't both go, and leave the children.'

'Perhaps I can help out.'

'How?'

'I could keep an eye on them for an hour on Sunday morning.'

Maggie found it difficult to suppress a smile. 'You don't know what you'd be letting yourself in for.'

He laughed. 'I'm willing to take a chance.'

She became serious. 'Why can't you go to church yourself and listen out for what people have to say?'

Harry raised an eyebrow. 'Do you really think people will open up to me, a typical blond-haired Englishman? You, Maggie, on the other hand, look more Spanish than English and you have a Madrileno accent. Besides which, I'm not a Catholic.'

'I never thought of that.' She hesitated, then said, 'Harry, you spoke about helping us escape from the city if things flare up. Does this include the children?'

'If you were forced to leave Madrid I'd make sure they went to a good orphanage…'

'What?' Maggie pushed back her chair and got to her feet. 'Forget it. If you want my help you must be prepared to save all of us.'

She picked up her bag and went to the door. Harry fumbled in his pocket for pesetas to pay for their coffees, then rushed after her.

'Maggie, wait!'

He caught up with her at the edge of the kerb, and grasped her arms, swivelling her round to face him. She tried to wriggle out of his clasp and snapped, 'Let go!'

But a bus swept past them and he only just managed to pull her clear. She looked at him with startled eyes as her cheek brushed his. She could smell Imperial Leather soap, a make she recognised from her brother using it during his student days. The incident reminded her of England and, fleetingly, made her feel homesick.

'Are you all right?'

She nodded.

'I'm sorry,' he said. 'It's just that I can't give you any guarantees about the safety of the others. They're all Spanish citizens; their fate is out of my hands. But listen, Maggie, I promise if things come to a head, I'll do what I can to help them. I give you my word.'

279

She stared up at him, not knowing whether to believe him. He sounded sincere but trusting people was becoming more and more difficult these days. He was, after all, a Foreign Office official bound by government red tape.

'How do I know you're telling the truth? You could be saying that just to gain my trust.'

People were jostling them while the afternoon traffic trundled past. The sound of planes roared low overhead. Instinctively, the milling crowds looked up and with one accord, dived for cover.

Harry grabbed Maggie's hand, and with their heads bowed low, they dashed back into the bar and out the back to where the owner and waiter were taking cover in a makeshift shelter.

It was a short-lived air-raid - the first for many weeks - and it served to rattle the Madrileños out of complacency. When it was over, Harry thanked the owner for letting them share his shelter and they left the bar.

'I didn't expect that,' said Maggie. 'I must get home and check on the others.'

'I don't think they caused a lot of damage this time.' Harry was clearly trying to be reassuring. 'Come on, let's get you home.'

They arrived at the apartment to find Rosario looking frightened. 'Are you all right?' she asked them. 'Did you take shelter? I didn't even have time to get the children downstairs. God, I hope this isn't the start of another spate of raids.'

Harry seemed very serious. 'I must go,' he said to Maggie. 'Have you made a decision?'

She nodded, 'I'll do it. When do I sign on the dotted line?' Even a vague promise of help was better than none.

I'm a spy, thought Maggie as she lay in bed trying to sleep. *I've been recruited as a spy*. The thought both shocked and amused her. What would her grandparents have thought? She peered into the darkness trying to imagine their reaction, and that of her mother. Sleep claimed her at last but she woke up in the morning feeling sick with worry. It had been the raid that had decided her and Harry's promise to help the children, although in the cold light of day, she couldn't see how he could possibly help them if it came to the crunch. Perhaps the raids would ease and things would settle down again.

She threw back the covers but as soon as she put her feet to the ground, a wave of nausea swept over her. She just made it to the bathroom, and gasping for air, leant against the washbasin unable to believe that the problems besetting her had eventually taken their toll.

'Maggie!' called Rosario. 'Hurry up your coffee's getting cold.'

Coffee? Maggie wrinkled her nose in disgust. Tea was what she craved. She resolved to try and find a shop that sold it, even if it meant going through the black market.

'Coming,' she called, and after a hasty check in the mirror, she left the bathroom to join the others in the kitchen.

'You look awfully pale,' observed Rosario, looking up from the table where she was seated trying to encourage a spoonful of mash into Donato's tightly pressed lips. She clucked in exasperation. 'He doesn't like this.'

Maggie pulled a face. 'Neither would you. Perhaps he's ready for something more solid. After all, he's got several teeth coming through and he needs to chomp on them.'

'You're probably right,' agreed Rosario, putting the spoon down.

'Try him with a piece of toast.'

Maggie sat down at the table and looked at the oat cake Rosario had placed in front of her. She felt her stomach turn over and pushed the plate aside. 'I'm sorry, I can't eat this morning, Rosario.'

'You must keep your strength up,' chided Rosario, taking both the plate and Maggie's coffee cup away. 'This coffee's gone cold, I'll reheat it for you.'

'Don't bother,' replied Maggie. 'I really can't face it.'

She got up and poured herself a glass of water, letting the tap run for several minutes to clear the stream. Some days the tap water was not very appetising.

'Would you mind if I leave the children with you while I go shopping?' asked Rosario. 'Only they seem happy enough, chasing one another around the living room. I don't think they'll disturb you while you work.'

Maggie nodded. She didn't feel like working but knew that Harry was eager to receive the next section of translation. Next time she saw him, he would explain about the encoding. The night before the notion of 'spying' had seemed amusing, but in the light of day, it seemed rather frightening. Taking the glass of water with her, she shut herself away in the study and settled down to work.

Contrary to Rosario's assurance that the children would play happily, Fabio started screaming. On investigation, it transpired that he didn't want to play with Eva, and Ángel, bored with playing with children much younger than he was, made things worse by taunting the pair of them. Maggie gave up trying to work and went to act as peacemaker, sitting on the sofa between Eva and Fabio to read them a story.

'I'm going out,' Ángel announced.

'Where are you going?'

'Just out.' With these words, he disappeared from the apartment before Maggie could stop him. She sometimes wondered what had induced her to allow him to stay. Apart from the rare occasions when he came up with something helpful, he had caused no end of chaos in their lives.

She heard him sprint down the stairs, swinging on the wobbly newel post at the bottom. She didn't trust him and every time he left the apartment she half expected a call from the police.

As soon as Rosario came back, she told her she would go and lie down on the bed. 'I'm still feeling a bit nauseous,' she said.

'I expect you've picked up a bug,' sympathised Rosario.

'Let's hope I don't pass it on,' replied Maggie, shutting the door and flopping down on top of the coverlet.

She woke up an hour later, surprised to find that everybody had gone out. Although it was only May, the temperature had shot up and even with the windows wide open, the apartment felt stuffy. She made herself a weak coffee but couldn't drink it. Dragging herself into the study, she set to work on the latest translation, finding it difficult to concentrate.

Two days later she was still feeling unwell. Rosario began to worry. 'You ought to see a doctor, Maggie.'

Maggie shook her head. 'It will pass. I'm overtired, that's all.'

Harry called in looking somewhat annoyed. He had expected her to finish the translation more quickly, but when he saw her pale face and lacklustre eyes, he too expressed concern.

'Perhaps I'd better not give you any more work until you're feeling better. Are you worried about our arrangement?' He had to choose his words carefully with Rosario present, even though her English wasn't very good.

Maggie stiffened. 'Of course not. I said I'd do it so I will. Don't worry, I'll be all right in a day or two.'

In fact, the next day, apart from feeling slightly unsteady first thing, Maggie felt much better and this time, she didn't refuse Rosario's offer of coffee and a croissant.

'I must get on with Harry's work this morning,' she said, brushing crumbs from her lips.

She took the work to the British Library that afternoon. Harry was waiting for her.

'Are you feeling better?' he asked.

'Much better,' she replied. 'I must have picked up a bug. Thank goodness the others didn't catch it.'

He led her to a private office and spent a couple of hours explaining the role she would play in the undercover operation. Learning the encoding was a bit complicated but she felt sure she would master it.

'Take your time doing the first assignments,' Harry advised. 'You'll soon get used to it.'

Harry was right. By the end of the week, Maggie had mastered the encoding. The faster she got, the more she saw of Harry, and much to her surprise, this began to please her. She found they shared many interests, enjoyed the same books, the same music and laughed at the same things. Raul had not put in an appearance for a few weeks and she was relieved, although she had to remind herself not to forget that the comfortable accommodation they were living in was down to Raul and that he could turf them out if things went wrong.

Another worry niggled at her. She had noticed a slight increase in weight, putting this down to the better food they were able to afford with her increased earnings. However, as time went on, she began to suspect that she was pregnant. Once the idea took hold, it wouldn't go away. She brooded for days, withdrawing from the others, causing Rosario to puzzle over her change of mood. At night, she lay awake staring into the darkness, desperate to find a solution to her dilemma, certain now, that she was expecting. This made a visit to Tres Lomas to see Raul imperative. He would know what to do. She gulped in dismay. Would he suggest marriage? That would tie her to him forever, just when she had decided he was not the man for her. This possibility plunged her into even more of a panic. She had fallen for him so completely to start with, so how could she have fallen out of love so rapidly? Screwing the cotton sheet up in her hands, she pressed her fists to her mouth to stem the sobs that threatened to become hysterical.

Trying to think rationally, she told herself that, with the present state of affairs in Spain, Raul would no more want marriage and a child than she did. He was studying to be a doctor, wasn't he? He wouldn't want to jeopardize his career. Of course, he might turn her away, deny the child was his. She sucked in her breath. Maybe he would suggest an abortion. The prospect was terrifying. She had heard about the dangers of back-street abortions, quite apart from the fact that these were illegal. On the other hand, if anyone knew where she could terminate her pregnancy safely, it was Raul.

Opportunely, Tomás came back. He burst into the apartment, gregarious as ever. The two women were delighted to see him.

'You must tell us all your news,' said Rosario, hugging him. 'Raul said you'd been sent to Montjuic. How did you get away?'

Tomás let out a roar of laughter. 'The castle had a change of ownership.'

'You seem none the worse for your imprisonment,' said Rosario.

Maggie couldn't agree with her. She had noticed an angry scar on the side of the big man's face close to the hairline, a scar that hadn't been there before. 'Come and sit down, Tomás,' she said. 'I'll cook you a nice meal tonight and we'll open that bottle of Cava we've been saving for a special occasion.'

He sat down, slapping his large hands on his knees, clearly pleased to be given such a welcome.

'You're not cross with me anymore, are you?' asked Maggie. 'I'm really sorry I put you to so much trouble.'

He waved aside her apology. 'Did you meet up with your brother?'

'Yes.'

Something about the way she replied must have alerted him. 'It didn't go too well then?'

Maggie rushed to reassure him. 'Yes, it was fine, just different to what I expected.'

He shook his leonine head. 'I *did* warn you.'

'I know,' she said.

They had a jolly evening, with Tomás amusing the children, surprised to be introduced to Ángel. When Maggie was able to speak to him in private, she explained how he had helped her escape from Tres Lomas during the raid.

'He's a street urchin, *mujer*, you'll have to watch him.'

'I know. But he does come in useful sometimes. He's very resourceful.'

Tomás frowned. 'Be careful, you may wake up one morning to find half the furniture gone.'

Maggie gave a giggle. 'He wouldn't go that far.'

Feeling encouraged by Tomás' friendliness, she said, 'Are you going back to Tres Lomas soon?'

'Why do you ask?'

'I need to see Raul.'

His eyes twinkled. 'Be patient, he'll come and see you again.'

Maggie blushed. 'No, it's not like that. I just need to speak to him.'

'Surely it can wait.'

Maggie's jaw tightened. 'It can't.'

286

Tomás gave her a scrutinising look, then said, 'I'm going in a couple of weeks but I don't know when I'll be coming back. You could find yourself stranded there and you can't leave Rosario with all these children to look after.' He took her hand. 'Maggie, it just wouldn't be fair.'

She lowered her gaze, feeling both ashamed and intimidated.

Tomás' hand tightened around hers. 'What is it *nena*?'

His sympathy was too much for her. Before she could stop herself, she burst into tears. Tomás intuitiveness astounded her. 'You're carrying Raul's child.'

Fumbling for a handkerchief, she sobbed into it, mumbling, 'How did you guess?'

Tomás sighed. 'I've seen it all before,' he said. 'What do you intend to do once you speak to Raul?'

Maggie gave a sniff and looked up. 'I'm going to ask him to arrange for me to have an abortion,' she admitted.

'An abortion, eh? What makes you think he'll agree?'

Maggie looked startled. 'Why shouldn't he? After all, it's in his best interest. He won't want the responsibility of fatherhood, will he?'

'Maybe not, but perhaps you don't know…'

'Know what?'

'Raul trained for the priesthood before studying medicine.'

'And so?'

'He's a strict Catholic. He won't agree to an abortion.'

'How can you be so sure?'

'Believe me, I'm sure.'

Tears welled in Maggie's eyes as she choked back a sob. Pressing a knuckled fist to her mouth, she mumbled, 'What can I do? I can't possibly have a baby, not now, not in this situation.'

'Does Rosario know?'

'No one knows.'

287

Tomás got to his feet. 'I've got to go. Things to do before I leave for Tres Lomas. Don't worry, *mujer*, we'll sort this out.'

'How?'

'Have faith and patience. I'll be in touch, meanwhile don't do anything stupid, promise?'

'What have you got in mind?'

'Wait and see.'

With those words, he strode to the door and left the apartment.

Maggie felt confused. Was Tomás offering to help her or not? How could he be certain that Raul would refuse to agree to an abortion? She thought long and hard, trying to look at the situation from Raul's point of view. She was sure he wasn't in love with her so there was no reason why he wouldn't let her take the easy way out? Thinking too much gave her a headache, and she eventually came to the conclusion that Tomás was trying to put her off because he didn't like Raul very much. But why?

Rosario interrupted her train of thought. 'Where's Tomás?' she asked.

Maggie shrugged. 'He left rather hurriedly.'

Rosario looked offended. 'But he didn't even say goodbye.'

Maggie improvised. 'He meant to but time caught up with him and he had to leave.'

'When is he coming back?'

'He didn't say.'

The next few days seemed endless to Maggie. Her emotions were in turmoil as she went about her daily tasks, responding mechanically when people spoke to her. At night she agonised over her decision to have an abortion. Her grandparents would have been horrified, even her mother would have disapproved. Perhaps she should consult Raul, accept his opinion, take responsibility for her reckless actions. After all, he would surely feel obliged to help support the child. But a baby of her own would trap her even more. Over the past couple of months she had been hit by the impact of what she had taken on. Clearly, it wasn't safe to stay in Spain. She needed to take the children back to England in order to give them a better life. Why, there was a big empty house on Stanmore Common waiting to be filled with children's chatter and laughter! These thoughts had been unformed until now. Pregnancy had brought to a head the practicalities of her responsibility towards the four children - yes, she even included Ángel in this equation - and it weighed heavily on her.

After two more weeks, Maggie began to panic. She had cleverly hidden her condition from Rosario although the girl had given her one or two strange looks, remarking one day that she seemed to be gaining weight.

'Too much starchy food,' laughed Maggie.

But her main worry was that soon it would be too late for an abortion. She didn't know much about these things but while working at the translation agency she had overheard a conversation between two of her colleagues and had gleaned that there was a fairly early time-limit.

Then Tomás turned up again. Rosario scolded him for leaving without saying goodbye but he was swiftly able to counter her admonitions with his usual gruff charm. He called Maggie to one side.

'I've made all the arrangements,' he said.

Maggie's eyebrows shot up. 'You're taking me to Tres Lomas?'

'No, I've arranged to get you an abortion here in Madrid. Tomorrow suit you?'

Maggie clapped her hands to her face. 'Tomorrow?'

'Otherwise you'll have to wait another week.'

She began to panic. 'Is it safe? I mean, it will be hygienic, won't it?' She had heard rumours of backstreet abortion clinics in big cities, and Madrid was effectively a war zone.

He put his big hand on her shoulder. 'Don't worry, *mujer*.'

The following day, she made up an excuse, telling Rosario that she had to go to the British Library to see Harry, going instead to meet Tomás at a café on the other side of town.

Her legs were trembling as she went into the café. Tomás was sitting by the bar, a beer in front of him. She prayed that he wasn't drunk. Tomás in a boisterous intoxicated mood would be the last straw. She had brought money with her - thank God for that extra stipend Harry was now paying her! Rosario had no idea how much better off they were these days.

On seeing her, Tomás knocked back his drink and got up to greet her. 'so you came, *nena*.'

'Did you think I'd back out?'

'It wouldn't have surprised me.'

She felt irritated. 'Let's get on with it.'

He took her arm and guided her from the café and along the road to a doorway quite close by. 'In here.'

She hesitated momentarily, then allowed herself to be led inside and up a flight of stairs. On reaching a door on the ill-lit landing, she asked, 'It will be all right, won't it?'

Tomás didn't answer. He rapped on the door and they waited for what seemed to be an interminably long time. He rapped again. But Maggie had turned and run back down the stairs. He found her sitting on the bottom step, howling.

CHAPTER TWENTY-ONE

The phone call came in the small hours. Maggie was in such a deep sleep that she didn't even hear it. She was woken by Rosario.

'What's wrong?' she cried, sitting up and rubbing her eyes. 'Is there something the matter with one of the children?'

'No, they're fine. It's Raul. He's on the telephone.'

Why would he ring up in the middle of the night? Maggie leapt out of bed, nearly tripping over the rug. Stumbling into the living room, she snatched up the receiver.

'Maggie, is that you?' Raul sounded uncharacteristically anxious.

'What's wrong? Why ring at this hour?' stuttered Maggie.

'It's about your brother.'

Maggie clutched the telephone receiver until her knuckles shone white. 'Tell me!' Her legs felt weak, her heart raced.

'He's been admitted to hospital.'

So her brother wasn't dead! Panic followed initial relief. 'How bad is it?'

'He's got a nasty leg wound but it's not life-threatening. He wants to see you,' he went on. 'Can you find a way to get here?'

'Of course.' Maggie's mind raced. Her brother wanted to see her. Raul had made no mention of Dolores so perhaps his girlfriend wasn't with him. But how was she going to get there? Then she remembered the truck. If she could get hold of some petrol she could drive through the night. 'Tell him I'll be there as soon as I can,' she gasped.

Then Raul spoilt it. 'It would be so good for him, Maggie, because Dolores has got to report back to the squad. Esteban needs a bit of morale support from a member of the opposite sex.

'Of course he does.' So she wasn't her brother's first choice. He only wanted her because Dolores wouldn't be available to hold his hand. Maggie's emotions swung between anxiety and anger. 'Tell him, I'll come as quickly as I can,' she muttered hoarsely.

'How will you get here? I'd come and collect you myself but I'm needed at the hospital.'

'Don't worry, Raul, I'll find a way.'

As she put the phone down, Rosario worried gaze searched Maggie's face. 'What's happened?' she asked.

'My brother's been wounded. He's in hospital, I've got to go to him.' She clasped Rosario's hands. 'Will you be able to manage on your own for a few days?'

'Of course.'

But Maggie couldn't help feeling concerned. Ángel had been misbehaving recently, disappearing for hours on end, coming back with all sorts of items which he said he had found, but which both women knew he had pilfered. As if conjured up by thought transmission, the boy appeared in the doorway. 'What's going on?' he grunted.

Maggie explained, voicing her concern that Rosario would have to manage on her own.

'But she's not on her own?' he protested. 'I'm here to help her.'

Genuine good intentions showed in his face, and for a moment, Maggie felt a surge of warmth towards him. Her loving feelings for the other children had been spontaneous but she had always had trouble coming to terms with Ángel's rebellious nature. Did he mean what he said? Would he really give Rosario a hand with the younger ones?

She reached out to him. 'Thank you Ángel, Rosario would appreciate that.'

'How are you going to get to Tres Lomas now that Tomás has disappeared again?' asked Rosario.

'I'll take the truck.'

'You can't drive all that way in your condition.'

'Why not? I'm feeling fine now that I'm over the first three months.'

Maggie heaved an inward sigh. How supportive Rosario had been since she had told her about the pregnancy. Things could have been so different had the teenager passed judgement on her and refused to help. At this moment, Rosario looked close to panic. 'Maggie, don't be foolish, you can't go on your own.'

Ángel butted in. 'I'll go with you.'

Maggie smiled. 'You can't be in two places at once; you have to stay here and help out with the little ones.'

He lowered his gaze and muttered, 'Oh yes.' But Maggie could see that he would much prefer to take to the road even though it meant returning to the town he had been so keen to leave.

'I must go and get dressed,' she said, determinedly getting to her feet even though her heart was thumping with trepidation. Half talking to herself, she went on, 'I wonder how much petrol's left in the tank. I hope there's enough to get me to the edge of town; by then there might be a garage open.'

Rosario followed her into the bedroom. They both swivelled around when they heard the front door slam.

'Where's Ángel gone to?' gasped Maggie, looking panicky. 'Oh dear, I really believed he would help you, but he's back to his old disappearing tricks, even in the middle of the night!'

Rosario sighed, 'Never mind, I'll make up some cheese rolls and a flask of coffee while you pack a few clothes.'

'Can we spare the cheese?' asked Maggie.

'Of course we can. I managed to buy some more the other day. Don't you remember?'

Fondly Maggie watched Rosario head for the kitchen before flinging a few necessities into her old suitcase. Picking it up she went to the bedroom door, then second thoughts. Going back, she pulled open the small drawer in the chest and took out the gun Tomás had given her. Wrapping it in a silk scarf - one which her grandmother had given her many years ago - she slipped it into her bag.

'I do wish you weren't going on your own,' lamented Rosario when she joined her in the kitchen.

Maggie tried to reassure her. 'Don't worry, I'll be all right. After all, it's not a long journey and I know the way now.' She looked around. 'Where are the car keys? I'm sure I left them on that shelf.'

The two women stared at one another, realising where Ángel had gone. Maggie snatched up her suitcase and gave Rosario a brief hug. 'I only hope the little idiot hasn't done anything stupid,' she said, her voice cracking.

She had already guessed where Ángel would be. And she was right. He had backed the truck out of the shed and turned it around. She couldn't imagine where or how he had learned to drive. He was busy filling the tank with petrol from a series of receptacles lined up on the path next to the vehicle.

She didn't bother to question him. Now was neither the time nor the place to put him through a cross-examination. Clearly, he had had the foresight to either buy or steal fuel. Had he been planning to make off with the truck, never to be seen again? She pushed this possibility from her mind.

He heard her footsteps crunch on the gravel and looked up from his task. 'All done,' he said with a grin. 'That will get you there and back.'

He looked so ingenuous that she felt a pang of conscience for having doubted him. 'Thank you, Angel.'

He carried the empty cans into the shed and padlocked the door. 'I hope your brother will get better soon,' he said rather shyly, then added hopefully, 'I wish I could come with you.' Seeing her furrow her brows, he went on. 'But don't worry, I'll look after Rosario and the kids, you can rely on me.'

With that he ran down the path and out of the main gate, leaving her staring after him.

It was getting light by the time she reached the outskirts of Madrid. Focusing on driving kept her mind off worrying about her brother, but as she got closer to Tres Lomas, she realised she had an additional worry. How was she going to hide her pregnancy from Raul? At four months, she was beginning to show. She hadn't seen him since February. Would he notice her increased girth? Would he expect her to spend the night with him? No, since she had decided not to involve him, that would be out of the question. Robert's injuries gave her a convenient excuse. She would spend the night either at Robert's bedside or at the Hotel Almeria, pleading that she was too upset to share Raul's bed.

It was late morning by the time she parked the truck in front of the hospital. One of the nurses she had met on previous visits recognised her and ran over to greet her.

'Maggie, I'm so sorry your brother's been brought in. There have been lots of casualties recently. The fighting has really stepped up.'

'*Hola*, Maribel, I can't wait to see Esteban,' said Maggie, using her brother's chosen name. 'Is he recovering well?'

'As well as can be expected.'

Maggie recognised this stock reply. It often hid the truth.

Filled with anxiety, she followed Maribel into the hospital, bumping into Raul in the entrance. He greeted her affectionately and she hoped he would put her hesitation down to anxiety.

'This way,' he said. 'Your brother can't wait to see you.' He wagged a finger at her. 'Be warned, he's in a lot of pain and needs all the rest he can get.'

'I promise not to overtire him,' she said.

Maggie had prepared herself for the worst but it wasn't Robert's injuries that took her aback when she entered the room. Her brother seemed to be asleep although it was impossible to tell because his face was obscured by Dolores' dark head bowed over the bed. When Maggie cleared her throat to signal her presence, Dolores looked up, startled.

'*Hola.*'

'*Buenos díos.*' Maggie returned her greeting.

The hostility between them was palpable. Dolores made no attempt to make room for Maggie. Instead, she turned back and continued stroking Robert's forehead. Raul followed Maggie in, apparently unaware of the antipathy between the women.

She turned and looked up at him. 'You said it was a leg wound, Raul. You should have warned me there were other injuries as well.'

'You mean his arm. It's only superficial. The leg was our main concern, but don't worry, he's on the mend.' He pulled up a chair for Maggie to sit next to the patient.

'I have to get back to work,' said Raul, backing away and disappearing out of the door.

'I didn't think you'd still be here, Dolores,' said Maggie, after he had left.

'I was given extended leave.'

'For how long?'

Dolores pursed her lips in the pretence of a wistful smile and replied, 'I'm not sure. They'll call me when they need me back.'

'Were there other casualties when my brother was wounded?'

'Quite a few, some deaths too. My Esteban was lucky.'

My Esteban! Dolores' choice of words was not lost on Maggie. She felt threatened. How could she compete with this striking beauty? The aroma of her musky perfume wafted across the bed every time she moved. Maggie caught a glance of herself in the mirror over the wash-hand basin and almost shuddered, wishing she had had time to wash her hair and put on some makeup before leaving for Tres Lomas.

Her brother stirred and opened his eyes momentarily. All at once, Maggie felt angry. How dare this gypsy woman steal her twin brother? Robert had asked to see *her*, his sister, hadn't he? Gaining courage, she said, 'Dolores, If you don't mind, I'd like to spend a little time with my brother on his own.'

Dolores' dark eyebrows shot up and Maggie could see that she was about to protest, but Robert came to life. 'Maggie,' he said. 'You made it. Come and give your brother a big kiss.'

Maggie flashed Dolores a triumphant smile before leaning across the bed and planting a sisterly kiss on Robert's cheek. As she regained her seat, he winked at Dolores, saying, 'Leave us for a moment, *mi corazón.*'

297

Without uttering a word, the woman got to her feet and flounced out of the room. Robert laughed. 'Isn't she something?' he said proudly.

She certainly is, thought Maggie. But despite her annoyance, she was relieved to find Robert in such good spirits. Clearly, his injuries hadn't dampened his zest for life.

'How's it been?' she asked in Spanish, the language they had always used between them.

'Pretty bad but Dolores has been wonderful, staying with me during my darkest hour.'

'I would have been here sooner if I could have,' muttered Maggie lamely.

Robert reached out with his good hand and patted hers. 'I know you would.' He changed the subject. 'Well, little sister, when are you leaving for home?'

'What d'you mean?' She pretended to take offence. 'Do you want to get rid of me?'

'I meant when are you going back to England because Spain's a dangerous place these days?'

'Do you think I don't know that?'

'Where are you living?'

'In Raul's friend's apartment in the centre of Madrid. It's very nice and it's in a respectable area. I'm sure you'd approve.' She squeezed his fingers. 'Honestly, Robert, you don't have to worry about me.'

'I prefer to be called Esteban these days,' he said tersely. Then his expression softened. 'About Raul…'

'Yes?' said Maggie, a little too quickly.

'Is there something going on between you two?'

'Certainly not.'

'I'm glad. You know he's got quite a reputation as a womaniser?'

Maggie shrugged off this information. 'So what?'

Her brother went on. 'It's rumoured he got one of the nurses 'knocked up', although I must say he stood by her.

298

Offered to marry her by all accounts, but she would have none of that. She married her childhood sweetheart instead. You have to laugh, the poor chap believes the child is his. Some people are easily taken in.'

Maggie listened to the story with growing alarm. She hated hearing her brother talk like this but, worst of all, she couldn't help wondering what Robert would think if he knew that she, too, had been 'knocked up' by Raul? Indeed, what would Raul say if he knew? Would he offer to marry *her*?

'Come back, Maggie, you seem miles away.'

'Sorry, I got up half way through the night so I'm feeling a bit tired.'

'Where will you stay tonight?'

'Here with you of course.'

He laughed. 'That would make it a bit crowded with Dolores staying. It's her last day. Tomorrow she's going back to camp.'

Maggie received this information with mixed feelings. On the one hand she was angry that Dolores had the privilege of bedside nursing, on the other, tomorrow she would be gone and that meant she would have her brother all to herself.

The duty nurse came in. 'I think that's enough chatting for a while,' she said. 'The patient must rest.'

'Away with you, my sister's come a long way to see me,' jested Robert.

The nurse smiled. 'She can come back later. I've told the other lady to wait outside. You need your rest, Señor Morán, and I'm going to see that you get it.'

Maggie got to her feet. 'You're quite right,' she said. 'I'll go and check in at the Hotel Almeria and come back later.'

'Make it after seven o'clock,' said the nurse.

'Take care, Robert…I mean Esteban,' said Maggie, giving his hand another squeeze.

299

'Ouch!' he gasped. 'That hurt; you should be more careful.'

'That must be the first and only time I've ever caused you pain,' laughed Maggie. 'It serves you right after all the pinches and slaps you've given me over the years.'

Robert looked surprised. 'Did I really hurt you?'

'Not enough to cause visible damage.'

Maggie made her way to the Hotel Almeria. She left the truck in the hospital car park, safe in the conviction that, since Ángel had painted over Arnaldo's name, no one in the town would recognise it. She felt a twinge of guilt. Maybe old Arnaldo had a son or a nephew who could lay claim to it. Did Raul know his family, would he expect her to return it to its rightful owner?

The proprietor of the hotel welcomed her. 'How are you, *Señorita*?' he enquired.

'Very well, thank you,' she replied.

His wife came out to greet her, eyeing her somewhat strangely, giving cause for Maggie to wonder whether her pregnancy had begun to show. In her room, she undressed and flopped onto the bed to sleep solidly for three hours and waking when hunger pangs reminded her that, apart from Rosario's hastily put together sandwiches, she hadn't eaten since the day before. Since the onset of her pregnancy, she had developed a healthy appetite and she knew that nourishment was essential. She got dressed and found a small café which served a limited selection of tapas.

'Wine, *Señorita*?' enquired the waiter.

She shook her head. 'Water will be fine.'

The waiter seemed friendly, engaging her in conversation and describing the loss of life and damage the town had received during the recent bombing. She nodded in commiseration, telling him why she'd come all the way from Madrid..

300

'How are things in Madrid?' he asked.

'We've had a few raids but nothing too serious.'

'Will you be staying in Tres Lomas for long?'

'Only until my brother starts to recover. He was badly wounded, and I can't leave until I'm sure he's going to be all right.'

She glanced at her watch. 'It's time I was going. They said I could visit him after seven.'

'*Buena suerte!*' said the waiter as she left the café. 'I hope your brother makes a full recovery.'

Maggie made her way back to the hospital, hoping Dolores would have departed. She hadn't. She was leaning over the patient, enveloping him in an embrace. The draped sleeves of her flimsy blouse covered his face as she caressed his head with her painted fingernails. Where does she get such fancy clothes, thought Maggie, this is wartime and luxuries are few and far between? The contrast between Dolores in guerrilla kit and Dolores in mufti could not have been more striking.

When Robert emerged from within the depths of Dolores' apparel Maggie could see that he looked a lot better. He had more colour in his cheeks. She wondered whether this was due to his lover's fondling or simply that he was on the mend.

'Dolores has managed to delay her departure for another couple of days,' he announced.

Maggie's heart sank. Two days! That meant she would have to share him. She had planned to stay one more day - a day without Dolores - and then head back to Madrid. She could hardly leave Rosario looking after the children for any longer than that.

'Come here, little sister.'

Although irked by his insistence on addressing her as his 'little sister', Maggie nonetheless obediently approached the bed. Dolores flounced away, glowering as she watched Maggie greet her brother. She gave him an affectionate kiss and squeezed his hand more gently than on the previous occasion. 'You're looking better,' she whispered.

He grinned. 'You and Dolores are the best medicine I could possibly have,' he said. 'How long can you stay?'

'Only until the day after tomorrow. I must get back for the sake of the children.'

'The children?'

'Yes, I'm in charge of some youngsters and I've had to leave them in Rosario's care during my visit. One of them is only a baby.'

Robert raised his head from the pillow, looking bewildered. He gave a groan and sank back, closing his eyes. Then his eyes sprang open. 'You mean those children you told me about when you came to the front line. Who do they belong to?'

'They're orphans, I told you.'

'Why haven't you dispatched them to an orphanage?'

Maggie's hackles began to rise. 'I told you, I can't let them go to an orphanage. I explained all that.'

'I don't remember,' he mumbled.

'That's because you don't listen properly,' replied Maggie.

Dolores tilted her head and said defiantly as if giving an explanation to a child, 'Can't you see, he's got concussion.'

Maggie gave an inward snigger. Concussion indeed! Or could it possibly be her brother's total lack of interest in anything she told him? All at once, she needed to distance herself from this self-absorbed couple. Clearly, she didn't fit in with Robert's new lifestyle. Had she ever fitted in with it? Or had she simply viewed her twin through rose-tinted spectacles?

Dolores was leaning over him again, her face close to his. They seemed to have forgotten her existence. Maggie managed to stifle her anger by leaving the room on the pretext of needing to speak to the doctor in charge.

She found him at last, and after some persuasion, managed to pin him down.

'What are my brother's chances of a full recovery?' she asked.

'Very good. He's in great shape physically and as long as that leg heals he'll be all right. Thankfully, there were no internal injuries.'

'So he's not really in any danger now?'

'Not at all.'

After a few words, the doctor excused himself and left her standing in the corridor. The interview brought Maggie to a decision. Back in Madrid, she was badly needed, here, she was surplus to requirements, a hanger-on. Robert - or Esteban as he now liked to call himself - was bored by her presence. Facing the truth, she realised that he always had been self-absorbed. As for Dolores, she had made it clear that she couldn't wait to see the back of her lover's prim little sister.

Maggie returned to the ward and, speaking in English, told a white lie. 'I've had a message asking me to return to Madrid as soon as possible. I'm afraid I'll have to leave tomorrow morning. I'm sorry, Robert.'

She could see by his expression that he hated being addressed as Robert, particularly as she had spoken in English this time.

Dolores glared angrily at her lover, who quickly translated Maggie's words. Her expression changed and she said sweetly, 'We'll be *so* sorry to see you go, won't we Esteban?`'

'Yes we will, goodbye little sister, keep in touch and let me know when you're leaving Spain.'

Stifling a sob, she left the room, thinking melodramatically, *this is goodbye Robert, hello Esteban*. The Robert of her childhood no longer existed.

CHAPTER TWENTY-TWO

It was while she was pushing her clothes into her suitcase that Maggie remembered the gun. She nearly opened up the case to slide it inside but at the last minute, decided to leave it in her handbag, stowing both the case and the bag in the back of the truck before climbing into the cabin. She drove blindly, with tears in her eyes and was well on her way before she remembered she hadn't said goodbye to Raul. Her parting from Robert had been so stressful that it had driven everything else out of her head. Robert had not seemed concerned that she might leave Spain and that they would not see one another again for a long time.

Once her anger had abated she had spent the night worrying about him and, in a moment of self-analysis, she had been forced to admit to herself that she was jealous of Dolores. In fact, she had always been jealous of her brother's girlfriends even though, in the past, they had been nothing more than passing fancies. But Dolores was different; her influence over Robert was powerful.

The trouble started when she was about ten miles out of Tres Lomas. The engine became overheated and she was forced to stop. She had some water in the back - a precaution Ángel had taken - but she knew she must wait for a good half hour to allow the engine to cool down first. The minutes ticked past until, at last, it was time to fill the radiator tank. As she was finishing the task, the crunch of a footstep on the road startled her.

'Can I be of assistance, *Senorita?*'

Maggie dropped the can and twirled round to come face to face with a Nationalist soldier. He looked unkempt; his uniform was filthy, his boots dust covered.

'It's quite all right, I can manage,' she stuttered, trying not to show her alarm.

'Let me help you,' he insisted.

'No thank you.'

Endeavouring to behave normally, she took a determined step towards the driver's door, but the man snatched at her arm, pulling her close so that their faces were only inches apart. '*Ven aqui, cariño, damme un beso.*'

'Leave me alone!' shouted Maggie, backing away. But he gripped her arm even tighter, pursing his lips and indicating with thumb and forefinger. '*Ni un besito?*'

Maggie began to panic. She glanced around and saw that he was on his own, a deserter by the look of him. Fleetingly, she remembered her meeting with Palmiro, also a deserter. How different that had been. She had trusted Palmiro instinctively. Then she remembered the gun in her bag.

'I need something from the truck,' she stuttered, smiling and pretending to comply.

'Is there room in the back?' he asked in the belief that he had persuaded her.

'Maybe. Just a moment.'

With triumph shining in his eyes, he let her go. Maggie went to the back of the truck and reached for her handbag, pulling out the revolver. Swivelling around, she pointed it at the man. He stared back at her in astonishment, then laughed. 'You're not serious?'

Maggie's heart beat like a drum as she took a step towards him, urging him to back away. She tried to keep her hand steady and wondered whether, if the man tried to overpower her, she would be able to fire the gun.

'All right, all right.' Holding up placating hands, he took another step backwards, almost stumbling on the uneven verge. 'I meant you no harm. I was only joking.'

'I'm not,' snapped Maggie. 'Now get going before I lose my temper and this thing goes off.' She couldn't believe the words were coming from her own mouth.

'You wouldn't use it,' he scoffed.

Maggie released the safety catch. 'We'll see about that.'

She hoped he hadn't noticed that she was trembling, but clearly he had because he lowered his arms and came towards her.

This unnerved her so much that the hand holding the revolver seemed to take on a life of its own. Suddenly, the gun went off. The bullet hit the ground next to the soldier's feet, sending up a spray of dust. His mouth dropped open and, before Maggie had time to recover her wits, he spun around and ran away, nearly losing his footing as he took a look back over his shoulder.

Maggie was in shock. Once his retreating figure had become a mere speck in the distance, she sank down onto the running board of the truck and dropped the gun. Lowering her head into her hands, she broke into a paroxysm of sobs until commonsense told her to get going as quickly as possible. As if in a trance, she picked up the gun and replaced the safety catch. Getting to her feet, she climbed into the driver's seat and started the engine, relieved when it coughed into life.

She was badly shaken by the incident but she made up her mind to tell no one about it. This meant she had to keep her nerves under control. Concentrating on driving helped and, as she drew near to Madrid, she forced herself to focus on the future. She needed to do as much translation work as possible. After all, there would soon come a time when she would have her hands full with a baby. She intended to continue working right up until her confinement. Afterwards, she would be able to manage, relying on Harry to carry the work to and from the British Library. Yes, she told herself, everything is going to fall into place.

She drove the truck into the makeshift garage, collected her suitcase from the back and replaced the gun in her handbag. Then she took time checking her appearance in the rear view mirror. The others mustn't suspect that anything was wrong.

Rosario, Àngel and the younger children greeted her warmly.

'How's your brother?' Rosario asked anxiously, relief spreading over her features when Maggie told her that he was recovering well.

'Has everything been all right here?' asked Maggie.

Rosario looked downcast.

Maggie gripped her hands. 'What's the matter?'

'I think Donato's got the measles.'

'What?'

'Come and look, he's covered in spots.'

Maggie dropped her suitcase and rushed into the bedroom. Donato was in his cot. He was grizzling and looked sickly. When he saw Maggie, he held out his arms to her. Reaching into the cot, she picked him up and rocked him gently. '*Pobre muchacho*, you are spotty, aren't you?'

'I've been trying to comfort him but he wants you, Maggie. And besides, I had to give the others some attention.'

'Of course you did. Oh dear, I shouldn't have left you.'

'You had no choice, you had to go to see your brother.'

Maggie still looked concerned. 'How have you managed about shopping while I've been away?'

'Àngel has lived up to his name. He's been a godsend.'

307

'Where is he?'

'He's gone to get some milk. Honestly, Maggie, he's been wonderful.'

Maggie could hardly believe her ears. Rosario had always seemed intimidated by Ángel and she was surprised to hear her singing his praises. But she was in a quandary. Until now, the children had all kept well, apart of course, from Fabio's refusal to speak. The last thing she wanted was to register with a doctor and run the risk of enquiries being made. Then she remembered the walk-in clinic that Tomás had taken her too when she cut her feet during the storm.

'Has Tomás turned up?'

Rosario shook her head. 'I wish he would.'

At that moment, Ángel burst into the apartment, bringing with him the milk and some other commodities he had taken the initiative to purchase. '*Hola*, Maggie,' he cried. 'How's your brother?'

'*Hola*, Ángel, Robert's fine thank you. His leg wound's improving.'

She wondered whether the provisions the boy carried were necessities or treats but decided not to enter into a discussion which might provoke anger. After Rosario's reliance on him, it would probably be better to turn a blind eye. Turning back to Rosario, she asked, 'Do you remember the name of the clinic Tomás took me to last year?

The girl shook her head. 'I barely knew you then and I don't recall Tomás mentioning the name of it.'

Ángel chirped up. 'There's a free clinic on the other side of town,' he said. 'But you have to queue up for hours.'

'Do you know where it is, Ángel?'

'I could take you there. Why do you want to go?' He grinned mischievously. 'You're not ready to give birth, are you?'

Even Maggie couldn't restrain a smile. 'Not yet,' she said. 'But look at Donato.'

Ángel peered at the baby, then turned up his nose and backed away. 'He's covered in spots. Is it catching?'

'It could be measles but I want to check it out.'

'They might not let you in if it's catching.'

This thought had also occurred to Maggie but she brushed the possibility aside. 'If I wrap him in a shawl, they won't know until the doctor sees him, then it will be too late.'

As she spoke, Maggie realised how wrong this sounded. Donato could end up being responsible for infecting other children. Pushing the thought aside, she studied Eva and Fabio, wondering whether they would come down with it as well.

'Rosario, could you please prepare a bottle for Donato, I'm going to take him to the clinic.' She turned to Ángel. 'Can you show me the way?'

They caught the bus and arrived at the clinic to find a queue stretching round the corner. Maggie's heart sank. She was exhausted after the long drive from Tres Lomas and the incident with the soldier.

Ángel made no secret of the fact that he didn't want to wait with her, but she insisted. 'Donato is heavy and I may have to ask you to hold him for a while.'

'But he's all spotty!'

'Shhh! We don't want the whole queue to know.'

Ángel resigned himself to waiting but when he started shuffling his feet impatiently, Maggie thrust the baby into his arms. 'You hold him for a while, my arms are nearly dropping off.'

After holding the child for a short while, Ángel looked at her rather shamefacedly. 'Sorry, Maggie., I didn't know how heavy he was.' He hesitated, then asked,

'Did you have a good journey back?' adding in a stage whisper, 'Did you use the gun?'

Maggie stared at him in astonishment. 'How did you know I took it with me?'

'You would have been a fool not to take it,' he retorted.

Before she could stop herself, she started telling him about the soldier's attempted assault, describing how frightened she felt when the gun went off accidentally. They talked in low voices, their conversation drowned out by Donato's howls.

'You won't tell anyone about this, will you?' she begged him. 'Especially Rosario. She doesn't even know about the gun.'

'You can rely on me,' Ángel assured her, putting a finger to the side of his nose in a conspiratorial gesture.

It was dark by the time they reached the door of the clinic. Maggie felt faint with hunger and exhaustion. She wished she had had the foresight to bring a sandwich with her. Once inside the door, she took the child back from Ángel and urged him to push ahead of the queue to the reception counter. 'This is urgent,' she retorted when other people protested. After a heated discussion Ángel came back, followed by a young doctor, who introduced himself. 'My name's Dr Carlos Menzes, come this way please, *señora*.' He directed her to a cubicle.

'Is it measles?' asked Maggie, watching nervously as the doctor examined Donato.

The doctor shook his head. 'No, it's rubella.' When Maggie looked uncomprehending, he explained. 'German measles.'

'Oh dear!' gasped Maggie.

'Have you got any other children?'

'Yes,' said Maggie. 'Two others. Is it…is it contagious?'

310

He hastened to reassure her. 'It's quite a mild infection. The only possible danger is during pregnancy…'

'Pregnancy?'

He gave her a searching look. 'You're not pregnant, are you?'

Maggie shook her head, 'Of course not.'

She looked at Ángel willing him to keep quiet whilst, at the back of her mind, she recalled reading an article in a medical magazine, which had suggested a connection between German measles and deafness, blindness, even mental deficiency if contracted during pregnancy.

'Did either of you suffer from it as a child?' asked the doctor, addressing both Maggie and Ángel.

'I don't remember.'

'Well, I'm afraid that if you or the boy are going to get it, you've probably got it already; the incubation period is 14-23 days. And as for pregnancy, where there is concern the foetus will often abort spontaneously. Still, you don't have to worry about that.' Folding the blanket around Donato, he smiled at Maggie and said, 'As for this young fella, he'll be back to normal in a few days. Don't worry, go home and put him to bed. He looks tired, and for that matter, so do you. Now, please excuse me, I've got other patients to attend to.' With these words, he left the cubicle.

Maggie followed Ángel out of the clinic as if in a dream. Suppose she got rubella! Suppose her baby became infected! The prospect of giving birth to a damaged child filled her with horror. How would she manage? Consumed by these thoughts, she let Ángel find the bus stop, pay the fare and lead her off the bus at the appropriate stop.

'What on earth's the matter?' gasped Rosario when they arrived home.

'Nothing,' replied Maggie.

311

'It's rubella and she's afraid…' Ángel started to say.

Maggie cut him short. 'I'm not afraid. Donato's going to be fine; there's nothing to worry about except that the others might get it too.'

Handing Donato over to Rosario, she placed a finger to her lips and snatched Ángel's wrist, dragging him into the office. 'Don't tell Rosario what the doctor said. Please promise me you won't tell her.'

'There are a lot of things you don't want Rosario to know about. Surely it would be better to tell…'

'No it wouldn't,' she said curtly. 'This is between you and me. I want Rosario to believe everything is fine. After all, she's got enough to worry about without that as well.'

Ángel shrugged. 'If you say so. Can I go now?'

She nodded and watched him rush out of the room, leaving her wondering what teenage thoughts were hurtling through his head. She tugged at her bottom lip. She had entrusted him with two important secrets. Would he keep his mouth shut? She hoped so.

Two days later, Fabio went down with rubella, followed by Eva the very next day. Maggie tried to keep her emotions under control. The children quickly recovered, leaving only Ángel to fall foul to the infection and he showed no signs of feeling unwell. Rosario claimed she had had it as a child. Maggie tried to remember whether she and Robert had had German measles. She remembered having chicken-pox and being really ill with whooping cough, but couldn't recall any other occasion when either she or Robert had been really ill. Then, she woke up feeling unwell. Determined to think positively, she put it down to over-tiredness.

'If you're not feeling well, Maggie, go to bed and I'll take charge of the children.'

Maggie followed Rosario's advice and went back to bed, but anxiety kept her awake. She told herself there

312

was nothing to worry about. So far, her pregnancy had progressed smoothly. She had not got around to confiding in Raul about the baby, telling herself that with Robert lying in a hospital bed, it was sensible to keep that news to herself. She didn't want her brother hearing about it. Next week, she decided, she would write to Raul breaking the news. The recollection of how panicked she had been on learning that she was pregnant made her shudder. Over the past few weeks she had got everything under control. Nothing could go wrong now. Holding that conviction in her mind, she fell asleep.

She was woken up by Rosario.

'Sorry to disturb you, Maggie, but Harry's here with some more work for you. He needs to explain something. I told him you weren't well but he says the work's urgent and that you are the only one who can do it.'

'It's all right, Rosario. Just give me a minute to wake up properly. Tell Harry I'll be with him in a minute.'

So this was what it was going to be like. Short bursts of urgent work followed longer stretches of routine translation. She got up, put on her dressing-gown and shuffled into the living room.

'Hello Harry.'

'Hello Maggie, sorry to drag you out of bed…' Harry frowned with concern. 'You look under the weather. Perhaps…'

Maggie didn't hear any more. A terrible spasm of pain gripped her abdomen and she slumped to the floor, losing consciousness. She came round to see an unfamiliar face looming over her. The face disappeared and someone spoke to her but she couldn't make out the words.

Slowly consciousness returned and she found herself lying on the bed. Rosario and Harry were hovering nearby. She tried to sit up but pain forced her to lie back.

'Keep still,' urged Rosario and Harry in unison.

'Who was that man?' she whispered.

'Charlie Stevens,' said Harry.

'Who?'

'Charlie Stevens. He's an old pal of mine. We were at university together.'

Maggie's eyes widened. 'What was he doing here?'

'I called him. He's a doctor and he got here pretty smartly thank goodness.' He hesitated. 'Maggie, why didn't you confide in me?'

'I…I…' She gave up. It was too complicated to explain. With a rush of fear, she recalled the terrible pain she had suffered before passing out. 'The blood? I was bleeding.'

Harry and Rosario exchanged a glance. Harry came over to sit on the edge of the bed. He said quietly, 'I'm afraid you lost the baby.'

'No!' Tears welled in Maggie's eyes. She hadn't wanted the child; she had dreaded going through the next few months; feared the confinement; panicked at the thought of raising a child all on her own. With a sob, she realised that losing her baby, even as early as this was traumatic. And Raul didn't even know about it!

She blinked and looked into Harry's face, seeing a mixture of emotions. How he must despise her! Harry was a member of the establishment, a man with high morals. He would never trust her again. The sobs caught in her throat. It was bad enough losing the baby, was she going to lose Harry's friendship as well? She had expected to see shock but it was pity clouding his eyes. Shock she could cope with, but pity…!

Harry leant towards her. 'I know it's terrible at the moment,' he said. 'But time heals. That sounds trite but it's true.' Yes, thought Maggie, pity's his over-riding emotion, but his next choked words astounded her. 'It was Raul's child, wasn't it? Are you…are you in love with

314

him? Did he know about the baby?' That didn't sound like pity, it sounded more like jealousy. Was it possible?

The ensuing silence separated them. To break it she whispered, 'You're shocked and you hate me.'

'Hate you?' He reached for her hand. 'Oh Maggie, believe me, that's far from the truth. The truth is I began to suspect you were pregnant when you nearly passed out at El Bar de los Marinellos. At the time, I'll admit I was shocked.'

'A well brought-up young lady like me!' mimicked Maggie, turning her head away to hide another rush of tears.

'This is wartime, Maggie, and unusual things happen. Honestly, I admire you so much. You've got courage and tenacity. Not many young women would do what you're doing.'

'I don't know how I got myself into this mess.'

Harry brought her back to the issue of the baby. 'It was Raul's, wasn't it? Are you…are you in love with him?'

She shook her head. 'I was, or rather, I thought I was.'

Did she imagine it, or did Harry begin to relax? She noticed that Rosario had discreetly left them on their own. What a wise young person she is, thought Maggie.

'I need to sleep,' she said, withdrawing her hand from Harry's.

He got to his feet, a hurt expression flitting across his features. 'Of course, I'll call round tomorrow to see how you are.'

As he left the room, she smothered a sob.

Even if time wasn't the healer it was supposed to be, Maggie did find that keeping herself occupied certainly helped. And, in the event, there was no choice because translation and encoding work poured in, keeping her busy over the next couple of weeks. In quiet moments, she found herself weeping and woefully wondering what sex her baby had been. Had rubella brought on the miscarriage or was it pre-ordained that she would lose the child?

Work kept her in close contact with Harry, which was sometimes a blessing, sometimes not. She kept thinking about the glances he had thrown at her over the months. Had his suppressed smiles been manifestations of concern rather than disapproval? Was it possible? No it couldn't be...

Once she came to realise how much he cared for her, she avoided embarrassment by keeping their discussions strictly work related until, one day, the conversation became more personal.

'We'll have to leave Spain soon, Maggie.'

'We?'

'Yes, I shall be leaving within the month. You must leave too. I can't protect you if you choose to stay here, but I can get you safely away if we leave together.'

Maggie bit her lip. 'I know you care about me, Harry, and that you're only thinking about my safety, but I can't leave without the children.'

'I know that. I meant all of you.'

'All?'

'Yes, you, Rosario and the four children. I've found a way of doing it.'

Maggie's eyes lit up. She couldn't believe her ears. How he had changed! Only a short while ago, Harry had been very reluctant to take on the children. Had love made him change his mind?

He went on. 'Once we reach England, they'll be taken care of and all your troubles will be over.'

Maggie tensed. This wasn't quite what she wanted to hear. 'I'm not handing them over to a bunch of unfeeling authorities. Surely you don't expect me to accept one orphanage in lieu of another!'

'It's not the same back home. They'll be away from the war zone, they'll be treated properly, put with decent foster families...'

'No!'

Harry looked astonished by her reaction and gasped, 'I thought you wanted to get them to England so that you could dispense with the responsibility.'

'Dispense with the responsibility!' The colour rushed to Maggie's cheeks and her eyes shone with anger. 'I'll be looking after them myself. Don't you understand, Harry, they're my family, I won't abandon them.'

'How can you look after them? What with?'

'With my inheritance, of course.'

'What inheritance?'

'Listen, Harry, I've got it all worked out...'

He butted in. 'You're living in a dream world, Maggie. You've just lost your own baby and those inherent maternal instincts are clouding your judgement.'

'My hormones, you mean?' Her tone was acerbic.

'Like I said, you're living in a dream world.'

Maggie lost her temper. 'I'm not, and if you'll listen, I'll tell you what I'm going to do.'

Harry frowned. 'Go on then.'

Having gained his attention, Maggie lost no time in explaining what she had in mind, finishing with: 'So you see, I've got to get back to Robert. He's the key to my future. If Ángel can get hold of some petrol, I'll drive to Tres Lomas and get Raul to take me to him again. Then, we can make arrangements.'

'I'll come with you.'

'No! It's better if I go on my own. Raul will listen to me. He might not like it if you tag along.'

'Have you told him about losing the baby?'

'Why should I?'

'I think you owe it to him.'

317

Maggie jumped to her feet, her face red with anger. 'No, I don't. Besides, it's none of your business.'

'Oh…' Harry also got up and went to the door.

Maggie felt terrible. She could tell by the hunch of his shoulders that she had cut him to the quick. He was offering to help her and she persisted in rebuffing him.

'Harry, I'm sorry,' she called out. He turned to face her and her heart contracted at the hurt expression on his face. She went on. 'It's better if I go alone. I don't want Raul to know, not *ever*.'

Harry came across the room and took her in his arms. 'I'm sorry too. I shouldn't have shouted at you. I just want to protect you.'

He bent over to kiss her just as Rosario and the children came back into the apartment.

CHAPTER TWENTY-THREE

Maggie drew to a halt at the side of the road, folded her arms across the steering wheel and lowered her head onto them. She felt exhausted and frightened. Dizziness had persisted from time to time since the miscarriage, together with sharp pains in her lower abdomen, but she hadn't told anyone. Perhaps it was normal to feel like this during the early weeks. After all aborting a foetus was traumatic. She began to wish she had allowed Harry to accompany her, admitting to herself that once again, obstinacy had provoked her into going it alone.

After resting for fifteen minutes she continued on her way, arriving in Tres Lomas just after four in the afternoon. Raul was expecting her and she knew that it was going to be hard not to weaken and confide in him about the baby. She wished he would find himself a new girlfriend, but wondered how she would react if she saw him with another woman. Commonsense told her to remain detached. The affair was over, no harm had come out of it, or had it? She shuddered at her own callous thoughts wondering at how she had changed from the innocent young girl she had been only a year earlier.

'*Hola Maggie, como estás?*'

'I'm very well, thank you. How are you?' She knew her words sounded formal.

If Raul noticed he didn't show any sign of it. 'I've located Esteban,' he said. 'They're trying to keep him away from the front line for the moment to allow him to recover from his injuries. These things take time, you know. He shouldn't have gone back so soon. Dolores is keeping a close eye on him.'

I bet she is, thought Maggie, for once failing to reprimand herself for the uncharitable notion.. 'When can we go and see him?'

'Will the day after tomorrow suit you?'

'Can't we go tomorrow?'

'What's the hurry?'

Maggie sighed. This bit she could tell him. 'I need him to sign over power of attorney to me so that our solicitor will agree to release funds from our inheritance,' she explained. 'There are bills piling up and I need to settle them.'

This explanation seemed to satisfy Raul. 'Do you think he'll agree?'

'If he doesn't we'll be landed with a mountain of debts,' snorted Maggie. 'My own money's fast running out.'

'Well then, tomorrow it is. And don't worry, I'll back you up. I know what it's like to have money worries especially when you know the problem can so easily be resolved.'

His words puzzled Maggie. 'What do you mean?'

'My family has debts, big debts, but we can't get hold of our finances. They're all tied up due to the hostilities.'

This was the first time that Raul had ever hinted at his background. All she knew was that he came from Gijon and that his parents were both dead. So Raul had his problems too. Somehow knowing this gave Maggie a warm feeling towards him.

First thing next day, Raul arrived to pick her up.

'Sorry about the transport,' he said, grinning mischievously from the saddle of a battered motorcycle with a sidecar.

Maggie burst out laughing. 'I think this is going to be fun.'

'You might not think so when we hit the road. It's going to be a bit bumpy.'

'Why can't we use Arnaldo's truck?'

'The bike takes less petrol. I thought you ought to preserve the small amount you've got left for the journey back to Madrid.'

'I suppose so,' agreed Maggie, scrutinising the motorbike and wondering how bumpy the ride was going to be, and how much jolting her tender insides could take.

Much to her relief, her brother and Dolores were stationed in a nearby small town.

'Hi Sis,' he greeted her. 'To what do I owe this honour?'

'You'll see,' she replied. 'How are you?'

For the first time, Maggie noticed the earthy smell, which both Robert and Dolores carried with them. She put it down to the change of environment. On the battlefield, smells and dirt were acceptable, here, in a more civilised community, their unkempt appearance seemed out of place. Although Dolores' hair was tied back, some strands had escaped, and as she drew closer, Maggie couldn't help wondering whether those glossy locks were louse-free. Her fingernails too, beneath the scarlet nail varnish, showed signs of ingrained dirt. She's a freedom fighter, Maggie reminded herself, how can she be fussy under those circumstances? Nevertheless, she found the woman repugnant and experienced again that streak of jealousy over her brother, the niggling jealousy which had haunted her throughout her life.

'I'm well,' he replied. 'And I'll be able to entertain you this time. Let's go and get a glass of wine at the local taverna.'

The four of them found a table and ordered wine and tapas.

'Now,' said Robert. 'What's the urgency?'

'I needed to see you because I'm leaving Spain.'

Raul, who had been listening on the sidelines, looked surprised. 'Leaving?'

Maggie's twin, on the other hand, nodded his head wisely. 'I think that's a good idea, *hermanita*, this is no place for the likes of you. The fighting is escalating, who knows what will happen next!' He grinned at her. 'But I'm glad you didn't leave without saying goodbye.'

'I'd never do that, but in any case…hmm…I had to see you. It's about the will.'

'The will?'

'Mother's will. Don't you remember, I told you the solicitor won't release funds without your say-so.'

Robert face clouded. 'Is that why you've come to see me?' Maggie began to feel irritated. This was going to be more difficult than she had anticipated, but she had to win him over. Without her brother's signature she wouldn't be able to put her plan into action. 'What do you want from me?' he scowled. 'I'm not going to England.' Dolores dug her fingernails into his arm. 'I'm never going back,' he finished.

Maggie's temper flared. 'I'm not asking you to.'

'What d'you want then?'

'I want you to come into Tres Lomas and sign over power of attorney to me through the lawyer there so that I can claim my share of our inheritance.'

'Don't do it, Esteban! The greedy bitch wants the lot,' screeched Dolores. For a dreadful moment, Maggie saw her brother hover on the brink of uncertainty. 'Don't give up your legacy, Esteban, when this is all over, we'll need it to start over again. Don't listen to that scheming vixen.' She spewed out profanity in a guttural dialect.

Maggie held her breath. Would Robert listen to her? The woman's elbows rested on the table and her fists were tightly clenched. From striking beauty her features had been transformed by hatred into the face of a caterwauling witch. Then her boot-clad foot shot out and kicked Maggie's shin, making her gasp in pain. Raul and Robert stared at her in silent astonishment until she became aware of the spectacle she was making of herself. She stopped shrieking and, when no one spoke, launched herself at her lover, tugging at his sleeves, thrusting her face into his, begging him to see things her way.

Suddenly, Robert came to life. Shrugging off Dolores' hands, he raised his arm and swung it across her face, knocking her off her chair. She slumped to the ground, clutching her reddened cheek. Maggie gasped with shock, barely resisting the urge to rush to her aid.

Without uttering a word, Robert pushed back his chair, called for the check and strode to where Raul had parked the motorcycle. 'What are we waiting for?' he snapped. 'Let's get this over with straightaway.'

Raul had watched the whole proceedings in amazement, but he was quick to seize the opportunity. Glancing at Maggie, he reached out a hand and pulled her to her feet. 'Well, I must say, I didn't see that coming,' he muttered. 'Come on, the sooner we get out of here the better.'

Still recovering from shock, Maggie couldn't help stealing a surreptitious glance at Raul; womaniser he might be but she couldn't imagine him striking a woman.

Robert was already on the motorcycle, obliging Raul to ride pillion. Maggie climbed into the sidecar and, before she had even had time to settle herself comfortably, they were off.

On reaching Tres Lomas, Maggie and Robert went directly to the lawyer's office. As Maggie had already set up a provisional meeting he was expecting them.

'This shouldn't take long, Señor Morán,' he said. 'Your sister explained everything, it's just a matter of identification and signature. We'll need a witness to your signature but I'm sure my secretary will oblige.'

'You will make it clear that I only want my own share of the inheritance to be released, won't you?' said Maggie

'There's no need to worry about that,' butted in Robert. 'Let my sister have it. I don't want any of it.'

'I don't want it all,' protested Maggie. 'Just my share.'

The lawyer frowned. 'It's actually simpler, *Señorita*, if I give you power to access the whole inheritance,' he said.

'There you are. Go ahead, *Señor Abogado*, the simplest way is always the best.'

'I'll put your share into bonds straightaway, Robert,' said Maggie, fondly reaching for her brother's hand. 'One day you'll get married, set up home and start a family, then you'll need money.'

Robert threw back his head and laughed. 'Do you really think I'll last that long?'

Frowning, Maggie squeezed his hand. 'Don't say things like that.'

'Hmm, is it settled then? Shall I draw up the document giving your sister rights over the entire estate?' Clearly the lawyer wanted to complete the matter as quickly as possible.

'Yes please.'

Brother and sister left the lawyer's office in high spirits.

'Let's celebrate, *hermanita*.'

For the first time since arriving in Spain, Maggie felt comfortable in Robert's presence. Here was the old happy-go-lucky Robert, not the new, renegade Esteban. She found it difficult to equate the angry individual who'd slapped his girlfriend's face with the amusing young man whose company she was now enjoying.

'Why not?' she agreed. 'I know a nice bar not far from here. It will be lovely to have a cosy chat and catch up. After all, we've hardly seen one another for two years.'

'Umm., I've got a better idea, let's get Raul and some of the girls to join us.'

This wasn't quite what Maggie had in mind but she swallowed her disappointment, realising that perhaps it would be for the best. Confidential chats over a few glasses of wine might coerce her into spilling the beans. She didn't want Robert to know about her affair with Raul or about the miscarriage. Worse than that, she could be tempted to reveal the real reason why she needed the money.

The evening went well, although Maggie was careful to distance herself from Raul. She deliberately chose a seat at the restaurant between her brother and one of the interns from the hospital, opposite Raul. She couldn't help noticing that he cast her the occasional puzzled smile, but she chose to ignore it. Going back to the hotel on her own proved easier than expected because Robert had to spend the night in Raul's cabin, thus saving Maggie the embarrassment of refusing to sleep with her former lover.

The next morning, after a moving farewell, Raul and Robert drove off on the motorbike and Maggie drove the truck back to Madrid.

She arrived to find Rosario looking much happier. 'I've heard from Palmiro,' she told Maggie excitedly. 'He'll be home on leave fairly soon.'

'That's good news, Rosario.'

'Did you do what you set out to do, Maggie?'

'Yes, it's all done and dusted,' replied Maggie with a smile. 'I've got power of attorney. There's nothing to stop us leaving for England.'

'I've got to wait to see Palmiro.'

'Don't worry, it will take a week or two to organise…'

Rosario's eyes clouded. 'I'm sorry, Maggie, I won't be coming with you.'

'You must!'

'It's a splendid plan of Harry's, letting me travel with you as the children's nanny but…'

Maggie clasped Rosario's arm. 'You've got to come. You'll be safe in England. You can start a new life there, continue your studies and after the war, Palmiro can join you.'

The teenager shook her head. 'You and the children must go without me. I can't leave Palmiro or Luis.'

Luis! Maggie realised with a tremor of guilt that, in her eagerness to make plans she had overlooked the needs and wishes of those around her. Clearly, Rosario didn't want to leave Spain. And why should she when her boyfriend had taken up arms with the international brigades and her brother was fighting for freedom in Barcelona? Of course she wanted to stay close to them.

Trapped in tunnel vision, she had pushed aside the obvious pitfalls. She knew Harry would say it made no difference, that they should leave anyway but could she abandon her young companion, who had been her mainstay throughout her sojourn in Madrid?

With tears in her eyes, she hugged Rosario and although she knew it was useless, she couldn't stop herself from whispering, 'How can I leave without you? We're a family. The children will be devastated if you don't come with us. It's going to be hard enough getting them to understand we're leaving Spain, especially Ángel.' She paused, then tried another tack. 'Is it because you're nervous about going abroad?'

'Of course not. When I was a little girl, my parents took me to France.'

A surge of panic coursed through Maggie. She balled her fists and pressed Rosario further, 'Please come with us, you can't stay here on your own.'

'I was alone before you found me.'

Maggie looked scornful. 'Not for very long, only a few weeks. How will you fare if the Francoists invade the city?'

Rosario looked downcast. 'I'll be all right. Maggie, Palmiro will look after me.'

Before she could stop herself, Maggie burst out, 'How can he when he's fighting at the front?'

Rosario shook her head and burst into tears. Turning on her heel, she fled from the room.

When Maggie spoke to Harry, his answer was as she had anticipated. 'You can't make her come if she doesn't want to.'

They were seated in an alcove of their local bar, the bar where she had fainted before discovering that she was pregnant.

'I don't want to leave without her.'

Harry held her hand across the table. 'Neither do I and travelling with four children isn't going to be easy without Rosario's help, but in some ways, it gives us fewer headaches, fewer explanations when we cross the border.'

Maggie pulled her hand away. 'That's a heartless thing to say.'

'It's not heartless, just practical. See sense, Maggie, your responsibility isn't to Rosario, it's to those four orphans you've adopted.'

She lowered her head, unable to meet his gaze. 'I know, but it's going to be so hard leaving her behind.'

'That brings me to another point.'

'Yes?'

'We'll be travelling as man and wife…'

'Man and wife?'

'You'll have to wear a wedding ring and call yourself Mrs Fforbes.'

'What about my passport.'

'Leave that up to me. I'll get it altered.'

'That's fraud!'

'There *is* an alternative.'

'What's that?'

'You could marry me.'

Maggie burst out laughing. 'Marry you? Don't be ridiculous!' Her amusement evaporated when she saw the expression on Harry's face. 'You weren't serious?'

He brushed it off. 'Of course not.' Anxious to cover up the awkward moment, he went on, 'We'll anglicise the children's names: Donato will be Donald; Eva, Eve; Fabio, Fabian; and Ángel, Anthony.'

'How do you know they'll go along with that?'

'Trust me, they will if we make it a game.'

'I don't think Ángel will see it that way.'

'Ángel's old enough to be told the truth.'

Maggie looked pensive. 'I suppose he is, but he can be cantankerous at times. He might throw a tantrum.'

'We'll cross that bridge when we come to it. Now, tomorrow you must give me your passport so that I can destroy it and get a new one issued in my name with you as my wife.'

'Can't I keep my real passport?'

'I need the photograph.'

'What about the children?'

'They'll be included on my passport and, don't forget, you'll be Mrs Henry Royston Fforbes.'

Maggie's lips twitched into a smile. 'Henry Royston Fforbes? That's quite a mouthful.'

'I never use the name Royston; it's too pretentious. I prefer to be plain Harry Fforbes.' He hesitated, then added, 'I'll have to alter your age too.'

'Why?'

'Three children aged nine, seven and a year. You're only twenty-five, Maggie. Shall we say you're twenty-nine?'

'Twenty-eight?' she corrected him.

'Why quibble over a year?'

'Twenty-nine's too close to thirty. It makes me sound middle-aged. Anyway, what about Ángel? I couldn't be a mother to him.'

Harry's mouth twitched into an amused smile. 'He can be my son from my first marriage.'

'I didn't know you'd been married before.'

'I haven't.'

'Oh dear, I'm totally confused. I don't know what's fact and what's fiction.'

Harry chuckled, signalling to the waiter for the bill, and they got up to leave.

'By the way, there's another thing,' said Maggie as they went out into the street.

'What's that?'

'Will Raul agree to let Rosario stay in the apartment on her own after we leave?' She fell into step beside Harry, and threading her arm through his, said with a hint of mischief. 'You didn't think of that, did you?'

'You'll have to write and ask him.'

Maggie wrinkled her nose. That was the last thing she wanted to do, but clearly, it had to be done.

CHAPTER TWENTY-FOUR

The next few weeks flew past. Maggie tried again to convince Rosario to come with them but she wouldn't hear of it so Maggie dutifully wrote to Raul asking him to allow the girl to stay on in the apartment after their departure. He willingly agreed although he expressed the wish to see her again before she left. *For old time's sake, Maggie*, he wrote. He seemed genuinely sad so she wrote a carefully worded letter back explaining that there wasn't time, that Harry had made all the arrangements and that they would be leaving at a moment's notice.

She was concerned about how Rosario would manage financially, although the girl declared that she would be all right with her brother's money coming in regularly and no rent to pay.

'Have you heard how Luis is getting on these days, Rosario?' she asked.

'No I haven't but no news is good news, isn't it?'

Maggie wasn't so sure, but she knew that while the free accommodation was available to her, Rosario would at least have a roof over her head, although the question remained: how would she manage if Luis' money ran out? She decided to leave her a chunk of money to fall back on should the need arise.

'You can't do that, Maggie,' protested Rosario. 'You'll need all your cash for the journey. Who knows what lies ahead.'

'We'll be all right,' Maggie assured her.

There was no further news from Palmiro and Maggie could see that the teenager was worried. But it was Tomás who turned up and Maggie was only too pleased to confide in him about her misgivings.

'Will you keep an eye on Rosario for me?' she implored him.

'I will while I'm around,' he said. 'But the fighting takes me away most of the time.' He fished in his pocket, bringing out a grubby scrap of paper. 'Here, give this to her. It's a contact of mine, a woman whose reputation need not worry Rosario. Just tell her to look the other way.' He guffawed at Maggie's horrified expression. 'Belen may not be a pillar of society but she's got a heart of gold and if I ask her to help Rosario, she'll willingly do so.'

'The girl's very innocent,' Maggie reminded him.

'Belen's got a soft spot for the uninitiated. Don't worry, she'll respect my wishes; Rosario will come to no harm.'

'Thank you, Tomás.' She sighed. 'Oh dear, I'm going to miss you all so much.'

'Have you seen your brother again? I heard he was wounded. Is he on the mend?'

'Yes, I've seen him and he's almost back to normal. I just wish I could persuade him to leave Spain with us but his heart's been in Spain ever since he was a little boy.'

'Two sides of a coin, you and your brother!' observed Tomás.

Maggie was reluctant to hand over her passport to Harry. He came to the apartment when Rosario and the children were out.

'Please let me keep it, Harry. Take out the photograph and I'll hide the passport so no one will find it.

'That could be dangerous. We might be searched.'

'Searched?' Maggie was horrified.

'It's possible. These days customs regulations are stringent. It's not only leaving Spain and entering England, but remember, we have to go through France as well, and the French can be sticklers for officialdom.'

'I don't like it, Harry.'

'Don't you trust me?'

'Of course I do but...'

'It ties you too closely to me.'

'I didn't say that.'

Harry took her gently by the shoulders. 'Don't worry. Things will work out, you'll see.'

Her eyes filled with tears. 'I can't help feeling scared. Suppose something goes wrong and they take the children away. I couldn't bear that.'

He drew her close. 'It won't happen. At least not if we act out our roles properly.'

She leant her head on his shoulder, unwilling to confide yet another anxiety. She was experiencing stomach cramps nearly every day and she had been bleeding heavily during her monthly cycle following the miscarriage. Try as she might, it was difficult to push aside the niggling fear that something was wrong.

Harry drew her even closer, stroking her hair until impulsively he stooped to kiss her on the mouth. She responded almost without volition, finding to her surprise that his kiss was pleasurable and comforting and, for a fleeting moment, she allowed herself to melt into his arms. They pulled apart, and looking embarrassed, Harry said, 'I'm sorry, I shouldn't have done that.'

'No, you shouldn't,' she said, realising that intimacy at this juncture would be a hindrance rather than a help. If the journey back to England with all its potential pitfalls were to succeed, they needed to keep their relationship strictly platonic.

Turning away from him she started tidying up the room. Anything to avoid another close encounter. Picking up a cushion and giving it a shake, she asked, 'How is it that you've got all this inside information - forged passport, etc - Harry, tell me truthfully, are you a spy?'

He laughed out loud. 'Hardly. I'm just a menial civil servant who happened to get posted to a war zone.'

With this light-hearted riposte, he headed for the door. 'I'll see you tomorrow morning with the final encoding job. Will that be all right?'

'Of course it will.'

He left the apartment just as Rosario and the children came back.

'Is everything going according to plan?' asked Rosario.

Maggie crossed her fingers. 'So far, so good! Tomorrow we must start coaching the children to get used to their new names.'

The next day proved to be one of disruption. First of all, there was an air raid during the early hours. This caused three windows to break and unsettled the children. Ángel, of course, found the whole thing exciting and got angry when Maggie wouldn't let him go out after the 'All Clear' sounded.

'I want to see the damage,' he protested. 'I won't get in the way of rescuers.' His eyes lit up. 'I could lend a hand.'

Maggie wouldn't relent and for once he obeyed her. When she ventured forth, she found that several local shops had been hit, which meant going farther afield to buy provisions. It also meant wasting a great deal of time queuing up. And later in the day when it seemed that the danger of a repeat raid had passed, the three younger children lost their initial nervousness only to get carried away by the activity carrying on in the street below the apartment. Eva and Fabio chased one another around the apartment with Donato bringing up the rear. Ángel didn't help. He deliberately stuck out his leg when they passed him. This resulted in Donato frequently letting out a howl when he plunged headlong onto the floor, since at sixteen months he was still unsteady on his feet.

Hard on the heels of this chaos, Palmiro arrived. Rosario was overjoyed to see him although, she confided to Maggie afterwards, she had hoped to have a few hours' notice so that she could tidy the apartment and prepare a nice meal for him. The young Italian looked tired but didn't seem to mind the children's capers.

Ángel was in awe of him: a soldier from the front! He plied him with questions until, eventually, Rosario begged him to stop. 'Ángel, can't you see Palmiro's exhausted?' she said. 'He wants a bit of peace and quiet. You can talk to him again tomorrow.'

To his credit, the boy looked shamefaced. 'Sorry, I didn't think,' he mumbled. 'But there's just one more thing...' He then launched into another barrage of questions until Palmiro himself asked to be left alone. With a disgruntled frown he left the room.

Rosario told Palmiro about Maggie's planned departure. For a moment, he looked dumbfounded. 'Are you going too?'

She shook her head. 'No, I'm staying here.'

He gave a swallow and said earnestly. 'You ought to go, Rosario.'

A look of dismay swept across the girl's face. 'England's such a long way away.'

Palmiro grasped her hands. 'I know, but at least you'd be safe.'

'I'm safe here. Nothing's happened so far.'

Palmiro squeezed her hands. 'There's a false sense of security here in Madrid. In the end the city will fall to the Nationalists.'

'How can you be so sure?' protested Rosario.

'It's worse than you think,' he replied. 'Believe me, it would be better if you left.'

She tossed her head. 'I can't go in case Luis turns up. He might decide to come and collect me and take me back with him to Barcelona.'

Palmiro was adamant. 'He won't do that. Please go with Maggie, Rosario, you'll be reunited with your brother one day, you'll see.'

'You don't understand, I don't want to leave.' She cast her gaze downwards and shuffled her feet. 'We...we wouldn't be able to see one another and...'

Maggie's entry into the room averted an embarrassing moment for Rosario.

Palmiro turned to her and pleaded, 'Maggie, you *must* persuade Rosario to go with you.'

'Believe me, I've tried.'

He turned back to Rosario. 'Please go to England with Maggie. I want to be sure you're safe.'

Rosario shook her head. 'How can anywhere be safe when Europe's on the brink of war?'

The discussion petered out after that but, later on, Palmiro caught up with Maggie privately and begged her to make Rosario change her mind. She promised to try again but knew it would be futile. Rosario had made up her mind: she was going to stay in Madrid.

Palmiro's visit was brief. Much as Maggie had welcomed him for Rosario's sake, she found his presence an inconvenience. For one thing, it put paid to training the children to get used to their new personas. After his departure, she reluctantly took Ángel into her confidence, fearing that he would cause a scene by refusing to cooperate. To her surprise, the reverse happened.

'England? We're going to England?'

'Yes, the children will be safer there.'

'Fantastic!' he yelled and starting dancing about the room, waving his arms in the air.

'I'm glad you're pleased,' said Maggie. 'But you've got to be very grown-up.'

He stopped mid-spin. 'How d'you mean?'

'For the children's sake, we've got to pretend that we're playing a game. They've got to learn to answer to their new names.'

'What new names?'

Maggie explained about the anglicised names she and Harry had chosen. 'You'll be Anthony Fforbes, Harry's son from his first marriage.'

'Wow!' was all he could come out with.

Maggie heaved a sigh of relief. The problems she had anticipated with Ángel hadn't transpired. 'We'll be relying on you a great deal, Ángel - I mean Anthony,' she said with a grin.

He snatched her wrists and swung her around, an unusual thing for him to do. Generally, Ángel loathed touching people.

'I'm going to call the others in and start playing the name game,' said Maggie after he had let her go and she had recovered her breath. 'Will you help me?'

Enlisting Ángel's help proved beneficial. He encouraged the others to join in the game, making sure they responded to their new names. As Fabio still refused to utter a word, there was no fear of him slipping up except that he had to learn to react when they called him Fabian. With Donato it was easy. He was after all only just learning to talk. Eva was the main problem because she was a chatterbox. Maggie wondered how they were going to stop her from spilling the beans.

Harry duly arrived bearing the new joint passport. 'I thought you'd like to see it,' he said. 'It's got your photo inside as well as mine.'

Somehow, seeing the passport brought home the reality of what they were about to embark on. Maggie found it exciting yet terrifying, and covered her concern with levity.

'You look like a criminal,' she said with a giggle, pointing to Harry's photo. 'I suppose you are. I expect we'll all land up in jail.'

Harry didn't seem to think that was funny. 'For goodness sake, take this seriously, Maggie. How can you expect the children to behave sensibly if you treat the whole thing as a joke?'

Maggie bit her lip. 'Sorry,' she whispered.

'How are they getting along with their new names?'

'Quite well. Eva is the most difficult, but I expect she'll be all right once we get going. When are we leaving?'

'The middle of next week, probably Wednesday,' said Harry. 'July's a good time to travel through France. We'll merge into the tourist crowd.'

July! Was it only a year since she had arrived in Spain? How could so much have happened in such a short span of time!

'I'll bring you final details in a day or two. Make sure you pack a change of clothes for the children.'

'I've only got one suitcase,' complained Maggie.

'I'll get you another one.'

Harry turned to leave but Maggie called him back. 'I know what a risk you're taking,' she said. 'I didn't mean to be flippant just now. Please don't think I'm ungrateful.'

Looking embarrassed, he gave a grunt and left the apartment.

The next few days were a flurry of activity. Tomás called in and Maggie was surprised at how upset he was by their imminent departure. As for Rosario, she seemed to be acting a role, gliding around the apartment playing hostess, smiling at everybody, even making jokes.

'There's still time to change your mind,' said Maggie, clasping the teenager's hand. 'I wish you'd come with us.'

Rosario's façade slipped. 'I can't,' she stuttered. 'I've told Palmiro I'm staying. Please don't make this any harder for me, Maggie.'

'Sorry, love.'

Rosario went on. 'Besides, there's Luis. I haven't got time to contact him before you leave.'

'We'll delay our departure…'

'No, Maggie. It's better this way.'

Maggie could see there was no way she could talk Rosario out of staying on in Madrid. Resigning herself to the inevitable, she gave her a hug and made her promise to write even if the post did take a long time.

Harry asked Tomás to drive them to the train station in Arnaldo's truck, after which Maggie told him to dispose of it as he saw fit.

'It'll come in handy,' he said. 'Is it all right if I put it back in the garage for the time being?'

'That's fine as far as we're concerned,' replied Maggie. 'But bear in mind that one day someone could come back to open up the house again, or pull it down.'

Tomás grinned. 'Not for a while yet.'

On Wednesday, Harry arrived as arranged. 'I've packed everything into the truck,' he said. 'It's going to be a tight fit but we'll manage.'

Before leaving the apartment, Maggie primed the children yet again. This time, Eva took her more seriously.

'I like pretending,' she said with exaggerated confidence. 'I'm good at it, you'll see.'

Maggie caught Harry's glance, raising her eyes to the ceiling while he pursed his lips and gave a shrug in reply.

They had decided to travel back using the route Maggie and Tomás had taken to get to Madrid a year ago.

338

Trains were still running, although the timetable was unreliable.

The final parting from Rosario was tearful. Both girls sobbed uncontrollably while the children stood quietly by, not quite understanding that maybe they would never see Rosario again.

There wasn't much room to park outside the station. Everybody seemed to want to leave the city. Tomas seemed unperturbed by the crowds and even Harry didn't seem surprised, but Maggie was dumbfounded.

'I didn't expect this,' she said as she herded the children ahead of her into the station.

'There have been rumours about a Nationalist assault in the next few days,' muttered Harry.

Maggie felt foolish. She had been so busy, locked in her own world, preparing the children for the biggest adventure of their lives, that she hadn't listened to what was going on around her.

Saying goodbye to Tomás was cut short because he had to rush off to shift the truck. Police were everywhere, ordering vehicles to move on. The last Maggie saw of him was his rude gesture at a police officer before he drove off into the traffic. *Will I ever see him again?* she thought with tears pricking her eyelids. So many farewells in the past few days! It was all too much to bear.

'Wait here while I go and get the tickets,' said Harry once they were inside Atocha Station's large vestibule. 'Keep a check on those children, especially Angel.'

'I'm coming with you,' snapped the boy, and after a moment's consideration, Harry decided that wasn't a bad idea. At least he would know where he was.

Maggie waited nervously while Harry joined the queue for tickets. With Donato wriggling in her arms, Fabio looking dumbly around and Eva hopping impatiently from one foot to the other, she tried to stand her ground

339

against the jostling passengers, who threatened to push her further and further away from where Harry had left them. It was unbearably hot; the noise was deafening; the gritty smell of steam wafted through the station vestibule; police and army officials shouted useless directions at the crowds, and to add to the mayhem, a couple of lively musicians squatting in the corner, started playing a popular American hit.

At last, Harry and Ángel re-joined them. Maggie checked her watch. They had been waiting for nearly two hours. Her back was aching even though she stood Donato down on the ground from time to time. This wasn't very satisfactory because he immediately started to toddle away.

'Come on,' said Harry, taking the baby from her. He looked anxious, more agitated than Maggie had ever seen him. 'Anthony, take the suitcases. Eve and Fabian go with your mother.'

He had spoken in English and, for a fraction of a second, Eva and Fabio looked puzzled, but they soon recovered and each took hold of Maggie's hands. They pushed through the throng, a family indistinguishable from many others trying to board the train. Maggie was terrified of losing sight of Harry. He was in charge of their passport, their route out of Spain. If she lost contact with him, what would she do?

Harry glanced back every once in a while to make sure they were following him. Ángel, in charge of the suitcases, by-passed Harry and charged ahead, ever alert for the best place to board the train. He stopped eventually, near the front and waved them on to join him. Shoving the suitcases on board, he grabbed Fabio and hoisted the little boy up the steep steps into the carriage. Eva followed, Maggie next, with Harry carrying Donato, bringing up the rear. Ángel climbed aboard last, just as the guard blew his whistle.

340

The journey was punctuated by stops and starts. More and more people climbed on board, jostling one another and making the corridors inaccessible. There was a moment of panic when planes flew overhead, zooming low over the railway line, but it seemed their attack was destined for a different target.

At the border, they climbed out of the train onto the platform and waited with the rest of the passengers, who were still struggling with luggage, screaming children and aged relatives. To add to their problems, the temperature soared even higher.

Maggie tried to shield the children from the bustling crowd. 'This is awful,' she muttered.

'Everybody wants to get out of Spain,' said Harry. 'Let's hope the crowds will disperse once we reach the French side.'

'What are we going to do?' Maggie was close to panic.

He pointed ahead. 'Look, people are being directed out of the station along the road to Customs.'

She gave a gasp, reminded of the last time she had left the train, on the French side that time. Tomás, a formidable bearded stranger to her then, had explained that the French wouldn't allow trains to cross the border. Indeed, the French authorities hadn't seemed bothered about stragglers making their way across the countryside. With a shudder, she remembered how they had been obliged to scramble through shrub-land and brambles and wade across a stream to enter Spain. Clearly, inspections had been tightened up since then.

She realised Harry was talking to her. 'In normal circumstances, of course, Customs Officers would have boarded the train to check passports before letting us continue on our way,' he said. 'But these are not normal circumstances.'

Keeping the children closely linked to them, they followed the rest of the passengers along the road to

341

Border Control and, when they drew closer, Harry stopped and crouched down to talk to Eva and Fabio. 'This is where you have to be very good,' he whispered. 'Try not to talk…'

'Fabio doesn't talk,' chirped up Eva.

'Shhh…I know, but you do and for once, you have to be very quiet.'

'Like a mouse?'

'Yes, just like a mouse and you have to remember your new names. What's your little brother called?'

'Fabian.'

'And your big brother?' Harry pointed at Ángel.

Eva giggled. 'An…tho…ny,' she articulated very slowly.

'Well done!' said Harry, winking at Ángel, who grinned broadly.

They continued along the road, jostled by a couple of porters who were transporting two large laundry baskets from the Spanish train's luggage compartment to the French train. At the border, the customs officials insisted on opening one of them but waved the other one on. This distraction gave Maggie and her companions the opportunity to slip through almost unnoticed.

Eva played her part well. 'Come on Fabian,' she said, firmly pulling her brother along beside her.

Once out of earshot of the border guards, Maggie heaved a sigh of relief. 'That was easier than I expected.'

Harry didn't look confident. 'There are two more borders to cross,' he reminded her. 'And the last one, at Dover, could prove to be the trickiest.'

'Well, at least we've got this far,' retorted Maggie. 'Surely we'll be accepted in England. We're English.'

'We'll see.' Harry glanced around. 'Come on, with a bit of luck we might be able to find you a seat on the next train.'

They were lucky and found a carriage to themselves as a lot of people had dispersed, disappearing in different directions once they had crossed the border. It took an hour before the guard blew his whistle and the engine snorted into life. For much of the time, the railway line followed the coast and, at first, the children were fascinated to see the sea. None of them had ever seen it before. Maggie smiled at their wonderment, remembering her own first visit to the seaside when she and Robert had spent a rare family holiday on the Isle of Wight. But it was a long journey and the children began to get bored, especially Ángel. He got up and shuffled into the corridor.

'Where are you going?' asked Maggie.

'To the lav.'

'Don't be too long.' She turned to Harry. 'Perhaps you should go with him.'

'He's big enough to go on his own,' protested Harry.

'All the same…'

Harry frowned. 'Maggie, you've got to learn to trust him.'

Maggie wasn't so sure. Harry hadn't been the target of Ángel's thieving attempt, he didn't know the number of times she had suspected the boy of shoplifting. She didn't believe that going to the lavatory was the boy's only reason for leaving the carriage. He was restless and she guessed that he wanted to explore and find some way of amusing himself. The younger children had fallen asleep so that she no longer had to read stories to Eva and Fabio, which was a relief because the stomach cramps she had been experiencing for some time still persisted. She hadn't mentioned them to Harry. He had enough to worry about.

As she feared, Ángel was gone for a long time. Harry tried to appear untroubled, although she saw that he looked up from his book and glanced towards the

343

corridor from time to time. When he realised she had noticed, he took off his glasses and gave them a polish with his handkerchief. 'They keep getting steamed up,' he said.

Maggie really began to worry when they stopped at the next station. More people got on, crowding the corridor and making it difficult to get in and out of the carriage. 'I wish Ángel would come back,' she said. 'Perhaps you'd better go and look for him, Harry.'

'Give him a bit longer. He's probably gone the length of the train. Maybe he's met a boy about his own age and they're playing cards or five stones.'

Maggie couldn't imagine this happening but a wave of faintness made it impossible for her to be more insistent. Resting her head back, she tried to allow herself to drift off to sleep.

Maggie woke up with a start as the carriage door slid open. Ángel stood there, looking sheepish. 'Where have you been?' she demanded.

'Sorry, I got caught up.'

'Caught up? Caught up in what? I was worried sick about you. Why can't you ever do what you're told?'

Harry butted in. 'Maggie, let him explain.'

Ángel sidled into the carriage dragging with him a little girl. Maggie's eyes widened. Leaning forward, she said, 'Who's this?'

'I found her. She's lost.'

Harry put a hand on Maggie's arm to calm her. 'Where did you find her?' he asked.

'Don't be angry,' begged Ángel. 'I had to bring her along 'cos she's got nowhere to go.'

'Where's her mother?' gasped Maggie.

'She doesn't know.'

Maggie was close to hysteria. Didn't they have enough problems? What on earth were they going to do with a lost little girl? 'You'll have to take her back to where you found her,' she snapped. 'Harry, you go with him.'

'Calm down, Maggie, let Ángel finish telling us what happened.' Harry's unruffled tone exacerbated Maggie's panic.

She felt her head begin to reel. This couldn't be happening. Why hadn't she insisted that Harry accompany Ángel to the lavatory? As if in a dream she heard Ángel explain that he had wandered into the baggage compartment and heard a noise coming from a large hamper. 'She was crying,' he said. 'Someone had shut her in the basket...'

'While she was asleep?'

'She was awfully dozy. I think she'd been drugged,' replied Ángel. 'I couldn't leave her there, could I?'

'Of course you couldn't,' agreed Harry. Maggie saw him give a swallow and knew that he was as flummoxed as she was.

She blinked and focused properly on the small child clinging to Ángel's hand. She appeared to be almost comatose. Rubbing a fist across her eyes, she gave a sniff and seemed about to collapse.

All at once, Maggie came to life. Reaching out a hand to the child, she said quietly, 'Come here and tell me your name.'

CHAPTER TWENTY-FIVE

Stanmore, 1948

Maggie sighed as she drew back the curtains to let in the sunlight. How different the house on the common was now! No longer dark and forbidding, it had been transformed over years of hard graft and determination.

The garden too was different. When they had returned in 1938 it had been nothing more than a jungle. Harry had worked tirelessly to transform it, creating a vegetable patch, planting fruit trees, which now towered above her and needed frequent pruning. Of course, they would never have been able to afford the renovations if Robert hadn't given her power of attorney. The size of their mother's inheritance had been a pleasant surprise, much greater than she had anticipated. But the war years had been difficult. After Harry was called up, his sister, Caroline had stepped in to help her. A well-heeled divorcée, Caroline had never needed to work but she had felt it her duty to join the WVS and 'do her bit for the war effort' as she put it. An energetic sportswoman, she managed to find time both for her civic duties and to help out with the running of the house. Maggie had found her a little intimidating at first but she soon discovered that Caroline had a heart of gold and a lack of curiosity, which enabled Maggie not to have to explain certain aspects of how she came to have collected so many children and how she and Harry had managed to get them out of Spain.

During the war years, with the help of Caroline and Anthony, Maggie had given over the whole garden to vegetables. Anthony, especially, had entered into the spirit of the 'Dig for Victory' slogan, rushing home from school to grab a spade or get down on his hands and knees to plant carrots, potatoes and onions. All the children loved feeding the hens they'd kept, giving them Spanish names.

They had been issued with an Anderson shelter, which still stood at the end of the garden, covered with grass and weeds but hidden from view by the Wendy house, now used as a garden shed. There had been plenty of occasions when they had been constrained to seek shelter in the Anderson due to their proximity to Bentley Priory, the headquarters for Fighter Command, one of Hitler's main targets. After a while they had got used to the intermittent drone of German bombers and anti-aircraft gun flashes.

On reflection, Maggie marvelled at how well the children had coped with entry into world war so soon after their rescue from civil war. They took the threat of bombing in their stride, never bemoaning the fact that they had left one danger for another.

She had the house to herself today. Fabian was at college, Donald was at school. Eve was in London doing her nursing training and Anthony was studying law at Cambridge. Who would have imagined that little vagabond would have turned out to be so clever?

It was nine o'clock and she was still in her dressing-gown. Harry, up with the lark, had gone to work early. He liked to get in before everybody else in order to keep on top of his work-load at the Foreign Office. She was in a nostalgic mood as she glided through the rooms, tidying the mess the family had left behind them. She didn't mind being a housewife but sometimes she wistfully recalled the under-cover work she had done for Harry when they were in Madrid. She wondered whether she was still up to doing such complicated translations. Her happiness was tainted only when she thought about Rosario and Palmiro. It hadn't worked out for the lovebirds. Rosario had lost both her boyfriend and her brother within weeks of one another. Life can be so cruel, thought Maggie, recalling her shock when she'd learned that the young girl had entered a convent soon after Franco had brought an end to the civil war. As for Tomás, according to Rosario he had disappeared, never to be heard of again.

She thought fondly about Harry. All right, their relationship wasn't the great romance she had always dreamed of. The passion she had felt for Raul was missing and, of course, they had been denied children of their own. The hysterectomy she had been obliged to have on her return to the UK had seen to that. But they were happy. She gave a puzzled frown. Perhaps happy wasn't the right word; they were content with one another. There had been one sadness in their lives: the untimely death of little Nerea, or Nora as she had later come to be called. Maggie's thoughts flew back to the day on the train when Anthony had brought her to their carriage...

'Come here and tell me your name.'

Timidly, the little girl stepped forward. 'Nerea,' she said.

'Where are your parents?'

The child bit her lip.

'Do you know where your mother is?'

She shook her head.

'How old are you, Nerea?'

'Five,' she mumbled.

'How did you get inside the hamper?'

'I don't know.'

'I told you, she was drugged.'

Maggie looked at the twelve-year-old who had discovered her. 'We don't know that for sure.'

'*I'm* sure,' he said.

Maggie glanced up at Harry. 'What are we going to do?'

'We'll have to hand her over to the authorities when we get to Calais.'

'But do the French welcome refugees from Spain?'

'I've no idea, but what else can we do?'

Maggie blinked and muttered in a low voice. 'We could take her with us. She'd have a better chance in England.'

'Are you mad? How would we get her through immigration?'

'Of course, that was a silly idea.' She fixed Harry with a steady stare. 'You decide what to do.'

During the journey to Paris all the children except Ángel fell asleep. The new arrival rested her head in Maggie's lap. Donato snuggled up between Eva and Fabio, who uttered reverberating snores from time to time. He needs his adenoids taken out, thought Maggie.

Ángel seemed subdued. He sat staring out of the window only giving the occasional grunt when either Maggie or Harry spoke to him. As they drew into the station at Paris, he realised they would be getting off the train. Frowning, he said, 'You won't hand her over to the authorities, will you?'

Maggie looked startled. 'I don't know. It's up to Harry.

She had been puzzling about the situation for the entire journey, relying on Harry to make the difficult decision. When he announced that they would take her with them as far as Calais, Maggie heaved an inward sigh of relief. She glanced down at the sleeping child and couldn't hold back the urge to stroke her hair. She looked so pale. There was a translucent glow to her skin and, despite the heat, her forehead felt cool to the touch, not clammy like Eva's or Fabio's. Her arms and legs seemed thin enough to snap at the slightest knock.

The trip across Paris from Montparnasse to Gare du Nord went smoothly despite the difficulty of herding the bemused children through a major city with luggage in tow. Maggie was pleasantly surprised to learn that Harry had a fair grasp of French, which made things easier. They arrived at Calais by the evening. When she saw the crowds waiting for the ferries, Maggie's heart sank.

'What are we going to do? By the look of things, we won't get a ferry tonight.'

Harry looked thoughtful. 'Don't worry, we'll find a B&B. Wait here while I make enquiries.'

He left her then, surrounded by children and suitcases. Donato slept in her arms, while Fabio and the new child clung to her skirt. Eva, lively after her sleep on the train, hopped impatiently from one foot to the other. All at once, she realised that Ángel was nowhere to be seen. Maggie panicked. Had he gone with Harry or was he off on some adventure of his own? She gulped. This wasn't Spain. Ángel wouldn't be able to talk his way out of a tricky situation in a country where he didn't speak the language. Her gaze darted around as she tried to pick him out in the crowds without alarming the children.

Eva tugged at her hand. 'Where's Ángel…I mean Anthony?'

'I expect he's gone with Harry.'

Eva accepted this explanation but Maggie wasn't so sure. She cradled Donato in her arms until an English couple standing nearby offered her a seat on their packing case. This helped a bit but she felt close to passing out as the cramps in her stomach got even more severe. Ángel came back first but Maggie was too exhausted to ask him where he'd been.

'Let me hold Donato,' he offered and she was only too pleased to hand the toddler over.

At last Harry came back. 'I could only find one room but it will do for you and the younger children. I had to pay through the nose I'm afraid.'

'What will you and Ángel do?'

'We'll manage,' said the twelve-year-old, assuming a confident expression. 'I've slept in the open before now.'

She could well believe it. Hadn't he been roaming homeless in the streets of Tres Lomas when she'd found him?

The next day when she and the younger children joined Harry and Ángel in the queue for the ferry, she noticed how tired Harry looked. Ángel was as bouncy as ever but, she reminded herself, he didn't have the worry of conveying seven people safely to England. They got on the ferry at last. Maggie didn't remark on the fact that Harry made no further mention of handing Nerea over to the authorities and she assumed he preferred to deal with English rather than French officialdom. Slipping her onto the ferry with the other children had been surprisingly easy.

After several hours, the ferry docked in Dover Harbour. Maggie felt faint from exhaustion and nervousness. At times, stomach cramps almost doubled her in half but she was determined to hide this problem from Harry. The sight of the white cliffs gave her a feeling of intense relief. *You may be Spanish, Robert,* she thought to herself, *but I'm English.*

The disembarkation seemed to take forever. Her legs were trembling as they followed the other passengers down the ramp to passport control. She still didn't know what Harry intended to do and hated the thought of the little girl being handed over to the authorities.

Then a roar rang out from the crowd. 'Man overboard!'

351

Confusion ensued. Sailors ran hither and thither with ropes and life jackets. The disembarking passengers stood and gaped. All at once, Harry grabbed Maggie's hand.

'Come on, now's our chance,' he snapped.

Without stopping to think, Maggie dragged the children along behind Harry as he pushed past people on the ramp. At passport control, he flashed the passport in the officer's face, pushing the family ahead of him. With everyone's attention focused on the drowning man, they swept through without close examination.

It was only when they stood on the platform waiting for the train to take them into London that Maggie realised what a risk they had taken. How unexpectedly the situation had evolved! The confusion at the ferry, the opportune diversion when the man jumped overboard. They would never have got Nerea into the country if that hadn't happened. It gave them the chance to smuggle the little girl through. But what were they going to do with her? In her concern for Nerea, Maggie almost forgot that the other children were also illegal immigrants.

'We'll have to hand her over when we get to London,' said Harry. 'I'll do it. You take the others on to Stanmore and I'll join you later.'

Maggie couldn't go along with that. 'What's the harm of keeping her with us for a day or two? We can decide what to do about her later.'

She knew her argument was unconvincing, but for some reason, Harry went along with it and later, he didn't argue about not trying to find homes for the other children. Maggie smiled to herself, acknowledging that the experience of travelling together as a family had had a profound effect on him.

'We made it,' he said, the evening of their arrival after all the children had gone to bed.

They had arrived mid-afternoon and the house, empty for over a year, felt cold and damp despite it being July.

Sheets had to be aired before use. Fortunately, the weather was warm and Harry had rigged up a makeshift washing-line to hang out the necessary bedding. The little ones had been too tired to complain about going to bed and even Anthony - as he was now called - didn't put up much of an argument.

'I can't believe we're here in England. Harry, will you stay and help me sort things out tomorrow?'

He laughed. 'Of course I will. You didn't think I'd abandon you, did you?'

And stay he had. Even after taking up his post at the Foreign Office, he had stayed on in the spare room, travelling to London from Stanmore each day. Leaving Spain proved to be the open sesame for Fabian. Much to everybody's delight, he found his voice. Settling the children in, teaching them English, fixing up schools for them drew Harry and Maggie closer together. She came to rely on him. He also pulled some strings and managed to formalize the adoption.

In the early days, Maggie thought about her brother a lot. He had survived the hostilities, but at what cost? Sometimes, she wondered whether she should have been more insistent in talking him into coming home, although she constantly reminded herself that nothing on earth would have persuaded him to leave Dolores and his comrades in arms. A few months after Franco took power, Robert wrote to let her know he was living in a small house near Zaragoza. It's a bit of a dump, he said, and there's no telephone but it'll do for the time being. Since then, he had phoned her only once, from a bar.

'I'm so relieved you've settled down, Robert.' In her excitement, she forgot that he preferred to be called Esteban.

'How's the old *pile*?' he asked, a joking term they had always used for the house on the common.

'You wouldn't recognise it. Harry and I have done so much to it. And, Robert, the garden…well, it's been transformed.'

'What on earth did you do with all those children?'

'I wrote and told you. We've given them a home and they're all doing fine, except for Nerea of course.'

'Nerea?'

'The last one we picked up. She had a heart problem and sadly she died.'

'Maybe it was a blessing in disguise.'

'What?'

'I meant…as you have so many children to look after.'

'That's a cruel thing to say.'

'I didn't mean to offend you.'

Maggie gave a swallow and tried to push aside her brother's indiscreet remark. This was not the moment to quarrel with him. Changing the subject, she said, 'Are you and Dolores happy together?'

She didn't hear his reply because the line crackled and went dead. He never phoned her again, and although she kept writing, Robert seldom replied and when he did it took the form of a few lines on the back of a postcard.

As for marriage, that had been the last thing on her mind. When after a few months of living together in the same house Harry proposed, she gaped at him in astonishment.

'Marry you?'

'I asked you once before,' he said. 'And you accepted our fake marriage but you weren't ready for the real thing.'

Maggie giggled. 'If I remember rightly, you did spring that marriage proposal on me rather suddenly.'

'I really care for you, Maggie. I want to share my life with you.'

'I don't think I'm ready for such a serious commitment.'

'Maybe you never will be.' Harry's tone was curt.

'I didn't say that. It's just that we haven't been back in England for very long and...'

'I would have thought it was long enough.'

'We've still got so much to do here, and what about the children. What will they think?'

'It doesn't matter what they think.' He straightened his shoulders. 'If that's how you feel, I think it's best if I move out.'

'No!'

This was the last thing Maggie wanted. She had got used to having Harry around, he brightened her day, she looked forward to greeting him home in the evening. She relied on him utterly, and with surprise she realised that he had never again attempted to kiss her after the aborted embrace in Madrid. Was it because she never gave him the opportunity?

He frowned. 'We live in the same house, we eat at the same dinner table, we brush past one another forty times a day, but we're no closer now than we were on the day we met. It can't go on like this, Maggie, I'll be gone by the end of the week.' He turned and left the room before she could protest.

The incident left her mind in a whirl. Suddenly, it all became clear. They were living like brother and sister. Was Harry a substitute for Robert? If he cared for her as much as he said he did, she was being unfair to him. She cried herself to sleep that night, waking in the morning still feeling confused. It was only when, three days later, he appeared at the top of the stairs with his suitcases packed that reality hit her.

'You can't leave,' she begged him. 'Please don't go.'

'It's for the best,' he said. 'We'll still be friends and I'll call in from time to time.'

'No, don't go, I *will* marry you.' She hadn't realised how loud she had shouted until Eve and Fabian poked their heads out of their bedroom door, looking astounded.

'Can I be bridesmaid?' asked Eve.

The day of nostalgia passed swiftly: ten minutes doing some dusting, an hour of baking, followed by a trek to J Sainsbury's to stock up on some groceries. When she got back there were a few mending jobs to do: sock darning, as well as lengthening Fabian's trousers.

'Mum, I'm home.' Donald came racing into the house. He had always called her 'Mum' but the others called her Maggie. She put this down to the fact that he was the only one who had never known his real mother since he was only four months old when she was killed. Maggie sometimes worried about the future, about what would happen to the children once she and Harry had passed on; not that she felt their demise was imminent, but she wondered whether they ought to encourage the children to trace their Spanish relatives. However, as time slipped by and the children seemed happy in their adopted family, she allowed the idea to fade away.

Although she had long since lost any feelings for Raul she sometimes wondered what had happened to him. Did he return to medical school once the war was over? Did his family ever recover their former wealth?

She turned her attention to her young son. 'How was school today?'

He shrugged. 'The usual.'

'The results of your eleven-plus will be out soon.'

Maggie had high hopes for Donald. After his rocky start in life, she prayed that he would achieve a successful career. He was a lively boy, always in a hurry and rather erratic in his studies.

'You'd better go and do your homework,' she said.

'Yeah, ok.'

'Donald, I wish you wouldn't use those Americanisms.'

He grinned and gave her a peck on the cheek. 'Too many Yankee movies, Mum.'

Half an hour later Fabian got home. 'Coming out for a bike ride, Don?' he called upstairs to his brother.

'Yeah!'

'Supper's at six o'clock,' shouted Maggie as they disappeared out of the kitchen door, the homework forgotten.

Christmas that year was, as always, a family affair. Maggie loved having everybody home although, secretly, she felt there was one big gap in the circle. If only Robert could be there as well! At these times she yearned to go back to Spain, to look her brother up, to take up where they had left off. But she knew in her heart that this could never happen while Dolores had him in her clutches. She realised with a little shock that she had always hated Dolores. Before going to Spain, her life had been passive, emotionless; she had never borne anybody a grudge until she had been introduced to her brother's woman.

The result of her search for him during those Civil War years had not had a satisfactory outcome. Expecting to be reunited with the same old Robert, she had felt bitterly frustrated to find a changed man, not only in name but also in disposition. His carefree temperament had metamorphosed into single-minded fervour. She had tried to point out to him that, like her, he was British. Didn't he understand that he was fighting someone else's war? But her brief sojourn at the camp had shown her that these young men from so many different countries were like aliens. They lived for the moment, cocooned in an unfathomable loyalty to a cause which had nothing to do with their normal world. Of course, with hindsight, she saw that what had happened in Spain had had a direct effect upon the war in Europe which followed. But could these young men have foreseen this? She doubted it. And after all these years, she still felt a deep sorrow for the useless loss of life played out on the Spanish plains.

'Maggie, don't look so gloomy. It's Christmas!' Harry broke into her reflections.

'Sorry, darling, I was miles away.'

'A penny for them,' cried Eve.

'Just memories.'

Eve came over and tucked her arm through Maggie's. 'Were you thinking about Esteban?'

'Maybe, a little,' she admitted.

How did she know? Eve had surprised Maggie over the years with her intuitiveness. She wondered how much the girl remembered of her own terrible experiences. Had they scarred her for life? Her doubts were swiftly swept away when Eve whispered, 'My boyfriend's calling round tomorrow, I hope you don't mind. He's called Michael.'

'Of course I don't mind. Harry and I would love to meet him.'

'When's the feast going to be ready?' called Harry, interrupting the intimate moment between Maggie and Eve. 'Who's hungry?'

There was a chorus of 'We are, we are!'

Maggie hurried into the kitchen. With food rationing still a problem, she had managed to obtain a couple of medium-sized chickens to feed the seven of them. Caroline had also come to join them for Christmas dinner. Flour had recently been de-rationed so that Maggie had been able to make a cake, although dried fruit was still difficult to come by for the Christmas pudding.

The family sat down to their meal, laughing and joking when the Christmas crackers were pulled.

'Listen to this,' said Anthony. 'What does a frog do if his car breaks down?' They all came up with silly suggestions until he read out the answer, 'He gets it *toad* away.'

'Mine's better,' said Fabian. 'What lies at the bottom of the sea and shivers?'

'Don't know,' yelled Donald.

'A nervous wreck.'

'Have you heard this story?' Fabian launched into a shaggy dog tail which went on for ages. Everybody listened intently until the punch-line, which he expertly delivered.

Maggie looked at Fabian fondly. Who would have thought he would become such a raconteur? She barely recognised the little waif who had refused to open his mouth for so long.

Harry winked at her and mouthed, 'We did well, didn't we?'

CHAPTER TWENTY-SIX

September 1962

Over the years, communication with her brother had become erratic. Maggie knew this was due to the restrictions imposed by Franco's harsh regime, but by the early sixties, the dictator had changed tactics, opening up Spain to foreign tourists. She still missed Robert terribly. There was, after all, no one with whom she could share early memories, no one with whom to reminisce about *abuelo* and *abuela*. But now her fiftieth birthday was looming, and over the months, she became obsessed with the idea of spending her half century with her twin brother. When she put forward the idea to Harry, he tried to discourage her.

'It's risky, Maggie, you could find yourself in trouble. They scrutinize foreign visitors very thoroughly, especially as you have Spanish connections.'

'What? How could I be in trouble? I've got a British passport and…' She gave Harry a sly look. '…and an English surname thanks to you.'

'I don't want you to go. It could be dangerous.'

'Don't be ridiculous! It would be lovely seeing Robert again, catching up on all those lost years. What could possibly happen on a visit to see my brother?'

'You don't know what Robert's been up to since the war ended. How d'you know he's not caught up in some subversive movement?'

'Subversive movement!' scoffed Maggie.

Harry pressed on. 'I don't want you to be disappointed. Your brother may be different to the way you remember him. Twenty-five years is a long time. He may not be the gallant hero you imagine him to be. Besides, how many times did you come back from Tres Lomas upset by something he had said or done?'

Maggie got angry. 'That was because of the tensions of the moment. How do you know what Robert will be like? You've never even met him. Besides, we're both older and wiser now; it's only right that twins should get together after all these years.'

Harry gave a shrug. 'All right, I'll book our flight.'

Maggie stiffened. 'Not you. I want to go on my own. If things work out well, you can come with me next time.' She could see she had hurt him and hated herself for it.

He brushed off her rebuttal with, 'Eve might want to go with you.'

'Out of the question!' snapped Maggie. It was one thing for her to go back but there was no way she'd want Eve to risk returning. Eve's British nationality had been formalised by Harry at the time of their marriage, but just the same…

Realising how sharply she had spoken, she raked her mind for a more acceptable excuse, mumbling, 'And who…who'd look after their children? Michael can't take time off work.'

'I suppose that would present a problem,' admitted Harry.

'I'm going alone.'

Harry put on a brave face, bowing to the inevitable with a show of levity. 'Like you did in '37?' He laughed. 'For heaven's sake, don't come back with a brood of orphans this time. Seriously though, I'd rather you'd let me come with you. I'll keep out of your way, I'll stay in the hotel while you go and visit Robert.'

'Please don't insist, darling,' pleaded Maggie. Contrition made her words seem persuasive rather than emphatic, to the point where she could sense that Harry thought she might change her mind.

'What's wrong with an extended visit so that we can take a holiday over there?' he suggested in a light-hearted tone.

'No, I want to see my brother on my own to start with. Don't make it difficult for me, darling, we can go on holiday another time.'

His face clouded. 'I think you're mad but who am I to tell you what to do? A new age husband isn't supposed to do that.'

New age husband! Is that how Harry saw himself? She almost laughed out loud but a glance at his face told her to tread carefully as, for an awful moment, she thought the discussion was going to develop into a full-blown row. She didn't want that because Harry's logic always won an argument.

The image of her brother rose in her mind's eye. How lovely it would be to see him again. How he must have changed? A little tubbier perhaps, greying at the temples or maybe that thick hatch of hair was thinner now. She had always intended going back to Spain but during the earlier Francoist years it had been impossible.

She left Harry and went upstairs to the bedroom to stare at her own reflection in the full-length mirror. A still acceptably slim middle-aged woman stared back at her. The dark hair was peppered with grey but the contours of the face were still firm and the eyes had not lost their sparkle. She went downstairs again, praying that Harry would let the matter drop, but this wasn't to be.

'You'll write and tell him you're coming, won't you? I mean it wouldn't be fair to spring it on him, would it?'

'Spring it on him?' Maggie echoed indignantly. 'Why, if Robert were to turn up on our doorstep without any warning, do you think I'd turn him away? On the contrary, I would be delighted. Don't worry, he'll welcome me, his only sister.'

'I didn't mean that,' Harry tried to explain himself. 'It's just that you don't know what his circumstances are, how he's living, what his job is.'

It was true, Robert had never told her what he did for a living. He was a qualified engineer and she had assumed that at the end of hostilities, after POUM and the International Brigades had disbanded, he had gone back to his chosen profession. His brief messages had been uninformative about his personal life. For the first time she felt a stab of doubt. Until now, she had never imagined for one moment that he was not comfortably off. Surely if things were difficult for him he would have asked her to release his share of the funds from their mother's inheritance, which was still accumulating interest in the bank.

In the end, she took Harry's advice and wrote to Robert giving him the date of her intended arrival, and on the seventh of September, she flew from Heathrow to Barajas Airport. She spent a night in Madrid, taking the opportunity to look around the modern metropolis, which was barely recognisable from the war-torn city she remembered. It was difficult to believe that she had fled Madrid with a brood of orphaned children. How different those children were now! And strangely only one of them had wanted to visit Spain. Last year Donald had gone on a camping holiday to Asturias with some friends. He had come back full of enthusiasm about the hospitality of the Basque people. It got her wondering about his Spanish relatives. How sad that they would never know what had happened to him!

The others led busy lives. Eve had her hands full with two lively daughters, Fabian too was married with a couple of youngsters. He had developed into a talented artist and was running his own graphic design business. Thankfully, his heartrending sketches of death and destruction had long been abandoned. Anthony had moved to New York with his American bride. They rarely heard from him but Maggie knew that he lived life to the full and was making a lot of money practising law. His glamorous wife, who Maggie and Harry had only met once, was a top model. Donald was as yet unmarried although he wasn't lacking opportunity. He had had girlfriends aplenty.

With her head filled with nostalgia, Maggie didn't feel the least bit lonely on the journey. She was glad she had dissuaded Harry from accompanying her. It was better to exorcise the remaining demons from that bizarre interlude in her life on her own.

She got up next morning feeling excited and not a little nervous. She checked and re-checked that she had everything ready: photos of Harry and the children at different stages in their lives and a snapshot of the old *pile*. She was sure Robert would be interested in that.

She took the train from Atocha to Zaragoza. A young man helped her with her suitcase, loading it into the luggage rack. This reminded her of her first encounter with Tomás and the way he had taken charge of her suitcase on that occasion. What had happened to him, she wondered. Making a rough calculation, she realised that if he had survived, he would be all of seventy-five, maybe older.

It felt strange hearing Spanish again. She hadn't spoken the language for a long time since, once the children had settled into the British way of life, the family always spoke English. Maggie sometimes wondered how much of their native language they remembered.

On reaching Zaragoza she had no idea how she was going to make her way to Robert's village. He hadn't replied to her letter telling him of her arrival, although she had lied to Harry, telling him that her brother was expecting her. She hoped he hadn't moved away but felt sure that in such a small village someone would know where he had gone.

She took the local bus, which trundled slowly along. It's wooden seats were far from comfortable but she enjoyed the opportunity to gaze out of the grimy window at the familiar scenery. It looked peaceful now but she couldn't stop her mind from winging back to the days when she had driven an ambulance over a pot-holed road, fearing they could at any moment be blown up. At last the bus drew to a halt but Maggie knew she still had some way to go. Robert's house was tucked away in a remote area. She wondered why he had not taken up residence in the Toledo villa their grandfather had left him.

The bus drove on, leaving her standing on a dusty road with her suitcase beside her. Her navy linen skirt looked creased, a light breeze blew a strand of hair into her eyes. She brushed the hair aside, momentarily carried back twenty-five years earlier to another lonely road near Tres Lomas where Tomás had angrily dropped her off after she had smuggled a lift in his lorry.

Picking up the suitcase, she headed into the village and found a solitary shop. Inside there was no one to be seen. She waited for five minutes, then called out, 'Is anybody at home?'

The proprietor appeared from a back room. 'Can I help you?' he asked in Catalan.

'Yes please, I'm a stranger around here and I'd like to know whether there's a bus that can take me to Cantaveija.'

Recognising her Madrid accent, the proprietor smiled and immediately went into Spanish. 'Are you visiting someone?'

365

'My brother. Here's his address.' She drew out the piece of paper she had with Robert's address on it.

'Ah, I know the place. You won't get a bus out there. You'll have to walk.' He glanced down at her feet and saw that she was wearing a pair of high heeled shoes. 'Those shoes won't do. Why don't you buy a pair of espadrilles?' He pointed to a pair which were hanging on a rack by the counter.

'The espadrilles are a good idea!' said Maggie. 'But I hope it isn't far.'

'It's only a couple of kilometres but why not wait until later when it's not so hot. There's a café down the road. Spend an hour or two there.'

Maggie took the proprietor's advice, bought the espadrilles and tucked her high heeled shoes into her suitcase. Although it was now September, it was still very hot and she felt exhausted by the time she reached the café. She was getting old, she told herself, twenty-five years ago the walk up the hill to the café would have been easy.

She had a snack and a coffee, and to kill time, chatted to the waiter, who offered to look after her suitcase until she returned. She thanked him and, an hour and a half later, bade him farewell and started on her way. Even now, it was still hot and she wished she had worn something more summery. She took off her smart jacket and carried it but her silk blouse clung to her body.

She was startled when a farm cart drew up beside her. The driver reined in his horse, leaned out and beckoned her. He mumbled something in Catalan and even though she didn't understand the words, it was clear from his manner that he was offering her a lift. The cart didn't look very clean but the offer was too good to refuse. He moved over so that she could climb up and sit beside him and, with a flip of the reins, urged the horse on again.

Conversation was almost impossible because the man only spoke Catalan. However, she surmised that he was asking her where she was going and he told her he knew where Esteban lived. When he stopped at the edge of the road and pointed to a deserted-looking hamlet, she thanked him and jumped down from the cart. He went on his way with a cheery wave.

She glanced around. There was no sign of life. The buildings looked to be little more than hovels. Maggie was filled with misgivings. Surely this couldn't be right! All at once, some children ran out from an alley-way, prompting a flock of pigeons to take to the wing. They were shabbily dressed and the girl's hair looked as if it could do with a comb. On seeing Maggie, she grabbed the hands of two small boys and the three of them stood staring at her with a mixture of curiosity and alarm. Maggie held her breath, reminded of Eve and Fabian's reaction all those years ago when they had cowered away from Raul. On that occasion, she had been the comforter. Now, it seemed, she was the one to pose a threat. She smiled and extended a hand in an endeavour to put them at their ease.

A dumpy woman with a weather-beaten face appeared from one of the houses. She was dressed entirely in black except for a pair of bright blue carpet slippers. She beckoned to the children, who ran to her.

Maggie blinked and came to her senses. 'I'm sorry, *Señora*', she said. 'I didn't mean to scare your children. Can you tell me where Esteban Morán lives?'

The woman looked startled and pushed the children away from her. They turned and ran into the house.

Maggie tried again. 'Esteban Morán is my brother, my twin brother.'

Puzzlement cleared from the woman's face and she held out her arms. 'My Esteban's sister!'

'Your Esteban?' Could this be true? Maggie felt reality slipping away. Who was this woman? Surely not Dolores.

'I think I've made a mistake,' she stuttered.

The woman shook her head and hurried towards her. 'No mistake, I am Esteban's woman.' She nodded towards the house and said proudly, 'They are our children.'

Snatching up Maggie's suitcase, she ushered her into the house. Once inside, she called to her daughter, telling her to fetch a tumbler of water for their visitor.

'I'm so sorry,' said Maggie after gulping down most of the water. 'I should have been prepared. You see, I haven't seen my brother for over twenty years. Where is he?'

The woman shooed her children out of the house. Her face clouded as she fumbled with the hem of her apron and muttered, 'I'm afraid your brother died earlier this year.'

For a moment, Maggie thought she had misunderstood the woman's odd mixture of Catalan and Spanish. 'Died?' she gasped.

Through her shock, she could sense the woman's sympathy.

'You need to rest, *Señora*, come this way.'

As if in a trance, Maggie followed the woman into a dark bedroom. 'Tell me what happened,' she begged.

The woman started to explain but exhaustion and shock made it impossible for Maggie to comprehend her Catalan accent. Sensing her visitor's need for rest, the woman said. 'The details can wait.'

Soothed by her calmness, Maggie sank back onto a narrow bed and fell instantly asleep.

Maggie woke up to find the little girl standing by her bed holding a mug of coffee. The child smiled shyly and said, 'My name's Estelita.'

This revelation jerked Maggie into alertness. 'Of course,' she said. 'You're my niece.'

The girl had some difficulty with Spanish and started to gabble in Catalan. Maggie shook her head. 'I'm sorry, I don't understand,' she said.

At that moment, the woman came into the room followed by the two little boys. 'Did you sleep well?' she asked.

'Yes thank you. What time is it?'

'Nine o'clock.' Maggie could scarcely believe she had slept for four hours. The woman smiled. 'You must be hungry, I've cooked you a meal.'

Maggie followed the others into the main room, which was lit with oil lamps. The room consisted of a small kitchen area, a table and a sagging sofa. To her surprise, there was an old television set in the corner of the room. This puzzled her. If the house was powered by electricity, why were they using oil lamps for lighting?

The woman answered her unspoken question. 'The TV doesn't work. Since Esteban's death I haven't been able to pay the electricity bill.'

Maggie was astounded. She couldn't believe her brother had been living in such poverty. 'Have you always lived here?' she asked.

The woman shook her head. 'We had to move when my Esteban became ill.'

Maggie's heart beat fast. Why had Robert allowed himself and his family to end up penniless when there was money in the bank in England? She felt out of her depth and wished she had allowed Harry to accompany her.

'What's your name?' she asked the woman.

'Pilar Lopez. You've met my Estelita, she's twelve and the boys are Jaime and Javier. They're nine and ten.' The two little boys, who had been quietly listening, gave proof to their presence by chasing one another around the table.

Their mother smiled indulgently before gently urging them out of the door. 'Estelita,' she called. 'Keep an eye on your brothers.'

In answer to her mother's wishes, Estelita got up and ran out to join them.

'Esteban and I were together for fourteen years,' Pilar explained, sometimes repeating herself because Maggie didn't understand her accent. 'We had a farm not far from here but the work was hard and with my Esteban's failing health - you know he was badly wounded?'

'Yes, but I thought he had recovered.'

'He was wounded several times, most of the wounds were minor but towards the end his lung was punctured. He also got a bullet in his leg.' She sighed and twisted her hands in her lap. 'He had breathing problems and he couldn't bend his knee. This made farm work very difficult.'

'But why was he working on a farm when he's a qualified engineer? I don't understand.'

Pilar shook her head. 'Life hasn't been easy under Franco. Esteban had to keep his head down.'

'But surely someone with engineering qualifications would be able to find work in the city. Why stay here in this remote region?'

'We are country people,' the woman said simply.

'Robert's not,' burst out Maggie.

The expression on Pilar's face told her that she had said the wrong thing and she realised that the woman could have no concept of Robert's prior life. Her brother would not have taken the trouble to enlighten her as to their middle-class English childhood. Feeling uncomfortable, Maggie moved onto safer ground. 'When exactly did my brother die?'

'On the first of May.'

Robert couldn't have chosen a better day on which to die, thought Maggie bitterly, May Day! Perfect timing to

370

fit in with his left-wing ideals. She felt puzzled. If Pilar had been her brother's companion for fourteen years what had happened to Dolores? Why had Robert left her? Perhaps he hadn't. Perhaps Dolores had been the one to leave after he had become a virtual invalid, or…she wrinkled her forehead…maybe it was after Robert had signed over power of attorney.

'Why didn't he get in touch with me?' she demanded. 'I could have helped him.'

Pilar snorted with indignation. 'Ask for help? My Esteban!'

Maggie stifled a sob. Pilar was right. Robert would never ask for help. But surely he hadn't forgotten his inheritance. Then she remembered. When he had signed it over to her, he had said he had no interest in it. Pride had always been his downfall; there was no way he would ask for it back.

She recalled the house their grandfather had left him. She had told Robert about it when they met up in Tres Lomas. He had been as surprised as she was to learn that they had each been left a property.

'Why didn't you move to the house in Toledo? Surely Esteban told you about it.'

'It was razed to the ground during the fighting.'

Conversation between the two women was proving almost impossible. Pilar frequently lapsed into Catalan, and in her confusion, Maggie found it difficult to concentrate. It was bad enough summoning up her lapsed Spanish.

Then Pilar changed the subject. 'You resemble my Esteban as I knew him fourteen years ago,' she said sadly.

'Have you got any photos of him?' asked Maggie.

Without a word, Pilar got up and pulled open a drawer in the dresser, bringing out an envelope. With a sigh, she wiped her sleeve across her face and handed it over.

Maggie slipped the dog-eared snapshots out of the envelope. The images brought tears to her eyes. The first picture showed her brother as she remembered him: looking exhilarant, standing with a rifle thrust above his head, surrounded by his laughing companions. Then there was one with his arm clasped around Dolores' shoulder, the familiar red kerchief around her neck. These had clearly been taken in the early days before the full horror of war had knocked the smiles off their faces. The other photos were much less exuberant. There was one of Robert seated on a low wall, his arm supported in a sling. That must have been taken in 1938 when he returned to the front after she had visited him at the hospital in Tres Lomas. The last one showed an older Robert. Seated on a chair, his leg outstretched, he was leaning forward awkwardly, a vacant expression on his face. The three children stood next to him. There were no photos of Pilar.

Maggie studied the snapshots, feeling reluctant to hand them back. At last, she pushed them back into the envelope and offered them to Pilar, who shook her head. 'No, you take them.'

'I couldn't do that. You'll want to keep these photos.'

Pilar smiled sadly. 'Please take them. I have his children, you have only his memory.'

'Thank you so much. I'll have them copied and return the originals to you.'

The next day, after a restless night trying to sleep on the narrow bed, Maggie made her departure with a mixture of relief and regret. She had tried to communicate with the children but their Catalan was incomprehensible to her. She thanked Pilar and promised to send funds to help the family.

Pilar shook her head. 'There's no need.'

'Oh but there is,' declared Maggie. 'Esteban's inheritance is held in an English bank. It will have earned a great deal of interest over the years. There's no longer any need for you to live like this.'

Pilar's expression hardened. 'We manage.'

'You don't understand. By rights, this money's yours. I want you to have it. You can find yourself a nicer house, move out of here, go and live in a town if you want to. The children can go to a good school...' Seized by the need to convince the woman, she clutched her hands tightly, going on urgently, 'Esteban would have wanted his children to have a proper education.'

Pilar pulled her hands away and took a step backwards. 'No, those things are not for us.'

Maggie was flooded with despair. Twenty-five years ago she had rescued a group of children from hardship, giving them a good education and a better life, yet here were her own niece and nephews living in dire poverty with their mother refusing to be helped. It was untenable and she knew she would have to do something about it.

'At least let me send you some money,' she insisted. 'Then you can get the electricity switched on again, buy decent food for the children, get them new clothes. Wouldn't you like to see Estelita in a pretty dress?'

'I won't take charity,' muttered Pilar.

'It isn't charity,' shouted Maggie, getting more and more heated. 'You are my family. Esteban's children are my blood relations. You must let me help you.'

Alerted by the shouting, Estelita came over and took her mother's hand. She was a pretty child with her father's huge brown eyes. Pilar looked down at her and Maggie could almost read her mind. The child deserved a better life, warranted a few luxuries.

'Very well, for the sake of the children.'

Maggie grinned. 'I'll set up a bank account as soon as I get home and one day, I hope you'll all come and visit me in England.' She knew this was unlikely. For Pilar, travelling to England would be tantamount to visiting the moon.

Pilar arranged for a local man to give Maggie a lift in his pick-up truck so that she could collect her suitcase and catch the bus connection but the trip back to Zaragoza was not a happy one. On the outward journey she had been spurred on by hope, but disappointment clouded the homeward journey. Robert was dead. She had left it too late. How could she ever forgive herself? Meeting Robert's children had been disturbing. She realised that she couldn't take matters entirely into her own hands. How the money was spent rested with their mother. But she could hold some back so that there would be funds in the bank for their future.

On reaching Madrid she had time to spare, her flight home having been booked for the following morning. She phoned Harry, giving him the briefest of details, needing time to assimilate them herself before describing them in full. There was time to take the train into the centre of the city but her emotions were in such turmoil that she knew such a trip would only make things worse. Instead, she killed time by going to the cinema to see *Los Atracadores,* a recently released crime film. Afterwards, she could hardly remember anything about it. In the hotel restaurant she found a secluded table, hiding behind a novel she had brought with her in order to avoid eye contact with other hotel guests.

After a good night's sleep in a comfortable bed, she got up next morning feeling refreshed. Despite the misfortune of leaving the visit too late to catch up with her brother, she had at least met his family, a family that a few days ago she had no idea existed. All at once, she longed to get home to tell Harry all about it. He met her at Heathrow. She flew into his outstretched arms.

'My, my, that's some welcome,' he said when at last she drew away.

'I'm so glad to be home, Harry,' she whispered.

'Was it really awful, darling? It must have been such a disappointment learning that Robert had passed on. '

Maggie sniffed into the handkerchief he offered her. 'It was a terrible shock, though meeting his children was a bigger shock. Why didn't he tell me about them?'

'We'll never know.'

Harry cleared his Ford Consul through the traffic onto the open road. Maggie filled him in, describing the poverty in which Pilar and the children lived. 'I must do something to help them,' she said.

'Of course you must and perhaps one day you can persuade them to visit us.'

Maggie smiled. 'I'd like that.'

Eve, Fabian and Donald were at home waiting to greet her. Eager to hear all the news, they bombarded her with questions until late into the evening. Finally, exhausted, she excused herself and went to bed. Harry joined her an hour later. With a sigh of contentment, she snuggled close to him, relishing the familiarity of his presence and realising that this was the man with whom she wanted to spend the rest of her life.

EPILOGUE

Bilbao - December 1962

The old man yawned and rubbed his eyes with arthritic fingers. He had been dozing, lapsing into yesteryear as he was wont to do these days, reminiscing on what had happened and what might have been.

A black-clad nun shuffled up to him. He frowned and emitted a grunt. Why did she creep around so noiselessly? Her saintly tolerance was enough to spook anyone. If he had the strength he'd holler at the woman, shock her into life.

'You've got a visitor, Señor Montalvo,' she said quietly. 'Are you up to receiving visitors?'

A visitor? Outsiders didn't turn up very often these days. He couldn't remember the last time someone had paid him a social call.

'If it's that po-faced therapist, send her away,' he snarled.

The sister smiled patiently, antagonising him even more. 'This is an old friend, El Profesor Guzman. Do you remember him? I believe he occasionally writes to you.'

Of course I remember him, he bellowed in his head, *do you think I'm an idiot?* Aloud, he said, 'Show him in, Sister.'

When the nun beckoned to him, Raul Guzman strode across the dormitory, a hand outstretched. He saw his host's expression change from ferocious bad-temper to one of welcome as he struggled out of his chair to greet him.

'Raul, well I never!'

'Still the same old irascible devil,' joked the newcomer, gripping the old man's hand and taking him in a bear-like hug.

Tomás Montalvo's weather-beaten face creased into a grin, revealing tobacco-stained teeth. He swayed slightly causing Raul to steady him, but the handshake and hug were as strong as ever.

'What brings you here, *amigo?* Tomás demanded as he tentatively lowered himself back into his armchair. 'You've never visited me before. Surely you didn't travel all the way from Zaragoza simply to see an old dodderer like me.'

'What makes you say that?' said Raul as he took off his overcoat and hung it on the back of the chair.

'Come clean, there must be another reason to bring you to these parts.'

'Well…'

'The truth will out.'

'I'm operating in this area tomorrow. They needed a heart surgeon with my expertise at the Hospital de Basurto, so I thought I'd combine business with pleasure and pay you a visit.'

They were interrupted by the reappearance of the nun, who was carrying a tray of tea and biscuits.

'Thank you, Sister Mercedes,' said Raul, giving her his disarming smile. 'That's very kind of you.'

'We don't usually get biscuits,' snorted Tomás.

The nun looked flustered, prompting Raul to ask light-heartedly, 'I hope Señor Montalvo has been behaving himself. I'm sure he must be a bit of a handful.'

'Of course he isn't,' protested the woman, blushing furiously. Clearly she wasn't used to having such a distinguished looking man joke with her. Turning abruptly, she left the room, her rough woollen habit brushing against the furniture in her haste to cover up her embarrassment.

After she had left, the two men talked about Raul's career, his rapid rise to professorship when he went back to medical school at the end of the hostilities. 'I was lucky,' he said. 'Despite having lost so much, my family could still afford to support me during those difficult years.'

'Lucky, my foot! You showed extraordinary talent. The new regime couldn't afford to let you go.'

Accustomed to flattery, both with regard to his looks and his ability, Raul smiled modestly and said, 'Enough about me, how have you been?'

'Dying,' replied the old man. 'Little by little, day by day, hour by hour…of boredom. Why couldn't I have perished at the front and been hailed a hero like most of my comrades?'

He broke into a paroxysm of coughing and delved into his pocket for a handkerchief.

'It can't be as bad as that,' protested Raul, handing him his own handkerchief.

'You should try it. Those do-gooding vultures are always waiting to pounce. They enjoy funerals. I think they've got a stake in the local undertaking business. But I defy their efforts to hasten my end. I've come this far so I'll cling on for as long as I can,' replied Tomás once he had recovered.

'You always were an obstinate old devil. But seriously, do they treat you all right?'

'I suppose they do their best, given the funds available to them.' He gave a snort. 'That's enough of the ranting of an eighty-year-old fossil. Come on, tell me, what's been going on in the outside world?'

Raul grinned. 'There's something I thought would interest you.'

378

'Out with it, don't keep me in suspense.'

'Well…quite out of the blue, I came into contact with a patient who gave me some news about a mutual friend.'

'An ex POUM member?'

'Yes, Esteban Morán.'

'Don't tell me that rascal survived? The last I heard was that he was badly wounded. I really thought he'd bought it.'

'He died earlier this year.'

'So he hung on for more than a couple of decades?'

'Yes, but he suffered from poor health for the remainder of his life. But what's interesting is, according to my patient, just after his death his sister went to see his widow…'

'He was married?' Tomás eyes lit up with interest.

'Married with three children.'

'What a surprise! I never thought that woman of his would be interested in motherhood.'

'Dolores you mean?' Raul laughed. 'He didn't marry Dolores. She made off after he handed all his money over to his sister. He married a woman from one of the villages; they ran a farm together until his health deteriorated.'

Tomás sat forward eagerly. 'Tell me, what happened to his sister, the little *inglesa?* He winked. 'You were involved with her, weren't you?'

'For a short while.' Not wanting to dwell on that episode, Raul went on. 'Apparently, Maggie is going to set his family up with a trust fund. This is money taken from Esteban's inheritance so it's rightfully the widow's anyway. It seems, Maggie had no idea her brother was living in poverty - he was a qualified engineer you know - let alone married with a family.'

'Didn't they keep in touch over the years?'

'I'm sure she tried but you know what a bastard that brother of hers was. He was pretty offhand with her when she came to track him down way back in '37. He was so full of his own importance, he didn't appreciate how courageous she was, travelling out to the front line to find him.'

After another bout of coughing, Tomás asked, 'What happened to her? Is she living in England?'

'Yes.'

Raul's reluctance to expound on Maggie's circumstances fuelled Tomás' curiosity. He leant forward in his eagerness to learn more. 'Well, come on, tell me, did she get those children safely out of Spain?'

'Yes, what's more, she brought them all up as her own, including that young tearaway, Ángel. Would you believe it, he's a lawyer now?'

'I'll be damned! But I suppose she was a match for any member of the male gender. Did she ever get married?'

'Yes,' said Raul quietly. 'She married that British diplomat.'

'Harry Fforbes!' Tomás gave a roar of laughter as he flopped back in his chair. 'Well I never! That woman was the feistiest female I ever came across. D'you know, she would never take 'no' for an answer. Talk about stubborn! And to think that when I first met her, she was afraid of her own shadow.'

Raul joined in with his companion's amusement although privately he did not share his gleeful recollections. His memories were sad: images of a naïve young girl with whom he had had the misfortune to fall in love. No woman before or since had matched up to her. He had missed his opportunity, hampered by war and his own stupidity. He often thought about her, and wondered whether she was happy with her English husband. How different the Morán twins had turned out to be. Two sides of a coin.

Tomás carried on. 'And she refused to have an abortion…'

'Abortion? I didn't know anything about that,' said Raul, his shoulders stiffening.

Tomás immediately realised he had spoken out of turn. 'I thought she'd told you.'

'Was it mine?' Raul asked the question but he already knew the answer.

'Who else's could it have been?' Raul heard Tomás carry on speaking. 'She lost it anyway. In fact, she was seriously ill for a while.'

'She lost my child?' Raul echoed Tomás' words as if in a trance.

'I'm sorry, I thought you knew.'

'Why didn't she tell me?'

'Maybe you didn't given her a chance.'

The meeting that had started out so jovially came to an abrupt end. Making the excuse of a pressing engagement, Raul Guzman took his leave of Tomás Montalvo, leaving the room with the old man's shocking words still ringing in his ears. In 1938, linked by a brave English girl, they had shared so much. And not knowing what had happened to Maggie had united them. Having exchanged information, Tomás would be left to while away his remaining years with fond memories but Raul had heard more than he wanted to hear.

After bidding farewell to Sister Mercedes, he left the retreat knowing that, despite having promised to keep in touch, he would never visit Tomás again. With Maggie's secret revealed, the link between the two men was broken.

381

Lightning Source UK Ltd.
Milton Keynes UK
UKOW042118160513

210811UK00001B/2/P